I0635478

Unending

by

Cassie Laelyn

The Fallen Guardians

This is a work of fiction. Names, characters, places, and incidents are either the product of the author's imagination or are used fictitiously, and any resemblance to actual persons living or dead, business establishments, events, or locales, is entirely coincidental.

Unending

COPYRIGHT © 2023 by Cassie Laelyn

All rights reserved. No part of this book may be used or reproduced in any manner whatsoever without written permission of the author or The Wild Rose Press, Inc. except in the case of brief quotations embodied in critical articles or reviews.
Contact Information: info@thewildrosepress.com

Cover Art by *Diana Carlile*

The Wild Rose Press, Inc.
PO Box 708
Adams Basin, NY 14410-0708
Visit us at www.thewildrosepress.com

Publishing History
First Edition, 2023
Trade Paperback ISBN 978-1-5092-5099-8
Digital ISBN 978-1-5092-5100-1

The Fallen Guardians
Published in the United States of America

"Who did this to you?"

"You." Her wild gaze suddenly focused and locked on him. "You did this to me."

Dread twisted in his gut. Of all the states he'd found her in, her remembering the choices he made, what he'd done, was the absolute worst. He experienced that guilt every day. And it crippled him each time she remembered.

"I'm sorry," he whispered, the words burning a path up his throat.

Sorry wasn't enough. Such a simple five letter word that couldn't encapsulate the devastating loss he experienced each time she died. The grief. The anger and bitterness she harbored toward him for putting her first.

Yet, he'd continue to say that word until his last breath. Because until someone invented another, it was the only one which even remotely described how he felt.

She glared at him.

He ached to brush the tears from her cheeks, to cradle her face in his hands and kiss them all away. But he knew better. The last thing he wanted was to cause her more hurt.

"You're not sorry, Cole. You knew this would happen. You always do. Yet, you do it anyway." She sobbed as tears streamed down her flushed cheeks. "You banish me to Hell. Locked in a castle to endure nothing but the memories. The memories of what you did."

Praise for Cassie Laelyn

UNFORSAKEN, The Fallen Guardians, Book 1:
Best Paranormal Romance (finalist) - Australian Romance Readers Award

UNFORGOTTEN, The Fallen Guardians, Book 2:
Best Paranormal Romance Novel (finalist) - Oklahoma Romance Writers of America International Digital Award

UNSEEN, The Fallen Guardians, Book 3:
Romantic Book of the Year (finalist) - Romance Writers of Australia

UNTAMED, The Fallen Guardians, Book 4:
"Untamed gives us the ultimate enemies to lovers story" - The Lusty Literarians

Dedication

For you, for trusting me with your heart and soul every lifetime

Glossary of Terms

Azrael – Angels of Death who transport souls from the mortal realm to their final resting place in either the Heavens or Hell. Azrael have silvery-gray wings.

Chosen – A mortal created by Fate, whose destiny restores the balance in Fate's favor.

Dumahel – Half Azrael/half mortal, Dumahel possess the power to enter and manipulate dreams. They are rare and always born as twins.

Fallen – Once angels of the Heavens, Fallen now reside in the many realms in Hell and give their allegiance to the current ruler of Hell. Fallen have crimson wings.

Guardians – Fate's warriors, tasked with protecting Chosen mortals, so they can fulfill their fated destiny. Fate exiled the Guardians to the mortal world over three hundred years ago. They have black wings.

Nuriel – Half Fallen Raziel/half mortal, Nuriel possess the ability to cast ancient magic.

Purah – Crystalline water from the Eternal Fountain, found in the Heavens. Purah is toxic to Fallen.

Raziel – Angels who cast magic, commonly used to disguise the immortal world from mortal eyes.

Sareal – The Protector of the Heavens.

PROLOGUE

Blaine
Aralim, Hell
Roughly two years ago

"You either sit down and connect me with the Ice Queen or I send your sister to the Infernal Pits for a few centuries. The choice is yours." Fire burned in Blaine's belly, and he cursed himself for letting his emotions gain control.

The Dumahel before him looked as though she was one shock away from fainting right there in his living room. Her gaze darted between him and her twin, who he currently had in a chokehold. Ebony struggled, acting out her part to perfection. Though, a tiny part of his soul, the fragment he unleased only on special occasions, longed to squeeze tighter.

Threats weren't usually his motivation of choice, but even he had limits. And right now, he'd reached them.

"You said you wanted me to pull an angel into a dream. Not the creator of the universe," her voice quivered.

He didn't reply. To be honest, he thought this half Azrael had more fire and determination. After all, she'd single-handedly dreamwalked herself right into his realm.

1

"Please," her twin pleaded, pulling heart strings. If he had any.

He clamped his tongue between his teeth to stop from laughing. When this was over, he'd commend his new sidekick for her acting skills.

When the half angel's face softened, he almost cheered at the victory. Using her sister as leverage would always work. Angels couldn't help but tap into their compassionate side. It would always be their biggest weakness.

He wiggled his fingers, increasing the flame sparking in his free palm for a bit more incentive. He could do this all day. Actually, he did. But that was beside the point. He'd been in Hell long enough to know that sooner or later, everyone always bowed to his will. Mostly sooner. And those who didn't, well, they ended up with a fate far worse than the deal he offered them.

But this Dumahel tested his patience like no other. The half Azrael /half mortal possessed so much light in her soul it made him nauseous. He'd offered her twin's freedom in exchange for one measly dreamwalk, and still she whined about how he'd lied to her.

Even though he had the ability, he never lied. Unlike his brother and that band of Boy Scouts stranded in the mortal realm, Blaine could lie to his soul's content. Whenever he wanted. But where was the fun in that? There wasn't any. In fact, he found it rather thrilling when he told the truth, and the recipient didn't believe him. Until the moment…they did. A smirk lifted the corner of his mouth. The look on their faces when they realized he'd told them the truth all along? Worth its weight in hellfire.

If one could weigh hellfire, that was.

Semantics.

He'd been sitting in his living room for far too long, patiently watching Ebony convince her twin to agree to their deal. Without the angelic blonde, he couldn't achieve his plan. He'd have to wait for another Dumahel born in the mortal realm. And that could take centuries. Time was of the essence. The more he idled by, the stronger Zath's powers grew. He'd already sacrificed far too much time to have his plan fail.

Ebony had managed to trick her twin into fake-rescuing her from Hell where she had no intention of leaving. It wouldn't be long until the twin's soulmate, his former beanie-wearing brother, came for her one way or another. More setbacks were not ideal.

He had no intention of keeping the angelic twin. Not when he only needed her for this one task.

Stretching open his palm farther, he intensified the flame until the heat tingled his cheeks. "I'm losing my patience."

The Duhamel's eyes widened before she regained her composure with a sharp lift of her chin. Such determination in an angelic soul. A trait she surely got from her mortal mother.

When he considered using a different party trick to haul her across the line, she opened her mouth. "Fine. But then I'm leaving."

About bloody time.

He gave her a curt, rather annoyed nod, and snuffed the flame in his palm as a gesture of goodwill, releasing her sister.

Hailee sat back on the couch beside her twin, and he took his usual seat in the cushiony armchair that had seen better days. He rather liked old things. Why bother replacing something that wasn't broken? Unless that something was the king of Hell that had ruled for far too long. That was another story.

He motioned to the females. "Shall we try again?"

The goody two shoes twin glared at her father sitting across from her. He'd almost forgotten the Azrael was still there. He'd manipulated Asher into gifting him his twin daughters long before their birth. Though, gifting wasn't the word the Azrael would use. It sounded much less confrontational than compelling.

The Dumahel closed her eyes as power radiated around them. Slight at first, unpracticed, until it practically poured from her skin. Ripples in the cool air he'd become accustomed to in his personal realm. With a wave of his hand, he could improve the temperature, but he'd never been one for summertime and all things warm. Unless that warmth in his chest came from the sweet bloom of revenge. He kind of liked it then.

"I'm ready," the angel murmured.

About time.

He nodded to Ebony, a simple confirmation that she should proceed as planned and dreamwalk him while connecting with her sister. In an instant, Ebony transported his mind to a dreamscape realm, neither here nor there. A campfire burned in the center of an open space, surrounded by thick wilderness. The hint of fresh snow on the brisk night air. Dirt and dried leaves scattered the ground by his boots. Imagery he'd seen several times and never cared for.

He'd never been outdoorsy.

Once the dreamscape fully evolved, he wasted no time instructing Ebony. "Connect us with your twin."

She nodded before closing her eyes while, he presumed, she searched for his sister's unique signature. Even though he'd ensured Ebony believed she'd choose the destination, he had other plans. Instead of bringing the Dumahel and that Ice Queen here, he rather liked the idea of surprising them.

Mentally willing a swift landscape change, he highjacked the dreamwalk and diverted them to a location he remembered vividly. One burned into his memory from so long ago it still hid in the farthest recess of his mind just waiting to torture him. A realm he'd visited frequently, right up until the moment he…didn't.

As the sickly-sweet smell of cherry blossoms drifted up his nostrils, he opened his eyes. Heavenly light assaulted his soul, scratching at the jagged surface, battling with his darkness, trying to heal him. It wouldn't. He'd Fallen far too long ago and had accepted his fate.

He reveled in the shocked expressions on the Dumahel twin's faces, particularly Hailee.

He cocked an eyebrow. "Someone has come into their full powers."

Without explaining further, he focused his attention on the female he'd come to see.

Fate.

Ice Queen. Creator of the Universe. Known by many names, though at heart she was all things good and heavenly bundled into one beautifully vicious angel. Pale blonde hair tumbled down her slender shoulders. Shimmering porcelain skin. Eyes the color of the clearest ocean, swirling with silver. But her wings always captured his attention. Iridescent white. Each soft, delicate feather perfectly crafted to weave together into the most stunning wings he'd ever laid eyes on.

And ever would.

He'd spent endless time in Hell imagining them. How the velvety feathers would glide between his fingertips. How his belly would quiver as he trailed his palms over the curved, outer edges all the way to the tips.

What her wings would feel like in his hands…as he pinned them above his mantle.

"Hello, love. You're looking rather angelic."

Fate stood before gliding toward him, ignoring the gaping looks from both Dumahel. Just as he did. He also ignored the annoying twitch appearing somewhere in his chest. Had he expelled too much power?

"Hell suits you, Blaine."

So nice of her to notice.

Heated air soothed the twitching muscle, expanding his lungs until they almost hurt. "You betcha it does."

Now they'd completed the pleasantries, he offered the Ice Queen the crook of his arm. He was a gentleman after all. "Shall we?"

They had much to discuss. In private.

The moment Fate hooked her arm in his, she waved her free hand, dismissing the Dumahel and terminating the dreamwalk in one swift motion. A flaunt of power. But he let that one slide. He only required the Dumahel to connect the dream, his own power would maintain it for long enough to conduct his business. And sure, Fate had a decent power reserve which probably helped. Not that he'd admit that to her.

In silence, they meandered down the sand-colored

gravel path, weaving between the mature cherry blossoms. Their heavily laden branches arched over the pathway as though protecting them from the cloudless clear blue sky above. Pale pink and white blossoms fluttered through the air, leaving a familiar, almost nostalgic scent in their wake. Lifting his gaze, he tracked a white blossom as it twirled above them, caught in an imaginary gust of wind. Spinning and tumbling, it battled against gravity until it finally lost and snagged in Fate's heavenly locks. Using his free hand, he plucked it from her hair, holding the fragile, almost innocent petal between his fingers before doing something that confused the hellfire out of him. He pocketed it.

With a grunt, he focused again on the path ahead.

"Zath's powers are increasing," Fate murmured, breaking him from his thoughts.

Just as well.

"I'm aware. It's intensifying quicker than I anticipated."

Which was the primary reason he'd initiated this dreamwalk.

Fate lowered her gaze, only for a fleeting moment, but that twitch in his chest returned. He really should focus his attention on their conversation, the objective of this dreamwalk, not the foreign sensations occurring in his body. They no longer mattered. But before he could think better of it, he placed his free hand on top of hers still looped through his arm. To aid her balance. Not to ease her burdens. That would be silly of him.

The vicious Ice Queen needed comfort from no one.

Remember that, Blaine...

"You need to stop him before he possesses the power to escape Hell."

Did he imagine Fate shiver? Surely, he did.

"He'll destroy the mortal realm. Everything I've created."

In the distance, he spotted his intended destination. A double chair swing, hung beneath a thick, sturdy branch of the tallest, oldest cherry tree in this realm. Releasing Fate's hand, he motioned for her to sit, then joined her, kicking off a gentle swing.

He looked back down the path they'd followed in more ways than one. Fate remained quiet beside him. He didn't know what was more confusing. The fact she barely spoke or how her gaze grew distant in the same direction as his.

He should draw her attention back to the task at hand, while they still had time. Yet instead, he found himself asking something else entirely. "What troubles you, love?"

Specks of silver flickered through her eyes as her skin radiated with the same unearthly glow. He recognized the signs having witnessed Fate's foretelling on more than one occasion.

"The book is missing."

Some soothsayer she was. He already knew that.

"Yes. A rather unfortunate turn of events. But don't worry, I'll retrieve it when you reincarnate the Nuriel."

She blinked a few times before looking at him. "This will be her last life."

He figured as much. They'd played this game for far too long now. Before, with Zath incapacitated in his Hell prison, the chase excited him. Challenging himself to locate the reincarnated soul quicker each lifetime. The thrill of tracking down Cole's soulmate before he did. The joyful power it gave him to know he was one step closer to achieving his goal.

Becoming the king of Hell.

He'd already envisaged a crown for the occasion and itched to finally place it upon his head.

"When will you reincarnate her soul?" he asked, excitement already bubbling in his belly.

Good, something productive to replace the annoying twitch higher up.

"Soon."

A sudden breeze whipped through the cherry trees, swaying the branches and propelling blossoms into the air before they reattached to the stems. The landscape wobbled slightly.

He stood, offering Fate his hand as she joined him.

She closed her eyes briefly and when they reopened, a sheen of silver coated her irises. "The Guardians summon me."

He couldn't stop the smirk from lifting the corner of his mouth. "Most likely because I have EJ's soulmate in Aralim."

Their time was almost up. He knew it wouldn't last long, but now it was nearly over, that bloody twinge returned with a vengeance, transforming his smirk into a sneer. Clearly, he'd eaten something rotten. Or perhaps it was a result of centuries in Hell where smoke and ash now coated the lining of his lungs preventing them from functioning properly in this clean and wholesome realm. Regardless, his dreamwalk with the Ice Queen should end. Now. Before…well, before he suffered more indigestion.

Fate straightened. The blossoms in her crown thickened as more flowers bloomed right before his eyes. "The fate of all the realms depends on you stopping Zath."

"Look at the two of us," he lightened his tone, even though the darkness inside him roared to life. "Immortal enemies, working together to take down a common adversary. Isn't this fun?"

Fate blinked. "Delightful."

"There she is." He chuckled. "I've missed your sense of humor."

"This is your last chance, Blaine. You're *only* chance. Don't fail."

He snatched her chin between his thumb and forefinger, tilting her head back. Violent bursts of silvery light erupted in her eyes.

Leaning down, he lowered his voice to a harsh whisper, a mere breadth away from her rosy, pink lips. "Be careful, my love. Underestimating me will be exactly how I pluck the pretty little crown right off your pretty little head."

"I look forward to it."

CHAPTER ONE

Cole
Infernal Pits, Hell, current day

One day he'd save her from Hell. But today wasn't that day.

Until then, he'd walk through fire for even the slightest glimpse. Literally. Like now, this very moment. Each step threatened to melt the soles of his boots, sizzling the leather like hot coals dipped in cool water. Ash fluttered from the sky. Dark gray, thick residue as delicate as snowflakes, only far more sinister. It choked his lungs, constricting his throat. Or maybe his inability to draw a breath was from the thought of seeing her again.

Last time he'd made this journey, she told him to leave. Actually, she swore at him and begged him to end her soul. He'd already done that countless times before, right? What was one more? The accusation had shocked him and left him a trembling, empty shell.

She'd died by his hands so many times he'd lost count. No, that wasn't true. He knew the score, having used the memories to torture himself over and over until their history repeated once more.

A pretentious castle loomed in the distance. Tall, blackened pillars stretching into the fire drenched sky as though they could spear the oversized sun. If it weren't for the scorching landscape, he could almost imagine one of those mortal movies where a princess tossed her hair out the highest window. Long raven curls would tumble down the side of the stone tower, begging a prince to take hold and rescue her.

One day.

And on that day, the princess would die her final death. He'd end her torture. He'd mist her to a place filled with endless summer days and warm cozy nights. A realm where her soul would finally be at peace.

But today wasn't that day either. Regardless of how much she'd beg him, he couldn't save her from here. Until she reincarnated into the mortal realm, he could only plead for her forgiveness. For her to trust him one final time.

Fate had given him her word. The next time his soulmate was reborn, would be the last. He'd asked for it. Bargained for it. Though now, he wasn't sure he was ready.

Scrap that. He knew he wasn't.

Keeping a keen eye on the farthest tower, the tallest of all the pillars, he strode across the narrow foot bridge with sluggish steps. Below, some hundreds of feet down, fiery lava bubbled, spurting explosive fireballs toward him. But it didn't deter him. Nothing would prevent him from seeing her. Not lava. Not Fate.

Not his soulmate.

She could hate him for eternity, but he'd never give up. They were destined.

One day, their paths would align. Until that day, he would maintain hope.

On the other side of the bridge, he followed the shattered cobblestone path, making his way through the twisted streets weaving between the towers. Hundreds of them in all different directions, each leading to different entrances. Different prisons. Each one for a different tortured soul.

Fate banished souls to this twisted part of Hell for their crimes in the mortal realm. A period of adjustment as she called it. But Devoid, soulless mortals, and Fallen under Zath's command, frequented the Pits, indulging in the sickest version of themselves endlessly torturing the soul.

Thank Fate Zath wasn't aware that his soulmate occupied one of these towers. If he ever found out...

He snuffed that thought with a sharp shake of his head. No good would come from wandering that path. Zath wouldn't discover Evie. Before long, she'd arrive back in the mortal realm.

He should be thankful Fate didn't banish Evie to the Infernal Pits permanently. She possessed the power and the means. Instead, Fate cursed his soulmate to reincarnate every fifty mortal years.

Up ahead, at the end of the uneven path, he spotted his destination. Pausing for a moment, he willed his heartrate to steady while he imagined her beauty peering down at him from the sole glass-less window at the top. How she'd beckon him to join her with a simple wave and gorgeous smile. He would unfurl his wings and lift through the stale, humid air. Much quicker than walking. Using his wings though would alert any lingering Fallen that an angel was nearby. Then, someone would discover exactly who hid in this restricted tower.

Besides, taking those stone steps, ascending one at a time, built sweet anticipation deep within his soul. It also gave him a few precious moments to anticipate which of the many greetings he'd face. He had experienced more than he cared to count. Everything from her hurling stones at him the second he opened the door, to finding her huddled in a corner sobbing. Each time, the sight of her stuck in a never-ending hellish loop in this Fate forsaken wasteland, broke his damn heart.

Misting her from this place would incinerate her soul until she was nothing but embers in the ash filled sky. Leaving her here blackened his.

An eternity wasn't enough time to seek her forgiveness.

Yanking open the heavy door, he began the ascent. One step after the other, circling the narrow, twisting stone staircase, all the while focusing on his destination. Nearing the top, he caught her scent through the sulfuric undercurrent. Sweet and spicy. A soft floral scent that had always reminded him of dark red roses right before they bloomed. One step from the top, he stopped as another scent ambushed his nose. Awareness prickled his nape.

A Fallen was inside her tower.

This tower was accessible only to him. Fate assured him of that. He couldn't remain in the realm for long periods without risking his soul Falling. He'd Fall for her, but then his yearning to give her peace would fail. Making frequent, short visits was the most he could manage.

Rounding the final curve, his step faltered.

Blaine.

The Fallen leaned his shoulder against the door to Evie's chamber as though he had not a care in the universe. Of course, he didn't. Fate hadn't banished Blaine's soulmate to a desolate realm of Hell and made him watch the light fade from her eyes year after year.

His muscles tensed, coiling heat through his blood.

"How did you get in here?" He didn't have the patience to play nice.

Anger and resentment rolled off him in waves and he struggled to contain it. So much for each step calming his nerves. Seeing Blaine only elevated other less helpful emotions.

"Where are your manners?" The Fallen pushed off the wall and flipped up the collar on his aged leather jacket. Why he wore a jacket in Hell when the temperature felt like a million degrees, he'd never know.

One dark look from Blaine replaced his anger with shards of ice scraping down his spine. Had Blaine done something to Evie? Intercepted her path? Entered her chamber?

No. He wouldn't dare.

Yet, when he tilted his head, studying Blaine's pitch-black eyes, that ice morphed into an avalanche in his stomach.

He barged toward the door—

Blaine snagged the arm of his tunic, twisting it in his fist, yanking him backward.

"Let. Go."

Blaine fought against him. "You and I need to chat first."

His heart plummeted to the fiery lava moat surrounding the doomed towers. He'd sensed something was amiss. In the ancient connection tethering his soul to Evie's, he'd felt a burst of energy followed by...nothingness. The sharp change had prompted him to visit her earlier than planned.

Last time he was here, she told him never to return. It didn't matter what she said, he'd continue to come back. Seeing her in this tower, enduring her torture right alongside her, was his penance for the decisions he'd made. They'd made. The choices that had placed them on this path.

Sensing Evie still safe inside, he shrugged off Blaine's hand. "What do you want?"

"Word on the street is that your soulmate is transitioning to her next life shortly." He gave an exaggerated gasp, hand flat on his chest. "Oh, wait. My mistake. Her *final* life."

Another unwelcome reminder.

Fate had vowed that the next time Evie left this tower would be her last. He'd known the countdown had started the moment he agreed to help EJ rescue his soulmate. How long ago was that? One mortal year? More? With the time difference in Hell, he'd only seen Evie a handful of times since the bargain with Fate. He'd promised her everything would be all right soon.

Was he ready for the end?

Blaine moved toward the staircase. "It seems the hunt is about to begin once more, my friend."

As Blaine descended the first step, adrenalin spiked in his blood. "This is her last life. I won't let you take it from her."

The Fallen peered over his shoulder, eyes darkening. "Are you threatening me? I thought we were friends?"

Friends. That concept seemed so foreign. Maybe they'd been friends a long time before Blaine Fell, but since then, Blaine had only hurt those closest to him.

"I mean it, Blaine. I'll find her before you. At any cost."

Blaine's lip curled in a smirk. "The chase is half the fun, is it not?"

Without another word, Blaine continued his descent until Cole heard the heavy door groan open at the bottom.

Blaine being here, inside this tower wasn't a good sign. Protecting Evie during her last life was his priority. Especially when Blaine planned to end it.

Every choice Cole made had led to this moment. He wouldn't accept failure.

After shaking off the lingering unease, he steadied his breath and entered. A single lantern flickered on the opposite wall, casting ominous shadows even he shrank from. Blistery ice chilled the air despite the scorching temperature outside the tower.

He inched farther inside. "Evie?"

Whimpers sounded from the far corner, concealed in darkness. Raising his hand, he called his own shadows, using them to chase away the others. The sight almost brought him to his knees. Huddled in a tight ball on the stone floor, his soulmate buried her head between her arms.

He rushed to crouch by her side. "Evie?"

Whimpers deepened into violent sobs, shredding his heart. Her shoulders shook with each ragged breath. Her once glossy raven hair was now a matted mess atop her head as though she'd tried to tear the strands out.

He eased his arm around her shoulders to draw her into his embrace.

"Get away from me!" she shouted, shoving him

backward.

He stumbled, taken by surprise, but quickly recovered.

Over the centuries, he'd found her in countless emotional states when he visited. Distraught. Anxious. Irritated. Vulnerable and once, excited to see him. But now? This was by far the worst. Her tattered black dress bore deep gashes as though a wolf had ripped it to shreds, leaving her in nothing but the remains. Similar claw marks marred her legs. Sunken, dark patches beneath her eyes. And her eyes...her usually bright golden eyes were now glassy and unfocused. No, not unfocused. Skittish. As though uncontained fear raged behind them.

"Evie?" he murmured, crawling closer.

"Evie. Rosaline, Cicely, Nora! Which name will I have next?"

A vise squeezed his heart until it almost flatlined. "Evelina. You'll always be Evelina to me."

Her lips parted on a sharp inhale, and he thought for a second, he'd broken through her fear. Until the light dimmed behind her eyes once more.

"Names don't matter. What matters is us. Our souls." He reached for her hand, but she swatted it away. Pressure ached in his jaw as his gaze slid back to the gashes in her legs and the matching ones visible through the ripped fabric barely covering her arms. "Who did this to you?"

"You." Her wild gaze suddenly focused and locked on him. "You did this to me."

Dread twisted in his gut. Of all the states he'd found her in, her remembering the choices he made, what he'd done, was the absolute worst. He experienced that guilt every day. And it crippled him each time she remembered.

"I'm sorry," he whispered, the words burning a path up his throat.

Sorry wasn't enough. Such a simple five letter word that couldn't encapsulate the devastating loss he experienced each time she died. The grief. The anger and bitterness she harbored toward him for putting her first.

Yet, he'd continue to say that word until his last breath. Because until someone invented another, it was the only one which even remotely described how he felt.

She glared at him.

He ached to brush the tears from her cheeks, to cradle her face in his hands and kiss them all away. But he knew better. The last thing he wanted was to cause her more hurt.

"You're not sorry, Cole. You knew this would happen. You always do. Yet, you do it anyway." She sobbed as tears streamed down her flushed cheeks. "You banish me to Hell. Locked in a castle to endure nothing but the memories. The memories of what you did."

Her fingernails dug into her calf and he suddenly realized how she'd gotten the scratches. Not a hellhound or mystical torture device. Her own nails.

So overwhelmed with emotion and…hatred toward him, she'd caused herself physical harm.

Nothing could've prevented the sinkhole splitting open his chest, engulfing his heart and soul in one swoop. Yes, each lifetime, he knew how it would end. What awaited them both on the other side. But he'd make that same choice again and again because the alternative was something he couldn't bear.

Drawing even closer, he tentatively curled his fingers around one of hers, easing her hand away from the bloodied cut in her leg. "I know it hurts, baby girl, but I promise you, it will end. This pain will end."

"When?" Her gaze lifted, wet lashes blinking back the last of her tears. "I...can't take any more, Cole. I would rather..."

He tightened his hand around hers. For countless centuries, he'd replayed the decision, their choice, and every time he arrived at the same conclusion. The precious time they spent together in the mortal world outweighed this torturous loop in Hell. Seeing her like this though, on the brink of destruction, emotionally wrecked, made him want to overturn all the choices he'd ever made. If he'd only let her go that first time. If he hadn't fought for her. Maybe then they wouldn't be huddled on the cold floor in the farthest corner of the Infernal Pits. Maybe, he could've spared her this pain.

Her hand slipping from his jolted him from his thoughts. He reached for it again, but his fingers ghosted through hers. Not just her hand, her whole arm...faded. Dissolved right before his eyes.

Alarm screamed in his head. "No."

"It's happening. I'm...returning." Her determined gaze pinned him, her voice hardening. "Don't find me. I don't want you to find me. Let me be. Let me live a full life."

"I love you. I'll always find you. Not finding you is never an option."

Nothing could stop him. She was his soulmate. Even for a few months, they would be together. Time didn't matter. He would protect her, fall in love with her all over again, rejoice in her soul awakening.

Grasping for her, he tried to hold onto her body, but her corporal form faded by the second until she was nothing but a ghostly shadow. Soon, her soul would reincarnate in the mortal realm.

His heart thumped back to life, already eagerly awaiting their reunion. This time would be different. This lifetime he'd fight to give her the ending she deserved.

Before she disappeared, the skin around her golden eyes tightened. "Find me and I'll never forgive you."

CHAPTER TWO

Cole
Mortal realm, current day

Cole dumped his duffle bag on the top step outside the Guardian mansion. Not knowing how long he'd be in the mortal realm, he stopped off at a department store and grabbed necessities. Being permanently in this realm might affect his ability to conjure simple items such as clothing. He wasn't sure. Every other time his soulmate reincarnated, he continued his duty, frequently misting to the mortal realm. For her last time though, he wanted to switch things up.

A gentle, wintery breeze swept across the porch, capturing dried, colorful leaves, swirling them through the air. Before her, he'd never stopped to appreciate the change of seasons in the mortal realm. Always focused on one task or another before returning to the Heavens. But everything was different now. Everything reminded him of her. Even the golden crumpled leaves sparked the memory of the last time he'd seen his soulmate. How she'd vowed to never forgive him if he found her.

Was it possible to protect her from a distance? To never reveal himself? He hung his head as the answer was always the same. No. One lifetime he'd tried, but in the end, the pull between their souls, the connection, drew them together regardless.

Or Fate intervened.

Either way, he'd rather his soulmate was safe and hating him, than…

Swallowing, he lifted his gaze back to the front door. He could've misted inside, like every other time he visited, or even strode through without knocking. But this visit deserved a bit more…formality.

He lifted his hand to press the doorbell, but the door swung open before he got the chance.

EJ stood in the doorway, ice-blue eyes narrowed. "Convenient timing, Reaper. Hails just made a fresh batch of cupcakes. It's like you have supersonic smell or something. Or you monitor her baking schedule."

"It's a cupcake kind of day, brother."

EJ frowned, eyeing the duffle bag by Cole's feet. "Going on a vay-cay?"

He lifted the duffle, mustering his best smile even though inside someone hacked at his chest with a pitchfork. All his earlier bravo seeped down his legs into the ground beneath his feet. He'd thought moving in with the Guardians would be easy. He'd aligned himself with them anyway. They were his…family. And ever since he'd aided EJ in rescuing Hailee from Hell, he'd spent more and more time with them in the mortal realm.

But now…he'd made that move permanent.

EJ stilled, his arms rigid, gaze distant, focused on something over Cole's shoulder. Silvery sparks glittered in the Guardian's irises. A look he knew all too well. Fate had sent EJ visions on and off since she banished the Guardians to the mortal realm over three hundred and fifty years ago on a mission to save Blaine, their fallen brother. But the Guardians weren't the first angels Fate cursed.

No, that title belonged to him.

The sinkhole in his chest widened, threatening to drag him under while he waited for EJ's vision to end. From what he knew, the visions captured a future where EJ would fail. Of late though, the Guardian had managed to change each outcome. He'd saved Aric before he chose Hell with his soulmate. Then he saved his own soulmate when Blaine had kidnapped her. More recently, he'd had a vision of Raine prowling toward Zath, a long sword dragging through the dirt behind her.

All those visions had ended differently. Was EJ having one now about Cole? About Evie? Invisible hands squeezed around his neck, making him sway.

When EJ blinked a few times, his eyes returning to their usual color, Cole stepped forward, urgency in his voice. "Is it her? Has she been reincarnated?"

EJ's mouth tightened. "Looks like Fate made good on her deal, Reaper. This is her last life."

Cole nodded, words stuck in his throat. Fate had vowed that this would be his soulmate's last reincarnation. That the torture would end.

What had EJ seen in the vision? Part of him yearned to know every tiny detail, even if the outcome could change. Though, another part, at least for a few moments more, appreciated the serenity of not knowing. That way, he could pretend that his soulmate lived in the Heavens where she belonged, surrounded by endless sunny days and peace. Instead of the Hell loop Fate cursed her with until her final day. Which was now sooner than he cared to admit.

When he'd begged Fate to end his soulmate's

torture, he hadn't expected her to agree. Let alone actually follow through.

EJ stepped back, opening the door wider for Cole to enter. "We better find you a room. One farthest away from the kitchen so you can't make midnight cupcake raids and piss off my soulmate."

He chuckled to himself, following EJ upstairs to the entertainment room where he found the other Guardians mingling over drinks, probably before a few of them headed out for patrol.

"Guess who's finally making it official?" EJ announced to the room.

Raven's gaze lifted, darted to the duffle bag in Cole's hand and back. "It's happening?"

They both knew this day would come. Heavens, it had been brewing for centuries. But every time Cole thought of it, it felt too soon.

"Happened. I had a strange feeling, so I went to visit her. She faded in my arms." He dumped the duffle bag in the hall. "After she disappeared, the entire tower crumbled around me. I barely made it out. There's nothing left."

Conversation erupted between the Guardians, but his mind shut down, refusing to focus on the vision of his soulmate's tower becoming nothing but a pile of fiery rubble. Sweet coconut drifting through his nose lured him to the couch where he grabbed a cupcake. The one with light pink sprinkles over white icing. Closing his eyes, he took the first bite and allowed the explosion of tropical flavors to transport him to a happier place.

"Groan much, Reaper?"

He opened his eyes to EJ glaring at him. "They're

good."

From the couch across from him, Hailee chuckled. "You're welcome, Cole. There's plenty, so don't hold back on account of EJ's smartass remarks."

"Sweetness, if you encourage him, he'll never leave."

"Don't pretend that wouldn't make you happy." Hailee patted EJ's cheek. "Besides, you can always lick the bowl."

The Guardian leaned over and whispered something in Hailee's ear, making her blush, before he moved behind the bar.

On the nearest barstool, Aric took a long draw of his drink. "Give us the low-down, man. How old will she be? Where will she be?"

Dusting crumbs off his shirt, he sat beside Aric, mainly so he wouldn't outstay his welcome on the first day by gorging on Hailee's treats. "It's never the same. Usually, by the time I find her she's about to…" He swallowed the tightness in his throat. "Even when I find her with enough time to…get to know her, I try to keep my distance. Knowing she'll die by my hand helps to keep me away."

Raven perched on the armrest next to Tayla. "Last time we found her, it was only a couple of days before her twenty-fifth birthday."

"Don't remind me," he mumbled.

Eating that cupcake was a bad idea. Now it churned in his stomach ruining all future cupcakes.

He and Raven had always had an agreement. A pact. A vow of protection for when he couldn't be in the mortal realm. Though, it never changed the outcome. It always ended the same way.

Hailee straightened on the couch. "Twenty-five? The magic age when she becomes immortal?"

A Duhamel, half Azrael/half mortal, became immortal at twenty-five. Hailee had gone through the same change. Only, in each lifetime, his soulmate was still mortal. She never transitioned. Her dying at that age was probably a sick joke on Fate's behalf.

He swallowed, forcing the cupcake back down. "No. At twenty-five, she...dies."

Silence.

Raven, Aric and EJ had been in the mortal realm for longer, had aided him for many of his soulmate's reincarnations. They knew the outcome was always the same. The others didn't. The last time his soulmate appeared in the mortal realm was fifty years ago.

"Then the loop starts all over again," Raven added.

"Not this time."

Raven drew back. "Why not?"

He peered at EJ, still busy squashing mint leaves and ice in a glass. "You didn't tell them?"

EJ shrugged. "I didn't get a chance, what with us busting down Hell to rescue Hails, then all the shit that went down with Raine's frickin' magical sword."

Had all of that happened between his deal with Fate and now? He'd lived in his own tortuous Hell for so long, sometimes he lost track of time and forgot others had their own trials. He swiveled on the stool to address everyone at once. "When I agreed to share my shadows with EJ so he could enter Hell, I asked—"

"Demanded." EJ scoffed. "Reaper stood toe-to-toe with Fate and frickin' demanded it. I thought she was gonna kick you into the next realm."

Pride swelled in his chest remembering the

moment. "Anyway, I told Fate the next time she reincarnated my soulmate, I wanted it to be the last. She agreed. When she dies in this lifetime, her torture will end. She can finally be at peace."

"Right." River sat on the pool table with his legs crossed. "If she just poofed out of Hell, does that mean you have like, eighteen years to wait until she's...an adult? I hate to tell you, but you're super early."

"It doesn't work like that." He was so accustomed to their unique situation, he struggled to explain it. "Her mortal form is already born in this realm but soulless. When Fate reincarnates Evie's soul, the mortal female is always twenty-four. It doesn't matter what she looks like because it's her soul I love. That's how I recognize her."

"That's so sappy I want to puke." Raine groaned.

Tayla laughed before turning to him. "Couldn't you search for a soulless mortal female and find her before Fate reincarnates her soul?"

"I attempted that once. There are billions of mortals in this realm, it was impossible even for me to locate all of them. And it also wouldn't surprise me if Fate created more than one potential Evie to foil that plan."

"Sounds like something she'd do." Aric shot back his whiskey. "How do we stop her from dying this time?"

They didn't. But how could he say that?

He surveyed the room and the immortals gathered around him. Despite Fate banishing them to the mortal realm on an impossible mission, they'd come out victorious. Nearly all of them had found love, their own soulmates, and happiness away from the Heavens.

Contentment. He didn't dare hope that could happen for him one day. The best he could hope for when this ended was Fate finally permitting Evie into the Heavens.

Not the darkest pits of Hell.

Surely, Fate, after all this time, was capable of forgiveness. If not, he planned to bargain.

He opened his mouth to reply, but a prickle erupted at the back of his neck. A Fallen was on the property. The others must've sensed it too, given how they froze. Raine reached for the dagger strapped to her thigh before bolting out the door, followed close behind by Slater, her once-Fallen soulmate.

He and the others raced after them. Lifting his palm, he summoned his shadows. Partly to ensure he still had the power after choosing to permanently reside here.

Outside, Ebony, Hailee's twin sister, stood in the center of the manicured lawn. Dressed all in black, her crimson wings were a stark contrast. She tilted her head, glaring at the sun as though the damn thing did her wrong.

Hailee separated herself from the others, moving closer with EJ right by her side. He doubted the Guardian would let her out of his sight again, and he didn't blame him one bit. If he had the opportunity to have his soulmate by his side for all eternity, nothing would get in his way.

Hailee paused a few paces from her sister. "Ebony, what are you doing here?"

"Hey, sis. Long time no see. Can't chat though, I've come for the book."

Tingles raced through his blood. Book? What

book? Surely, she didn't mean...

"We don't have it." Raine tossed a dagger in the air and caught it before tossing it up again.

His heart beat faster, spiking adrenaline through his blood.

"You stole it from me. I saw you. Blaine wants it."

Book...Blaine...

As though time slowed, he turned to Raine. "What...book?"

She frowned at him, still tossing the dagger. "Some ancient grimoire this low life Fallen had in a cave while she tortured an innocent Raziel."

No. It couldn't be.

Sweat beaded on his brow, sudden heat making his vision waver.

"Don't get your panties in a knot. The book..." Slater threw his hands in the air. "Vanished just after we got it. Disappeared into thin air."

Vanished. *The book.*

Something snapped his last tether of restraint. His vision righted, zeroed in on Raine. "You had the book and didn't tell me?"

Someone cursed behind him. Possibly Raven.

Raine and Slater exchanged confused looks which irritated him further.

"You had the book in your possession? The one object that Blaine desires more than anything, which will ultimately lead to Evie's soul dying forever, and you didn't think to mention it?"

How had he not sensed it at the mansion? In the mortal realm?

Slater inched forward, stepping slightly in front of Raine. "Listen, buddy. We had no idea you were looking for the book. Had we, I'm sure Raine would've told you. Now, check that attitude."

He raked his fingers through his hair, pulling the roots as he roared at the Heavens.

A steady hand squeezed his shoulder. "We didn't know, my man. I've never seen it."

Raven.

He knew the Guardian spoke the truth. Not just because he couldn't lie, but because they'd always had each other's backs. Besides, he'd never told them of the book's importance.

If only he hadn't kept that to himself all these centuries. Only him, his soulmate, and Blaine knew about the book. Oh, and Fate. Now, it seemed Ebony and the other Guardians did too.

That damn book.

Many centuries ago, his soulmate had acquired it. Since then, this never-ending nightmare had tortured them both and commenced a life-size game of cat and mouse every fifty years.

Blaine needed the book.

Cole needed to destroy it.

"Blaine wants the book. If you're hiding it, he won't be happy," Ebony said.

Raven stepped closer to the Fallen. "How about you tell my brother, the next time he wants to send a message, he can deliver it himself."

With a sneer, Ebony stretched out her wings before misting away.

Raven turned back to face him. "Tell us everything, Cole. Starting with why the fuck Blaine wants a book."

CHAPTER THREE

Evelina

Evelina strolled up and down the corridors, double checking that everyone had left for the day. Too often, she found a couple or an obsessed book nerd hiding in the rear stacks secretly hoping someone locked them in overnight. Sure, the idea of hanging out in the library wing, surrounded by almost three thousand historic texts, gave a buzz to a select few. But surely after the lights went out, and the alarms turned on, then the practical side would kick in. Who could go all night without snacks? Not her. She'd die of starvation.

No food or drinks were permitted in the upper levels of the library housing the more restricted collection. Hard no. Everyone knew the rules. If visitors happened to miss the ten signs in big, bold text posted at various heights along the connecting corridor, the main reception desk caught them when they checked bulky bags.

The reception staff took their job seriously. Sometimes, a little too seriously, but that was another story.

Unfortunately, though, bag checks didn't weed out stupidity. On occasion, more than she cared to count, couples seeking more than a buddy read would sneak in some adult time between the stacks. Believe it or not, the comfy couches were for reading. Not canoodling.

Canoodling? Good lord, how old was she? This job had aged her. She should've studied something trendy like marketing or how to become the next socialite. Not ancient history where she'd ended up working in a library rather than as a museum curator or out on an actual dig site discovering hidden treasures.

Again, another story.

Fifteen minutes before closing time, she rounded the last stack and found a young couple snuggled on the couch. Given the whispered panting coming from their locked mouths, and their wandering hands, they weren't here for the books.

Evelina strode right up to them. "Sorry, the library is about to close."

The girl's perfectly shaped brows shot up on her flushed face, but she made no move to climb off the dude's lap. "Oh, we hadn't realized how late it was."

Sure.

She continued staring them down until they got the hint and untangled themselves to stand. The dude was kind of hot. She couldn't blame the girl for indulging in a piece of him while surrounded by books. But not on her shift. She checked her watch and forced herself not to tap her foot to hurry them along. If she didn't wait until they left, they'd only hide somewhere else in the library. Possibly somewhere she'd already checked. Then, in the morning, she'd find used condoms beneath the couch. Eww. If couples went to all the trouble of sneaking in to have sex, the least they could do was take their evidence with them.

The guy packed up their reading material before draping his arm around the girl on their way toward the exit. "Have a great night."

"You, too," she replied, holding back her smirk.

Plan foiled. How sad.

She peered over the railing to the ground floor, watching their backs as they made their way past the front desk where her grumpy coworker barely even lifted her head as they walked out.

After adjusting the seat cushions, she headed to the final upper section. Now, if she were to hide out in the library for the night, with snacks of course, she'd set up between these stacks. She checked this section last each night for that reason. Ancient history. Even brushing the pads of her fingers along the spines sent a heated thrill through her blood. No wonder no man lived up to her expectations. All the good ones were dead or fictional.

Lost in thought, she turned back to the corridor.

Her step faltered.

A man stood at the entrance to the stack with his forearm casually resting on a shelf. He wore all black, everything from the T-shirt beneath his aged leather jacket to his military style boots. Frowning, she lifted her gaze to his face. His almost black eyes stared back. Recognition tickled the far recesses of her memory. Had she met this man before? Not that she remembered, yet there was something undeniably familiar about him.

Beneath the soft lighting, his haphazardly styled black hair almost reflected blue. Longer strands fell in his face. His whole demeanor screamed old money and wealth, even if his attire said the opposite.

But his eyes. Endless pools of darkness. They called to her, lured her in until she took a step toward him.

"Hello, love."

A regal English accent wasn't unusual in Ireland. Nor were American ones, like hers.

She cleared the fog invading her mind and forced her feet to stop gravitating toward him. "Do I...know you?"

The corner of his lip kicked up in a devastating smirk. "Not in this lifetime."

Strange answer. But also kind of...cute.

Although fluttery wings erupted in her belly, she sensed this guy wasn't here to rattle her. Even if he portrayed a bad boy capable of murdering her and hiding her body so deep in the forest no one would ever find her, she didn't feel threatened by him.

She turned her attention to a nearby book, adjusting the spine to align it in a neat row with the others on the shelf. "Do you need something? The library is about to close."

When she stole a glance across her shoulder, he flashed a smile that would shatter the hearts of millions. If that were his intention, she had no interest.

Right?

"I'm glad you asked." He stepped into the stack. "I'm looking for a particularly rare book and wondered if you could help me."

The flutters quickened for an entirely different reason.

Rare book? *You bet.* After all, locating rare artifacts was her specialty. Her heart's calling. She rarely had the chance because the overentitled staff always beat her to it.

Instead of squealing in delight, or doing cartwheels down the stack, she opted for a more professional demeanor. "I'd be happy to assist. We open again tomorrow at nine."

His smile widened. Clearly, this guy was used to getting what he wanted. "It will only take a moment."

Any other night, she'd insist he return tomorrow. But something about him was different. Something she couldn't identify. The sense she'd met him before, or he knew her. *Really* knew her. Besides, hardcore collectors or historians rarely came here in person, opting for email over face-to-face conversation. Fire had destroyed a large portion of the artifact collection in the southwest wing about ten years ago, including rare texts. Only a few remained on display behind temperature-controlled glass cabinets.

He was probably looking for one of those.

She turned to him. "I'll do a quick search on the main catalog, but any more than that will have to wait until tomorrow."

"Of course." He stepped aside, motioning for her to lead the way.

Walking one step behind, he followed her down the long corridor to the front entrance of the library. Her coworker had already flipped the closed sign on the door and must be turning off the lights on the ground floor display cases. That woman had their closing routine down to the second.

When he continued to follow her around the reception desk, she quickly replaced the rope preventing him from entering the staff only section. Though, that same strange feeling told her if it suited him, he'd enter regardless.

Awakening the catalog computer, she readied on the search engine. "What's the name of the book?"

"It has no title."

She frowned, lifting her gaze. "No title?"

Just another good-looking dumbass wasting her time.

"That's right."

Fine. She'd humor him for a tiny bit longer, but only because she...didn't want him to leave. Not that she'd admit that to anyone but herself. There was something about this guy that...she didn't know. Captured her attention? Sure, all that dark hair, bad boy vibe energized her in a strange way. He also smelled good. Sinful. Wicked. Leather with a fiery undertone. But there was more. As though they'd not only met before but had a long draw-out history together.

Impossible.

She'd remember him.

She shook off the feelings and readied her fingers at the keyboard once more. "Who's the author?"

"You wouldn't believe me if I told you."

On second thought, this guy was hellbent on keeping her past closing time on a Friday night. Margaritas beckoned.

Plastering on a polite smile, the same one she'd mustered thousands of times before, she said, "I'm sorry, without an author or title, I can't find the text you're looking for. You're welcome to come back when you have more information. Even the year it was discovered or published would be a start."

From the inside breast pocket of his jacket, he withdrew a crumpled photograph, unfolded it, and placed it flat on the desk in front of her. "How about a picture?"

Damn him! Curiosity curled its claws around her

and raised her hand to the paper. She could almost hear the guy's satisfaction through his charming smirk. Lucky for him, he didn't gloat otherwise she'd kick his ass to the curb. And keep the picture.

"When was this taken?"

A long time ago given the crumbled edges and faded image. Yet, the quality, the detail, said otherwise. Instinctively, she flipped it over, looking for a date.

"Several centuries ago."

She almost scoffed. The quality of this photo wasn't possible centuries ago. Unless he meant the text inside the book?

While he remained quiet, studying her, she focused on the book in the photo.

"It's definitely old," she said. "Some would say before our time, but I can't confirm the century without seeing it for myself."

From what she could tell, it resembled a grimoire. Chunky, maybe two hundred or so pages. The paper was thicker, so that would bulk it up. The cover secured with a leather strap, knotted on the side. Small indentations marred the surface, as though stamped into the leather but she couldn't make out the detail. She'd never seen anything more stunning.

Her blood sung whimsical tunes at the thought of reading the secrets inside.

"These markings." Just above the photo, she followed one of the lines with her finger as it intertwined with the others. "They remind me of something, but I can't figure out what."

Her heart beat a little faster. Of course, it did. She lived for finds like this. Ones where she could bury her nose in the musky smell of aged parchment and inhale the history.

Orgasmic. Who needed a man?

A little breathless, she lifted her attention to the stranger. His eyes had lightened a touch, but still resembled deep, dangerous, forbidden pools. They continued to draw her in.

"I…" She cleared her throat. "This is really fascinating, and I'll admit you piqued my interest. But I can't find the book without knowing a bit more information."

When she offered the picture back to him, he held up his hand. "Hold onto it, maybe it will trigger a memory."

She slipped the picture into her pocket so she didn't accidentally leave it lying around for someone else. "What do you want with the book anyway?"

"It's a family heirloom of sorts."

This guy chose some strange words. Instinct still told her he held back the real reason for wanting the book, which of course, was his own business. But it made her crave to find it even more. The places she could see, the contracts she'd commission. One find could fund her for a few years, and she wouldn't have to work in a library, wishing for greater things.

The guy flashed a sinful grin, one that would make Jemma collapse in a puddle of swoon. "You'll help me find it?"

Her hand brushed her pocket. All she had was a damn picture. No title, no author. Not even an accurate year. The book could be anywhere, quite possibly in someone's private collection. But wasn't that half the fun? The research. The rabbit holes. She'd never backed down from a challenge, never given up. Never taken the easy road. Some would say she had the fire of a dragon inside her belly once she discovered a loose thread. The drive to unravel it consumed her.

Uncovering mysteries was her jam. A modern-day treasure hunter without the expeditions.

Oh, what the hell. It couldn't hurt to at least do a bit more digging. She had nothing to lose.

She shrugged one shoulder, reining in her excitement. "Sure. Why not?"

His smirk deepened, as though he never had any doubt she'd agree. Why did it suddenly feel as though she'd signed over more than her research skills?

As he turned to leave, she stopped him. "Wait, I don't know your name."

"Yes, you do, love. You simply don't remember it." He gave her an exaggerated, low sweeping bow. "Blaine."

CHAPTER FOUR

Cole

After unpacking his limited belongings in a guest bedroom on the second floor, Cole made his way down to the lower level of the Guardian mansion following the chatter and laughter to the formal dining room. At the open doorway, he paused for a moment to truly appreciate the sight. Usually when he visited the Guardians it was to drop in and say hi, maybe share information, help them out with a situation. Steal a cupcake or three. After all, he was already there. It wasn't like he visited solely to eat Hailee's cupcakes. That would be ridiculous.

But rarely, if ever, had he joined them for a formal meal. Something about this moment, like the one earlier when he walked through the front door rather than misting, felt defining. New. Branching down an unchartered path.

The Guardians and their soulmates were all seated around a large table, passing trays of hot food between each other. Mixed scents of freshly baked bread, seared meats, sweet pastries filled his nose, relaxing his shoulders. Homely, comforting. Several conversations carried on at the same time and he couldn't help but smile. Each Guardian never ventured far from their soulmate. Always touching in some way, whether it be

41

with their hands or lingering gazes. Many times, Raven had told him about how the Guardians had made the most of their banishment from the Heavens. How they'd formed a family outside the shimmering gates. A home away from home.

Family. A sense of belonging.

He witnessed all of that here.

A dull ache settled low in his chest, adding weight to his already sluggish legs. He'd wanted to give this to his soulmate. To Evie. But when he'd first met her, Fate had already marked her soul for Hell. Ripping Evie's dreams, wants, needs, right out of her hands. He'd never had the chance to offer her more. Since then, each lifetime he'd tried his best to keep his distance. Tried everything he could to break the curse thrust upon them. Nothing worked. They'd had to endure the motions of each lifetime knowing it would end the same.

She'd never live past twenty-five. Never experienced joy such as this—a family gathered for an evening meal surrounded by love and hopes for the future.

She'd never truly be his.

Previously, the most he could offer her was a few precious weeks or months, when he didn't interfere with her life. This time though, she'd made it clear that if he did, she'd never forgive him.

But could he stay away? Would it make a difference? No. Blaine would still find her, even if he didn't.

That was a fate far worse than any curse.

Despite his best intentions or whatever vow he made to himself, the pull between their souls always triumphed. He always found her. She always died.

By his hands.

"You gonna join us?"

Raven stood beside him, hands in his pockets, a slight frown on his face. So lost in his own thoughts, he hadn't even noticed the Guardian get up from the table.

"I..." He shook his head, not sure how to convey the destructive storm wreaking havoc with his emotions.

"We'll find her, Cole. We always do."

He eyed the Guardian. The one he considered a brother more than a friend. Friend seemed too cold and distant for the bond they shared between them. He thought back to the time when Raven had lost his own soulmate and the devastation that followed. He never wanted someone to experience the crushing weight of watching their soulmate die. Yet, he carried that weight year after year. Decade after decade. Century after century.

Now, this lifetime, the curse would end. Not his pain, not his anguish, only the curse. His soulmate's torture.

Peace was all he had left to offer her.

"This is the last life," he said, his voice scratchy.

Raven's gaze travelled back to the table, in Tayla's direction, who threw her head back laughing at something EJ had said. "Then we hold nothing back." After a long moment, he turned back to Cole. "Even if it means playing dirty. We're all in with you, my man. We have your back."

He swallowed, casting his gaze to the other Guardians gathered around the table. To beat Blaine, they'd have to play dirty. That Fallen would stop at nothing to obtain the book and Cole's soulmate.

But neither would Cole.

No one should underestimate what he'd do to finally grant his soulmate the peace she deserved.

A familiar quiver rippled through him making his shoulders sink. Souls. As an Azrael, he was bound to collect souls and escort them to their final resting place in either the Heavens or Hell. He'd hoped Fate would pause his duty while he searched for his soulmate, but he wasn't that lucky. And Fate wasn't that accommodating. She'd granted him permission to reside permanently in the mortal realm for Evie's last life, but he still had to fulfill his Azrael obligations.

If he left it too long, ignored the pull until it forced him to respond, it would cripple him. Infect his own soul with a poison like darkness that would leave him reeling here in the mortal realm. He'd learned that lesson early on, back when Fate had forbidden him to return beyond the shimmering gates of the Heavens. Back when she'd cursed him and Evie.

His stomach clenched, twisting into tight vicious knots making him wrap an arm around his middle.

"Souls?" Raven asked, a reassuring hand on Cole's shoulder.

He nodded, straightening once the clenching subsided.

"How long's it been?"

"Too long." Usually, he could go for a few days without collecting souls, letting them bank up so to speak. After all, he wasn't the only Azrael. There were many more who also retrieved souls and escorted them to their final resting place. Only, those other Azrael had the advantage of accessing the Heavens, or more accurately, the healing power of heavenly light. Once Azrael ventured beyond the shimmering gates, the healing rays would eliminate any lingering side effects. They wouldn't suffer the nausea and crimpling migraines like he did. They'd heal and carry on as though they'd collected the soul immediately after death.

Not him.

He suffered that shit for days after. Then the cycle recommenced.

Sweat coasted down his spine as another tremor coursed through him. "I haven't escorted any souls since before I saw Evie last. In Hell."

Raven swore. "You gotta go. We haven't seen you for almost a fortnight."

He should've escorted souls before misting to the Guardian mansion, but he'd been so eager to search for his soulmate, to make it official, that he'd neglected his other duties. Would it kill Fate to give him a day off? A much-deserved vacation?

He'd surely earned it.

But she wouldn't.

Despite every fiber of him urging him to stay in the mortal realm and look for Evie, he couldn't. He needed to be at his best, physically and mentally, to beat Blaine.

With a heavy sigh, he nodded once more. "I'll be back as soon as I can."

"In the meantime, I'll get EJ to start searching for Evie." Raven squeezed his shoulder. "We'll find her."

With a final nod, he misted from the mortal realm, reappearing in his own. A waiting room of sorts. Stark white. So blinding, he blinked a few times until his vision adjusted. He'd never been to another Azrael's realm, only his own, so he couldn't comment on whether they were all the same. If they were, he pitied the others. Unlike the dining room at the Guardian mansion, this place lacked that homely, comforting feel. It resembled more of a mortal hospital crossed with a morgue. White walls, white floor. No windows or doors. The place needed a plant or two.

A brightly colored cupcake stand.

Beyond the long white corridor was the waiting area where he knew more than a dozen or so souls awaited him. They couldn't see each other. Probably thought they were the only souls in the room. But he could see all of them, and the thought of them rushing him the second he stepped into the room always made him restless.

Today though, he focused on what he needed to do afterward. *Get in and get out. Find Evie.* Once he finished here, he could recover at the Guardian mansion, then find his soulmate.

With renewed purpose, he strode down the hall and into the waiting room. Instantly, the transparent souls bombarded him with questions. Some shouting, some sobbing. Grabby hands pulled at his shirt. Others fell at his feet pleading for him to take them back to their loved ones. A few hung back at the outer edges of the room eyeing him with suspicion. Most didn't even realize they'd died. That they'd reached the end of the line. But some, particularly those destined for Hell, knew. Those were the souls he dealt with first. The darkness from those souls infected him the most on the flip side, and while Evie was on her last life, he couldn't risk being out of action for too long once he returned.

A middle-aged guy with a poor haircut and a fresh bullet hole in the middle of his forehead caught his attention first. He pushed through the souls crowding around him, beelining for him.

As he reached out to touch the guy's shoulder to mist him to Hell, the guy spoke. "Are you the Azrael Cole?"

Strange question. Not many mortals knew the names of the angels who escorted them. Come to think of it, no mortal had ever called him by his name.

The knowing glint in this guy's narrowed eyes made him pause. His legs and arms tensed. He gave a curt nod.

"Blaine has a message for you."

Air rushed from his lungs. Surely, he'd misheard. "What did you say?"

"Blaine sent me here with a message."

Blaine.

How had Blaine sent him a message via a dead mortal? Only Fate allocated souls to Azrael. Blaine couldn't possibly know this mortal would end up assigned to Cole. Such a huge gamble, it surprised him that Blaine would take it.

Why didn't Blaine track him down and deliver the message himself? Or even mist to the Guardian mansion.

Ice trickled down his spine as wariness crept in.

The only reason Blaine would not deliver a message himself was if something else demanded his attention. Or someone.

Evie.

He gripped the dead guy by the neck of his scruffy

shirt, shoving him against the wall. "Tell me."

"Blaine said to tell you he found her. That he beat you again."

Fury erupted inside him. Blaine beating him wasn't possible. The Fallen couldn't have found Evie before him. Cole had left Hell immediately after Evie's soul reincarnated. Even though time moved differently in the mortal realm, if Blaine had already found her, he must've known where she'd been reborn. He must've had help. Trackers on every continent. Even then it would take days, if not weeks to find her.

Unless…Fate.

No. Impossible. She wouldn't aid Blaine.

He shoved the soul again, harder this time. "You're lying. Enjoy Hell you piece of shit."

Without another word, he misted to the fiery gates and threw the mortal inside before he had a chance to protest. He didn't have time for distractions. Especially lies delivered to him with the intention of throwing him off his game.

Returning to the waiting room, he escorted the remaining souls without sparing them a single glance. Though, the quiver in his stomach remained, as did the first guy's words in the back of his mind.

Once he cleared his waiting room of souls, he misted back inside the Guardian mansion. The nausea hit him like hellfire straight to the gut. He doubled over at the waist, heaving. Putting one foot in front of the other, he stumbled down the hall toward his room. Halfway there, EJ slung Cole's arm around his shoulder, bearing the weight, and helping him to his room, lowering him to sit on the bed.

"First, Reaper, you look like shit. Second, while

you were away, a courier pigeon in the form of a crimson-winged evil Fallen delivered an invitation from Blaine."

He leaned over, cradling his churning stomach. "Blaine?"

EJ crouched and waved the invitation in front of his face. "Creepy ball at an even creepier castle. But that's not the creepiest thing."

Pushing aside another wave of nausea, he lifted his head. He loved this Guardian, but today wasn't the day for riddles. Not when at any second, he might throw up on his shoes.

"Inside the invitation was a name. Evelina Fairburn."

What were the odds? Daggers stabbed his temples, and it took all his effort to stay conscious.

"Turns out she's a twenty-four-year-old female living in Ireland."

Oh, Fate. All the pieces stitched together. The soul he'd escorted to Hell was right. Blaine had found Evie. It had to be her. Why else send him an invitation with her name on it? Blaine had set this entire plot in motion and now wanted to gloat.

"When's…" He gagged as bile burned the base of his throat. "When's the ball."

EJ disappeared into the adjoining bathroom before returning with a glass of water and wash cloth. "Rest up quick, Reaper. You're getting your fancy on tomorrow night."

CHAPTER FIVE

Evelina

Someone knocked on the glass doors to the library. Evie jumped so high her knees slammed the underside of the desk. On the other side of the door, Jemma balanced takeout containers in her hands with a bottle of wine tucked under her arm.

Laughing, she unlocked the door for her friend to enter. "You gave me a freaking heart attack."

"You forgot our lunch date," Jemma grumbled, zipping past her to the desk. "I bet you don't even know what day it is."

"Sure, I do. It's Thursday." She reengaged the lock on the door.

Spoiler alert: she had no clue what day it was. Which often happened when she caught a trail. All her energy diverted to finding the next clue. And given the library had closed for the holidays, she didn't even have the routine of work to keep her occupied and on task.

Nope. The hunt for this mysterious book had consumed every waking thought.

During the holiday break, library staff often came in to catch up on cataloging or research without having to deal with the public. But given the forecast for heavy snow today, she doubted anyone besides her would venture out. Her and Jemma.

Jemma transferred the takeout onto the desk, then swung around, throwing a dramatic hand on her hip. "I knew it. You're obsessed with something. Spill."

Her best friend knew her too well. So, she should, they'd been best friends since college when Evie had studied abroad, and they'd lived together for their final year.

"I can't help it. I have an addictive personality."

Jemma patted her shoulder, ushering her to the food. "I know. That's why I'm such an awesome friend and brought you lunch."

The delicious smell of barbequed meat drifted into the air making her tummy go from not hungry to hangry in an instant.

"And it's Sunday by the way, not Thursday."

Had it been over a week since the mysterious Blaine gave her the photo?

Trying to rein in her shock at losing so much time, she forced a smile. "I knew that."

"No, you didn't, but you're forgiven. Now, tell me everything."

As Jemma set about opening and arranging the takeout containers, she poured wine into coffee mugs from the break room while confessing her latest obsession.

"You remember how I told you about the strange guy that came here looking for a book?"

Jemma nodded. "The cool one that looks like a witchy book?"

"Yeah. That's what I thought at first, but the more I search for it, the more I think it's…I don't know."

She couldn't find the words to describe the connection she felt to the book. How her skin tingled every time she glanced at the photo, as though she'd seen it before. Not only that, she still couldn't shake the sense that she'd also previously met Blaine. That they'd known each other well. But she couldn't remember how or when. Even stranger was how he'd told her that she already knew his name.

Now, she enjoyed a good margarita on a Friday night at the local bar, but she'd never been drunk enough to forget meeting someone. Let alone someone like Blaine.

Who could forget him?

"Can't you do a search for it?" Jemma waved a fork at the computer screen.

She shook her head. "I have. Many times. I've tried different keywords, different databases, even looked under mythology and folklore searching for a mention in a non-fiction book. Nothing even remotely accurate. It's like the book doesn't exist anywhere but in this photo."

"Did you ask one of the dragon ladies for help?"

The reference to dragon ladies made her chuckle. The hardcore librarians who worked in the back room, living and breathing books but lacked…human personality. "No way. This one is mine. They stick their noses up every time I ask for a research task, like I have to be a thousand years old to have enough experience. I'm not telling them anything."

"You go girl." Jemma clinked her mug with Evelina's. "But have you considered that it's not real?"

She chewed a mouthful of noodles, contemplating Jemma's comment. That had also crossed her mind. What if Blaine was a weirdo who got his kicks by sending women on wild goose chases for fake books?

Maybe he'd return to the library after the holidays and laugh in her face that it had been one big prank. Or perhaps he wouldn't even reveal the joke, letting her search for the book forever while the thought of never finding it ate away at her soul.

Even with those possibilities, and really, she couldn't speak for the guy's character, a strange thrum in her blood told her the book was real.

More to the point, she'd seen it firsthand.

"I don't know how to explain it. It's like…I've…seen it before."

Jemma paused, fork at her mouth. "You've seen the book before?"

Just because they'd been friends for years, didn't mean Jemma wouldn't find her crazy and ditch her. She only had one close friend. Losing her would…she couldn't even consider it.

"Yes? I know it's improbable. Crazy even. How could I have seen it before?"

Jemma's brows dipped, taking her time to finish the mouthful of food. "What if you have? You love to search for weird old books. Maybe you saw a picture when you were looking for something else? Maybe it's in another library?"

She took a long sip of wine. What Jemma said made sense, but that wasn't it. She hadn't seen a picture of the book before, she'd…seen the actual book. In person.

"A book this old would be on display under glass and if that were the case, it would be cataloged in a database somewhere."

Jemma flopped her feet up on the desk, leaning back in the swivel chair. "What clues do you have?"

Excitement erupted in her belly as she pushed aside her takeout container. Plenty of times she'd subjected Jemma to her ramblings about some search or another and the thrill of sharing that with her best friend never faded.

She opened the document on her personal drive, where she kept all the research she found, no matter how small. Also, in a location not accessible by the dragon ladies. "Okay, there's no author or title on the cover from what I can see, and Blaine confirmed that. Because it's not in any database, I can't find a publication year. Which means, all I have to go on is a hunch."

Jemma sipped her wine. "When do you operate on anything but a hunch?"

"That's true." She clinked her mug with Jemma's again. "My hunch tells me the book is a family heirloom, just as Blaine said. But if that's correct, it's probably in someone's home library gathering dust. Or buried in an attic."

Jemma swooned, pressing the back of her hand to her forehead as though she were about to faint. "I'm getting beauty and beast vibes here." Her eyes sparkled as she slipped her feet off the desk to lean forward. "Imagine if the Blaine dude collects rare books for his huge library. Next, he'll marry you in a big lavish wedding so his beauty, you, can live with him in his ancient castle. And you have four magical little babies and live forever surrounded by swoony words."

Her eyes widened. "That's rather specific."

Jemma laughed, feet back up on the desk. "It might be a fantasy of mine. Don't judge. You of all people should totally understand."

"Next time he comes in, I'll give him your number."

They both laughed and clinked their mugs once more. For the next hour, she took Jemma through her research notes. The places that were dead ends and the others she wanted to investigate further. Searching for a book in someone's personal collection was like finding a four-leaf clover on a blistering summer's day. But she'd never walked away from a challenge, and this time was no different.

Midafternoon, as they packed up the evidence of their lunch, a sudden prickle at her nape made her turn to the closed doors.

A man stood behind the glass, dressed in a fancy suit straight out of a magazine, his hair slicked back. Eyes dark, almost black.

"Miss Fairburn?" The guy raised his voice so it penetrated the door.

She and Jemma exchanged looks that silently questioned which one of them would call security.

"I have a delivery for you," the guy said, holding up a black envelope with her name written on the front in gold, old-fashioned cursive.

"Open the door, Eve," Jemma whispered beside her.

"You open it," she whispered back.

Realizing neither of them were about to move, the guy tucked the envelope under the door and pushed it through to their side. With a curt nod, he turned and left.

They both rushed from behind the desk, but Evelina snatched the envelope off the ground before Jemma.

"What does it say? Show me!" Jemma squealed.

On the underside, a lavish crimson wax seal held it closed. The embossed symbol in the center looked like a flame.

"Oh my god! Evie-Eve, is that an invitation?"

She stared at the envelope in her shaky hands. Why was she so nervous? "I don't...know."

"It's a little weird that someone delivered an invitation on a Sunday when the library is closed for the holidays." Jemma frowned. "How'd they know you were here? Who cares? Open it before I die of excitement!"

Her heart thudded, pounding her ribs. Why did opening the envelope feel as though she was about to release Pandora's box? She didn't even know who it was from. Though, she had a suspicion. Only one guy she'd met lately could pull off this old-fashioned wax seal while still making it trendy and...sexy.

Back at the desk, she slid the letter opener along the top and slipped out the invitation, holding it between her and Jemma so they could read it together.

"A masquerade ball!" Jemma squealed again and slapped her arm. "Oh. My. God. It's from the beast dude. It has to be."

Heaviness sank on her chest making it hard to inhale. She staggered back, the invitation fluttering to the floor. Something flashed in her mind, so fleeting she couldn't grasp it, but the image stirred dread in her belly.

A tower...fire...foreboding.

Jemma touched her shoulder. "Are you all right?"

The edge of another piece of paper peeked out from the envelope on the desk. Swallowing to moisten her parched throat, she pulled it out. Written in the same beautiful cursive were the words:

To the commencement of our hunt. Blaine.

"This is ridiculous." She couldn't catch her breath. "I'm not going to a party. To a ball. I don't even know this guy. And I haven't found the book he wants." Words came out in a rush. "For all I know, this beast might lock his beauties in the library as prisoners."

Jemma tipped her head back as though swept away by romance. "So worth it."

"I'm not kidding, Jem. All I know about this guy is that his name is Blaine. That's it."

"And he loves old books and probably has a massive library that would make your knees weak."

She raised an eyebrow.

"Before you say no, first think about it." Jemma collected the invitation from the floor and read it again. "The party is tomorrow night at…oh, my god!"

"Will you stop saying that?"

Any minute now, Jemma's screams would alert the afterhours security team to come running.

"Did you see where it is?" She waved the invitation in Evelina's face. "At freaking Castle Sarael. A castle! You've been invited to a masquerade ball at a castle!"

She had to admit, the idea was…exciting. But accepting was reckless. Who invited someone they barely knew to a ball?

"The invitation is for you and a plus one." Jemma pointed to herself. "Me! I'm your plus one. We'll look out for each other. Nothing will happen if we're together. And, you know, if he turns out to be a serial book girl collector, I'll sacrifice myself for you to escape. I'm a good friend like that. I will become his prisoner, locked in his extravagant library forever with his talking teapot."

Evelina groaned, rolling her eyes. And Jemma thought once Evelina latched onto an idea she never gave up. Pot meet kettle.

"Besides, we'll never get another invitation like this. Ever. We have to go." Jemma took her hands, squeezing them tight. "Please can we go. Please? Pleeease?"

She couldn't stop her grin from widening. She also couldn't deny the excitement at the idea of dressing up for a masquerade ball hosted at a castle. Of course, she saw castles all the time, but she'd never attended a ball at one. Think of the history. The hidden corridors. The staircases lurking behind bookshelves leading to dusty basements and mysterious rooms. Plus, as Jemma said, if they were together, they could look out for each other. If it turned out this invitation was for a party of three, they could high tail it out of there before stepping across the threshold.

She took one last lingering glance at the invitation. So much effort went into planning a ball. From invitations and fancy wax seals. It would be rude to decline. Besides, it would give her more opportunity to ask Blaine questions about the book. A research trip, disguised as a ball. That could work.

"Fine. We'll go."

Jemma squealed with excitement, taking her hands to spin them around the room. "We're going to a ball at a castle!"

CHAPTER SIX

Evelina

"This is the bomb." Jemma giggled with the excitement level of a toddler on a trip to the zoo, her face squished against the tinted car window. "I have no regrets about getting in this random car."

As she and Jemma had exited their apartment, a car had pulled up out front driven by Invitation Guy, courtesy of Blaine. She'd argued with Jemma for a good fifteen minutes about the dangers of getting into the car while the driver patiently waited by the open rear door. If it weren't for Jemma hopping in and refusing to get out, she wouldn't have accepted the ride. Nothing like peer pressure to convince her to get in a stranger's car.

Goodbye life.

"I feel like it's the most reckless decision I've ever made. The driver's probably taking us to some dark forest to murder us. Maybe Blaine hired a hitman."

She swore the driver chuckled at her comment. More evidence.

Why wasn't there a privacy screen?

Besides that, how the heck did Blaine know where she lived? A question to ask him later...if they survived.

Jemma sipped the glass of champagne she refused

in case it contained poison. Or a date drug. One of them needed to stay sensible.

Speaking of sensible, Jemma also hadn't applied that concept to her outfit, wearing a strapless deep burgundy mermaid cut dress with a slit all the way to the top of her thigh. How did she move in it? Or breathe? Whereas Evie had chosen a more conservative navy gown with layers of tule in the full skirt and lace, cap sleeves. Fairytale worthy, not that she'd admit that to anyone but herself. They were going to a ball at a castle. Part of her demanded to feel like a princess, even in a thrift store dress.

"Really, what would a hitman have to gain from murdering us? What would this Blaine guy gain? If he murdered you, he'd never find his mysterious book."

Good point.

"Besides." Jemma downed the rest of her champagne. "We're here…and would you look at that, we're still alive."

The car slowed to a stop a moment before the driver opened the door. "Miss Fairburn." He held out his hand to help her from the car.

From inside her purse, she slipped on the delicate mask she'd purchased with her dress, fasting the black ribbon behind her head before placing her hand in the driver's.

Even if she were destined to die tonight, she felt magical, important, special. Deserving. As she waited for Jemma to exit the car, her gaze followed the dark red carpet leading to the castle entrance.

Sharp pain sliced through her head, gone as quickly as it arrived. She squeezed her temples bracing for another bout that never came. For the past few months, she'd experienced the fleeting migraines on and off. As a teen, they'd lasted for days, but the older she got, the less intense they were. The downside was they now occurred more frequently. Sometimes accompanied by bizarre images.

She should see another doctor, but every test they'd subjected her to as a teen came back negative for all the nasties. It's just hormones, they'd told her. *There are no specific triggers. You'll have to learn to live with them.*

Why bother seeing more doctors only to have the same result?

"Told you." Jemma nudged her shoulder, breaking her thoughts. "I know you met the guy first, but I'm going to totally marry him. Sorry, not sorry."

She took in the castle in front of her. All words vanished. The scene was straight out of an historical movie. Torches flanked the stone steps leading up to the most magical castle she'd ever seen. And, being a lover of history, she'd seen her fair share. Tilting her head back, her gaze roamed over levels upon levels, magnificent turrets reaching into the cloudy night, countless windows, many of the rooms lit inside, and the main keep proudly positioned in the center for all to admire.

Grand. Old wealth. Untold history.

At least with the absence of a moat and drawbridge, they could escape if needed.

Again, a strange sense of déjà vu fluttered in her belly. This castle was one of the few she'd never visited. Though, on several occasions, she'd admired it from afar. Privately owned, it didn't open for tours during the tourist season. The castle wasn't the biggest, but definitely the most mysterious. No one she knew had seen inside.

Excitement replaced the fluttering unease making her heart flip. She'd be one of the few people to venture inside. Elite. For whatever reason, Blaine had chosen her to find a book clearly important to him.

She'd do whatever it took to find it.

A wispy breeze chilled her warm cheeks while she and Jemma waited at the bottom of the steps. Several more cars delivered other guests, confirming their invitation wasn't a hoax. Or murder plot. Such a relief.

Jemma linked her arm in Evelina's as they ascended the wide steps before presenting their invitation to a gentleman dressed in a tuxedo that probably cost more than their apartment. Without a word, he tipped his chin to another smartly dressed guy, who pushed open the heavy ornate door and motioned for them to enter.

She leaned close to Jemma. "Do you have your cell? In case we're separated or…kidnapped."

"Yes, Miss Paranoid, I have my cell." Jemma's eyes glazed over as they entered. "Again, not that I'd mind being kidnapped by the beast who owns this place."

She rolled her eyes.

Inside the castle was even more lavish. Women in stunning ball gowns and equally beautiful masks glided around the spacious foyer. Mingling with men in suits straight out of movie sets, most with black masks. Servers weaved between the guests, carrying silver trays of tiny delights. Modern instrumental music played from an adjacent room. What was Blaine celebrating?

Jemma slipped her arm free as a server appeared,

offering drinks. This time she grabbed a champagne. One couldn't hurt. And if someone poisoned it, they'd all die.

Pausing on the outskirts of the main foyer, she took a moment to catch her breath. Four large golden candelabras hung from the expansive ceiling, detailed artwork graced the walls, and the black and white marble floor gleamed in the candlelight. On the opposite side, twin staircases swept up to a second level where she presumed was the main residence. Though, no ropes or barriers prevented people from venturing up there. A sudden thrill zipped through her body at the thought of exploring beyond the common areas. Discovering the history of the castle and its occupants. To uncover more about Blaine.

"The ball must be through there," Jemma said, linking her arm in Evelina's again.

Double doors on the left opened to another room. Exploring upstairs was rude, and not why Blaine invited her. Though, she couldn't stop her gaze from drifting back to the staircase.

Maybe later. If the opportunity arose.

Instead, she and Jemma followed the other guests into a large ballroom. If she thought the foyer was luxurious, it had nothing on this room. The entire castle screamed old money. A lot of it. Had Blaine's family owned this castle for generations? Or had they acquired it fully furnished?

Another waiter appeared with canapés and Jemma asked questions about gluten free options. While they chatted, Evelina drifted through the crowd, drawn to an oversized portrait of a guy with similar features as Blaine. His ancestor maybe. But as she studied the painting, she couldn't help that feeling of déjà vu again. As though she knew not only Blaine's relative but had met him in person. Ridiculous.

Glancing back, she found Jemma chatting with some other guests, totally engrossed in the conversation. Parties were more Jemma's scene. She made friends so easily. Everyone loved her. While Evelina felt more comfortable among stacks of ancient books than in a room filled with people she didn't know. Sure, the champagne loosened her shoulders and gave her false confidence, but she still felt out of place.

When she considered slipping back into the foyer, the band stopped playing and everyone's attention turned to where Blaine stood, on a stage. He wore a similar outfit to when she'd seen him last, and nothing like the expected attire. She had a feeling Blaine never did what everyone expected.

Wearing a vintage leather jacket with black jeans and unlaced boots, the only effort he'd made was a mask. Dark red fabric with black swirls. She narrowed her eyes, squinting at the upper edges of his mask. Were they miniature flames? Yes, flames. Surely, she must be seeing things. If his mask were on fire, the fabric would burn. Besides, no sane person would wear a flaming mask.

"Is that him?" Jemma whispered, sidling up to her.

"Yeah," she replied, not taking her gaze from Blaine. "Are those…"

"Flames. Yep. So cool. Very…intense. I'm definitely marrying him."

There she went again.

Blaine cleared his throat and the voices faded away as everyone gave him their full attention. He sure knew how to control the room.

"I'm not one for boring, drawn-out speeches…Oh, wait, of course I am."

The crowd chuckled.

"But tonight, I welcome you all on my team so to speak. Enjoy the festivities." He lifted his drink in the air. "To…world domination."

The crowd echoed his words, toasting him before erupting into cheers. The music began again, and everyone resumed their conversations. Some even moved to the dance floor.

She stood there dumbfounded, gaze locked on Blaine as he weaved through the crowd, greeting everyone as though he knew them personally.

"Did he seriously say 'world domination'?" she murmured.

Jemma chuckled. "So hot."

Wow. Blaine might be super rich, with charisma and charm in spades, but perhaps he had a few screws loose. The strange fluttering in her belly returned, coupled with tingling at her nape. Had someone turned up the heat? Maybe just nerves from being around so many people in a strange place. Sensory overload.

Placing her empty glass on a nearby table, she turned to Jemma. "I'm going to find the bathroom."

Jemma waved her off and Evelina weaved through the crowd, back to the empty foyer. For a brief second, she considered finding a bathroom on this level. Then, she eyed the staircase. It called to her. Lured her up the burgundy carpeted stairs to the second floor.

It couldn't hurt. Just one look.

After a quick glance to make sure no one was watching, she gathered her dress, lifting the hem off the floor and quietly tiptoed upstairs. Heading left at the top, she followed the long-carpeted hall until she found a bathroom and slipped inside.

After taking care of business, she washed her hands and inhaled a deep breath before venturing back out. Instead of returning downstairs, she veered in the other direction, drawn to the library.

How did she know this castle had a library? Didn't they all? Maybe. But that didn't explain how she knew the library was the last door on the right. She must've seen the floorplans in one of her many hours of falling down rabbit holes on the internet.

Her heart beat faster, bouncing around behind her ribs the closer she drew to the closed door. Her hand stilled on the doorknob. Curiosity or something much more powerful was at play. Too many times over the past week she'd felt as though she'd met someone or seen something. Or been somewhere before.

Like now. The library behind this door beckoned her. Taunted her with secret knowledge. Consumed her thoughts and actions until, despite common sense warning her not to, she opened the door and slipped inside.

CHAPTER SEVEN

Cole

Cole stilled. His entire body vibrated with awareness as a familiar sensation thrummed through his middle. No, his blood. Evie. She was here. Nearby.

He gravitated closer to the open doorway leading into the library. He'd stood outside on the balcony for only Fate knows how long, allowing snowflakes to sprinkle the shoulders of his suit jacket and melt in his hair. Frozen in place and time. Unsure why he didn't return inside. That wasn't true. He knew why. But sinking into the endless pit of memories wouldn't change the past. It wouldn't change what had happened on this balcony almost one hundred and fifty years ago.

Even knowing the outcome, he'd choose the same destiny. Every time.

He'd come to this pretentious ball convinced Evie would appear. That he'd catch a glimpse of her beauty while maintaining his distance. Protect her from afar. But when he arrived, he hadn't sensed her soul in any of the mortal females.

Until now...

While still partially hidden by the heavy drapes, he peered inside the library, dimly lit by only a few lamps. A female stood on the far side with her back to him. Her navy full-length gown billowed out behind her as she glided by the shelves, her fingertips trailing the spines, with a mask dangling from her free hand. Equally dark, wavy hair tumbled down her back.

Evie.

He knew it with every fiber of his being. Her soul a beacon of heavenly light, guiding him to her.

Did she sense him as he sensed her? Had she unconsciously wandered to this room, drawn to it by some unknown force? By their connection.

Or did she remember the last time she'd joined him on this balcony?

His jaw tightened. If she remembered, then they were almost out of time. Her memories always returned shortly before she died.

For once, he longed for her not to remember her past lives. For her memories to never return. For them to start over. Properly. Without the guilt, without the history. Without the burden of knowing that once she remembered, their time would end.

He'd give his soul for her to fall in love with him for the first time.

For her to live.

But none of that would happen. No amount of wishing could change the past.

Spellbound by the door, he admired her beauty from a distance. Allowed his mind to recall the many times he'd tunneled his fingers through her thick locks. Was it as silky as he remembered? Softer? Her gown accentuated the curve of her hips. On more than one occasion, he'd longed to rest his hands there, hold her steady as he peered into her eyes. What color would they be in this life?

Her scent drifted across the room, seeping into his

lungs with a deep inhale. Soft and delicate. Roses. A whole garden of blooming buds dusted in dew on a crisp spring morning. Just as he remembered. During her time in Hell, the sulfur and brimstone stench had concealed her own beautiful scent. He'd missed it.

Remaining still, he continued to watch her as she ascended the staircase to wander the top level of the library. Her soul shone as bright as ever, a blazing light he couldn't turn away from. It blinded him. Called to him. Captured him. Although, for a mortal the tether between them would feel more like a sixth sense rather than a mystical connection between two souls.

Soulmate. His one and only.

Fate had destined for them to cross paths lifetimes ago, so long a mortal couldn't comprehend the time. He'd experienced every one of them. Over the centuries, he'd witnessed this beautiful soul reborn, each time, more breathtaking than the previous. His love for her never faded. In fact, with each reincarnation, his love strengthened.

For a moment, hot anger flashed through him at the thought of Blaine inviting Evie to this charade, at setting her up. But it didn't matter what Blaine did. His soul colliding with hers was inevitable. Eventually, Fate always got her way.

This time would be no different.

All he could hope for was a quick and painless death. An end to the suffering.

If all went to plan, they'd eventually reunite in the Heavens.

Her fingers stilled on a book, head angled toward the main door into the library as though she'd heard something. Or sensed. Had she sensed him? Every screaming thought told him to remain on the balcony. Keeping his distance kept her safe. She'd also begged him not to find her in this life. To let her live.

Yet, he couldn't stop his feet from dragging him across the threshold into the room.

She wouldn't remember him anyway. One conversation, to hear her voice, to capture her smile for his memory, wouldn't spiral her life out of control. Then he could leave her alone. Focus on finding the book and ending this torment for her.

By the time she remembered her past lives, he'd have destroyed the book and saved her.

He shoved his hands into the pockets of his tailored slacks and steadied his racing heart with a deep inhale. This would be their last first meet.

Ever.

"Evie?"

She whipped around, hand at her the base of her neck. "Oh my gosh. I thought I heard a noise but didn't realize someone was already in here. I'm so sorry for intruding."

Mystical hands twisted his lungs, constricting his ability to breathe. His blood tingled. Her eyes. Even in the dim light, he saw the golden irises. Thrusting him back to the first time he'd found her almost five centuries ago.

The organ behind his ribs ached at the memory.

Pushing through the anguish, he found his voice. "Don't be. I...didn't mean to startle you."

Her fingers curled around the banister, peering down at him. "No, it's my fault. I...shouldn't be in here."

"Neither should I, so I guess we're both breaking

the rules."

In more ways than one.

She chuckled and the sound reverberated deep in his soul. If it wouldn't block his vision of her, he'd close his eyes and drift away on the mystical notes.

Moving closer to the staircase, she motioned to the bookshelves. "Don't tell me you also have an obsession with history."

If only she knew how deep his obsession ran. He lifted one shoulder. "There's nothing quite like escaping into the memories of other times."

Her brows knitted as she studied him. How he ached to ascend that staircase and take her face in his hands.

"I guess that's exactly what I do. I never thought of it like that, but you're right." She looked back at the perfectly arranged books. "All the words on these pages are memories. Whether real or make believe, they're still thoughts from someone."

His traitorous feet gravitated closer once more. They no longer listened to his head.

As though she also felt the pull, she drifted to the top of the staircase. He held his breath as she bunched the front of her gown, lifting it slightly to descend the steps. His heart thumped harder, stronger until it almost burst from his chest. When she reached the last few steps, he offered his hand to guide her to the bottom.

Her hand slipped into his, and it felt like time stood still. How fitting. For centuries, he'd wished for time to stop so they could have more together. The realm would carry on around them, he knew that, but now, alone in this library, it felt like someone had finally granted his wish.

He'd grown resentful of Fate, and to an extent, of Evie. How she forgot the pain, how she lived a happy, blissful existence until she met him. How she carried on while he stood in the shadows drowning in the memories. But memories were what propelled him forward. Knowing he'd see her again. Knowing one day, they'd break the cycle.

At the bottom of the stairs, she stopped before him, her hand still in his. "Thank you." Her deep golden eyes glistened in the dim lights, flickering with specs of pale amber. "I'm Evelina."

The lightness in his chest expelled with a rush of air. Evelina. Each life she had a different name, the one given to her mortal form at birth. How fitting that this lifetime, her final life, she'd have her original name.

Searching inward, he concentrated on their connection, the light trickling from his soul to hers, holding on by the barest thread.

Her original eye color. Original name. Meeting him for the final time.

Their souls had orbited around each other for centuries and finally aligned.

"Cole." Lifting her hand, he placed a gentle kiss on the back. "The pleasure is all mine."

Pink dusted her cheeks as she slipped her hand from his to meander the lower-level shelves. He had so many questions. How old was she? How did she know Blaine? What did she remember?

Answers would tell him how much time they had left. But instead, he opted for ignorance. Choosing to appreciate their moment in time. Their countdown was inevitable, this time he didn't want to watch it tick away.

Once they departed the library, he'd focus on the book and let their destiny unfold as it should.

He shoved his hands back in his pockets. Mainly, so he refrained from reaching for her every second. "How has no one noticed your absence? I would've thought a significant other would want you on their arm."

Okay. One question wouldn't hurt. Only to know if he was about to escort a male's soul to Hell this evening.

"Smooth." Her eyes sparkled back at him. "Is that what you would do?"

A racy sensation in his chest made his blood simmer as he stepped closer. "I wouldn't let you out of my sight. The most beautiful woman at the ball deserves to have my devoted attention for the entire evening."

Her mouth opened before closing again as she turned back to the books. "I'm here with a friend, not a…significant other."

Fresh, cool air swept over his heated skin.

She perused the shelves once more. "I know it sounds strange, but I kind of wandered here. Like the books called to me."

Not strange at all. Though, it wasn't the books that called her.

"What's your favorite?" he asked.

She turned to him once more, a soft smile curving the corner of her mouth. "My favorite book? Clearly, you're not a reader. That's a question only a non-reader would ask." She motioned to the bookcases full to the brim. "How could I possibly pick one book out of the millions published? Each one makes me feel something different."

He didn't care how much time they had left together. He only wanted to spend every remaining second locked in this library listening to the excitement in her voice. He moved closer until his shoulder brushed hers and her floral scent replaced any thoughts of leaving.

"What about you?" Her voice breathy, as though he affected her as she did him. "Why are you hiding in here?"

Coldness seeped into his bones when he thought of the true reason he'd wandered to this part of the castle. "Maybe the room called to me, too."

"Can I tell you a secret?" She turned to face him, her chest rising and falling, distracting him.

How he yearned to capture all her secrets. All her kisses.

He nodded, unable to form words around the memories that clogged in his throat.

"I have the strangest feeling that I've been here before. Everything is so familiar."

He reached out and touched her hair, sliding the strands between his fingers. "Like in a past life?"

Dangerous ground. But he…couldn't stop. The yearning to be near her, to touch her, to…have her, too great.

She scoffed. "Silly, right?"

He peered into her eyes, so close their fronts almost touched. An inch more and he'd have her pressed against him. Like before, time seemed to grind to a halt. The air heavier, thicker that a second ago. Heavenly light sparked between their souls, grasping for the other, desperate for connection.

He should back off. Leave. Let her be. But…he was an asshole. The worst soulmate in the history of soulmates because all he wanted to do was crush her mouth against his and drown in her taste forever. As though she read his thoughts, her lips parted on a sharp inhale, golden eyes darkened. Her pulse thrummed in his ears.

One kiss. Then he'd leave her to live her life, free from him.

Thankfully, he could lie to himself.

Letting her hair sift through his fingers, he moved his hand closer, cupping the side of her jaw. She dragged her bottom lip between her teeth, and he couldn't hold back his moan.

To hell with Fate. To hell with all of it.

When Evie lifted on her toes, he tossed aside any remaining common sense and met her halfway.

Stars. Glittery stars exploded behind his lids as his mouth pressed against hers. Warm and soft. Heavenly light pulsed in his soul, dancing to the tempo of his pounding heart, beckoning her. He refused to think about it. To let their past dictate their future. For once, he longed to pretend it was only the two of them in this realm, that nothing could come between them.

Cradling her jaw with both hands, he angled his head. Evie opened her mouth, and he captured her moan, sweeping his tongue inside to deepen their kiss. Nothing compared. Some lifetimes they barely met, let alone touched, but he always remembered her taste. Sweet. Otherworldly. Beautiful like the Heavens.

Her fingers curled around the lapels of his jacket pulling him closer. In this moment, he'd give her anything. Everything. The entire mortal realm if he could. Nothing would stop him.

When her fists tightened, he backed her against the bookshelf, desperate to have their bodies pressed together, to lift her—

The memory slashed through him. *Evie in Hell…begging him not to find her.*

I'll never forgive you.

His heart stilled. What the Fate was he doing? Her only request was to not find her, and he'd done the complete opposite.

He recoiled, putting much needed distance between them. Distance he should've maintained. Not kissed her like his soul depended on it.

Fate.

Damn her.

Evie touched her lips, breath punching in and out, her eyes dark pools of golden lust.

"Shit." He turned away. "I'm sorry. I don't know what came over me."

She took a long moment to answer. "I…do I…oh, wow."

Such a stupid move. Kissing her could've triggered her memories. Could've shortened their time, expedited their end. Why didn't he ever learn?

He dragged a hand through his hair, eyeing the door. "I need to go."

"Don't. Please." She touched his arm, stilling him. "Why don't we get some air?"

Without waiting for his answer, she headed to the balcony doors.

Panic clawed at his chest. She couldn't go out there. Blaine had set up this meeting knowing their history, knowing Evie had once fallen from that balcony.

"No."

Her smile faltered when she glanced back at him, and the hurt in her eyes stabbed his twisted heart. "Are you afraid of heights?"

Nausea rose, curling sharp fingers around his throat. His stomach clenched. He couldn't do it. He couldn't stop her from going outside without telling her why, which would initiate a devastating rippling effect.

"No." His voice came out harsher that he intended. "I'm afraid of Falling."

She'll remember. Then, she'll die.

But that didn't mean he had to stand there and watch history repeat itself. He wasn't prepared for her life to end.

Not yet. Not ever.

As Evelina glanced between him and the balcony, he turned away and stormed out of the library.

CHAPTER EIGHT

Evelina

After Cole, the alluring, mysterious man who'd kissed her, fled the library in a storm of angry shadows, Evie took a moment to catch her breath. He'd kissed her. A stranger, who she'd barely met, had kissed her. She let him. Craved it. And it felt...good. No, more than good. Right. Magical. Calling it destiny grasped at straws, but no other word described it better. As though all her life had led to this moment. The joining of their two mouths. Breathing the same air.

Her skin still tingled with residual heat. They'd spoken for barely five minutes. How could he consume her thoughts like this? Deep in her belly, the fluttering returned at the thought of how he'd looked at her. Like any woman, she appreciated someone admiring her, but Cole looked at her as though he truly saw her. He didn't just know her name, which was also weird, he acted as though he knew *her*. Because beyond the layers of clothes and flesh, his intense silvery-gray gaze had penetrated every barrier, captured her, and refused to let her go, leaving her exposed and shivering it its wake.

Wow. Okay. All that work to catch her breath just flew out the window.

After Cole had left her in the library, an ominous feeling held her back from the balcony. Not because he'd refused to join her. That was silly. But she had to admit, the dangerous scowl on his face when he'd said no freaked her out. As though he resented the idea of going outside. Or the balcony itself.

Stupid, right?

She thought so, too. Until she'd moved closer to the doors, intending to ignore his warning, and a dark, icy shiver halted her at the threshold. Now, she wasn't a huge believer in relying solely on a sixth sense, but there were times when she listened to her gut. Times like that.

Smoothing out the creases in her gown, she took a few deep breaths. She couldn't stay hidden in the library all night secretly hoping he'd return. No, she needed to get back to Jemma. And the reason she'd come to the ball in the first place. Question Blaine about the book.

Straightening her shoulders, she left the events of the library behind and returned downstairs to the ball. She wouldn't chase Cole, but if she happened to run into him again, she might just exchange numbers. Maybe she'd circle the crowd once to make sure he made it back downstairs. That he hadn't lost his way. Wasn't locked in a bathroom or something.

Sure, tell yourself whatever lie you need.

Disappointment clipped the fluttering wings in her belly when she didn't spot Cole as she entered the ballroom. By now, the ball was in full party mode. The band had switched to more upbeat music, luring most to the dance floor, servers weaved between the partygoers refilling glasses. She spotted Jemma solo dancing with champagne in hand, having the time of her life. She should join her friend. Yet, her gaze drifted beyond the full-length windows, mesmerized by the falling snow. Not enough to pile on the ground, but enough to bring this magical castle to life. As though she really were in a fairytale. Only the man who stole her attention wasn't a beast. Mysterious, yes. But not the villain of the story. And since meeting him, she couldn't get him out of her thoughts.

A dull ache pushed forward in her head. No, not tonight. She didn't want a migraine to ruin another evening.

Spinning in small circles, Jemma danced her way over, a champagne flute held high. "Where have you been party-pooper?"

They were chalk and cheese. If anyone listed their individual qualities on paper, they'd never believe they were friends.

"I wandered upstairs." *Met a drop-dead gorgeous guy who kissed me in the library as though I were his long-lost love.*

"Ooh, you rebel!" Jemma tossed back the remaining champagne and placed the empty glass on a tray as a server passed them. She leaned in, lowering her voice. "Tell me everything. Does my beast have a library to die for? A secret deranged wife chained in the attic? Maybe a hidden fortune locked away in a vault in the basement?"

She laughed, wishing she had half the zest for life Jemma did. "I can't confirm a fortune or secret wife, but he does have a stunning library."

"I knew it!" Several people turned to them at Jemma's squeal.

Jemma snagged her arm, ushering them away from prying ears. "Did you find the book?"

She mentally smacked herself. In the library, she'd completely forgotten about the book Blaine asked her to find. Mainly, because a certain hot guy in a tux had distracted her. Though, surely Blaine wouldn't ask her to find a book which was already in his library.

She shook her head, a smile lifting her lips as she recalled her secret kiss. "I was…a little distracted."

Jemma narrowed her glassy eyes for a moment before realization dawned on her face. "You met a guy, didn't you? In the library?" She raised on her toes, scanning the crowd. "Which one? Oh my god, is he cute?"

Evie tugged her back. "It's not like that. Well…it is kind of, but that's not the point." She couldn't stop from also scanning the crowd. *Stop looking for him!* "He probably left already. I haven't seen him since he left the library."

"Oh, you have to tell me all about him. Like, now." Jemma draped an arm around her shoulder guiding them out to a small, uncovered patio extending from the ballroom.

Chilly wind stirred her hair, sprouting goosebumps on the back of her neck. Lifting her shawl, she wrapped it tighter around her. Thankfully, someone had turned on the heaters, so they didn't freeze. She peered out into the night. Had Cole left? Was he in one of the countless rooms in the castle? Was he a figment of her imagination?

Did he know Blaine?

"So…" Jemma nudged her arm. "Spill."

She needed to focus on finding the book rather than some hot guy in an equally gorgeous tux that probably cost more than her yearly wage. She had neither the time nor the inclination to swoon over a man, not matter how delicious. It had been so long she wouldn't know where to start. Besides, Jemma went through enough men for the both of them.

"There's nothing to tell. I met him in the library, we had a conversation and then..."

Jemma leaned closer, excitement lighting her eyes.

"He kissed me." Her traitorous heart flipped at the reminder.

Jemma covered her mouth to muffle a squeal. "Girl, all you need to do is dress like a princess and hide in a library for a hot prince to swoop in. Is he cute? How was it? Did he kiss like a hot villain or a swoony hero?"

A server offered drinks and they both grabbed a glass. The bubbles did nothing to ease the increasing tingles along her skin. Nor cool the fire erupting inside her.

"All I'll say is that if he came back for seconds, I wouldn't say no."

Jemma winked. "I'll take that as 'it was amazing, Jem. You are now free to marry the beast.'"

Evie laughed.

Jemma rested her glass on the railing as she turned to face her. "Do you think he's looking for the book, too? It's a possibility if he was in the library while a fancy ball carried on downstairs."

"I didn't ask."

"Girl, you need a lesson in secret agent business. First rule: seduce the opposition to gain all the answers."

A giggle quaked her chest. "Is that right? What are the other rules?"

Jemma drew back. "What do you mean? There aren't any other rules."

She slung her arm around her friend and laughed. If only finding an ancient book was as easy as seducing a guy. Especially when said guy captured her soul, kissed her, and then bolted the second she wanted to go outside.

Seduction clearly wasn't her strong point.

Lowering her arm, she peered at the fire torches flickering in the garden. Her heart skipped. The guy from the library stood with a few others.

"That's him," she whispered.

Jemma followed her gaze. "Which one is Library Guy?"

She leaned forward as though it would help her vision. "The one in the tux speaking to Blaine. I don't know who the other two are."

A bald guy, dressed in all black stood on one side of Cole, while a woman with platinum blonde hair pulled into a tight bun, dressed in a blood-red short gown and mile-high heels, stood on the other side. Was that Cole's date? Had he come here with someone else and…kissed her?

"Your library guy doesn't look happy with Beast," Jemma said, also fixated on the conversation.

She went to correct her, Cole wasn't her man, but as she opened her mouth, his gaze shot to her. She froze, unable to move or hide the fact she stared back from the patio. This far away, she couldn't see his expression clearly, but the hard set of his body told her he was furious. Because she'd caught him with a date? Or was it something to do with Blaine?

Beside her, Jemma sucked in a breath when Blaine

turned their way. A slow smile lifted his cheeks. He said something she couldn't hear. If only she could lip read.

As Blaine turned back around, Cole shoved him in the chest. Fixated, she couldn't turn away. It looked as though Cole wanted to beat the ever-loving shit out of Blaine, but the other guy and the woman grabbed his shoulders and held him back.

"Ooh, this is interesting. I wonder what our beast said," Jemma added.

Her heart thumped behind her ribs. She wondered, too. Had Cole told Blaine that he'd kissed her? No, he didn't strike her as the type of guy to kiss and tell. Then why was he so angry?

The two exchanged heated words and she braced herself for a fight to break out. Only it didn't. After another glance at her, Cole spun and stormed down the driveway, followed by his two buddies.

Blaine waved before turning back to the castle. She and Jemma twisted, pretending they hadn't stood there the entire time watching a private argument they had no right to view.

"That was weird," she whispered to Jemma, leading them back inside.

"You're telling me. There's some juicy history between beast dude and Library Guy that's for sure."

Jemma had that right.

"Maybe it's about the reward."

She froze. "What reward?"

Jemma did a quick look around the room before huddling closer. "I overheard someone saying that Blaine has offered a ridiculous amount of money for the return of his book. So many zeros I couldn't count."

She opened her mouth. Then closed it.

"Right? I wonder why he didn't tell you about it?"

Huh. Was it because he assumed money didn't motivate her? He clearly didn't know that she'd spent the last of her savings hiring a private detective to track down her birth parents, hoping that one day, she'd feel like she belonged somewhere. Or at least to someone. Only for them to find nothing. Zip. How was that even possible?

Every time the PD had come to her with a lead, it wound up at a dead-end. Until the money ran out and the PD stopped contacting her all together. With more funds, she could hire someone else. Not knowing her heritage, her story, if she had any family out there, ate at her. How could anyone expect her to write the middle and ending to her story if she didn't even know the beginning?

"I need to find that book."

"We. After that scuffle outside, I'm not letting you embark on a dangerous quest all on your own."

Her grin widened. "A dangerous quest? It's an antique book, Jem. Did you hear anything else?"

Jemma stared at the ceiling for a long moment. "One guy who danced with me said something about a quaint antique store in Inverness. But I wasn't really paying attention so I didn't catch the name or anything else."

Excitement sparked. "Inverness? There is loads of history there, but I already searched the museum and library databases and didn't find anything resembling the book."

"But as you said before, if it's in a private collection, it won't be in any databases. We could check in person."

She and Jemma had traveled back and forth, mainly on weekends, after they'd both scored full time jobs and could afford a tiny bit of luxury, visiting all the historic sites.

The butterflies in her belly regenerated their wings. Searching for the book suddenly felt like a modern-day treasure hunt. They couldn't be better suited for the task. Her love for history, and Jemma's ability to…acquire information. She lifted her gaze to Jemma, finding the same excitement reflected in her friend's bright hazel eyes.

"So…we're going to Scotland?"

Her smile widened. "Why not? The library is closed for another fortnight. We have nothing but time."

Sudden dizziness swept through her, making her reach for the table to steady herself. *Nothing but time.* If that were true, why did she suddenly sense a ticking clock looming over her?

CHAPTER NINE

Cole

Cole paced back and forth by the lit hearth in Slater's hideout. One of his many hideouts apparently. "I'm so furious I could throw a cupcake."

From the couch, Raven snorted.

Cole didn't even question why Slater had acquired several places in the mortal realm. He had his own shit to unpack. Like, how the Fate Blaine had found Evie so quickly. Thank the Heavens Slater and Raine had returned to the castle to keep watch, otherwise, no one could hold him responsible for tearing that Fallen's head off.

He and Raven had left the masquerade ball about an hour ago and unease still slithered through his blood, curling his fingers into fists. Blaine had set him up. Of course, he had. As if he thought the night would go any other way. The moment he'd found Blaine outside Evie's Hell tower, he should've known something was off. That Blaine would trick him. Though he'd never expected Blaine to have prior knowledge of Evie's rebirth.

That Fallen had not only found Cole's soulmate before he did, but Blaine had also squirmed his way into her life. Again.

Talk about repeating the past.

Just like all the other lifetimes Fate reincarnated Evie, Blaine managed to somehow gain her trust before Cole ever had the chance to warn her. Now, instead of keeping his distance, his only hope was to win her over before Blaine convinced Evie to find that wretched book for him. If he hadn't already. Raine and Slater had mingled with the mortals at the ball and overheard a few mention the book. Word was already out. It wouldn't be long before Evie fell for Blaine's trap again.

Not for the first time, he wished she'd never laid eyes on it.

He wished Evie had never known its power.

"Did Evie say anything of use? Does she remember anything yet?" Raven asked from the armchair, nursing a bourbon.

The Guardian had also attended the ball. For support, he guessed. There weren't exactly any Fallen dressed up in suits waiting around for them to send back to Hell. Only Blaine. And a ball full of mortals. He'd never wanted to shove a Purah dagger in the Fallen's heart more than he did tonight. He'd barely restrained his shadows from strangling Blaine. If Evie hadn't been outside watching…

Staring at the fireplace, he shook his head. "I wanted to ask her so many things, but I…"

He trailed off, unable to finish. He had wanted to ask her, to warn her, to…anything. Instead, he allowed himself to fall under the spell of her beauty, their connection, the way her long dark lashes swept down before she smiled.

"I get it, my man. I get it."

So much for keeping his distance. Fate's sake, he

could barely stifle a groan when thinking of how her taste still lingered in his mouth. When his gaze had dipped to her full dark red lips, firing a thousand questions at her was the farthest thing from his mind. Kissing her leaped right up to the top. What the Fate was wrong with him? One second, he'd convinced himself to keep his distance for Evie's safety, so she could live a full life as she wanted. The next second, he'd cradled her jaw and thrust his tongue in her mouth.

What a kiss though. He'd never taken their kisses for granted but none owned him quite like the one tonight. Ripped his soul apart. Shredded it. Then pieced it back together with one damn whisper of her breath. The way she'd clutched his jacket and yanked him closer made him want to storm that castle, throw her over his shoulder and mist her away. Right in front of fucking Blaine.

"Earth to Cole," someone said.

"What?" he snapped, blinking a few times to regain his composure.

Raven tipped his chin to the cell facing up on the table between them. Shit. He'd forgotten they were on speaker.

"I said, what's the plan?" Aric's voice came through the cell.

Cole cleared his throat. He really needed to get himself together. Things were not going as planned. Again. "We need to find out as much as we can about her in this lifetime. Where she lives, works, her friends. She was standing with someone outside. Who was that? Evie obviously knows Blaine well enough to attend the ball and venture to the upper levels of the castle."

Did someone growl? Was it him?

"Does she look the same?" Raven asked.

He nodded as a boulder dropped in his throat. She looked as beautiful as the day he'd first laid eyes on her. Stunning black hair, mesmerizing golden eyes, an angelic face that had been starred in every one of his dreams. "Original features with original name. It can't be a coincidence that this is her last life. Her mortal form was born before I even made the deal with Fate. She's messing with my fucking head."

"We'll call you back. EJ said he's going to see how much he can dig up." Aric murmured something away from the cell before the line ended.

He thought of those who came here to help him. Raven, the Guardian he'd trusted with Evie's protection each time she was reborn. Raine, although they hadn't known each other as long, he had no doubt she'd lay her immortality on the line for those she cared for. Her admitting that out loud was another story. He just hoped her being here tonight meant he included him in that category. And Slater, the once Fallen Azrael who he'd known since the beginning of time.

They'd become his family, his home away from the Heavens. But could they help him save Evie? When the time came, could they help him destroy the book?

His fist twisted the front of his shirt, above his chest. "I feel this ache to return to the castle, to make sure she's all right. To smash Blaine in the face for setting this up and making such a spectacle of our first meeting in this lifetime. He knew Evie would gravitate to that damn library, and he bet on me doing the same." The ache spread to his clenched jaw. "He's as manipulative as Fate."

"Tell me something I don't know." Raven watched

him with a knowing look. "But keeping your distance is the safest option, Cole. If Evie remembers too soon…"

Raven didn't need to remind him of what happened when his soulmate remembered her past lives. Especially when she recalled the choice Cole made in the final moments of each of them.

A choice he'd made countless times and regretted not even once.

The pressure squeezing his chest became unbearable. He knew where she was, yet he wasn't with her. He couldn't see her, touch her, protect her. Kiss her again. Was that what she wanted?

How could she live a full life with Blaine intervening?

"This time is different. This is her last life. Her last…"

Death.

He couldn't even say it.

Raven leaned forward, bracing his forearms on his thighs. "Which is even more important. More is at stake this time."

"What could be more important than her life?"

Raven's gaze held his. "I meant the book. If she remembers before she finds it, Blaine won't hesitate to turn her."

Damn Fallen. "I won't let that happen."

Just like every other time, he'd made the choice to end her life so Blaine couldn't destroy her soul.

He stopped to stare at the ceiling as though Fate was laughing down on him. He'd sensed her at play ever since that dead mortal had delivered Blaine's message. The subtle drive in his blood pushing him forward, forcing him to make choices he wasn't prepared for. Of course, Fate predicted his path before he chose it, but that didn't make his decisions any less important. At any moment, he could change his course. Choose another path. Could Fate still predict the outcome?

Something told him that even if she did, it wouldn't change Evie's destiny. Death was her only option.

Was he ready? Could he do what he needed to when it came down to it? He had to. Because the alternative, banishing her soul to Hell for eternity, was a path he wouldn't accept.

"We have to find the book before Blaine."

Raven's deep blue gaze darkened as he studied Cole. "And then?"

"I'll destroy it. Blaine can't get his hands on it. But I need to do it before Evie remembers. I can't let her use it. Nor can I stomach her looking at me like…"

Raven blew out a curse. "Destroying it before she remembers? You know what that will do, don't you?"

His heart slammed against his ribs, raging to break free. "Fate could end her life."

CHAPTER TEN

Evelina

Hell. In the form of a grueling road trip, subjecting her ears to a compilation of boy bands, courtesy of Jemma's playlist. Finally, though, they'd arrived in Inverness. A city so filled with history it made her heart burst at the seams. She'd been here a few times now and each visit left her enriched, her well full to the brim. This time though, it made her think of Cole. In particular, the way she'd sensed, deep within her, a connection with him. That they'd met before. The mysterious dark-haired guy who waltzed into her life ready to throw her over his shoulder and make her his with one mind-blowing kiss. Talk about fairytales.

Great. Now their encounter in the library last night moved to front and center in her mind. More accurately, how his steel gray eyes had washed with silver right before he leaned down and kissed her.

Ugh. She shifted in the passenger seat.

As Jemma navigated the busy, narrow streets, Evie gazed out the window catching couples walking hand in hand, some sneaking kisses in front of iconic landmarks. Others, sharing a meal along the riverbanks. Love and history, seamlessly molding into one. Everywhere. Did the city have to shove it right in her face?

Coming out of a self-imposed man drought would be fine for one interested guy. But two? One who turned up at her workplace with a carefree, bad boy attitude and panty-melting accent, luring her in with a treasure hunt and extravagant ball. While the other, a devastatingly handsome stranger who'd caught her in a library, captured her with his handful of swoony words and...kissed her. Kissed the living hell out of her. Devoured her mouth. Made her knees wobble and toes tingle. But just because Cole was quieter, more reserved, didn't mean he was any less dangerous. She sensed both of them could easily rip out her heart, crush it, and toss it in front of the car for Jemma to run over.

Not that she was dating either of them. Or interested in dating. If she were honest, yes, Blaine intrigued her and had captured her attention, but he wasn't the guy who's face, and heated touch had kept her awake all night.

That crown belonged to Cole.

The car's navigation spoke, directing them to a parking lot a block from the antique store where they ditched the car and continued on foot. Good, she needed physical exercise to stop her mind from wandering. Nothing good came from fantasizing.

Traditional music and the smoky scent of whiskey layered the chilly air as they rounded a corner and spotted the store up ahead. For a bustling tourist destination at lunchtime, the backstreets lacked the same excitement as the main ones. Thank goodness. They only passed a handful of people, all scurrying in the opposite direction as though late for a meeting. No one locking lips in front of monuments. Anyone would've thought they'd entered a dead part of town, instead of a street containing so much hidden culture.

Shit. Maybe the store closed for the holidays? Had either of them checked?

As she opened her mouth to ask, they arrived at the entrance. Open. Whew.

A bouncy ball pin-ponged behind her ribs. "This is it."

"Onward we go." Jemma didn't hesitate. She linked her arm in Evie's and opened the door.

A bell chimed, sounding their arrival to…no one. Inside, the small shop opened to a narrow, vacant reception desk across from a few scattered armchairs. Also, vacant. Farther in, were several glass displays encasing what looked like books and artifacts, positioned around the small room. Dim lighting made it hard to see past the foyer, but it seemed like more antiques were through another entryway on the far side.

"There's no one here," she whispered, pausing by the reception desk.

Shouldn't someone at least be here to charge admission? Or monitor the customers coming in and out?

Cold fingers slithered down her spine as the bouncy ball from earlier deflated with a nervous hiss. Something seemed off. Sure, businesses closed around the holidays, but plenty of people were still out and about on the main streets. Plus, the store was open according to the sign on the shopfront window. Surely, at least one other person would be in here, not just her and Jemma.

The dusty and damp air made her think the store hadn't been open all year. Even though the lights were on inside, the walls seemed to cave in on her. They shrunk, forcing her farther into the center while critters scurried in her belly, urging her to flee.

Jemma must've sensed the same unease because she tightened her arm around Evie's. "Maybe we should come back tomorrow? Or next year? Or...never?"

They'd come all this way because someone from the ball had mentioned it in connection with the book. They couldn't turn back now. Besides, from what she'd seen so far, the store consisted of only the foyer and one other room. Two, tops. They could easily search it in a few minutes. Plenty of time to get in and out before whatever loomed in the sinister shadows caught up to them.

Mind made up, she tugged Jemma toward the second room. "Let's be quick."

"Okay," Jemma whispered back. "We'll cover more ground if we split up."

Good idea, even though the thought of separating darkened the ominous shadows. "You take that side, and I'll take this one." She leaned closer so only Jemma could hear. Not that anyone else was within earshot. "This place is giving me the creeps."

"Right?" Jemma shivered. "So creepy. Hurry up and let's get out of here."

Before darting down the first section, she handed Jemma the picture Blaine had given her of the book.

In another time, or place to be honest, she'd love to read all the inscriptions describing the encased objects, but this wasn't the time. The sooner they got out of there the better. Searching for a book with a bounty was one thing. Dying was another.

Dying? Maybe a little dramatic considering they

hadn't even seen another person in here. But the cold fingers tightening around her throat said otherwise. She darted through the doorway and began searching.

Within minutes, she'd covered her side of the large room and met Jemma in the middle. "Any luck?"

"It's not here." Jemma pocketed the picture. "I guess decent treasure hunters never find the treasure at the first place. That would make for a boring movie."

She snorted, covering her mouth. "That's true. I guess we're back to square one. Maybe we could ask around in town. Now let's get out of—"

"You shouldn't be here."

They both squealed. An older lady stood in the internal doorway leading back to the foyer.

"Oh," Jemma was the first to recover. "Sorry, we thought you were open."

The lady who had to be in her late sixties, with silvery-gray hair pulled into a tight bun at the back of her neck, didn't spare Jemma a glance. No, the lady locked her narrowed, pale blue gaze on Evie.

Those critters from earlier scrapped their nails along the pit of her belly trying to claw their way out.

She backed up, tugging Jemma with her.

The lady matched their step, entering the room and pointed at Evie. "You."

"Excuse me?" Evie squeaked. So tough. Some treasure hunter she was.

She eyed the door they'd come through—their only exit—but the lady blocked their path. Briefly she considered pushing past and knocking her over. Maybe. But that seemed a bit violent, especially when directed at the elderly.

The lady gravitated closer. "They'll find you here."

Okay, that was enough weirdness for one day. Time to leave.

"We were just going," she said, urging Jemma to move, but her friend dug in her heels.

Jemma unlinked her arm. "Who? Are they looking for the book, too? Maybe you can help us find it first?"

"Are you serious?" she hissed at her friend. "Let's get out of here."

Tiny hairs on the back of her neck stood to attention. This was bad. They needed to run before whatever hid in the shadows pounced on them. She grabbed Jemma's hand and tugged her.

The lady continued to stare at Evie. "You shouldn't search for it."

"Do you know it?" Jemma asked, reaching into her pocket. "We have a picture—"

"Do you think they won't find you? That they won't check here? Or all the other places?"

Enough was enough. "Listen, I don't know who you think I am. I'm just looking for an old book, that's all." She snatched the picture from Jemma and shoved it in her own pocket. "We're leaving now."

"You made my grandmother vow not to tell you where she hid it. I won't break that."

Evie froze.

What. The. Hell?

Never in her life had she met this lady, let alone her grandmother. Why would she tell someone she'd never met about a book she'd never seen? Until a week ago, she never knew the book even existed. This lady was crazy.

And this antique shop was a dead-end.

Before she answered, the bell tolled at the entrance

to the store. Through the doorway, she saw two figures storm into the foyer. Black leather jackets, military style pants, boots. Buzz cuts. Their demeaner screamed hitmen. But what were they hunting?

They scanned the foyer before one spotted her. She backed up.

Impossible. Her mind couldn't comprehend it, but at the same time the evidence was right in front of her. His eyes were…red.

"Run." The old lady stepped in front of her and shook her shoulders with a forceful grip that seemed beyond her ability. "Your life depends on it."

CHAPTER ELEVEN

Cole

Spontaneity wasn't Cole's thing. For one, it was dangerous, especially when flying. Without a destination, it felt like flying blind, which was never ideal. And two, he damn well hated surprises. He'd had enough surprises to last an eternity.

The biggest of which, was always finding Evie.

Given his inability to track her soul like a normal soulmate, thanks to Fate and her twisted curse, each lifetime he had to rely on other methods. Feelings. Sensations when he was near her. Or now, when he knew without a doubt that something was wrong.

He paced back and forth in the spare room at Slater's hang out, cell phone to his ear. "Damn it, brother. Can you hurry up?"

The vise inside his chest started constricting ten minutes ago and had worsened every second. He knew the feeling all too well. Evie was in danger.

"Get your skates on, Reaper," EJ said from the other side of the phone. "I found her."

About damn time. "Tell me."

Cole pressed the speaker button and tossed the cell on the bed as he slipped on his jacket. No more formal Azrael tunics for him for the time being. He couldn't exactly walk around the streets of the mortal realm wearing them. People would stare. Come to think of it, maybe he'd give them up for good. Escort souls in jeans and a T-shirt from now on, at least until his permanent stint in the mortal realm was over. They were a heck of a lot more comfortable. And less breezy.

"I tracked her phone to this place in Scotland. Internet says it's an antique store, but Ric thinks it's a front. I kinda agree, with all the weird frickin' witchy stuff—"

"Fuck." He didn't swear a lot, but now seemed appropriate. "Tell me the address."

The unease stirring in his gut intensified, making him nauseous. He'd misted to Scotland a handful of times, including once with Evie. Like all her other lifetimes, it hadn't ended well. History was destined to repeat.

EJ rattled off the address as Cole laced up his boots.

Evie was already hunting for the book. He should've realized that when he found her in the library last night. Each time she reincarnated, he found her closer to twenty-five. The age when everything went to shit, including his plan to break the curse. This time, knowing Fate would keep her word, he'd go directly for the book instead.

Find it. Destroy it.

Unless Evie found it before him. If that happened…He couldn't think of that right now. He had to stay on the path. For Evie to enter the Heavens, he'd have to pull out all the stops.

"Rae and her shadow sidekick will meet you there," EJ added.

Slater had misted he and Raine back to the

Guardian mansion last night while he and Raven stayed in Ireland. Even though he could mist anywhere in this realm in the blink of an eye, he couldn't bring himself to leave the city. Thankfully, with modern technology, EJ tracked Evie through her cell. Invasion of her privacy? Perhaps. But when it came to protecting her life, he'd do whatever was necessary. Walking away wasn't an option.

"Thanks, brother."

He ended the call and took a second to calm his erratic pulse. Raven had left an hour ago to investigate the library Evie worked at. It amazed him the information EJ uncovered with only a name, and approximate age. He texted an update to Raven before tucking the cell in his back pocket.

Misting was second nature to him. A form of transportation he'd relied on for millennia. But with his mind so focused on protecting Evie, beating Blaine to the book, and making sure his soulmate didn't die another horrible death, his nerves resembled a burned, crispy cupcake. If he didn't focus on his destination, he could end up anywhere, including crammed inside a tomb with an ancient mummy. Been there, done that.

Closing his eyes, he conjured an image of Evie from last night in his mind. How light from the lamps had reflected in her golden eyes making the amber specs shimmer. The tiny creases at the corner of her eyes when she'd laughed at him after he asked about her favorite book. The relief that had soared through him when she mentioned attending the ball with a friend, not a date.

Heavenly light buzzed in his blood, energizing his limbs. Calm enough to mist, he visualized his destination. Gradually, his corporeal form dissolved into millions of molecules, transporting him through the ether before binding him back together in the alleyway behind a pub.

Slater and Raine materialized beside him a second later.

He cocked a brow at Slater. "You're like a Guardian Uber now."

The once Fallen Azrael smirked but didn't take the bait. Always on his best behavior in front of his stabby soulmate.

Prickles flashed over his nape at the same time Slater's gaze shot down the alley.

Raine flipped a dagger in her hand. "Fallen."

At least two of them.

Slater cracked his neck. "See if you can beat me this time, my queen."

"Oh, I wasn't even warmed up last time." Raine cocked her brow. "I was bored waiting for you to catch up."

Instead of interrupting their bizarre foreplay, he took off, running toward the antique store with Raine and Slater close behind. Just as he reached the shopfront, a screamed echoed from inside. Evie. Without hesitation, he summoned his Azrael shadows, raising them in his palms at the ready before busting open the door and storming inside.

Metal sliced through the air in front of his face. He recoiled just in time as the dagger sailed past his nose, slamming into a wall. The Fallen charged at him, another dagger raised ready to throw. He shot his shadows forward, snagging the dagger and disarming the Fallen before tossing the weapon on the floor. Cole escorted souls, he didn't make a habit of killing. But things were different now.

He lifted his shadows, about to strike when another set of shadows, darker than his, shot forward, curling around the Fallen's neck. The Fallen froze, eyes wide. A sickening crack sounded a second before the male flopped to the floor.

"Find Evie," Slater said, now beside him. "Raine and I have these fuckers."

He still wasn't used to Slater being back on Team Fate. But he'd take all the help he could get. With a curt nod, he dashed toward another room, grunts and sounds of battle echoing as Slater and Raine fought Fallen. Sharp tingles constantly erupted at his nape as more and more Fallen misted to the antique store.

He ducked a swinging fist, and skidded into the main store, heading to a door labeled staff only. He eyed two mortals huddled together in the far corner of the room. Not in immediate danger. He'd come back for them if he had time.

Crippling pain shot through his chest making him stumble. Evie. Regaining his balance, he bolted to the door before kicking it open.

He blinked twice to adjust his vision. A Fallen had Evie pinned to the wall, held off the ground by a hand around her throat. Fire exploded through his blood, heightening his rage, thickening the shadows in his palm.

He shot a shadow, wrapping it around the Fallen's neck. "Get your hands off her."

The Fallen squeezed tighter. Evie's eyes bulged as she sputtered. Someone slammed into his back, and he stumbled forward. With his shadows tightening around the Fallen's neck, he shot another at the second Fallen. His arms shook, raising both Fallen off the ground, squeezing their throats. He should rip their souls from their bodies and send them back to Hell. But until Evie was safe, he settled for snapping their necks. Both Fallen toppled to the floor.

Planting his feet shoulder width apart, he circled his arms in the air, summoning a dense layer of shadows to block the doorway.

Evie whimpered, huddled on the carpeted floor a few steps from him. The scene threw him right back to the last time he'd seen her in Hell. Lead filled his lungs. He'd done this to her. Every lifetime, Blaine attacked her to draw him from the shadows. She was once again terrified, fearing her life, because of him.

He'd vowed to himself this life would be different. That he'd focus on destroying the book rather than laying these horrors at her feet. Yet, he'd failed. Regardless of her wish for him to not find her, he always would. Whether he intended to or not. Their paths were one. Linked. Destined.

Fate made sure of that.

Now, he'd make things right.

He crouched, holding out his hand to her. "Evie. We have to leave."

Her watery gaze lifted to him before widening at something over his shoulder. She screamed. He spun as a Fallen, wings unfurled, swiped his talons at the shadows blocking the doorway. Cole grunted, pushing with everything he had to increase his shadows and hold them in place.

The Fallen stilled, eyes wide. A second later, the Fallen exploded to a gritty mist and one of Raine's daggers bounced on the ground.

Evie scrambled to stand, backing away from him. Her gaze darting to the doorway.

Oh, *fuck*.

"You." She raised a trembling hand to stop him from approaching.

If only he could pretend he was just a guy she'd met at the ball. Not her soulmate, cursed long ago to endure an eternity of torture. If only they could live a normal happy existence. If only he could grant her wish. He'd rather Evie live a normal mortal life, without knowledge of the immortal war raging around her, but that wasn't her destiny.

They would always meet.

For once though, a part of him craved so bad for her to…choose him. To choose to find *him*.

"Evie." He reached for her again, but she backed against a wall.

"What…was…that?" Her eyes darted between him and the doorway. "What…are you?"

If history had taught him anything, he couldn't walk away. Even if Evie remembered nothing now, if he left her, she'd continue to hunt for the book. She'd continue retracing her steps, even unconsciously. Because that was what she did.

Centuries of reincarnation had taught them nothing.

And this would be no different than any other lifetime.

He promised to free her from this pain, from the repetitive torture, not subject her to more.

When the sounds of battle ceased beyond doorway, he recalled his shadows. Blaine wouldn't be pleased they'd eliminated the Fallen sent to draw Cole to Evie. But he'd done exactly as Blaine wanted. He'd stepped out of the shadows to protect his soulmate. As always.

"Evie, you need to come with me. It's not safe anymore."

Her gaze darted back to the doorway. He heard Raine and Slater in the other room speaking to the mortals.

He held out his hand to Evie. "Evelina, please."

"How did you…find me?"

A fist squeezed his heart when he recalled the betrayal in her voice in Hell after he'd said he would always find her. But she didn't remember him from then. Only from the ball Blaine had thrown to kickstart this never-ending chase. Still, the confusion in her eyes made him second guess himself. If only for a moment.

I'll never forgive you.

Maybe so. Maybe she could hate him for all eternity. But tough times called for even tougher choices. He wouldn't lose her, and he wouldn't walk away. Not now, not ever.

This was their destiny. She was his destiny.

He softened his voice, urging her to take his hand. "Come with me. I'll protect you."

Heat flashed along his nape alerting him to Blaine's presence somewhere nearby. Besides him and Evie, no one knew the importance of that book more than Blaine. No one wanted it more.

Even though he still intended to destroy the book, he wouldn't leave Evie here with Blaine. She could hate him all she liked later. At least he'd keep her safe. Nowhere was safer than with him.

Before Evie had a chance to protest, he grabbed her arm, threw her over his shoulder and…misted.

CHAPTER TWELVE

Evelina

"Let me out of here!" Evie slammed her fists on the locked door. Surely, if she kept at it, the door would eventually break. Or at least crack. Hopefully, the racket she caused would draw attention to her captors, and someone would call for help. How close were the neighbors? Could they hear her?

Raising her voice, she screamed louder, "Help!"

She sensed Cole nearby, his presence a constant tingle on her skin, coming from the other side of the door. As though he'd tossed her inside this room and paced the hallway to keep watch. Who the hell was he? Or more to the point, *what* was he? Back at the antique store, he'd taken down those monsters with a flick of his wrist. If that weren't scary enough, then he threw her over his shoulder like an empty library bag. Her stomach whirled before she passed out and woke in this bedroom.

With the door locked.

The luxurious fixtures and decadent bedding wouldn't tempt her from trying to escape. Not in the slightest. This was how people died. She'd warned Jemma.

How long had she been unconscious? Where was Jemma?

Patting her pockets, she searched for her cellphone, only to come up empty. It had either fallen out somewhere during the attack at the store or Cole had taken it once he tossed her into the room. Either was plausible.

She had to find her friend. Claw her way out of here through the walls if it came to it. Nothing would stop her.

At the oversized window, she shoved open the drapes and lifted the window. Brisk evening air stole the heat from inside the room, carrying a hint of fresh snow. At least they were still in the same hemisphere. Her knees wobbled as she eyed the drop to the ground. Possibly two levels. If jumping from the window was what it took to free herself, then she'd do it. Maybe. It was a long way down. And the gravel landing pad would hurt. Bad. Was breaking her neck worse than remaining a prisoner in the locked bedroom?

Possibly. Definitely.

She needed to think smarter, not make hasty, reckless choices which would end in her death.

After lifting the windowpane farther, she leaned forward—

Bright teal light burst in front of her eyes and knocked her backward.

What the actual hell?

More carefully this time, she eased her hand out the window. The teal light once again erupted, tingling her palm, sending little shocks through her blood, making her hand recoil.

Magic. Not the garden variety. This magic was strong, powerful. Old. If Cole practiced dark magic, real dark magic, then this situation was worse than she'd thought.

Wait a second. Since when could she distinguish between different magics?

A knife stabbed her temples. She cried out, cradling her skull, staggering back. As quickly as it came, the pain vanished. One epic migraine brewed in her head, and she couldn't blame her mind for wanting to incapacitate her for a bit. Everything that had happened in the past few days had rolled into a giant trigger.

Breathless, she backed away from the window.

Getting out of here was her number one priority.

The door flew open in a rush. Cole stood just beyond the doorway. His silvery-gray gaze scanned the room before landing on her. "What happened?"

His fists clenched by his sides while his gaze darted between her and his feet as though he forced himself not to step into the room.

Screw him.

Rage exploded like a thunderstorm inside her. "You kidnapped me!"

He opened his mouth to speak, only to think better of it and close it again.

Was he serious? No explanation? "Nothing to say?"

Those dark eyes narrowed at her. "What would you have me do, Evie? Leave you there for others to kidnap you instead?"

Now it was her turn for stunned silence. The guy had a point. A good one. *Whatever*.

"How would I know?" She threw her hands in the air. "You could be just as dangerous."

He flinched.

No longer content with filling the doorway with his broad shoulders, he barged in, stopping just out of reach. Her breath quickened. Especially when a distinct smell of winter drifted around her. Nighttime. Dark wintery nights by a fire. It lured her a step forward. Called to her.

She dragged her gaze over his shoulder to the open doorway. Could she make a run for it before he caught her? Why didn't she want to? He kidnapped her! They wrote horror stories about this. Yet, her feet wouldn't move.

"Let me leave," she whispered.

His gaze softened, dipped to the floor before returning to her. "I can't. It's not safe for you."

She shifted her feet as boulders tumbled inside her belly. "Why? What were those...things?"

His steadfast gaze held hers. "It's not important. What's important is that you're safe."

She drew back. "Oh. So only you get to decide what's important? I don't think so." She stepped back, her brain finally coming on board. "How did you know where I was? Have you been stalking me? Is that why you seem familiar?"

Again, he flinched. "Not exactly."

Another backward step toward the window. Could she jump through the magical shield?

Cole's chin dipped slightly. "I'll explain everything, I promise. Only...not yet. It's too much all at once and it's...too soon."

"When? How long do you plan on keeping me locked in this room?" She gritted her teeth as a fleeting pain sliced through her temples again. Cole reached for her, but she held up her hand halting him. "Don't touch me."

Something stirred in the far recesses of her mind, but before she grasped it, wispy dark gray shadows floated from Cole's fingers. They reached for her.

Magic.

She staggered backward until her back flattened against the wall. Pain lashed her temples again, lingering just long enough for her to cradle her head, before disappearing.

"Tell me what's happening." Cole's soothing voice warmed her. "Do you...remember?"

The shadows drifted closer, surrounding her, and for some reason she didn't understand, they didn't scare her. Instead, they calmed her. Floated around her body as though wrapping her in a comforting, protective blanket.

So weird. Yet strangely...familiar.

She was losing her mind.

This guy had taken her against her will. From a terrifying situation, sure, but did that make it okay? No. But right now, he seemed concerned with her wellbeing.

Why? That was the mystery.

She straightened and shooed away the shadows. "Get those things away from me."

"Evelina, please."

His raw, raspy voice tugged at her chest, but she couldn't show any weakness. To make it out of here, she had to go head to head with him. When she didn't answer, his shoulders dropped causing the shadows to snap back inside his fingertips. Yes, *inside.*

He turned to the door.

"Wait! My friend, Jemma. Where is she?" Her

stomach twisted when Cole didn't turn to face her. "Oh no, tell me you're not so heartless you left her at the antique store with those monsters."

How long had it been? Jemma was probably going out of her mind. Or worse…the others had captured her.

"Slater misted her back to her apartment. She's safe."

Misted?

And who the hell was Slater?

"Are you serious?" She had the biggest urge to punch him. "She's not safe. Those monsters saw her. They attacked both of us. The old lady knew who I was. You have to protect Jemma."

Cole swore under his breath. Without another word, he stormed from the room, slamming the door shut behind him.

She bolted to the door to twist the knob. Locked. Damn it!

"Let me out!" She punched the door, even knowing it would make no difference.

Her breaths heaved in and out. Was Jemma safe? Was she in more danger?

Sourness seeped low in her gut, churning, making her gag. With her back to the door, she sank to the plush carpet, refusing to think of how lovely and cushiony it felt.

Nope. Nothing would make any of this okay. And it also appeared, nothing would free her.

****

Cole

Cole paced back and forth in the entertainment room of the Guardian mansion, down the hall from where his soulmate…resided. A much nicer word than imprisoned. Yes, he'd kidnapped her. Holding her against her will was a far better alternative than Blaine capturing her. Or using her as bait as he had last time.

Now, Cole weighed his choices. Collect her friend or not?

Slater had done a simple mind manipulation when returning the friend home to make sure she didn't worry or call the authorities. Was that enough to keep the friend safe though? Would Blaine target her? The friend wouldn't be any use to Blaine in Hell, but he could use her as bait.

He'd never paced a room so much in his Fate-damned existence.

"Technically mortals are forbidden at the mansion," Aric said, interrupting his thoughts. "But that was before Raven brought Tayla here. And before you kidnapped your soulmate. Also, something Raven did, let me add."

Did rules even apply in this situation? Why couldn't Evie's last life be without incident?

He turned to Slater standing by the pool table beside Raine. "Was the friend's apartment safe?"

"Not in the slightest."

The back of his throat tightened. "I saw her friend at the ball when she spoke with Evie on the balcony. Blaine would've seen, too. We have to bring her here."

"You know, Reaper, I didn't think you had it in you. Kidnapping not one, but two mortals," EJ piped up from behind the bar.

He shot him a dirty look.

Raven slid his empty glass on the bar top. "I technically kidnapped Tayla from the middle of a forest to save her, and regret nothing. It's not kidnapping if it's your soulmate."

At least someone had his back.

"This is your home, Raven. I'm only a guest. Are you fine having another mortal here until this blows over?"

Aric grunted. "This isn't blowing over anytime soon, man. Bringing Evie here just kicked this war up a level. But if it helps, I would've made the same choice had it been Willow."

It did help knowing they supported his choice. But that wasn't the only source of his worry. What frightened him the most though was Evelina remembering. Each lifetime she remembered at different stages. Sometimes, he had months with her before she hated him, other times she remembered as soon as they met. In this life, he'd only just found her, but that didn't mean her soul hadn't been in play for a lot longer. Blaine had had enough time to orchestrate their meeting, so he'd known where she was for days, if not weeks, longer than him. Given how she cradled her head earlier, he'd bet that her mind was already beginning to remember. When that happened, she'd remember where she hid the book.

He didn't have long.

"Cole," Raven interrupted Cole's panicked thoughts. "We have plenty of room here for another mortal or otherwise, especially if she's connected to your soulmate. My concern is another mortal knowing about our world. We can't walk around under the same roof pretending to be something else. You'll have to explain everything."

He read between the lines. Explaining everything to the friend meant also explaining everything to Evie.

Thrusting them both into the middle of an immortal war they never asked for. No doubt triggering Evie's memories of her past lives.

Tempting Fate.

Too late for that.

Slater crossed his arms. "I only lightly covered the friend's memories until she knew Evie was safe. It won't take much to unveil them."

He of all immortals knew about the long-lasting effects of tampering with memories. They almost never resorted to that power, unless absolutely necessary.

One at a time, he peered at those around him. The immortals who'd welcomed him with open arms when he'd needed it most. The Guardians who'd given their protection to his soulmate when he couldn't. The family who never batted a single feather when he'd sought help.

Maybe this was all part of Fate's plan. Perhaps she'd planned every step from the moment Blaine Fell from the Heavens and kicked off this chain reaction.

Together, he and the Guardians could end not only Evelina's hellish cycle, but the war between the Fallen. Maybe this was another step in the endgame to return Blaine to the Heavens.

Again, a hunch told him Fate had already predicted that exact thought process. If so, he had nothing to lose.

"Evelina is right. The friend is in danger by association. I wouldn't put it past Blaine to use her when he can't get his hands on Evie. He knows this is his last chance." Slowly, he nodded, more to convince himself. "We need to retrieve the friend and bring her here."

CHAPTER THIRTEEN

Evelina

A soft knock sounded on the door. Before Evie had a chance to turn, it opened and Jemma barged in, racing to her. "Oh, my god, you're alive!"

Evie stumbled backward as her friend collided with her, squeezing her in a tight hug. Relief burst free along with tears. Jemma was safe. Only now, they were locked in this prison together.

Over Jemma's shoulder, she caught sight of Cole lingering by the door. Dark shadows lined the sunken skin beneath his eyes, his brows drawn tight as he looked at her. When she mouthed "thank you" his lips pressed together almost in a grimace. Had no one ever thanked him before?

Probably because he made a habit of kidnapping people.

Jemma leaned back to pinch her cheeks. "Yep. You're still alive. Okay. Explain."

The door softly shut, and she felt Cole's absence in the sudden coldness that swept through her. Gosh, there were so many strange and unexpected feelings she needed to decipher, but now wasn't the time.

Grabbing Jemma's hand, she pulled her to the bed, sitting beside her. "Are you okay? Did they hurt you? How did you get home from the antique store?"

Jemma waved her hand in the air. "I'm fine. I want to know more about this fortress. Does it have hidden tunnels? Where do they hide the treasures?"

A giggle quaked her chest. Typical Jemma. More interested in chasing a fairytale than her own safety. "I don't know where we are. The last thing I remember is those…people attacking us at the antique store and Cole showing up to fight them. Then when I wouldn't leave with him, he threw me over his shoulder, and I woke up here."

"Girl, that is next level romantic. The way he looked at you before he left the room was like you were the most precious cargo and he'd burn down this realm before he let anyone hurt you."

Realm? Jemma had an unhealthy obsession with this fairytale.

"Umm…that's not romantic, it's creepy. This is not a fairytale, Jemma. We're locked in this room because a guy kidnapped me." She squeezed Jemma's hands. "How did you get here? Do you know where we are?"

"Library Guy turned up *inside* my apartment. One second, he wasn't there, next *poof*! He did some hand trick and suddenly, I remembered what happened at the antique store. Then he told me we were both in danger and that he'd take me to you. Of course, I agreed, so he grabbed my hand and we magically appeared here."

She frowned. "You just left with him, no questions?"

"Oh, I had plenty of questions, but he answered none of them."

"What if Cole is the bad guy? What if leaving with him put you in more danger?"

Jemma screwed up her face as though the answer

119

should be obvious. "I'd rather be stuck in the baddie's lair with you, than without. What a boring life I'd have if you never came back. Ugh. Besides, I'm not sure how I feel about this guy yet." She leaned in and whispered even though they were the only ones in the room. "Blaine still seems like a better choice. He'd never kidnap you. There's that whole thing about consent to consider."

She stared open mouthed at her best friend for a long time. Was she on drugs? Sure, she had one of those full of life, hyperactive personalities, but this seemed...different. Crazier. On the other hand, one lifetime wouldn't be enough to show Jemma how much she valued their friendship. The second they'd met in college they hit it off and had been inseparable ever since. But...Jemma trusting a guy to whisk her to who knows where just so they could be together, took their friendship to the next level. They were both in this now. And they'd both leave here. Alive.

First things first, they needed information, and three questions came to mine: Where were they? Who were these people? How would they escape?

She jumped off the bed, ready for business. "Did you see anyone else on your way to this room? Any clues that might give us hints as to who he is or where we are?"

"Not a soul. But I can tell you, this place is nice. Like the beast's castle nice, but not as old." Jemma peered around the room. "Give me the low down. Are we escaping or not? I mean, I haven't seen the library yet so I can't judge his taste, even if Library Guy is hot. Like, hot-hot. Maybe we should stay until we have all the info?"

Well, they agreed on something. Cole was hot. Even though she'd only seen him twice, three times if she included inside this room, she'd noticed his physique. A good foot taller than her with a sharp-angled jaw and broad shoulders. Clearly strong, given how he'd effortlessly thrown her over his shoulder. Dark hair and a dusting of stubble had always been her weakness, so he easily gained points there, too. Oh, what she'd give to squeeze his biceps or drool all over his forearms. A brief glimpse of them would turn her into a puddle of lust. Just like his firm chest had when she'd clawed at it while he devoured her mouth in the library.

But just because the guy was gorgeous didn't excuse the fact he'd kidnapped her. And then proceeded to kidnap her friend.

Hold up. She'd…asked him to bring her friend and he…did. He didn't kidnap Jemma, he did her a favor by bringing her here.

Oh, man. She was in big trouble.

Jemma waved a hand in front of Evie's face. "Earth to Evie-Eve. Escape or live a life of imprisoned luxury? We could always invite Blaine, and they could battle it out for your affection."

Only a few days ago, Evie admired both guys yet now, she wasn't sure if she wanted anything to do with either of them. All because of a damn book.

She inhaled a deep breath and paced the room to sort her thoughts. "Okay. There isn't a mystery we can't solve, so let's treat it like a regular Wednesday whodunnit podcast. Cole is clearly something other than human. No ordinary guy can appear out of nowhere, do magic things with his hands, or look that good. We can also assume Blaine and Cole know each other. Something tells me they're not friends. Which means we possibly just landed in a feud. Maybe over the book. Maybe rival families?" She moved to the window, peering once more at the white-painted edges showing no sign of the magical barrier keeping her in. "The windows are spelled with something preventing me from putting my body through even though it allows the breeze in."

She pushed her hand in the opening to show Jemma, and the magic illuminated, tingling through her arm. It didn't hurt. In fact, the tingling sensations reminded her of…something she couldn't quite pinpoint.

"Magic." Jemma nodded. "My granny dabbles in magic. So did my aunt. It didn't end well for her."

"What happened?"

"She made an attraction tonic and gave it to the wrong guy. Insert restraining order."

What the hell?

Jemma tilted her head, giving her a long quizzical look. "You know, I always sensed magic in you. I'm usually spot on with those kinds of things."

"In me?"

Ridiculous. She'd never tried magic in her life. How would Jemma sense it? Unless one of her biological parents practiced witchcraft? Did witches even exist anymore? Another downfall of never knowing her ancestry.

"Yes, siree." Jemma waved a circle in front of Evie. "You have a strong aura."

Aura? "Riiiight."

Jemma laughed, dismissing Evie's shock.

"Everyone has an aura, Evie-Eve. Yours is just a bit...extra. Don't freak out on me now. Keep it together."

Umm. How the hell did she respond to that? "Thanks? I think. I didn't know you were so into magic."

"My family hails from Ireland, honey. Magic is in my blood, but don't worry. I don't run around with a voodoo doll or anything."

Of course, she knew Jemma came from a country known for witchcraft and magic dating back centuries, but she'd never connected the dots until now. Plus, her friend had never delved into it. "Okay. Right."

Jemma explored the room, opening and closing doors, drawers, leaving no space left unturned. On her way out of the bathroom, she motioned to the door leading to what Evelina presumed was a hall. "Have you tried the door? We could sneak round. This place looks huge, and I'd love to get a layout on the inside. I doubt Library Guy can watch us all the time. He'll slip up soon enough." She collapsed on the bed, disappearing in a mountain of throw cushions and pillows. "Or we could live a life of luxury here. Really, there are worse things. But as your friend, I'll support your decision."

Her eyes widened. "Jemma!"

"What? Wait!" Jemma jolted upright. "What if the beast comes for you?"

"Blaine? Why would he come for me?"

Jemma lifted a brow.

"Just because I saw them arguing in front of the castle doesn't mean he'd bust down the door to save me. He probably doesn't even know Cole kidnapped us."

"Oh, I'm sure he does. My guess is Cole is hunting the book too, and he kidnapped you to take out the competition. Or use you as ransom." Jemma snagged a pillow and hugged it to her chest. "Either option is totally plausible."

Was the book important enough for Cole to go to such extremes to find it before her? Which begged the question: what lengths would Blaine go to?

"Clearly, I underestimated the book's value." She moved to the door again and paused with her hand on the knob. "We have to get out of here and find it. We need to be ahead of whatever those two are planning."

Jemma bounced off the bed, landing on her feet. "Perfect. I was getting a little cabin fever in here anyway."

This time when Evie twisted the knob, the door swung open.

CHAPTER FOURTEEN

Cole

Sporadic energy buzzed through his limbs making it impossible to stay still. He couldn't sit, relax, stop tapping his foot, nor follow the one-sided conversation with EJ. Thank Fate that Guardian could hold a conversation with himself. Because right now, nothing could steal Cole's attention from the staircase leading up to the second floor where Evie and her friend were. Evelina. His soulmate. He'd brought not just her, but her friend here as well.

He didn't even know himself anymore. Especially when it came to the Hell he'd endure to keep her safe. Though, having her in the same house was far from Hell. In fact, it was the sole reason he couldn't stay still.

He'd go for a flight to calm himself, but that meant leaving her.

If the Fallen had captured her at the antique store, Blaine would've won. Blaine would've forced Evie to find the book and then taken her soul to Hell. Granted, it would've been in record breaking time. For centuries, he'd prevented Blaine from getting his twisted hands on Evie and the book, while simultaneously doing everything in his power to make sure she didn't use it.

The only way to end this for good was to destroy the book. But that risked Fate's wrath.

Which he'd face, when he knew Evie's soul would enter the Heavens.

"Reaper? Are you even listening?"

He shook the troubling thoughts from his head. "Not in the slightest, brother."

EJ mumbled something about everyone ignoring him, but Cole shrugged it off.

Heat flashed through his blood a second before two pairs of footsteps tiptoed down the stairs as though trying to sneak out. They couldn't leave. Raine had given her word the Raziel spell on the outer perimeter prevented mortals from exiting.

Mortals. Not immortals.

Locking Evie in the room by using his shadows was a low move, but he needed to ensure she was safe until Raine finished the spell. He couldn't let her go now. If Blaine found her...

Thankfully, Fallen couldn't enter the Guardian mansion. That spell had ensured the Guardians' safety for over a century.

A slight grin lifted his lips when Evie paused at the bottom of the stairs, her friend a step behind. His heart squeezed before tumbling over in his chest. When her gaze found his, the earth fell from beneath his feet sending him into a never-ending freefall. He'd never tire of the feeling. Nor would he ever tire of looking at her. The bronze glow dusting her cheeks, her full pouty lips, the way her dark brows furrowed as she studied him. But her eyes were what captured his heart, how her seductive deep brown irises lured him in until it felt as though they were the only ones in universe. All that mattered was reaching her. Touching her. Caressing his fingers along her jaw one more time.

But he did neither of those things. Instead, for a long moment, he simply held her gaze, embracing the light streaming through his blood from their connection, warming his chest. It wasn't often that he had the opportunity to admire her, drown in her beauty before all the shit between them roared to the surface. Once she remembered him, remembered their story, she'd hate him. After all, she'd vowed to never forgive him.

He had to find the book and end this. Only then could he truly be worthy of her forgiveness.

He cleared the rocks in his throat. "Hey."

Hey? Surely, he could do better than that. He was an immortal for Fate's sake, not a nervous male talking to a woman for the first time. He'd had plenty of practice with Evie. He should be an expert by now. Except, each time they met, nervousness overcame him, and he ended up doing something stupid.

Like kissing her in a library.

"Hi," she replied, still standing on the bottom step.

Her friend, Jemma, nudged her out of the way to step in front. "Right. Which one of you is going to explain why we ended up in this extravagant abode? We feel we deserve more information before making a final decision."

His mouth kicked up at the corner. "A decision about what?"

Evie lifted her chin, moving closer to overlook the landing into the living room. Her gaze darted to the front door only a few feet away, raising the hairs on the back of his neck. "Whether we leave or stay."

Even though he knew it wasn't possible, his stomach still lurched at the thought of her leaving him. Again. He steadied his voice so he sounded more confident than he felt. "Leaving's not an option."

Great. Now he just sounded like an asshole.

But it wasn't safe for either of them, didn't she understand that? The quickest way for Blaine to win was to force Evie to remember and given she was the only one who knew the book's location, Blaine's patience would only last so long.

"Why can't we leave? You can't keep us locked in here forever."

The thought had crossed his mind.

But this time was different, he needed to keep reminding himself of that. He didn't have an eternity to improve his courting, he also didn't have an eternity of first meets, first kisses, hearing her tell him for the first time that she loved him. They were on borrowed time. Less than usual. And if Fate had anything to do with it, which of course she did, that time would run out real damn quick.

Fate wasn't one to concede defeat. Nor was she an angel who looked kindly on someone who defied her, especially if that someone was a mortal.

This lifetime, he had to speed things up. Skip the part where Evie got to know him before he told her he was an angel. He didn't have time to slowly earn her trust. He'd lay it all on the line and hope the feathers fell in his favor. Surely if she knew the reasons why he'd brought her here, she'd trust him enough to stay willingly, rather than him locking her inside the mansion. Which, for the record, didn't sit right with him.

They needed to hunt for the book together.

He glanced at EJ who'd relaxed on the couch, drink in hand, a slight smirk on his face as though he couldn't wait to see how Cole handled Evie's question. Would be nice to have some of that cockiness, some…natural seduction to smooth things along. Alas, all Cole had was the fact he and Evie were destined.

That was all he needed.

He didn't have to rely on sex appeal or seductive words, he just needed to tell her the truth.

"Evie, I know this will be a lot to take in, but…" He swallowed any remaining nerves. "I'm an angel and you're my soulmate."

EJ spat out his drink. "Smooth, Reaper. Real smooth."

He ignored the Guardian. This wasn't Cole's forte, but surely Evie would sense that.

Besides, he'd said it now, he couldn't take it back. At least she didn't laugh at him or make a run for it. A good sign. He should keep going while he was on a roll. "We've met before, many times in fact, because your soul is reincarnated every fifty years."

Evie held his gaze, a slight frown on her face, her lips squished together tight, for a long moment until she…burst out laughing. So hard in fact, she pressed the heel of her palm to her eyes and leaned over at the waist. If the rocks hadn't returned to his throat, he might have enjoyed the sound. Instead, he shifted his feet. Then to pluck another feather from his wings, her friend joined in, bracing one arm on the banister, laughing so hard she snorted.

No wonder he needed centuries to get this right. His last opportunity to explain things for the first time, and she'd laughed at him. What the Fate did he do now?

He glanced at EJ.

The Guardian lifted the glass in front of his face, obviously trying to hide his own smirk.

"A little help, brother?"

EJ's chest quaked as he lowered the glass onto the coffee table to stand. "All right, Reaper. But only because I owe you. And I also happen to like you." The Guardian squeezed him on the shoulder. "That was like watching Rae gut a Fallen…using only her toothbrush. So cringy."

"Thanks for the confidence."

EJ laughed again before turning to Evie and Jemma. Thankfully, they'd also stopped making fun of him. "Hey friend, how about we give these kids some privacy and I show you around? I make a mean cocktail."

Jemma held up a finger silencing EJ. "Tempting. One moment please." She lowered her voice, leaning closer to Evie. Little did they know, both him and EJ could still hear every word. "What do you say, Evie-Eve? Explore or escape?"

When Evelina looked back at him, albeit with glassy eyes from laughing so hard, her hand lifted to her chest, almost as though she felt the pull between them.

That made two of them.

Maybe he'd gone about this all wrong. Maybe, her soul already recognized him.

She gave her friend a slight nod. "Explore."

CHAPTER FIFTEEN

Evelina

"Okay, rockstar, lead the way." Jemma motioned to the guy standing beside Cole. Black ripped jeans, form-fitting T-shirt, and arms covered in tattoos. He looked familiar, she could've sworn she'd seen him before, but where? When? Was he at the ball with Cole? Or...now, here was where her mind dipped into crazy mode. Had her soul really been...reincarnated?

To be fair, she had suggested that to Cole at the ball, right before he kissed her. The feeling that she'd been there before, seen things before, met people before.

She mentally smacked herself. No. It wasn't possible. Was it? Sure, she believed in the afterlife and the possibility of reincarnation. But believing it happened to her was a completely different concept.

Wasn't it?

As Jemma and the other guy disappeared down the hall, she turned her attention to Cole. Her heart fluttered, just like it had when she'd first seen him in the castle library. Two kindred spirits seeking the pleasure of books. Two...soulmates? Once again, she slapped herself.

Don't be stupid.

Back then, his appreciation for literature and the

131

way he'd filled the fine tailor-made suit had struck her stupid. Awoke all those sensitive lust receptors between her legs so her brain could no longer focus. But that didn't excuse his actions. Even if he did believe they were soulmates. Was that even a thing?

Also, how was it possible for the same guy to look equally mouthwatering in jeans and a T-shirt? Surely that broke some law.

How did one turn off their lust receptors?

"Tell me what you're thinking." Cole's deep voice swirled over her body like lowering into a warm bath on a wintery night. Somehow, without her noticing, he'd gravitated closer to stand by the stairs.

"If you're an angel, can't you just read my mind?"

He tunneled his fingers through his thick, dark hair, making the strands move in all different directions. "I've never been very good at this."

"At what? Reading minds or kidnapping people? You seem quite proficient at that in my opinion."

She meant it as a joke, but the way he flinched made her immediately want to take it back. Maybe she should cut him some slack. He was right earlier. Bringing her here saved her from those other creatures who would've surely done worse. Sure, he'd taken her without consent, but she wasn't exactly in the right frame of mind to answer anyway.

Besides, the poor guy looked as though he balanced the weight of the world on his shoulders.

She shifted to face him, leaning her forearm on the banister. "If I'm your soulmate, wouldn't I know you? Remember you from a previous life?"

He inched closer until she could reach out and brush her fingers along his stubble. Would it be soft or prickly? Once again, her belly flipped as his decadent scent consumed her every breath, doing wicked things to her blood. It lightly stroked the surface of her skin until every nerve ending zapped and tingled.

"You eventually remember me. Us. But each time I find you, it's like meeting you for the first time all over again."

Damn if that wasn't the most romantic thing she'd ever heard. Jemma would've melted into a puddle on the floor.

Was it so farfetched to believe in soulmates? A connection that reached beyond normal comprehension. The conviction in Cole's voice was so convincing, as though he believed every word. Which made it hard for her to dispute. Yes, she adored history books, but believing in real-life fairytales was Jemma's thing, not hers.

"That sounds kind of sad."

"Maybe." His gaze held hers as he moved even closer. "Tell me you don't feel the pull."

As though on command, a strange tug in her chest demanded she step closer. She couldn't speak. For one, how did he know she felt a connection to him she couldn't explain? Did he...did he feel it, too?

No. Not possible, the reasonable part of her brain reminded her. She barely knew Cole. She'd only met him yesterday. She needed a lot more information from him before she trusted him. Let alone believed they were soulmates. To start with, how did he know Blaine?

She stepped back, which did nothing to clear her thoughts. "Are you looking for the book?"

Muscles in his jaw popped, and those strong board

shoulders stiffened. "Have you found it?"

How stupid of her. She should've known his story was some bogus coverup just so he could find the book first. She wasn't his soulmate. He was using her to get the bounty.

Fine. Two could play this game.

"No, but I intend to."

His shadowy gray eyes darkened as he massaged the back of his neck, giving the hallway a fleeting glance.

"That's why you were in the library."

A deep frown indented his forehead. "Give me today to explain. To…convince you we're on the same team."

Telling her she was his soulmate was a brand-new pickup line experience. Come to think of it, guys rarely used any pickup lines on her that didn't involve slurring and spilled beer. Even if she could understand them, she was hardly ever interested in giving more than a polite "no, thank you." Something held her here. Not only in this house, but right here, standing with Cole. She couldn't quite explain the urge to hear him out, for him to tell her everything. A niggling flutter whispered that he was interested in more than the book. She should listen to all the facts so she could make an informed decision. If it turned out he was just another person Blaine had commissioned to hunt for the book, then she and Jemma could be on their way. But…if it turned out Cole told the truth…well, she'd cross that bridge if she got to it. If.

On the other hand, maybe Cole knew something about this sought-after book and would slip up by telling her its location. She could use their close proximity to her advantage and gather information.

She crossed her arms, mainly so her change of direction didn't show. "Okay. You have twenty-four hours."

Gosh, his heavy, almost relieved, exhale did strange things to her belly. If he lied, and meant her harm, surely he wouldn't have given her a choice. Nor would he be so relieved that she'd agreed to stay. Unless he had a weird set of morals. One of those morally gray villains Jemma lusted over.

Cole motioned to a door at the end of the long, carpeted hall. "Let's talk over food."

With a nod, she followed him through the dining room and into the kitchen where she perched on a stool while Cole stared at the stovetop looking as though he'd stumbled into a different world.

Eventually, he lifted his gaze to her, his expression grim. "I, uh, haven't been in the mortal realm for long enough to learn how these appliances work. But I can vouch for those cupcakes." He pointed to a stack in a sealed container on the counter.

Could this guy be more adorable?

"Cake and I are best friends."

His mouth lifted in a slow smile. "We've always had that in common."

Cole grabbed two cupcakes, offering one to her. With the first mouthful of creamy icing and fluffy cake, she might've died and gone to heaven. "Oh, wow. These are good."

Only now did she realize Cole had been watching her while she took that first bite, and the thought diverted all that sugar to her head, making her dizzy. When she licked a smear of icing from her lips, his intense gray eyes smoldered, dipping to her mouth. A sudden ache flared to life between her legs while indecent images of him licking the icing from her lips flashed before her eyes. *His hot lips crashing into hers. Groans of pleasure as she swept her tongue over his to taste more of that sweet, sugary goodness in his mouth.* Tingles erupted over her sensitive skin, his look caressing her, pulsing in her heated blood.

It would be so easy for her to climb onto the counter, tuck her legs around his waist, tunnel her fingers through his thick hair. Would he kiss her back? Would he grip her backside and rock his hardness against her aching core?

His Adam's apple bobbed and…oh, jeez. Did he just moan or was that her? How was she so sexually attracted to a man she barely knew? How did he control her most intimate feelings and thoughts with only a look?

Aroused didn't even come close to how hot she felt. She'd take off her sweater if it weren't so obvious. Oh, great. Thinking of taking off her sweater only did the opposite, filling her overstimulated mind with thoughts of him trailing that sugar-coated tongue down her neck to skim her nipples.

Cole cleared his throat, his fingers curled over the edge of the countertop.

Surely, he didn't know how much she throbbed between her legs. He couldn't, right? Then why was he suddenly looking in every direction but hers?

She shifted in the seat, diverting her attention back to the cupcake, forcing her thoughts out of the gutter.

After a few tense minutes, Cole's deep voice finally broke the sexually charged silence. "EJ's soulmate makes the cupcakes. While I'm living here, I'm trying hard not to overindulge, but…it's difficult."

The way he said overindulge made her think he referred to activities, not cupcakes.

"EJ?"

Cole dusted crumbs off his shirt. "The one you met in the living room."

Okay, they'd navigated out of the lust fog into a normal conversation. Mentally, she listed questions in order of importance.

"Do you not usually live here?"

Well, she could've picked a better first question. She was warming up.

"No."

When he didn't elaborate, she asked another. "You said you're an angel. Is EJ one, too?"

Cole pushed aside his empty plate to lean his forearms on the counter. "Yes. Ten immortals live in this house, including me."

Chewing slowly, she considered his response. It sounded so ridiculous. Absurd. Ten angels, living in a house together, baking cupcakes? Another giggle threatened to unleash, but she bit the inside of her mouth to suppress it.

She finished the cupcake and dusted her hands over the plate.

"Another?" Cole gave the container a longing look.

"No, I probably shouldn't. I may love sweet treats, but alas my hips don't." She sat up straighter, causing those gray eyes to drag back to her. They pulled her in so easily. Note to self. "Let's cut to the chase. What do you want with the book?"

He bowed his head for a moment, and when he

lifted it again, the pain behind his eyes cut a thousand slices in her chest. For someone so troubled, he didn't act it.

"What did Blaine offer you?"

She drew back, surprised by the question. How much did he know about the book? That was the real question. "I'd get the same reward as you, I suppose. A bounty for the return of his book."

Why did it sting to realize she wasn't the only one Blaine approached to find the book? And why didn't he offer her the reward up front. If Jemma hadn't heard about the bounty at the ball, she might have never known.

"Return?"

She frowned. "Blaine said it was a family heirloom and someone stole it from him. Why? What did he tell you?"

His granite jaw tightened, muscles popping out the sides. "Let's just say I'm searching for the book but for different reasons."

That piqued her interest. "Like what?"

He straightened, crossing his arms over his chest. Her gaze immediately diverted to the delicious biceps stretching his T-shirt. Bad move. The tingles were back.

"It doesn't matter why I want it. What matters is that we find it," Cole said with an air of finality in his tone. "I'll help you. We'll find it together."

That sounded great, but what happened with the bounty? Would they share it? Would Cole double-cross her? She barely knew the guy, could she trust him?

Though, if they pooled their resources, including ten so-called angels and two humans, they could find the book quicker. That strange shiver of awareness she experienced each time she looked at Cole assured her she could trust him. That perhaps, he was the only one she could trust.

Despite her common sense, she found herself leaning toward his offer. "What's the catch?"

"When you find it, and you will, I have no doubt, you don't give it to Blaine."

Oh, that was a mega sized catch. The two of them working together to find an ancient text for apparently different reasons, but when she found it, she…what? Keep it instead of giving it to Blaine as he'd asked? She wouldn't have known it existed if he hadn't told her. Unless…Cole wanted it for himself. Was he related to Blaine? Or from a rival family? "Is this some kind of mafia war I've walked into the middle of?"

"I don't know what mafia is."

He didn't speak for the longest moment, until she was sure he wouldn't elaborate. But when she opened her mouth to explain, he beat her to it. "The others are upstairs, I'll introduce you."

Introduce her to the ten angels. Not that she'd seen proof of these angelic claims. Surely, angels didn't walk around like ordinary humans. Didn't they have wings? Could they go outside during daylight? Oh, wait, that was vampires. She'd read a lot of ancient texts that referenced angels but like many other myths, they were exactly that. Myths. Weren't they?

"Wait a minute. You didn't answer my question. Are you and Blaine enemy angel families?"

"You could say that." Fury swirled in Cole's gray eyes, darkening the rims, making her pulse spike. "Blaine's dangerous, do you hear me? If there's only one thing you remember, remember that."

What if Cole was just as dangerous?

CHAPTER SIXTEEN

Cole

Cole led Evie upstairs to the entertainment room, hands shoved in his pockets, so he didn't reach over and entwine his fingers with hers. So desperately, he wanted to calm her nerves, reassure her that she was safe with him. To tell her everything would be okay.

If only he had Blaine's ability to lie.

But the truth was all he had in his arsenal. When she'd asked about Blaine, he almost blurted out everything. Throwing large amounts of knowledge at her in one go would gain her memory back quicker with potentially devastating consequences. That would diminish the light in her golden eyes sooner than he cared for. Just once, he'd give anything to have time with her without all the hurt of their past.

But he couldn't allow things between them to progress, no matter how much he ached for it. Remembering the lust in her eyes and the decadent scent of her arousal back in the kitchen almost brought him to his knees. What he wouldn't give for one more kiss. One more embrace. A chance to taste more than her mouth. Each time he thought of wanting more, he forced himself to remember her final words in Hell.

I'll never forgive you.

That sure snuffed out the flames.

At the entrance to the entertainment room, Evie skidded to a halt just inside the doorway, and he cursed himself for resting a reassuring hand on the small of her back. So much for keeping his distance. That lasted three point six seconds.

Clearing his throat, he introduced Evie to the Guardians and their soulmates. In turn, each waved, saluted with a drink, or welcomed her with a hug. Her friend, Jemma, looped an arm in Evie's, diving into a chaotic retelling of EJ's tour, once again underestimating immortal hearing. It made him smile. The female was practically bouncing on the spot and kept ensuring Evie that this place was better than the beast's.

Whoever the Fate that was.

A drink landed in his hand, courtesy of EJ, but he didn't take a sip. He couldn't stomach more than cupcakes with the team of acrobats somersaulting in his belly.

Jemma and Evie sandwiched themselves between Hailee and Tayla on a couch, and as usual, he found himself gravitating closer just to breathe the same air.

Standing by the bar, Raven cleared his throat. "How much does she know?"

Before he answered, Jemma cut in. "We know you're all immortals, that this is some hidden mansion in the middle of the forest, and Cole is also looking for the same book as Eve." A smirk, crossed between smug and boastful, curled on Jemma's mouth. "Of course, Evie-Eve will find it first. Her investigation skills are on point."

Maybe now was time for that drink.

Raven shot him a baffled look and Cole just

shrugged, having no idea how to handle that much energy squeezed into a tiny female form. "Right. Let's get down to business."

"Hang on." Evie narrowed her eyes at him. "I never agreed to work with you to find the book. What happens to the reward? Do you expect us to spit it in…eleven shares?"

"Twelve," Jemma muttered.

"Sorry, Jem. Twelve shares?"

Cole moved closer, until he stood right beside the couch. "I have no interest in money. And considering you're the only one who can find the book, we need to work together to—"

"What did you say?"

He frowned. "I have no interest in money."

"No, after that."

Prickles burst inside his chest along with giant red, flashing sirens warning him to slow the Fate down. Back the fuck up. The more information he told her, the quicker she remembered. The quicker she'd hate him.

When her eyes softened, almost pleading for him to tell her something, he lost the battle. He'd never make a skilled Guardian.

"You're the only one who can find the book," he whispered the words, hoping she didn't hear them.

Evie's eyes narrowed as she studied him. "That's nice of you to think so, but I'm sure you can find it just as quickly. Especially with all your…angelic abilities."

At least she believed him. That was a start.

He almost forgot the others were in the room when he moved to crouch in front of her, resting his hands on her knees as though they belonged there. "You hide the book in a different location every lifetime. Only you know where. It's important that we find it before Blaine."

Her eyes widened, and she drew back.

Shit. He'd said too much. He squeezed her knee, but it did nothing to lower her frantic pulse thumping in his ears as if it were his own.

"Okay, that's enough." She pushed his hands away to stand and he joined her. "Thank you for your hospitality, it's been, um, enlightening. We'll be going now."

Jemma remained seated, her gaze darting between he and Evie. He sensed she'd help him convince Evie to stay, but a twisted part of him wanted to do that all on his own. For her to stay because he'd asked her to. Because she wanted to.

"You can't leave," he blurted when she turned to the door.

"You said that before, but here's the thing. I have a job, people who will notice that I'm gone. I have a life outside of this magical bubble of castles, angelic beings, and immortal treasure hunts. As much as I'd love to search for an ancient text with a household of...angels, I need to get back."

She winced, squeezing her forehead as though fending off a headache. More like memories. He recognized the signs. He needed to tread carefully, one truth at a time otherwise the sudden onset of memories would do more harm than good.

He totally sucked at this.

Instead of doing things differently, he'd done everything backward. As though he'd learned nothing during their past lives. Perhaps instead of doing things differently, finding a way to earn her trust, her love, he should accept the inevitable. No matter what he did, in the end she'd still resent him. She'd still wish he had never found her. But at least, if all went to plan, her soul would enter the Heavens.

Nothing would stop him from granting her that peace.

Not even her threat to leave. He brought her here to keep her safe. If he stopped pretending to be something other than himself, this would all be over before they knew it.

He raked his fingers through his hair and puffed out a hot breath. "I already asked EJ to notify your workplace that you had a family emergency and needed an indefinite period of leave. I also misted to your apartment, gathered your personal items and anything I thought you might need."

If looks could kill, her volatile glare would incinerate him. But he didn't stop. The sooner he made their position clear, the quicker they could progress to finding the book, then the quicker he could destroy it. After that, she could hate him all she wanted. At least her soul would still live.

That wouldn't happen if Blaine took her to Hell and sacrificed her.

"There's no going back, Evie. You're staying with me."

CHAPTER SEVENTEEN

Evelina

"Can you believe him?" Evie shoved open the door to the bedroom which Jemma closed behind them.

Her bedroom.

The room where Cole had conveniently delivered her personal belongings because this was her life now. Screw him. He'd given her nothing, no answers, no reason to trust him, hadn't even told her why he wanted the book. And that bogus story about her being the only one who could find it. Bullshit.

She stomped around the room, hands on her hips like a cranky librarian who'd discovered a row of mis-shelved books. "He thinks he can just swoop into my life, kiss me like the world is ending, and then spin me a tale about lost soulmates." She turned to Jemma who sat cross-legged on the oversized bed. "What is so important about this book anyway? It has to be more than a family heirloom. Cole and Blaine are going to extreme lengths to find it."

"I'm conflicted, Eve. On one hand, you thrive on uncovering mysteries so I'm not sure why you're fighting this one. On the other, meeting angels is super cool."

She almost threw a pillow at Jemma's head. "We don't have proof that they really are angels. I mean, sure, the creatures who attacked us at the antique store had red eyes and scary looking wings, but what if these people are worse? What if they're the bad guys, not the ones with red eyes? What if Cole didn't save me because I'm his so-called soulmate? What if he stole the book from Blaine and wants to make sure no one finds it?" She threw her hands in the air. "Again, what's so special about this damn book?"

"Speaking of our beast, have you heard from him?"

She shook her head. "I haven't seen my cell since I got here. For all I know, I dropped it at the store."

She made a mental note to ask Cole about it once she calmed down. She'd stormed out of the room in such a rage, he probably expected her to sulk in here for years.

Jemma bum-shuffled to the edge of the bed and opened her hand, preparing to count. "All right. Let's list what we know. Blaine approached you first and said the book belongs to him, that someone stole it from him." She tapped her index finger. "Cole said you're the only one who can find it and that you hide it each lifetime. Which I think is totally badass by the way."

"Not helping, Jem."

She smiled, tapping her third finger. "Cole said Blaine is the bad guy, and his group of tightknit immortal buddies agree. Cole also believes you're reincarnated."

"Not possible, right?"

"Maybe. Maybe not. The way he looks at you is...intense. As though he already loves you more than life itself. No, it's deeper than that. He looks at you like he wants to devour you but at the same time, the thought of touching you causes him physical pain."

Her stomach whirled. She'd caught that exact look back in the kitchen but hadn't wanted to read more into it. What would happen if he did touch her? Which, of course, brought her full circle to wondering if being soulmates with an angel was possible. How did she reincarnate? How did she...die?

Ferocious tornados slapped the pit of her stomach, waves of bile rising in her throat. On second thought, how she died wasn't something she really wanted to know.

She paused by the window, peering at the deep magenta sunset casting a mystical haze over the thick pine forest. How many times had she considered leaving, escaping, walking out the front door and daring someone to stop her? But something kept her here. Not finding the book, that was the farthest thing on her mind. The pull, the strange grounding sensation that stopped her from running had something to do with Cole. A...connection she'd felt to him ever since they met in the library. Not simply lust because of their big-screen worthy kiss and the way her body lit up in his vicinity. The sensation stemmed from his silvery-gray eyes, how they recognized her, knew her, saw through hers right to the heart of her soul. Those eyes told her the truth, that she was his soulmate, that they were destined to meet again in each lifetime. And as impossible as it sounded, she couldn't dismiss it. Until she knew for sure, she couldn't leave.

Turning back to Jemma, she leaned against the cool glass. "We still don't know much about the book, nor do we have proof Cole is the good guy. We need more answers. Until we get them, I think we should stay."

"He's good, I sense it. Almost too good." Jemma

giggled.

If only she trusted her own senses.

Warmth bloomed over the back of her neck, and she spun to see Cole stride across the manicured lawn heading to the forest. The sensation, the flutter in her belly, the extra pulse in her blood, all supported Cole's belief that they knew each other from a different time. More than what was possible from two encounters.

Jemma appeared beside her, brushing her arm with hers.

They watched Cole on a mission to the trees, his long strides crossing the grass with steady purpose. The guy was just as beautiful from behind. Otherworldly. Everything from his board, muscular shoulders, down to his perfect ass. Okay, fine, she didn't make it past his ass. Who could blame her? It was as breathtaking as the rest of him. She bet he was the kind of guy who could give a girl a dirty, sinful night of pleasure and then wake her up with flowers and breakfast.

Would it hurt to give him a chance? Really, she had nothing to lose. If he wasn't in it for the money, then why did he want the book? What was he hiding? She should go down there, talk to him, ask him. Demand answers. Something, anything, to prove the crazy world he spoke of truly existed. That he was who he said. That she could trust him.

As though he sensed her burning stare, he turned at the tree line and lifted his gaze to her window. She couldn't read his expression from this far away, but she sensed his pain, his yearning in the sudden ache behind her ribs.

He held her gaze for long moments while the ache thumped in time with her pulse. More than craving answers, she ached for something to explain the connection with him. Proof she was his soulmate. Maybe then she could—

She sucked in a sharp breath, her hands flying over her mouth.

Holy shit.

Huge, majestic wings unfurled from behind Cole's back in one swift woosh. Yes, wings. Large, muscular...wings. Extending in a wide arc out to his sides, they swept up and down as though in slow motion, swaying the grass at his feet.

She leaned forward, pressing one hand on the cool glass, her quick breaths fogging the space in front of her mouth. Silvery-gray feathers matched the color of his smoky eyes. They shimmered beneath the fading sunlight, setting off a kaleidoscope of sparkles.

Mesmerizing was the only word that came to mind.

An image appeared in her mind, as crystal clear as if it happened in real time, right in front of her. *Cole appearing before her, his wings proudly unfurled behind his back. He smiled and he held out his hand, told her she was safe now...*

Her breath stalled. Not a random thought...a memory.

Cole placed his palm on his chest, right over his heart and mouthed something she couldn't hear. But she didn't need to. His vow seeped through her skin, into her blood, right to the center of her soul.

He'd told the truth. He always told the truth, every time they found each other. Cole was an angel, one who'd long ago fallen for her and would forever do anything to keep her safe.

Her soulmate.

Jemma curled her arm around Evie's, giving it a squeeze. "Well, Evie-Eve, I guess that's your proof."

****

At some point during the evening, Tayla, Raven's soulmate whom she'd met earlier, invited them down for dinner, but she and Jemma had opted to eat in their room. She wasn't avoiding Cole. Well, maybe a little bit, but who could blame her? Everything he'd told her had been the truth. She felt it as his gaze held hers from across the lawn.

Discovering he was an angel was one thing, something she could accept as bizarre as that sounded, but realizing she had a soulmate, that they'd met in many lifetimes, blew her mind. Also, why the hell couldn't she remember any of her past lives? How unfair, not just for her, but for Cole also. Given he was a freaking angel, she doubted he died over and over as she clearly did. It must've been devastating for him to watch her die again and again.

Instead of hiding in the room avoiding their conversation, she should tackle it head-on. For a while, she thought maybe if she stayed in here long enough, everything outside these walls would resolve itself and she could return to normalcy when she stepped out the door. That wouldn't happen though. The conversation she needed to have with Cole would still be waiting. The whole thing about the book and why Blaine wanted it, wouldn't go away just because she was too cowardly to face the hard truths.

Also, the more she paced the room, the more questions she added to her list. For starters, did Blaine know who she was when he asked her to find the book? Did he know her connection to Cole? Is that why he told her she knew his name but didn't remember it?

It all made sense now.

She paused her restless pacing to peer at Jemma, snuggled under piles of bedding, sound asleep, as though she were in her own bed back home.

If only she had some of Jemma's resilience. No, not exactly resilience, more of her free spirit, her ability to quickly adapt to an ever-changing environment. Change was tough. Anyone would think that foster care would've strengthened her character, but instead, she seemed to crumble with uncertainty. This year, she'd vowed to step outside her comfort zone, take a risk or two, which was what had prompted her to accept Blaine's proposition.

Look where that got her. Plummeted her into an immortal world of angels and soulmates.

Gosh, she needed air or to lose herself in a room overflowing with books. What she'd give to smell a dusty old tome. Actually, she'd seen a decent collection in the living room when she and Jemma first ventured downstairs. Maybe all she needed was to curl up on the couch with a book. Everything else could wait until morning.

With Jemma softly snoring away, Evie wrapped a throw blanket around her shoulders and slipped out of the room. Lamps illuminated the quiet hallway in a soft warm light, and she winced at each creak in the floorboards as she made her way downstairs. Nearing the bottom, she stilled when the soft strum of an acoustic guitar drifted up the stairs. She waited and listened, recognizing the music, but she couldn't quite grasp the piece. A few chords here and there with lengthy pauses in between, linked together by emotion rather than sheet music as though the player simply strummed for comfort but couldn't bring themselves to finish the entire song.

The haunting tone sprouted goosebumps along her arms even though she was anything but cold. It called to her. Fueled the desperation she'd felt a couple of times lately when she'd been near Cole.

Sorrow. Pain. History.

She experienced it all, the aching melody holding her ribs in a vise, slowly squeezing them together until she thought her lungs would collapse. She pressed her hand over her heart to make sure it still beat.

As lightly as she could, she tiptoed closer to the corner, the sound luring her in. At the bottom, she peeked around the wall. With his back to her, in almost complete darkness except for the flickering fireplace, Cole sat on the edge of the couch, a guitar rested in his lap.

The strumming paused, but neither of them moved or acknowledged the other's presence.

Millions of thoughts rolled around and around in her head. She shouldn't interrupt, she should be in bed like the rest of the household. This moment felt personal, private, she should wait until morning to talk to him. Yet, all those reasons and excuses fell away with her long exhale. Of all the rooms she'd felt drawn to tonight, Cole was in the same one. Surely, that meant something. Didn't it?

Still facing the fireplace, Cole began strumming once more. This time when the chords blended in the familiar melody, pressure heightened in her chest. A slight throb began at her temples, and she braced for a spike of pain that never came.

How was everything about Cole so familiar? Did her soul recognize his even though her mind didn't. Was that why he consumed her thoughts, why each time she stepped outside her room she hoped to find him standing in the hall waiting for her? Sure, he was attractive, more than that, the guy was gorgeous, but was she ready to believe her attraction was more than physical?

Reincarnated soulmates? What if the feelings she experienced now were from a past life? How could she distinguish between them?

Thinking about it transferred the pressure from her chest back to her head.

Although she had loads of questions, and a connection she couldn't explain had drawn her to this room, she should leave him be. The moment felt too personal to interrupt.

As she pushed off the wall to walk back upstairs, the strumming paused once more.

"Join me?"

Slowly, she looked in the living room to find Cole watching her. "Sorry, I didn't mean to interrupt."

Firelight reflected in his gray eyes, giving them an unearthly glow that reminded her of his wings. "I'm glad you did."

He leaned the guitar upright by the couch and without her even realizing it, once again she gravitated toward him. In the living room, she stood for a moment and watched the logs crackle in the fireplace while her breath somewhat steadied. Awareness tingled over her sensitive skin, heating her blood before pooling low in her belly. She felt Cole watching her, his gaze a warm, silent caress.

The tightness constricting her ribs almost became too much.

How could one person affect her like this?

Heat bloomed as his quiet footsteps neared, stopping so close behind her that she swore she could feel the steady, strong beat of his heart. A base line so in time with her own. His cool, wintery scent wrapped around her like his arms once did.

Wait.

Slowly, she turned and peered up into those mesmerizing eyes. A memory flashed in her mind, hard and fast, fragments of a previous life. *Cole standing before her in the darkness, lifting his hand to her cheek...* Sharp pain sliced through her temples, and she sucked in a breath.

Cole cupped her face. "Evie?"

The pain vanished and her vision cleared. She refocused on his furrowed brows, the sexiest goddamn frown she'd ever seen, when realization hit her.

Her headaches came when she...remembered.

Before meeting Cole, her migraines came with flashes of moments she'd thought were dreams. Only, they weren't, were they? They were memories. Past lives. Each time they vanished, they left a gaping hole in her chest, filled with longing for something she'd lost...but hadn't realized what.

She sagged into his embrace, staring up at him, itching to sweep her hand over the dark stubble dusting his square jaw, to tunnel her fingers through his hair.

His gaze searched hers. "What's wrong?"

"I...I think I'm remembering things."

Cole's expression hardened for a split second before he dropped his hands and stepped back, half turning toward the fireplace. "You should be asleep." His voice sounded strained, no longer concerned, now bordering on frustrated. Hurt, maybe.

"I couldn't sleep. I thought sitting down here might help." She wrapped the blanket tighter around her shoulders. "What song were you playing? It sounded familiar."

His gaze shot to her. "You recognized it?"

"Yeah, but I couldn't quite place it. Was it from a…past life?"

Something flashed in those haunting gray eyes. He opened his mouth to speak but closed it again without saying a word, instead choosing to put more distance between them by sitting back on the couch. "It's an old song."

Part of her considered pressing for more information but held back. Even though she swore she'd heard it before, given his standoffish reaction, it clearly meant a lot to him, and something told her the memories weren't at all happy.

CHAPTER EIGHTEEN

Cole

Why? Why did he torture himself? When all the Guardians were either out patrolling for Fallen or snuggled in bed with their soulmates, he sat in the dark living room strumming chords to a song he'd written for Evie almost two centuries ago. A night he remembered so vividly, as though it were only yesterday. Snow had fluttered from the sky, much like tonight, in the belly of a cave, warmed by a small campfire. That night he'd told her who he was, what he was, and what she meant to him.

That night he'd told her he loved her.

In that lifetime, her family had lived in a small farming cottage on the outskirts of town, and for three nights in a row, she'd snuck out after nightfall to meet him at the cave. Back then, he naively thought they had more time, that he could court her as she deserved, that she'd fall in love with him rather than the idea of their history.

History had taught him nothing though. Because once he told her who he was, she remembered everything else the following day and hadn't returned to the cave. Instead, she'd searched for the book.

Leaning forward, he rested his forearms on his thighs, wishing for a drink in his hands so he'd stop reaching for her.

Why did he keep doing this to himself? To her?

He should focus on the book, not fall in love with his soulmate again. He exhaled a shaky breath. Who was he kidding? He'd never fallen out of love.

Evie quietly lowered onto the opposite couch, curling her legs up beneath the blanket wrapped around her shoulders. Having her nearby always calmed him, and tonight was no different. The second he'd sensed her tiptoe down the stairs, the boulder sitting on his chest gradually shrunk until it weighed no more than a stone. In return, an ache twisted his heart into knots.

"Cole, there's so much I don't understand. Things I feel like I know but don't remember." Her gaze captured him. "I need you to be straight with me."

That was the least he could do. But at the same time, scared the shit out of him.

He twisted his fingers together and nodded for her to continue.

"You said earlier that Blaine is dangerous, and that I'm the only one who can find the book he wants, but I feel like you're leaving a lot of information out. Important information. And I need you to tell me, especially if I'm going to…stay here."

That organ behind his ribs thumped back to life.

"Believe it or not, in this decade, guys can't just whisk in and save girls with no explanation. Even if they do have…wings."

He snorted. Fate, he'd missed her snark and stubbornness.

He'd gone about all this the wrong way, again, he realized that, but he of all angels knew he couldn't change the past despite how much he wanted to. All he

could do was focus on the here and now, tonight, and the decisions he made for the future.

Their future.

Because at the end of this, after he destroyed the book and Evie's soul safely resided in the Heavens, this torture would end.

He cleared his throat, shifting in the seat to face her. "Ask away."

"What's so special about the book?"

Of all the questions... "You're leading with that? Could you not have eased into the hard questions? Talk about the Heavens, angels, how I'm here, what I do, how I fly? Anything before throwing that question at me?"

She laughed and the sound swept over him in a comforting caress, awakening life inside him. "Sure, I want to know the answers to all those things, but let's get the hard ones out of the way first. We have plenty of time for the others."

If only she knew how little time they actually had.

Before Evie, he didn't believe Fate could reincarnate a soul with the same personality traits as the previous life. Although Evie's name changed, sometimes her hair was a different shade or style, at the heart, her essence was always the same, because her soul was the same. She had curiosity and determination to rival even the Guardians. Countless times, her drive led them together but at times, it also tore them apart. She craved more information than he could give without the risk of hurting her.

Because each time he gave in, fed her the answers she desperately craved, she found the book. Then he ended her life.

This lifetime though, he had to have faith that Fate wouldn't screw them over, not when this was his last chance to make things right. Fate had vowed to allow Evie's soul to enter the Heavens on her final death and he bet, because of that, Fate expected him to bow down and hand over the book. No way.

Even Fate wouldn't foresee this ending.

He leaned back in the couch, trying to relax despite his insides fluttering around hyperalert. "The book contains angelic spells. Not like mortal witchcraft, spells that can only be crafted by someone possessing angelic powers."

"Like you?"

"No…like you."

Her deep brown eyes narrowed, studying him, waiting for him to continue, but really, he'd rather not. The more he said, the more she'd remember. Then he was back to the ancient struggle where he yearned for her to remember as much as he hoped she'd forget.

"Hang on. Are you saying I have angelic powers? Are you serious? If I'm going to help, Cole, you have to tell me the truth, not some farfetched tale."

If only she realized how much she asked of him. At this point though, what did he have to lose? He needed her to remember something so she could find the book, so he could destroy it. Without her memories, they would flail around in the dark until a frustrated Blaine decided to retaliate or worse, cut his losses by ending Evie. But he longed for just a bit more time with her.

Perhaps if he fed her small bits of information, he could control the damage. That sounded reasonable. Unlike him unfurling his wings in the middle of the lawn just so she believed him.

Dumbass.

He fiddled with the head of his guitar. "There are mortals like you, who possess angelic powers. Nuriel. Those mortals have Fallen Raziel blood in their veins. Not enough to grant them immortality, but enough to craft spells. Some though, practice dark magic. Like the spells in the book."

"Are you sure I'm one of these Nuriel?"

He nodded.

She shifted, nudging the blanket up higher. "I guess Fallen are dark angels? Who are Raziel?"

"Angels who cast heavenly magic, usually protection spells to conceal the immortal world from mortals. Sometimes, they harness a higher magic and imprint that on objects, like Raine does with her weapons."

Her lips twisted as she thought for a moment, and he braced himself for her next question. "I presume someone casting the spells in that book is a bad thing?"

"It depends which side you're on. If the book falls into the wrong hands, like Blaine, it could have devastating consequences. For a Nuriel though, it could make the impossible, possible."

Dangerous territory right there.

"If what you're saying is true, there's potentially a lot of Nuriel in the world disguised as witches or people who practice some sort of magic. I mean, look at Jemma's family. Maybe they're all Nuriel, too? What makes me so special? Why am I the only one who can find the book?"

For Fate's sake. He never saw that question coming. Not yet anyway. Talking to her about the book or even her powers was one thing. But how did she link with the book? Why she was the only one who could find it? He wasn't ready for that conversation, not in a million lifetimes.

"Evie." He leaned forward again, resting his forearms on his thighs. "I don't want to overwhelm you and bring on more headaches, especially considering all you've learned tonight. How about we talk about the book in the morning?"

That way, he could seek guidance from Raven, so he didn't screw it up. The Guardian had been his eyes on the ground each time Evie reincarnated, protecting her from afar while Cole couldn't because he was collecting souls or out of action, of course, until Fate simply stepped in and collided his path with Evie's whether he wanted or not.

He had to do this right.

Her eyes darkened in a challenge he'd witnessed so many times. "You think this poor human with Fallen blood can't handle it?"

He fought back a grin, realizing he loved her more than he ever thought possible. "Oh, I know you can."

"Then by all means, carry on."

Warmth seeped into his blood, loosening his shoulders, lifting his spirits. Why did he treat her like an ordinary mortal? When she was far from ordinary. "Only you have the ability to cast the spells in that book."

"Don't you think I'd know if I had powers? Wouldn't I be able to do things?" She shrugged. "Like, make the library tidy itself? Or find this book everyone wants?"

He held her gaze, hoping she saw how serious he was. "You may not know how to wield the magic yet, but you will. I think you already sense it, but you're not sure what you're feeling."

She didn't flinch or try to deny it. Nor did she howl with laughter like she did when he'd told her he was an angel. Each lifetime, she swore she'd sensed power inside her, had a feeling right before she discovered her gift. Each time though, her powers had grown stronger, faster, scaring the Heavens out of him. At the rate she progressed, maybe she'd be able to take on—

No. He couldn't let it get to that. Ever.

If that happened, her soul would end forever.

Her blanket slipped, exposing her shoulder, and although she wore a shirt, he couldn't help but long to trail his lips over her smooth skin. To bury his face in the crook of her neck. To nibble on her fleshy earlobe.

"What's it like? The feeling?" Evie whispered, diverting his thoughts.

He paused for a moment. Having never been without his powers, he struggled to describe the sensations. "It's…a steady thrum in your blood. As though there's a thread of warmth buzzing beneath your skin just waiting for the moment for you to call on it."

Turning one hand upright, he called forth his shadows. Her breath hitched as he increased the darkness, swirling it in the air between them. "For angels, powers are second nature. We call upon them at will. For half mortals, they're not born with innate knowledge and need to learn how to summon and wield their powers. But once they master it, they can operate them at will."

Leaning forward, she reached for his shadows, gently slipping her fingers through the tendrils. Heat flashed through his body. He didn't exaggerate earlier when he said his powers were an extension of himself, they were. He felt every touch that connected with his shadows.

Each Azrael honed their shadows and skill set in a particular area, usually guided by Fate. Slater's shadows tracked souls better than any Azrael he knew. But his own connected with emotions. A pretty shit deal when it came to collecting souls and transporting them to their final destination. He experienced every emotion as though it were his own. The mortal's death, their longing for more time, their grief. He'd once thought it made him more compassionate. But when a mortal wasn't so upstanding, he experienced the torment and hatred eating away at the mortal's soul until he released it in Hell.

When that happened, "tortured soul" took on a whole new meaning.

Shaking the darkness from his thoughts, he focused on Evie's emotions as her fingers drifted around his shadows. Wonder and amazement tingled in his blood, while her curiosity tickled his skin. He could delve deeper, but over his many millennia in this realm, he'd learned that some emotions, particularly ones hidden beneath the surface, were better left undiscovered.

Tiny sparks sputtered at her fingertips as they swept through the thick, gray shadows, connecting his powers to hers. She'd unknowingly progressed father than he thought. Even though she wasn't aware of her magic, it was there, ready to ignite at her command. All she needed was guidance.

Gradually, he withdrew his shadows and lowered his hand.

Evelina inspected her fingertips, before lifting her

gaze to him. "Will you teach me how to use my magic?"

Every other lifetime, he'd refused. Power equaled pain. Power also equaled death. Because regardless of how talented she was with her magic, she couldn't use it to fend off Blaine. She couldn't use it to change the past. And she also couldn't use it to defy Fate.

But maybe he could.

He lost himself once again in her deep brown eyes. Each lifetime had ended the same for them and this time he'd vowed it would be different. Maybe that started with her learning about her magic. Maybe, just maybe, it would make her stronger when Blaine came for her.

Maybe in this life, she could fight to live.

For the first time ever, a spark of hope dug its claws deep inside his heart and refused to let go. Perhaps, this time he could change the future.

Because *he* would defy Fate.

A pivotal moment he was all too familiar with. A fork in the road as Raven called it. Even with the risk of retaliation from Fate, he found himself nodding at Evie.

She leaned back on the couch, a victorious grin on her face. "Okay, I'll help you find the book. But while we're negotiating, I'd also like someone to lift the spell that prevents me from leaving this house."

He choked. "Negotiating? I hadn't realized we were negotiating. Maybe you'd like cupcakes delivered to your room daily, instead? I can absolutely organize that, I'm glad you asked."

"I'm serious."

"So am I. You'd be appalled at the lengths I'd go to for a daily cupcake."

Her eyes narrowed, bringing a smirk to his face. "I want to be able to come and go as I please."

"It's not mortals who are after that book, you understand that don't you? It's *immortals*, and one dangerous Fallen in particular. It's not safe outside these walls."

"You expect me to instantly trust you, but you forget that I only just met you. This is a lot to take in." She crossed her legs, resting her hands in her lap as the blanket fell from her shoulders. "I didn't say I'd bolt out the door and never come back. I'm just asking you to trust me in return. Let me have freedom while I'm here."

Freedom. Fate, he ached to give her the world, all she'd ever wished for, a full happy mortal life not tangled with his. And he'd cross every immortal to make that happen. He realized the error in his judgement and wouldn't lock her inside the mansion. But his heart, no matter the distance between them, wouldn't ever let her go.

So, for now, he'd grant her request. And when the time came, he'd seek her forgiveness.

"I already asked Raine to remove the barrier spell. But Evie, promise me, if you leave the property, you have either me or one of the Guardians with you."

She screwed up her face. "Really?"

"That part is non-negotiable."

He'd lost her too many times to have Blaine pluck her from the mortal realm the second she stepped outside the property unprotected.

She studied him for a long moment before replying, "I accept your term."

Relief washed over him in the form of a heavy

sigh. "Are you sure you don't want to reconsider adding the cupcake clause?"

She laughed. "I'm good, thanks." She straightened all business like. "Okay. Tomorrow, we begin the hunt for this magical book."

Words failed him as dread cursed through his belly like oily dark shadows. Tomorrow, they would start searching for the book.

Tomorrow, their countdown began.

CHAPTER NINETEEN

Evelina

The next morning, Evie found herself in what the Guardians referred to as the "war room." A large space, with a long oval boardroom type table in the center. A little comical really. Why did a brotherhood of immortal Guardians need a...boardroom table? To strategize their immortal war plans? To move around empires in the hope of defeating an evil, powerful king? Or were they going for more of a corporate takeover feel?

The entire room was a cross between medieval and high-end tech firm. Strange.

Despite their reason for the room, she took a seat beside Cole, ready to find the magical book. True to his word, Cole had in fact lifted the spell surrounding the house, and she and Jemma were free to move outside. As long as they had an angelic chaperone, of course. Another ridiculous concept. She was almost twenty-five years old, and she hadn't needed a chaperone for some years.

If Blaine was such a dangerous immortal, why didn't he kidnap her when he had the chance? He'd had the opportunity at the library and again at the masquerade ball, and by the sound of it, he also had motive. Evil villains didn't host wildly expensive

parties to get what they wanted. They took it. Didn't they?

The jury was still out. At no point during their encounters had she felt unsafe around him. In fact, maybe she should demand answers from Blaine himself. That might clear up this mess and they'd all be on their merry way.

An idea for later.

The other Guardians filed into the room and took seats at the table, except for the huge scary looking dude named Slater. He'd taken, no, *misted* as Cole called it, Jemma back to their apartment earlier this morning so she could collect more of her clothing. Staying at the mansion was all well and good, but she'd appreciate her sweatpants and baggy T-shirts so she didn't have to live in jeans twenty-four-seven.

Raven took a seat at the head of the table, forearms resting on the top. From this point forward to be known as the CEO. She stifled a giggle when Cole side-eyed her, his brows furrowed. EJ, the rockstar, as Jemma had nicknamed him walked in with a tray of cupcakes, placing them in the center of the table, followed closely by his partner Hailee.

A board meeting with pink iced cupcakes.

EJ tipped his chin at Cole. "One at a time, Reaper. You hear me? Don't embarrass yourself in front of your soulmate."

Cole grunted a reply, but that didn't stop him from reaching forward and swiping a cupcake and placing it on a napkin in front of her. Then proceeded to grab one for himself.

He'd given her a cupcake.

She stared at him, trying to figure out what went on

in that mind of his. One second, he kissed her in a library, the next he saved her from beastly demons. And now, he fed her sweets. He either wanted to fatten her up or...or this was him, showing her what she meant to him. Her sudden onset of dizziness had nothing to do with sugar.

Cole lifted his cupcake to his lips and paused...oh, no he didn't. She'd just about combust if he licked the icing.

She held back a groan when his tongue darted out, licking a line of icing in one long sweep. Heat flashed through her so hard and fast it stole her breath. She melted into a puddle right there on the chair as he licked the pink whipped sugar for a second time. Captivated, he continued, making her mouth dry. Could he...how did he...oh, man, that *tongue*. Wicked images flooded her mind, speeding up her pulse. Inappropriate images. Way too inappropriate. Especially when she sat in a boardroom full of angels.

She gulped.

The corner of his lips kicked up in a half smile as he turned his head to her. She diverted her gaze quick smart. The last thing she needed was him seeing her expression, which no doubt said, "lick me like that."

Thank goodness he couldn't mindread. Wait. Had she confirmed that?

She cleared her throat, brushing imaginary crumbs off the table.

"What's your plan, Cole?" Raven asked once everyone had sat, thankfully interrupting her embarrassing fantasy-for-one session.

Cole swallowed a mouthful of cupcake before addressing Raven. "Given that you found the book in the store in New Orleans, I thought I'd try there first. Work backward."

"Slater and I didn't find it at the bookstore," Raine answered, standing near the side table. "The evil twin already had it when we arrived."

"No, Ebony likely found it there."

"Hang on. You found the book? If you already have it, why are we looking for it?" she asked.

Cole's shoulders stiffened as he balled up the napkin in his fist.

"Oh, boy," the guy wearing the colorful shirt muttered—River?—leaning so far back in his chair any minute now it would topple over.

She twisted to face Cole, waiting for his answer. Or the lack of it.

Eventually, he reached for her, only to take back his hand. "Each lifetime your soul is reincarnated, you make the book…reappear somewhere else."

Just when she thought this situation couldn't get any weirder.

"You realize how crazy that sounds, right?"

He cocked a brow, leaning closer. "Crazier than searching for a magical book with an immortal angel?" He straightened, addressing the others. "The bookstore is on the list."

"What list?"

He cast a downward glance as though carefully choosing his words before looking at her. "The list of places you've…previously found it."

"Is the antique store on that list, too?"

"No, but the castle where Blaine paraded around like the king of Hell is."

Meeting Cole at that ball felt like a lifetime ago.

"It could've been at the castle. I didn't do a thorough search."

Cole shook his head, shifting in his chair. "I did. It's not there."

"How far did you get into your search?" EJ asked her.

"Not far. I'd eliminated a handful of state libraries, and smaller ones, plus some collections which have special exhibit rooms that could accommodate a book as old as that one. I reached out to a historian I knew at college but haven't heard back yet. If only I had access to the database still."

"The library database?" EJ asked.

She nodded.

"Easy. I'll hook you up."

Add illegal hacking to the rap sheet for these immortals. Maybe they operated outside the law like the mafia she'd first assumed they were? Or maybe they considered themselves above basic human rules. Did the Heavens have a police department or someone to hold rogue immortals accountable for their actions?

Another strange train of thought.

She turned back to Cole. "What are the odds that the list I started has some of the same places as your list?"

"Very high."

Excitement straightened her back. "We need to get it. It's in my drawer at work."

Was she even employed anymore?

Cole diverted his attention to his cupcake wrapper, picking bits of crumbs from the lining but never eating them. "We don't need to. I remember all the places the book appeared. Every one of them."

The gruffness in his voice made her heart clench. This guy carried so much pain on his shoulders, she wondered how he even stood. Or flew.

A loud crash made her jump, and everyone turned to find River, flat on his back, the chair still underneath him. Laughter bubbled out of her, lightening the pressure in her chest. The others joined her laughing, while someone grumbled something about how an angel could be so uncoordinated.

Such an ordinary family. Not at all what she expected from immortals.

Aric held out his hand to River, helping him up. "All I saw was a streak of sunshine right before you hit the floor."

Someone snorted.

Unfazed, River righted the chair and threw a candy in his mouth. "I was distracted."

Raven cleared his throat. "Now that River is safe and well, let's get the hell out of here. EJ, you sort out the tech access for Evie while Cole and Raine check out the bookstore again to see if it's reappeared there."

Before she threw a tantrum and stomped her feet about Raven excluding her from that excursion, Cole beat her to it.

"Thanks, brother, but Evie and I will be fine. No need for Raine to come."

"Thank Fate," Raine muttered. "That's one place I don't need to revisit. Last time I was there, Slater came back with a damn cat."

More laughs ensued, but they faded away as Cole dusted the crumbs from his hands and twisted her chair to face him. "We'll head there tonight."

****

Cole

Outside, the brisk evening air tumbled dried leaves in a flurry over the manicured lawn. He glanced back at the Guardian mansion, the place he now called home, and instead of a feeling of family, a sense of belonging, all that ran through his blood was impending doom. A ticking time bomb, slowly counting down in the form of a heavy weight on his chest. The dread could also be a result of the souls he'd ignored for the last couple of days because he'd been too preoccupied with remaining close to Evie.

That need drove ninety-nine percent of his actions and thoughts.

It always had.

The Guardians spoke of their love for their soulmates, and he saw it in their heated glances, the spark between their souls, the heavenly light surrounding them when they embraced. But he also knew it firsthand. He'd experienced those sensations centuries ago, only to have it disappear and reappear more than a dozen times now, each absence leaving a wider hole in his heart.

Dwelling on it or dreading the end wouldn't help anyone. It certainly wouldn't retrieve the book and it wouldn't make Evie fall in love with him any faster. Usually, he'd relish the slow build of their relationship, but this time he willed it to happen quicker as much as he yearned for it to never end.

If anyone deserved a happy ending, it was them.

As though she'd sensed him thinking of her, or perhaps because he'd told her to meet him here, Evie exited the front door and strode toward him. Slater and Jemma had returned a short time ago with a suitcase each of belongings for Evie and her friend. And now, she wore a pair of navy jeans, a slim-fitting sweater with a scarf wrapped around her neck. Since seeing her earlier, she'd tied her hair back, but raven-colored waves fell from the loose bun, shaping her face.

Hands squeezed his heart when her gaze caught his, bringing a smile to her face.

Fate, her smile was beautiful. Full of undiluted joy. She should've been an angel.

When she reached him, she rubbed her shoulders. "I should've brought a jacket, but we'll be inside, right? I hate having to lug a coat around and only wearing it for a few minutes."

Without thinking, he took off his jacket and wrapped it around her shoulders. "Have mine. That way you can hand it back when you no longer need it."

Her returning smile tightened the hold on his heart.

"Okay, so how does this work? I don't remember much of the last time you...*poofed* us here. Or will we..."

Fly. He sensed the word on her lips. "I'll mist us to the bookstore and back. It's a fair distance, and given how cold it is tonight, it's more practical than flying."

"Right. Because you have wings."

He bit back his smirk. "Yes. I have wings. Big ones."

She held his gaze for a solid ten seconds before howling with laughter. "Big ones. I bet you say that to all the girls." She burst into a new fit of laughter. "I'm sorry. Give me a minute."

He tried not to take it personally. She wasn't laughing at him, was she? Regardless, the sound did something wicked to his blood, filling him with joy and the biggest urge to wrap her in his arms, squeeze her tight and never let her go. Laughing at his expense was a small price to pay. The happiness she projected lit up his soul like the blazing sun. Fiery, explosive, never-ending.

Closing the distance, he reached out and brushed his thumb along her cheek, wiping away a tear. Her breath hitched as her gaze lifted to his. Small puffs of cold air collided in the sliver of space between their mouths. His thumb tingled as it trailed her cheek, down to her jaw, all the way to her pouty bottom lip. Fate, he missed touching her. Having her in his arms, whispering dirty thoughts in her ear to make her giggle. This close, when he inhaled a deep pull of air, he scented her unique sweet, floral smell. Otherworldly. Old. He'd never smelled anything even remotely like her in all the realms.

His soul recognized it immediately. *Mine.*

Yes, his heart, his body belonged to her. It always would. They were made for each other.

Her lips parted and anticipation shivered beneath the surface of his skin. The need to kiss her. All he had to do was lower his head a few more inches, maybe less. His mouth watered, imagining having her lips on his, sweeping his tongue over hers, capturing her breathy moans.

Reality smacked him in the face with a cold sheet of ice.

This version of her, this mortal version, barely knew him. To her, he'd only met her a few days ago. She didn't have the benefit of centuries of memories to understand he loved her with all his soul, that he was in it for all the right reasons. For the long haul. She didn't know their history.

She'd told him not to find her. One day, when her memories returned, she'd remember her words and when that happened, he didn't want her to regret anything. He couldn't stomach kissing her now, only for her to hate him more for it.

And until she remembered it all, until he could be completely honest with her and lay everything on the table between them, he wouldn't take this any further. Couldn't. No matter how much it ate away at him and twisted his body into knots. Or more accurately, his balls.

The wait would be worth it.

Without a doubt.

When Evie rose on her toes, her eyes shadowy with desire, he lowered his hand and stepped back. "We should go before it gets too late."

Pressure squeezed his chest when her gaze lowered and she retreated a step, straightening the hem of her sweater. "Of course."

In that moment, he ached to confess his secrets. But it was too soon. He was a selfish bastard for wanting more time with her.

With a heavy sigh, he held out his hand.

She frowned.

"I need to hold your hand or…touch you in some way while we mist. It prevents your soul from shooting off in another direction."

"Oh. Okay."

She entwined her fingers with his, and he cleared his throat, trying to dislodge the unwelcome lump. Closing his eyes, he misted them, reappearing in the dark alley outside the bookstore. This late, the streets were almost deserted.

"That was really weird." Evie stared at her hand, turning it back and forth.

"It's an attractive superpower though, isn't it?"

She cast him a cheeky grin. "To match your big wings?"

"You bet."

When she laughed again, he took her hand and led them to the entrance of the bookstore. Holding his hand over the doorknob, he summoned shadows to unlock it in one swift motion. Showing off? Perhaps. Every guy, immortal or otherwise, needed their ego stroked now and then.

He held open the door as they slipped inside.

"Wow. There are books everyw—" She grunted, doubling over at the waist, squeezing her head in her hands.

"Evie, what's wrong?"

"My...head. It..." Her painful groan sliced him in half.

He wrapped his arm around her waist, supporting her weight. "Memories."

He held her tight, all the while cursing himself for ever putting her in this situation. If only he'd obeyed Fate the first time. If only another Azrael had collected her soul.

No. As much as it pained him to see her suffer like this, he didn't regret his choices. If another Azrael had escorted her soul, he would have never met her. If he had bowed at Fate's feet, Blaine would've taken Evie's soul to Hell. He would've seen her, touched her, experienced the soulmate connection with her for a fleeting moment and then never again.

How could he ever wish for that?

Evie inhaled a few deep breaths before straightening.

He swept the hair off her face. "The pain is your memories trying to break through."

"I figured that. Last night when we talked, I think some pieces fell into place."

He clenched his jaw, needing to know the answer to a question he didn't want to ask. "How...old are you?"

He'd avoided it for too long. EJ probably already knew the answer from the information he'd discovered so far, but a huge part of Cole had avoided finding out. Every lifetime, Evie died on her twenty-fifth birthday. Every time. And she usually experienced an increase in headaches right before that day.

"Don't you know it's rude to ask a lady her age?" She must've seen the seriousness on his face, because a second later, her grin disappeared. "Twenty-four."

Fuck. "When is your birthday?"

His stomach plummeted all the way to Hell. How much time did they have? How long until he needed to end her life for the final time so she could find peace?

"In two weeks."

CHAPTER TWENTY

Evelina

"I'm not sure how my age, or my birthday for that matter, is relevant." Evie exited the front door of the mansion, with Jemma right on her heels. "But Cole acted as though me turning twenty-five was a death-sentence. It's not that old."

"That's weird."

"Right?"

Morning sunlight chased away the chill in the air as they crossed the lawn to a bench beneath a towering pine. Most of the house was still sound asleep as they'd beelined down the hall and outside, needing to break free. To use the brisk air to clear her thoughts. Cole had acted so strange two nights ago when he'd taken her to the bookstore that it still rattled her this morning.

Perching on the bench, she bent her legs, wrapping her arms around them as Jemma sat beside her.

"When I told him my birthday was in two weeks, he freaked out. Like, really freaked out. Practically ransacked the bookstore, cursing to himself before he grabbed my arm and misted us back here. I couldn't even get a word in before he dumped me on the porch and left on what he called angel business."

"What kind of business is angel business?"

She scrunched up her face. "I have no idea. Is there

someone up there handing out daily work orders?" She shook her head. "You're missing the point. Why would he freak out like that?"

Jemma plucked a soggy brown leaf from the seat and tossed it to the ground. "I've been going with the flow here. None of it surprises me anymore."

"It should though, shouldn't it? I mean, this whole situation is so…unbelievable. Yet, at the same time, staying in a house with angels, finding a magical book, misting from one place to the next, seems…normal. Familiar."

Jemma took a bite of the pastry she'd swiped from the kitchen before they headed outside. "You're his reincarnated soulmate, right?"

Her pulse chose that moment to accelerate. "Yeah. Again, unbelievable, yet it feels like the truth."

"We studied history, ancient civilizations who believed they would join the gods in the afterlife. Become gods. They didn't believe their body would waltz into the next life, they believed their soul would. Yes, it's not every day you shack up with a bunch of angels, but I kinda believe it all." She chewed another mouthful, staring back at the house. "Is that EJ and Hailee on the roof?"

Sometimes being best friends with someone with a short attention span kept her on her toes. Never a dull moment.

Sure enough, EJ and Hailee sat curled up in each other's arms on the rooftop, facing away from them as though watching the sunrise. She felt a sharp pang in her chest when she looked at them so blissfully in love. Suddenly, she wanted that. She wanted all of it. A love that lasted the ages, a guy who looked at her like she was his entire world.

Someone who looked at her like…Cole.

"He's somewhat intense though," Jemma whispered.

"EJ?"

"Yeah, he is, too in a different way. But I was talking about Cole." Jemma pointed her half-eaten pastry at her. "People write books about the way he adores you."

The way Cole adored her? Sure, he made the idea of their past lives sound romantic, and the way he kissed her, how he cradled her face in his hands made her feel like she was special. Worshipped. But at the bookstore, he'd looked at her as though her mere presence caused him physical pain. Especially after she'd told him how old she was.

She sighed, leaning back on the rickety bench to stretch out her legs. "Maybe I've been a bit too hard on him. Too dismissive of our history. Maybe I should cut the guy some slack."

"Nah, you can't make it easy for the men folk. They need to work for it." Jemma dusted crumbs from her jeans. "But while we're here, you could hear him out. Maybe get a little something-something from that fine male specimen."

A laugh exploded right out of her. "Jemma!"

"What? Don't tell me you haven't noticed how fine he is. And he's got your name tattooed on his forehead."

Secrets still lurked in the darkness, she felt them lingering behind every word Cole spoke, but maybe she hadn't given him a chance to open up. Talk to her the way they had in the middle of the night by the fire. If she listened harder, maybe she'd understand more about the book, about him, about their story.

Jemma patted her knee. "I'm going to shower. See you inside for breakfast?"

"Didn't you just eat?"

"Nope. That was pre-breakfast."

Laughing, Jemma leaped off the bench, hightailed it back across the lawn and inside the mansion. By the look of it, EJ and Hailee had also ventured back inside. A coil of unease tightened in her gut when she realized she was alone. Cole had asked her not to venture away from the house without him or another Guardian. Was it really that unsafe? Of course, it was. She'd witnessed the danger firsthand at the antique store. But surely here on the bench, in plain view of the front door, she was safe. If something bad happened, she'd sprint across the lawn screaming for help.

Leaning her head back, she tilted her face to the cloudless sky and took the opportunity to clear her mind. To listen to the wispy breeze rustling the forest, the early morning bird chirps, rejoice in the sunrays warming her cool cheeks. Before long, a path presented itself. She'd already agreed to help Cole, and before that, Blaine, find the book. But until now, she'd been completely blind to their motivations and history concerning it. That stopped now. After breakfast, she'd make Cole tell her everything before they progressed any further.

Opening her eyes, she straightened, peering at the mansion. Although the coil in her belly had long ago unwound, pins and needles took its place, scurrying beneath her skin. The sensation spread, fanning out until it infiltrated every cell in her body with a mass of tingles.

A branch snapped behind her. She spun on the bench, searching the forest. By now, the sun had risen, but darkness still lingered between the towering trees, broken only by a few patches of sunlight sneaking through the branches.

A shadowy figure appeared beside a tree trunk. Cole? She hadn't heard from him since he disappeared on so-called angel business and all but dumped her back at the mansion. Had he come to apologize? To talk? To tell her the real reason why he wanted to find the book?

She stood and straightened her jacket.

The person waved before stepping into a beam of yellow sunlight.

Oh, no. Not Cole.

Blaine.

Her heart clawed all the way up her throat. How did he find her? Had he come to demand why she hadn't found the book? Rescind his bounty that he never told her about? Or worse, had he come to take her?

She shot a quick glance at the house. Cole had reminded her on more than one occasion that Blaine was dangerous. Yet, all her interactions with him had been the complete opposite. He'd never hurt her or given her any reason to worry for her safety. In fact, she'd been more than comfortable in his presence. Quite comfortable in fact.

Cole had insinuated that Blaine had orchestrated the attack on the antique store, but she'd seen no evidence to support that. For all she knew, those monsters attacked of their own accord.

Blaine beckoned her with the crook of his finger.

Was talking to him reckless? Dangerous? *Probably*. But…was it worth the risk to ask him face to face why he wanted the book and what his history was with Cole? She inhaled a deep breath and thought long and hard while Blaine watched her from inside the forest. *Yes*. Something told her that if anyone was brutally honest with her, it would be Blaine.

He had no reason to protect her feelings. After all, she wasn't his soulmate.

Before reasoning kicked in, she ducked between the trees and walked to Blaine.

"Hello, love."

His crooked smirk and haphazard style were the same as when she first met him in the library. Leaning his shoulder against the tree trunk, he fiddled with a piece of bark as though he didn't have a care in the world. If he knew what the Guardians thought of him, or how they warned her, it didn't seem to bother him.

"How did you know I was here?" she asked, stopping a few feet before him.

He waved a hand in the air dismissing her concern. "The Guardians and I go way back."

Yet, they treated him like the enemy.

Blaine offered the crook of his arm. "Shall we take a morning stroll?"

That coil of unease bubbled in her belly again, warning her to say no. Who did she trust? The angel who swore she was his soulmate? The one who'd saved her at the antique store but kept her partly in the dark? Or the guy who'd originally approached her at her workplace seeking a book that had been stolen from him?

Despite her sense that Cole still withheld information from her, she trusted him. Trusted that connection she couldn't explain but also couldn't deny. Talking with Blaine was one thing, probably something she shouldn't engage in, but allowing him to lead her away, or take her from the safe confines of the Guardians, was a step even she wouldn't cross.

"You have my word we won't depart the property, if that's your concern," Blaine added, as though he'd read her mind.

"Can I trust your word?"

"Like my wings depend on it."

With a small nod, she looped her arm in Blaine's. He covered her hand with his and they strolled through the forest at a slow, casual pace. Just when she thought staying with immortals and stories of reincarnated souls were the most unbelievable concepts. Now, she wandered the Guardian property on the arm of their enemy.

Her morals were all over the place. Not to mention her loyalty.

Blaine guided her around a tree, diverting from the main path. "My offer still stands, love."

"To find the book?"

He nodded. "Despite what the Guardians told you, the book belongs with me."

"Why is everyone so fixated on finding it? What's so special about it?"

Blaine remained silent for a long moment as they continued meandering between the giant trees with nothing but their footsteps and distant bird calls keeping them company. Up ahead, he held her forearm to help her over a fallen tree trunk. This guy had old-school manners as though he'd lived in another time.

"It's very special to me," he eventually replied. "I found it not too long ago, but the Guardians stole it." He returned his hand over hers as they recommenced their stroll. "I only want it back."

She stopped, slipping her arm from his. "How did you find it? Cole said I'm the only one who can locate the book."

A wicked smirk curled at the corner of his mouth. "And here I was afraid he'd keep you in the dark."

That kind of stung. Especially when she knew Cole hadn't told her everything because he was afraid of bringing her memories back in one rush. But Blaine didn't need to know that, so she kept quiet. Maybe if he thought she knew everything he'd unknowingly feed her more information.

"I'm quite familiar with your pattern by now. Besides, an...associate of mine, stumbled upon the book while she was looking for a method to activate a sword."

Magical books...magical swords...another day in the life of an immortal.

"I presume they told you the book reappears each time Fate reincarnates your soul?"

She nodded. Who the hell was Fate?

"Good." He clapped his hands together as though she should get it. Spoiler alert: she had no idea.

Blaine tilted his head, studying her. "Is there another incentive you'd rather than money? Something to convince you to look a tad harder for my book? The truth perhaps? I can give you answers to all those pesky questions plaguing you."

Uh-oh. The fact that her pulse quickened at his

offer should've been enough to warn her. Cole had never refused to answer her questions, he simply avoided it or skirted around the truth. But gaining the answers from Blaine made her stomach churn.

Blaine stepped closer. "Perhaps you'd like to know why you die every lifetime at the young age of twenty-five?"

She gasped. "What did you say?"

"He didn't tell you? I'm surprised your soulmate would withhold such vital information from you." He waved his hand in the air, dismissing her increasing panic. "Anyhoo, I really should skedaddle before your bodyguards come charging into the forest with their swords raised."

Air whooshed in her ears, muffling the sounds of someone shouting her name.

"Too late. Think about my offer, love." Blaine swept his arm in a low regal bow. "Until next time."

Before she said a word, Blaine vanished right before her eyes, leaving her standing there frozen with nausea churning her stomach.

CHAPTER TWENTY-ONE

Evelina

"Cole!" Evie shouted as she stormed across the lawn seeing nothing but red. It pulsed in time with the fury whirling through her blood. Why didn't Cole tell her? Twenty-five? She was going to die in less than two weeks. Twelve days. No wonder he freaked out when she told him her age. He knew.

Why the hell did he continue to keep secrets from her?

Raven waited on the gravel drive, his eyes narrowed. The hard set of his jaw told her he knew exactly whom she'd been with.

Good. She wanted the Guardians as angry as her.

She strode past Raven to the front door. He didn't deserve the brunt of her anger, Cole did. He wanted her to trust him, but he continually kept her in the dark.

"Wait," Raven commanded the second her fingers reached for the door handle.

She spun, glaring at him. "Where is Cole?"

"He's not here." Raven stepped closer, his voice low but layered with a rumbling warning. "What did Blaine tell you?"

"Are you serious?"

"He lives to meddle, Evie. Blaine would love nothing more than to cause a rift between you and Cole.

A rift he's caused countless times before."

"Because I've lived countless lifetimes I can't fucking remember." She closed her eyes and inhaled, trying to steady her anger before reopening. "He told me I die at twenty-five? Is that true?"

Raven shoved his hands in his pockets.

After several moments, she realized he wouldn't answer. She scoffed. They were all the same. Of course, they would protect their own. Raven would side with Cole. Maybe Blaine was the only one who told her the truth.

"He's afraid to tell you because each time he does, you remember."

Her heart stilled. "Would remembering be so bad?"

"Remembering leads to your death."

The sharp pain through her chest felt like she'd swallowed a letter opener. *Remembering leads to your death.* Was that why Cole didn't tell her? Was he protecting her? Again.

Warmth burst over her nape a second before Cole appeared on the lawn with his majestic gray wings unfurled. His disheveled hair and slouched shoulders caused her to stumble forward a step, but she quickly stopped herself.

When he made no attempt to walk to her, opting to stand on the lawn waiting, she took matters into her own hands. No more lies. No more hidden truths. This time, if he didn't answer, she'd leave.

Raven stepped aside as she strode to Cole, focusing her attention on the task with each long step. When she reached him though, a little of that resolve slipped. The dark sunken skin beneath his eyes, the deep creases in his forehead. When did he last sleep? She'd seen him the other night. What had he done?

Cole's gaze flicked over her shoulder, before pinning her with an angry stare that no doubt matched her own. "Blaine was here."

How did he know? What a great conversation starter. "You lied to me."

"I told you how dangerous he is, and you still went outside to see him. While I wasn't here."

"Excuse me? Don't put this blame on me. Blaine came here, I didn't go off searching for him."

"You met with him," Cole raised his voice. "How can I protect you if you don't listen to me?"

"You don't own me or get to tell me what I can or can't do," she shouted back.

Cole furrowed his fingers through his hair, tugging at the ends. "For Fate's sake, Evie, this is what he wants. It's what he does. Turns you against me."

His wings glided up and down grabbing her attention, reminding her that she was right in the middle of an immortal world. Not living the life of Evie Fairburn, Research Librarian. Instead, she was Evie, reincarnated soulmate with Fallen blood running in her veins. She'd never felt so out of depth.

Sighing, she looked Cole in the eyes, pleading for the truth. "I feel like Blaine is the only one telling me anything."

He shuddered, bending forward before straightening again. "I can't do this right now. I have to go. I'll explain everything when I get back."

She threw her hands in the air. "Of course. Important angel business. What could be more important than telling me the truth?"

When had she become such a bitch? Part of her

knew Cole didn't deserve her outburst, but she couldn't help it. For the past few days, she felt as though she'd been dragged into a war she didn't belong in. On a quest to find a missing book she knew nothing about.

No longer would she stand here and fumble along behind Cole, doing what he asked because she was supposed to trust him. Trust was earned, not given.

"Evelina…"

She gritted her teeth at how her named rolled off his lips as though he'd said it to her a thousand times. Instead, she lifted her chin. "Will I die when I turn twenty-five?"

The pain in his eyes caused that letter opener to slice her heart in half.

When he didn't answer, she lowered her voice, "Tell me, Cole."

"Yes."

Even though Blaine had told her earlier, having Cole confirm it was like a sucker punch in the chest. Pressure squeezed her ribs.

When Cole stepped forward, she held up her hand, stopping him. "How could you keep that from me?"

He grunted, pressing the heel of his hand to his sternum. His whole body…flickered in and out. What the hell was happening?

"I wanted to spare you the pain of knowing. Of the countdown."

The countdown to her death.

Bile rose in her throat. "Why do you treat me like I'm fragile? Like I can't handle the truth?"

His gray eyes darkened as he growled. "Damn it, Evie. You *are* fragile. In under two weeks, I'll watch you die in my fucking arms. Again. For the ninth time."

Words clogged her throat.

She'd died in his arms? Eight times already?

He bent over again, grunting as his body wavered, as though half here and half somewhere else. Instinctively, she almost reached for him, but she still couldn't move her legs. His pain-laced words had rendered her frozen.

When he straightened, a bead of sweat dotted his temple. "I can't hold it any longer. I promise to answer your questions when I return."

"Maybe I'll just ask someone else."

The second the words tumbled from her mouth, she wanted to shove them back in there and zip her lips shut. Sure, Cole kept information from her, but now she kind of understood why. Watching her die, in his arms, at least told her the reason he withheld the truth came from a place of sorrow, not malice.

Muscles popped in his jaw as he closed the distance between them. Air evaporated in one swift woosh when he peered down at her, his dark gaze burrowing right to her soul. "Blaine will use you for his own gain. And once he gets what he wants, he'll toss you aside. You'll be nothing. Your soul will be dead."

She whispered, "Is that what you'll do?"

"Never." His shaky hand lifted to cup her cheek. "Everything I do is *for* you. To save you. And if that fails, I'll do everything in my power to ensure mine ends right alongside yours."

Before she replied, he vanished just like Blaine had, leaving her trembling in the center of the lawn.

****

Cole

"Fuck!" Cole screamed into the nothingness.

Sulfur burned his nostrils with each gulp of air he sucked in, trying to regain control. He'd left his soulmate trembling on the lawn of the Guardian property. She already hated him, and she had every right. Although he'd never lied to her, he hadn't exactly told her the full story. Didn't she understand that everything he'd done had been for her? To secure her freedom, her happiness, passage to her soul's final resting place.

Every. Single. Thing.

Shooting forward, he grabbed the sick bastard by the collar of his fancy shirt and hauled him to his feet. He'd been in the process of escorting this scumbag to Hell when Evie had called his name. Summoned him. He hadn't even known she could do that. Her powers were stronger in this lifetime. Probably because she was almost twenty-five...

"Hey, man, you look like shit."

It took every ounce of willpower not to punch the guy in his perfect face. "Yeah? Maybe because I have to escort sick souls like you day in and day out."

The male frowned, peering at their surroundings as though he'd only just realized he was no longer in the mortal realm.

Since leaving Evie after the bookstore, he'd spent far too much time ferrying souls to both gates. His own fault. He had neglected his duty for too long, until he could no longer ignore the pull. Some days, being an Azrael was like being at Fate's beck and call. Whenever souls required escorting, he had no choice but to obey. The tether connecting him to Fate's magic was too strong.

"Where are you taking me?"

Oh, now the male wanted to be nice? Too late. Cole was no longer in the mood.

"Welcome to Hell."

Usually, he stood by the entrance, facing the gates until they opened, at which time the mortals would fight kicking and screaming until Hell summoned them inside. This time though, he didn't have the patience, nor the energy to wait. Every cell in his body pulled him back to Evie.

She was no longer safe without him there to protect her. Especially since Blaine had made his intention clear by proving how easy it was to reach her.

With a growl, he shoved the mortal forward. The gates opened.

The mortal tried to fight the pull.

"Doesn't matter what you do, one way or another, your soul will end up in there."

Without waiting for the mortal to build up the courage, or for Hell to suck him in, Cole grabbed the male by the neck of his shirt and all but dragged him as he stormed through the gates. Inside, he dumped the mortal on the crumbled cobblestone and continued down the street.

As an Azrael, he could enter Hell for short periods without tainting his soul. Lately though, that period had become shorter and shorter.

Behind him, the mortal screamed as Hell's magic sucked his pitiful soul right from his corporal form before a whiff of air signaled the gates closing. Dangerous, dark emotions slithered beneath his skin, making him gag. Usually, he spaced out his visits to Hell, escorted souls to the Heavens in between. But he'd been in the mortal realm more since Evie reincarnated, and instead of escorting small numbers at a time, here and there, he'd let the souls build up.

He had to be more careful.

Without access to the Heavens, this misstep would take him too long to recover. He didn't have the time. Any day now, Evie would remember. Or worse, she'd leave.

He needed to find the book and end this.

Striding down the main street, he used the time to push aside his worry for Evie, the sickness he felt building in his stomach, and focus on his destination. He hadn't meant to lose his temper with Evie, but when he found Blaine, he wouldn't hold back. For far too long that Fallen had meddled in Evie's life, with the singular objective of using her to craft a spell so powerful it would end her soul.

But again, and again, Blaine underestimated what Cole would do to prevent it.

Stepping through a partly demolished shopfront, he walked straight through a gateway, appearing in a dense forest in Aralim. Blaine's own realm within Hell.

A gloomy, decrepit castle loomed in the distance. A fitting residence for an equally dark fallen.

Chances were, Blaine wasn't even here. Especially if he'd just been in the mortal realm tormenting Evie. But Cole would leave no stone unturned until he tracked him down.

At the entrance, two Fallen bodyguards stepped in his path, crimson wings splayed wide as though warning him. Which he ignored.

"I'm here to see Blaine."

"The boss is busy."

Cole snorted. In one swift movement, he

summoned his shadows thrusting them forward to wrap tendrils around the Fallen's neck, tossing him through the air. The Fallen thudded on the ground somewhere in the surrounding forest.

The other Fallen wisely stepped aside.

Blaine waltzed to the open doorway, clapping his hands. "Look at that, a visitor. For me?"

Cole gritted his teeth so hard his jaw ached. "Stay the fuck away from Evie."

"That's no way to speak to your friend."

"I'm not your friend."

"Don't forget, Azrael." Blaine narrowed his eyes as they flashed with crimson. "You're in my realm. Perhaps show a tad more respect."

Warning sirens set off in his mind. He was in Blaine's realm. From what he knew of Aralim, Blaine could draw on the realm's powers to amplify his own. If he were an ordinary Fallen, Cole would stand a chance, but Blaine had been in Hell for centuries, no doubt syphoning power from souls for almost as long. Given the Fallen was powerful before Falling from the Heavens, he imagined by now, Blaine's powers were unparalleled.

Just as Fate had predicted.

Besides, he'd come here to tell Blaine to back off, not to start a fight.

The second Fallen bodyguard wandered along the perimeter of the castle, clearly satisfied his...*boss*...no longer needed protection.

He jerked his chin to the weapon strapped around Blaine's waist. "Are you intending to wear the Empryen for the rest of eternity?"

The only sword crafted with a mixture of Raine

and Fate's magic. Capable of destroying an entire realm with one strike.

"I wouldn't dare be complacent with such a valuable possession." Blaine cocked a brow. "Unlike you."

Bullshit. He hadn't lost the book, neither had Evie. She'd hid it from this twisted Fallen so he couldn't get his toxic hands on it. Blaine had a knack for slithering under his skin, and this was another effort.

"Hiding and losing are two completely different things."

Blaine shrugged one shoulder. "Semantics. Lose the book, lose your soulmate. Either way, you're not very good at holding on to what matters."

His fists clenched. He wasn't usually the violent type, but lately, he didn't know himself. Right now, he wanted to make Blaine pay for what he'd done, and what he intended to do. Make the Fallen's soul burn in the Infernal Pits for all eternity.

Even though he knew that couldn't happen.

With every ounce of strength, Cole kept his shadows under control. If Blaine sensed a threat, the Fallen wouldn't hesitate to retaliate.

Cole eyed the sword. "Why not fight Zath and end this already?"

Blaine's hand rested atop the hilt. "That would be convenient for you, wouldn't it?"

When Blaine ended Zath, he'd also end the Infernal Pits. A hellish torture realm for trapped souls. He'd destroy the one place Fate kept returning Evie's soul.

Blaine descended the steps to stand before Cole. "How about you step aside and let me take her from here? I give you my word I'll make it painless."

His stomach churned. There was no way Blaine could make what he planned painless. The thought alone had driven him mad for centuries.

"Your word is worth nothing when it comes to obtaining what you want."

Blaine placed his hand over his heart in mock horror. "Harsh, my friend. Harsh."

Maybe. But he was here to make his intentions clear, not reinforce non-existent friendships.

"Fate vowed this would be Evie's last lifetime. Let her live it."

Prickles raced along his nape as Blaine smirked. "Previously, I might have considered that request. If I didn't already know what you intend to do with the book."

How could Blaine know? He'd purposely concealed his memories and thoughts for so long, fearing if Blaine caught even a snippet, his plan would unravel and fail. If that happened, everything he'd done would be for nothing. Evelina would once again end up in Hell. Only this time, she would never leave.

Blaine withdrew the Empryen from its sheath to examine the black lettering along the flat side of the blade. "I need her magic and the book. One does not function without the other." Slowly, he returned the sword and lifted his crimson gaze. "On that, I will not compromise."

"If only Fate could see how far you've Fallen."

Crimson flames sparked in Blaine's eyes. "Oh, she will, don't worry your angelic little head over that." Using the pointed nail on his index finger, Blaine sliced his palm. Dark crimson blood pooled at the cut and held it out for Cole to do the same. "Do we have a deal?"

"Never."

Blaine's laughter churned his stomach as he withdrew his hand. "Such hostility."

Enough. He'd tried the honorable path by approaching Blaine and asking him to back down. Nothing would stop him from granting Evie her final wish. All he'd ever done had led to this moment, and he wouldn't fail.

Barging past Blaine, he ascended the porch, heading to the gateway inside the mansion.

As he stepped through the entrance, Blaine called out, "See you at the finish line."

CHAPTER TWENTY-TWO

Evelina

Evie hadn't seen Cole for four days, seven hours and roughly forty-three minutes. Although the days seemed to roll into one since he'd left, time felt as though it dragged along in slow motion. She'd wandered aimlessly around the Guardian mansion lost in a daze. Wingless critters scurried in her belly, and she couldn't shake the feeling something was wrong with him. Where had he gone? How long until he returned?

Was he okay?

Tingles continued to sprout along her nape as though sensing impending doom, but she couldn't figure out if it was because of Blaine's words, her upcoming birthday, or something more sinister.

Like the fact she usually died in just over one weeks' time.

Jemma had adapted to their new lifestyle with ease and confidence. In fact, her friend fit in so well it was as though she'd lived here her entire life. For once, Evie wanted to feel the same, truly, but something held her back. Nothing connected to her old life, that was for sure. So why did she feel stuck in limbo?

In the beginning, she'd accepted the request from Blaine because it challenged her. Sparked her thirst for mystery. Treasure hunting. Then, finding out about the reward drove her even harder. She could use the money to search for her birth parents. That now seemed pointless given one of them wasn't even human. Since Cole's absence, Raven had been more forthcoming with small bits of information. Nothing major, but a few pieces to lock into place in the jigsaw of her life. When she'd queried about her parents, Raven had explained how Fate placed her soul into a soulless mortal each lifetime. This body was a shell for her soul. A loan.

Seriously, she shouldn't have asked. It only made her head threaten to explode.

Peering out the attic window, she scanned the forest, and mountains beyond. Dark, angry storm clouds built in the distance. If only they unleashed their fury. Screamed over the land with thunderous rain and lightning. Released the tension laced in the evening air.

Released the chokehold on her heart.

Heat flashed at her nape, jolting her to attention. A second later, it simmered until it became a slow, achy burn through her entire body.

A sensation she associated with Cole.

He'd returned.

Turning from the window, she hurried down the stairs and along the hall. In front of Cole's bedroom door, she hesitated with her hand raised, ready to knock. Retching sounds came from the other side, followed by guttural groans that made her heart sink.

Was he sick? Did angels get sick?

Was that why he hadn't come back earlier?

Busting down his door and demanding answers from him now seemed cruel. Petty even. Sure, she wanted to know more about the book, about her past lives, about why she died at twenty-five, but now, all those questions fell away with his painful groans on the other side of the door.

As she placed her hand on the doorknob, the retching started again.

If she were in that state, the last thing she'd want would be Cole coming in and seeing her head in the toilet. Were they at the point in their relationship that he'd want her to care for him? In this lifetime, anyhow. Or was Cole a suffer-in-silence type of angel?

She hesitated a few more moments before drawing back and forcing her feet to continue down the stairs to the living room to ask someone who knew him better. At the bottom of the stairs, two Guardians swiveled in their seats to face her.

"Is…Cole, okay? I heard him being sick."

Raven motioned for her to join them in the living room, where she sat on the spare couch.

"How much has Cole told you about his duty?"

She leaned forward, clasping her hands together. "Hardly anything. I know he's an angel, that's about it."

Raven took a long sip from his drink before answering. "Cole escorts souls to their final resting place. He's part of a faction of angels called Azrael. When a mortal dies, Azrael collect the mortal's soul and transport it to either the Heavens or Hell."

She thought for a moment. Was that why Cole disappeared? Had duty called? Why didn't he just tell her he had to work?

I have angel business to attend to…

Damn it. He did tell her, but she thought it was an excuse. When would she just give him a break? Believe him for once? Trust his word.

Now.

She'd start trusting him now.

"If that's his job, why does it make him sick?"

Raven looked at Slater sitting across from her. "Care to answer that one?"

The other Guardian leaned back on the couch, his leg crossed, ankle resting on the opposite knee while he petted a purring kitten snuggled in his lap. "When an Azrael collects a soul, they absorb emotions. Darkness. It's an occupational hazard."

"Do you...escort souls, too?"

"Once. Long ago." He lifted his hand and a thin tendril of dark gray shadows slithered from his fingertip, swirling in the air before retreating. The same shadows as Cole.

"When an Azrael denies the compulsion to collect a soul, the souls build up. Cole has been careless in that respect as of late, so I imagine there was a shit load of souls waiting in limbo for him to move on. He's now suffering the hit of all those emotions at once instead of a few here and there." Slater shrugged. "He'll get over it."

Get over it? Cole was up there, alone in his bedroom, purging his stomach because he'd escorted too many souls at once? Her chest tightened. He'd been careless in his duty because of her. Because of the stupid book. Instead of focusing on his angelic job, he'd been running around after her, saving her from monsters at the antique store, appearing out of thin air when she screamed his name after Blaine visited. Trying to convince her to stay.

And all she'd done in return was second guess everything he said. He'd kept information from her because he didn't want her to know when she died.

She was such a bitch.

He'd done nothing but shower her with kindness and she'd thrown it back in his face. How could she have been so heartless?

Lifting her gaze to Slater, she asked, "Is there anything I can do to help him?"

"Nah, he'll be fine once it passes in a day or so."

"A day or so?"

Slater shrugged. "Around one hundred mortals die every minute in this realm, and there's only so many Azrael assigned to escort them. My guess, he had hundreds, if not more, waiting in limbo."

She thought back to the few margarita Fridays where she and Jemma had too much to drink and one of them ended up sleeping on the bathroom floor. Although Cole's hangover wasn't quite the same, maybe treating it the same could help. Lucky for Cole, through college, Jemma had perfected an epic, guaranteed hangover cure. With any hope, it would work for an angelic one.

She jumped up from the couch. "Do you mind if I raid the kitchen?"

Raven pointed down the hall. "Go for it. Treat this place like it's yours."

The Guardians resumed their conversation as she headed into the kitchen. If nothing else, it couldn't make Cole feel any worse. He'd done so much for her, taking care of him was the least she could do.

Rummaging through the fridge and pantry she grabbed a cold energy drink, bottle of water, and a handful of strawberries. Strange, yes, but the combination worked. Did immortals take painkillers?

She added two to the tray just in case. If this didn't help, she could always order a greasy burger.

Upstairs again, outside Cole's room, she angled her ear to the door. Silence. Maybe he'd fallen asleep? She could sneak in and leave the remedy for when he woke.

Balancing the tray in one hand, she slowly opened the door and nudged it wider with her hip.

A single bedside lamp illuminated the room and…empty bed. Of course, her gaze shot straight to the bed. Like her mind slipped into the gutter. It wasn't like she'd never been in a guy's room before but stepping into Cole's personal space felt different. Significant.

Pausing by the door, she took in the rest of the extravagant room. Antique furnishings just like her room, a cushiony chair in the corner, and a small desk on the opposite side. Heavy drapes covered the two windows. On the far side, a pair of boots, jeans and shirt lay in a heap by a closed door with the distinct sound of running water coming from behind it.

Instant images of a naked Cole showering flashed through her mind. Hot water cascading over his toned, coiled muscles. The dark dusting of hair leading down his abs. His length, hard and thick. Going only by how his jeans had hung indecently low on his hips, she bet his body was drool worthy. Had she experienced it in a past life? Had she trailed her tongue over his smooth skin just to hear him moan? Had she felt him slide inside her as he whispered dirty words in her ear?

Heat thrummed in her blood, pooling low in her belly until she almost stumbled with the tray.

What was wrong with her? Here she stood in his room, uninvited, imagining the poor guy naked, after he'd spent the evening throwing up.

Leave the tray and back out the door was what she should do, yet her feet wouldn't move. He had no one to care for him. And right this second, she wanted to be that person.

The shower cut off, snapping her out of the daze. She tiptoed to the side table, placed the tray down and turned to the bathroom door just as it opened.

"Evelina?"

Her breath hitched. Cole stood in the doorway in nothing. Absolutely nothing. Completely naked encased in a cloud of misty steam.

Water dripped from his shaggy wet hair, landing on his shoulders before travelling down his defined pecs, over the ridges and grooves of his abs until it disappeared in a patch of dark hair.

She gulped.

His impressive length hung proudly between his legs, slowly coming to life as though warmed by her mental caress.

He didn't move or speak, nor did he interrupt her...ogling. Drooling. She should probably close her mouth. The poor guy had gone through hell escorting souls, giving them peace, and she stood there gawking at him.

Swallowing, she forced her gaze upward to collide with his.

Fuzzy fragments she now associated with memories flickered through her mind. *Lying on her side facing Cole, stroking her fingers over his bare torso as summer rain beat down on them.*

Cole cleared his throat. "As much as I welcome your attention, I don't think you're here for..." His voice sounded thicker. Deeper.

The guy was beautiful, yet in a damaged way. An angelic face with sharp edges. As though all his years—centuries?—of absorbing human emotions had taken a toll on him. Dark stubble dusted his jaw and she itched to graze her fingers over it.

He gravitated closer.

"I...ah." Her gaze darted to the hangover cure she'd forgotten about the second Cole strode from the bathroom naked. "I thought you might like some...well...Slater and Raven told me about what you do. I thought this could help with the after-effects."

Concentration was difficult now that he'd moved to within reach. Heat from the shower radiated from his skin, and it took every inch of control not to close the distance and press her body flush against his.

He held her gaze for a long moment. His usual gray eyes were now darker around the rim.

Her breath quickened. "Okay, well, I'll...leave you to it."

His hand lifted, and ever so slowly, swept a loose strand of hair behind her ear. An incredible ache burned inside her chest, stilling her heart. "Stay." His fingers trailed along her jaw and down her neck to halt at the shirt collar.

Her heart thumped, frantic beats echoing in her ears as his fingers traced a delicate path back up to her face, as though he reacquainted himself with her features. Or as though he couldn't quite believe she stood before him.

Her breath punched in and out, making her dizzy.

The urge to kiss him overwhelmed her. To taste him again. Ever since he brought her here, he'd acted as though their kiss never happened. But the memories of that night in the castle's library lived rent free in her mind. How he'd commanded her as though he knew exactly what she liked and how to deliver it.

Her gaze dipped to his mouth. Full lips slightly parted.

A shiver danced through her middle at the thought of his tongue colliding with hers again, of his groan as he'd deepened their kiss. How he'd hold his naked body against hers.

His hand shifted, curling behind her neck, fingers tightening. His eyes darkened. But something held him back, just out of reach. Was he waiting for her? For her to give him the okay? Was he nervous? No, when he'd kissed her in the castle, he'd been confident and somewhat possessive. Maybe this time he wanted her to make the first move.

Slowly, she lifted onto her toes and pressed her lips to his.

A strangled moan escaped his mouth a second before he swiped that control right out from underneath her. His lips dominated hers as he thrust his tongue inside her mouth, tangling with hers, making her head swim. This kiss was different. So very different. Hungry. Raw. Desperate. Nothing at all like the kiss in the castle where she'd likened it to a fairy tale.

This kiss supercharged every cell in her body.

Both his hands captured her head, angling it to deepen their kiss as her hands glided over his bare back, pressing him closer. His hard length nudged against her belly, stealing her breath, making her ache for more. More. More of this man. How could she have existed without him?

With a feral groan, Cole shifted to grab her ass and lift her to lock her legs around his waist. A few quick strides and he sat her on a low dresser. Lights danced before her closed lids as he ground his hard length against her center.

Praise the lord for thin yoga pants.

Pressure built between her legs. The low rumble of an impending eruption shook her middle almost to a painful level. His mouth buried in her neck, licking, sucking, sending her to unexplored heights. How could it be this good?

Squeezing her thighs, she locked her legs around his back as he thrust his hardness right on top of the building ache, working her into a frenzy through the barely-there material. The dresser creaked and groaned with each drive of his hips.

"Tell me what you need, baby girl," Cole crooned by her ear. "Show me."

She couldn't think let alone verbalize. Her body craved release. Anything. Everything. All at once. She gripped the back of his head, forcing him to look at her as she rolled her hips, rocking against his hardness, matching his pace. His eyes darkened even farther. Dangerous gray pools, so intense, almost feral. This affected him as much as it did her.

"I'm going to make you fall apart," he growled.

Done for. She was absolutely done for.

With a dark curse, Cole shifted his hands between them, pushing her thighs apart so his fingers could find her center, rubbing in rough circles through the thin fabric. He took her mouth in another searing kiss, controlling her, dominating, flinging her to the edge. An explosion ripped through her so suddenly and forcefully she threw her head back and cried out his name. Over and over intense shudders tore her apart as he continued to draw every ounce of pleasure from her heated flesh.

Dizzy spots cleared from her vision as the orgasm ebbed even though her breath remained heavy, labored. Her heart though…forget it. It would never be the same again. Nothing had ever brought her to such heights.

She ached to touch him, please him, explore his body. Make him fall apart just as she had.

Cole dipped his head, watching his fingers lazily stroke her center in lighter, soft motions. Her hands slipped down his sides, drawing a shiver from him as she reached for his straining length heavy against her thigh, glistening moisture at the head. But before she touched it, Cole swore.

His hands disappeared. Cool air rushed between them as he stepped back.

"We…*fuck*. I didn't mean to…" He tore at the back of his neck, retreating even farther. "I keep screwing this up."

"What? No. I…wanted this. Sure, I hadn't planned on sitting on the dresser, riding your fingers, but I'm totally okay with everything we did."

When his gaze snagged hers, he may as well have doused her in a bucket of ice water. Her cheeks flamed. Had she thrown herself at him? Did he not want to touch her?

No, the lust, the need in his eyes had reflected hers. The yearning wasn't one sided.

"You may not regret it now, but you will."

While Cole stormed to his closet and roughly threw on a pair of jeans, she slipped off the dresser, feeling as though she were the one naked. How had the mood suddenly plummeted? Had she totally misread his signals?

The back of her throat burned. "Why would you say that?"

Way to make a girl feel shitty.

She couldn't stomach figuring out what happened, not when nausea replaced the burn in her throat. In the castle, he acted as though he'd regretted kissing her almost immediately afterward, and just like then, now he barely looked at her.

Before she made more of a fool of herself, she straightened her shirt and stepped to the door.

Cole caught her wrist. "Don't go."

"Please, Cole. Save me some embarrassment."

Instead of granting her plea, he tugged her, twisting her around until he pinned her between him and the wall. Her core reignited, clearly reading the signals wrong yet again.

His hands braced the wall either side of her head. "Why would you be embarrassed?"

Did she really need to spell it out? This man was so confusing. "Because I...touched you and you pulled away."

Deep grooves creased his forehead. "You think I don't want you to touch me?"

"You kind of implied that when you backed away."

"Evelina." His voice deepened to a growl as he curled a finger beneath her chin to lift her gaze back to his. "I want you to touch me so bad it hurts. I dream of the day when you make me lose my fucking mind. When I'm inside your heat, claiming your body and soul."

212

If he thought that explained his actions, he thought wrong. That only made her more confused. "Then...why did you stop?"

His mouth twisted as though his thoughts caused him physical pain. "Because I'm...scared. I almost want you too much. Even knowing that when you remember, you'll hate me for finding you again."

All that nausea swirling through her body collided in one heavy mass behind her ribs. "I could never hate you."

She knew it with every fiber of her being. Regardless of how long she'd known him, she could never feel anything but this sense of wholeness whenever they were together.

"You say that now." His thumb swept over her bottom lip, sending bolts of heat through her middle. "Until you remember every word you said to me before this life, I won't risk it. I can't. I won't take that decision from you."

CHAPTER TWENTY-THREE

Cole

Ever since Cole had his hands on Evie in places he'd only ever dreamed of, he'd done everything possible to avoid her. And by avoiding her, he meant when he wasn't escorting souls, he'd disappear every time he sensed a tingling warmth at his nape right before she entered a room.

Coward. He was a damn coward.

But how in the Fate was he meant to look at her after he'd all but thrown her on the dresser and drowned in her bliss while her pants were still on? And she thought he didn't want her to touch him? Farthest thing from the truth he'd ever heard. Since their kiss in the library, he'd craved her hands all over him. Now, after touching her, no words described how badly he wanted a repeat of their bedroom action...minus her clothes.

Fate. Just thinking of the sweet moans she made when he ground against her sensitive flesh made him want to bellow her name to the rafters. She wanted him, he had no doubt, but would she when she remembered? Until he knew the answer, he needed to keep his distance. He couldn't allow them to be alone, not when he wouldn't have the same restraint.

But they were running out of time. Evie turned twenty-five in four days and the more he delayed searching for the book, the more he risked Blaine finding it first. Remembering that, and all the years Blaine had hunted her, should keep him on the straight and narrow. Along with the countless times she'd died in his arms.

That should do it.

Find the book. Destroy it. Save Evie.

As he wandered down the hall to the entertainment room, a giddy sensation quivered low in his belly at the thought of seeing her. Given his butterflies, anyone would think they'd only just met, that he hadn't loved her for hundreds of years. Yet like every other time, his breath caught when he entered the room and found her laughing with Jemma, Tayla, and Hailee.

He paused in the doorway for a long moment admiring her. How she'd tied back her wavy hair in a loose bun with stray strands framing her face. How flecks of amber sparkled in her dark brown eyes each time she laughed. How she slung an arm around Jemma's shoulders, seeming comfortable and at ease in her new surroundings. But mostly, he marveled at how his heart beat a bit faster upon hearing her voice.

As though Evie sensed him standing there, she glanced his way. Time slowed. The air around him felt thinner, lighter. An invisible tether connecting his soul to hers pulled him forward until he stood within arm's reach.

He really shouldn't touch her, that only heightened his need to kiss her and truly make her his, but he couldn't stop his hand from brushing her jaw. "Hey."

"Hi."

Her eyes sparkled. If she still felt an ounce of embarrassment from the other night, it didn't show.

"I thought we should try again to search for the book. Visit another place you've hidden it in the past."

The light in her eyes dimmed, just enough to kick him in the guts. Maybe he should apologize for his behavior in his bedroom? Reassure her he felt the same longing. Though, keeping their focus on finding the book was wiser and smarter on all fronts.

"Sure." She turned to the other females now lounging on the couches. "I guess I'll skip this movie and catch the next one."

Hailee waved. "Don't worry about the movie. This hottie will be here waiting when you get back."

A shirtless mortal male appeared on the massive TV causing a burning sensation in his chest.

"Girl, you have your own man. I already called dibs on all the Chris hotties." Jemma motioned to the TV.

As the others debated Jemma's statement, Evie turned back to him. "Where are we going?"

To ease the burn in his chest, he threaded his fingers in hers and led her outside to the gravel drive. "Two lifetimes ago, you found the book in an ancient cave hidden away in the Rocky Mountains." His thumb circled the back of her smooth hand, relishing the tiny zings through his blood with each stroke. He couldn't stop touching her, even in a small way. Even when he knew he shouldn't. "I thought we'd try there."

"Sounds like a strange place to hide a priceless grimoire."

That wasn't the strangest place. "You've always had a vivid imagination."

When Evie smiled, he inhaled a deep, cleansing breath and misted them to the mountains. Reorientating himself, he scanned the thick, gloomy wilderness for the cave's entrance. The last time he'd been here it was nothing but dense vegetation and rugged landscape, with hardly any foot traffic. Mortals didn't venture this deep into the mountains except for those who used the cabins for hunting. Severe snowstorms frequented this part of the country during the winter months and being caught without shelter was a death sentence.

Still holding Evie's hand, he wandered in the direction of the cave, drawn to it by memory rather than landmarks. To be honest, it felt nice to hold her hand, even if it wouldn't last. As though hand holding satisfied his desire to touch her without the risk of triggering memories. Like kissing would.

"Tell me about this lifetime," Evelina murmured, watching her step through the damp vegetation.

Chilly wind swept between the trees and Evie pressed her body closer, wrapping her arm around his. He should've worn a jacket, if only to offer her some warmth.

Instead, he kept his gaze ahead and mind on the cave.

"You were a teacher back then, and your family worked in lumber."

"Really? And let me guess, I was looking for a rare book for my class?"

"Actually, you'd already found the book when we met in that lifetime. Only, you didn't know what it meant." He closed his eyes for a second, remembering the details of that life and how he'd barely had three days with Evie before Blaine located her.

Wolves howled in the distance as the wind increased, cutting through his shirt. He wrapped his arm around Evie, tucking her closer to his body. In lieu of a jacket or to ease the dread pooling in his stomach, he wasn't sure. Either way, he wished he could shield Evie from all of it.

"Once I realized what the book meant, I hid it in a cave? How would I have even found the cave?"

And there it was. The source of that sour taste at the back of his throat.

When he didn't answer, she tugged him to a stop. "Cole? What's wrong?"

He couldn't lie to her. Not only because he physically couldn't lie, but he couldn't stomach the thought of stringing her along with a handful of half-truths. When this lifetime ended for her, he wanted her to know he'd been honest. He'd given his heart freely and openly. He'd laid his wings on the line for her.

But telling her the truth didn't come easy. It hurt. Each truth would reveal another memory. Hopefully, with a gradual process, she would avoid the physical pain of enduring them all at once.

Turning to her, he lost himself in her gaze and the words slipped from his mouth. "I showed you the cave. It was a place away from prying eyes, and somewhere Blaine wouldn't think to look."

"If that's all, why do you look so...devastated?"

He slipped his hand down to entwine their fingers. "You died in the cave."

She gasped.

"Each place we travel to is a location where you died."

"What?"

He lowered his gaze to the damp leaves coating his boots, catching filtered moonlight between the trees.

"In your final moments, right before I…right before your soul leaves, you reactivate a spell you placed on the book."

She stood there, eyes wide, staring at him like the time when she'd watched from the window as he unfurled his wings. "There are so many strange things about that statement."

His chuckle cut short when she winced, cradling her head in both hands.

Holding her shoulders, he leaned down, so they were eye level. "Another memory?"

"It hurts less than the others though."

Fate, it killed a piece of his soul every time he saw her in pain. This lifetime and every one before it. One consolation was her memories came back gradually, rather than in one agonizing dump. Lately, he wasn't sure what was better. Getting it over with and comforting her through the pain. Or prolonging the inevitable? At least with the latter, she could get to know him, trust him, perhaps even love him back, before she remembered that he was a selfish asshole.

Particularly the parts where he took her soul.

As quickly as the headache came, Evie straightened. "I'm okay, it's gone. It was flashes that I couldn't piece together."

He tilted his head, studying her.

"Really. I'm fine." She wiped her palms on the thighs of her jeans before pointing to the left. "I feel like the cave is over there."

He glanced in the direction. Nothing but darkness, thick trees and wild untamed wilderness greeted him. But beneath that, a lead weight settled in his gut as the knowledge hit him. This was the first time she'd sensed her past. Soon, she would remember everything, including where she'd hidden the book, and when that happened, he'd end this wretched cycle.

This was the beginning of their end.

He nodded, his throat too thick for words.

Leading Evie, he slashed his way through the undergrowth, following a steady incline until he spotted something familiar. "There." He pointed ahead. "Over by the boulders."

Mostly hidden by centuries worth of dirt and growth, he located the boulders concealing the entrance to the cave. After he'd escorted her soul back to Hell in that lifetime, he'd returned here, to preserve their memories. Or lock away the pain. Either way, he hadn't wanted another soul to step foot in the last place Evie had drawn breath.

Given its untouched state, his plan had worked.

Summoning his shadows, he raised his palms and used the tendrils to move the boulders aside to create a narrow opening for them to squeeze through. He turned on the light from his cell, waving it over the cave walls as they entered.

Evie peered over her shoulder at him. "What? No fire power?"

"Sadly, only mortal technology."

She laughed and the glorious sound echoed through the cave.

Guided by instinct or memory, Evie continued forward, trailing her fingertips over the damp, jagged surface until she stilled.

"Is it weird that I know there's a hidden nook behind this rock?"

That heaviness in his gut lifted to his throat. "No.

Your soul knows the way. It always does."

After handing Evie his cell, he jimmied the rock free to reveal a small nook about the size of a large…book. Inside, though, was nothing but loose dirt.

"It's not there," she murmured, lowering the light.

His shoulders sank. As much as he wanted this lifetime to last forever, they were running out of time. Evie would turn twenty-five in less than a week. Blaine wouldn't sit by and wait for much longer. If Cole didn't locate the book before she came into her powers at twenty-five, he'd lose her forever.

Evie touched his shoulder. "I'm sorry, Cole. I don't know how to find it."

He returned the rock where it belonged. "It's not your fault. You'll find it. You always do."

"Why is it…" Her mouth twisted slightly. "Why is it so bad if Blaine has the book?"

Because he'll use your power to perform the spell and your soul will die.

The words were on the tip of his tongue, but he couldn't bring himself to say them. Couldn't bring himself to cause her more worry. But keeping the truth, the severity of their situation, made his stomach churn.

"He…he doesn't just want the book, Evie. He wants *you* with the book." Even in the dim, patchy light from his cell, he caught her lip tremble.

"Because of what I am?"

Wrapping his arms around her, he pulled her tight against his chest and rested his chin on her head. "I'll protect you. I won't let him take you."

They didn't have time to waste, they should continue searching for the book, but sometimes he forgot just how much he wanted her. To hold her. To love her. To spend all his eternities with her. And moments like these, with her wrapped in his arms and her sweet otherworldly scent branding him, were the memories he'd cherish long after she departed this realm. The ones that would pull him through the darkest nights until they reunited in the Heavens.

These moments would make all the pain worth it.

He should take her back to the Guardian mansion, or to another previous location, but he didn't want their night to end like this. Laced with disappointment. When it was only the two of them, he could pretend, even for a moment, that they weren't searching for the book and that Blaine wasn't hunting her and that eventually, he'd take her soul.

One night they could just be them.

"How about a detour?" he murmured into her hair.

Evie leaned back, still within his embrace. "Another place I died?"

Shudders ran through him. "No. Somewhere fun."

"Are there margaritas, because I could use one."

A slow smile returned the color to her cheeks, and it made him want to burn down the entire mortal realm just to see it again.

"I can arrange that."

CHAPTER TWENTY-FOUR

Evelina

Evie's stomach whirled, her skin tingled, each cell exploding with burning light only to snap back together again in less than a second. Her legs swayed slightly before regaining balance in a narrow alleyway.

Cole peered down at her in his arms, his dark gray eyes somehow glowing in the moonlight. "You okay?"

He dragged his thumb along the edge of her jaw, leaning down so close his warm breath brushed her lips. She nodded because, well, if she spoke right now it would no doubt come out as a squeak.

Releasing her, he took her hand and led them farther down the alley, lit by a single streetlamp. "It's just up here."

Distant music echoed through the night, the air filled with smoky barbequed flavors making her mouth water. Forget the margaritas, she'd take two of whatever that smell was. Actually, food and a margarita sounded divine.

Toward the end of the alley, Cole paused by a blood red door with a single brass knob in the center. Oh great. Was he into some freaky sex club thing? Sure, she found him attractive. Who wouldn't with that stubble dusting his perfect jaw and the ridiculous muscles she now knew hid beneath his shirt? But...a sex club? Had their relationship progressed to that level?

At the entrance, she swallowed the giant lump in her throat as Cole opened the door and motioned for her to descend the narrow staircase, lit by several lamps hung high on the walls, leading to a second door.

At the bottom, she turned to Cole. "I realize you know me well from previous lives, and that we're soulmates, but I'm not into...well, I don't think I'm into, I guess I've never tried so I can't say for sure, but I think maybe we should get to know each other a bit more first."

His dark brows descended, bunching together in a tight frown. "I'm not following where this is going."

Oh, gosh. She had to spell it out for him. And she thought him pushing her away when she'd tried to touch him had embarrassed her.

She swallowed the lump down. She was a confident woman, comfortable talking about sex. No reason to make this awkward. "I've never been to a sex club before. That doesn't mean I won't like it, I just want you to know it's...my first time. At a sex club."

Cole held her stare for a long moment before he howled with laughter. Irritation itched her skin the longer he laughed, even bending at the waist to catch his damn breath.

She slapped his shoulder. "It's not funny. I'm not saying I won't try it, I just think maybe we should, you know, do more together first."

He inhaled a deep breath and straightened, though that stupid smirk remained. "You think I'm taking you to a sex club?"

"Aren't you?"

His mouth twisted as though holding back another fit of laughter. "Oh, baby girl, now I wish I was."

Wait, what? "Where are we then?"

"An immortal club. Sex no doubt happens behind closed doors, but it's definitely not out in the open for others to watch."

Relief washed through her in one giant wave leaving a slight, barely noticeable pebble of disappointment. Not that she'd admit that to Cole.

Cole motioned up the stairs to the alley. "If you'd prefer, we can go to a sex club, I can call EJ to ask—"

"No!"

He snickered again, louder this time.

She smacked his chest. "Stop it. It's not funny."

"It really is."

She grunted at him before turning back to the door.

Wrapping his arms around her from behind, Cole reached for the doorknob. His hardness pressed against her lower back as he whispered in her ear, "Now I can't get the thought out of my head."

She didn't respond and it took a mighty amount of strength not to tilt her head to one side and invite his mouth on her neck.

The door swung inward, and she all but stumbled down another narrow hall following the live music and glittery lights.

Wow. She stood gobsmacked at the entrance to the bar, taking it all in. With a long slab of timber running the length of one side, bartenders behind it flipping bottles and making drinks, a large dancefloor in the middle of the space, a band playing on a raised stage, and tables scattered around the room, it resembled a mix between a night club and a small-town bar and grill.

People danced together…with clothes on. Not a sex club. And now she felt like an idiot.

Still holding her hand, Cole led her to the bar where he pulled out a stool for her to sit. The bartender hollered from the other end before he vanished, only to reappear right in front of them. Did that bartender just…mist?

The bartender fist bumped Cole. "If it isn't my favorite Azrael. How long are you around for?"

"A few weeks. How you been, Dash?"

"Living the best eternity, as usual." The bartender motioned to the crowd. "You going to play for us? I'm sure I can find you a spot."

Cole's hand moved to the small of her back, drawing her closer. "Not this time. I'm here with Evelina."

Dash kissed the back of her hand. "Pleasure to meet you, Miss Evelina. Let me make you both a drink."

"We'll have margaritas, brother," Cole said without missing a beat.

Dash slapped the bar. "Coming right up."

Cole sank onto the barstool beside her and swiveled their chairs to face the band currently playing a slow rock ballad she hadn't heard before.

"Do you usually play the guitar here?"

He lifted one shoulder. "Sometimes."

In no time, two frozen margaritas arrived on the bar top behind them, complete with brightly colored paper umbrellas, right before Dash misted to serve another customer. So weird.

The tanginess of that first sip shuddered all the way

to her toes, squeezing her throat, but gosh, she'd missed it. If only Jemma were here.

Drink in hand, she scanned the club. "When you said immortal club, does that mean angels come here?"

Cole draped an arm on the back of her chair. "Angels, part-angels, mortals who know about our world, and the occasional Fallen." He scowled at a scantily dressed woman practically climbing on two guys at once.

"Have I…been here before?"

Cole took a long sip of his margarita. "In your previous lives, we never really had an opportunity to…relax."

"And we do this time? Between searching for the book, dodging bad guys, and finding out I'm some human-Fallen hybrid?"

His gaze grew distant, those deep creases returning to his forehead. "No. But I don't want you to miss out on moments like this. Not this time."

Something in his tone raised an alarm. Probably because she had less than a week until her birthday. Until she usually died.

Way to dampen the mood.

Content with sitting beside Cole, listening to the band, she allowed herself to relax. Enjoy the moment. Cole answered every question she threw at him without hesitation, and she asked plenty, until they ended up playing a game of "which kind of immortal" as she pointed to random people in the club.

Every time Cole laughed or when his hand rested on her knee or when he leaned closer to brush his thumb along her bottom lip, her body lit with a fire she couldn't contain. The push and pull between them drove her insane. Back at the Guardian house in his bedroom, he'd been all over her, eager, and hungry to please her. So much that she'd lost her mind in the pleasure. Then he'd told her he was scared. Scared she'd hate him once she remembered her past lives. Now, more than ever, she couldn't believe she'd ever have a reason to hate the angel sitting beside her.

Not now that she'd acknowledge the connection between them. Her feelings had only deepened.

"Hang on a minute." The lead singer signaled for the music to stop. "Is that Cole I spot at the bar?"

The entire dance floor turned to look at them.

"I'm not playing. Not tonight," Cole answered with a slight shake of his head.

The lead singer, clearly not convinced, encouraged the crowd. "Who wants to hear a badass angel raise the roof on this place?"

The crowd cheered, clapping, and stomping their feet as though Cole was some kind of famous musician.

Cole dismissed the growing unrest with a wave of his hand before he swiveled his chair to face her. But he couldn't hide the excitement sparkling in his gray eyes. He wanted to get up on that stage and…she wanted to hear him play. At the Guardian mansion, she'd only heard him humming and that had been enough to turn her insides to lava. What would he sound like here with a full band and acoustics?

She touched his knee, smiling. "They want you to play."

"I'm not here for them. I'm here for you."

Could he melt her heart anymore? She shot a glance to the stage where the lead singer hyped up the crowd even more. "*I* want you to play."

Their gazes locked for a long moment where the strange connection she experienced with him soared to life, swirling through her blood, drawing her closer.

"Azrael, come up here and show your girl what you've got," the lead singer called out over the microphone.

Your girl.

Two words she'd never anticipating loving as much as she did. Two words that exploded the lid off her feelings, making her yearn for more.

She tipped her chin to the stage. "Go. Play for me."

Cole tossed back the remainder of his margarita in one gulp before sliding off the stool. He tipped her chin up with his finger and kissed her hard and fast. If she hadn't been sitting down, she would've ended up in a puddle on the floor.

"One song," he said, striding to the stage.

A memory slammed into her. *Lying together under the branches of a weeping cherry tree, warm summer breeze whispering over her skin as Cole leaned down to place a gentle kiss on her forehead...*

In a blink, the memory vanished, leaving an achy hollowness behind her ribs. Why couldn't she remember everything? Why only fragments here and there? She wanted to, yearned to. If only to remember what her other lives had been like? Memories of her and Cole. Even something that told her how she died. Why it happened each lifetime at the same age. What if in one lifetime, Cole decided she wasn't worth the hassle? What if he didn't find her? That hollowness expanded like a black hole in her chest. Already, she couldn't imagine never meeting him. Existing in a life without him.

Before she sank into that downward spiral, the band's lead singer announced Cole's arrival on stage and cheers grew louder. Someone handed him an electric guitar. He flipped the strap over his head before fiddling with the tuning. He could stand there just holding that guitar and women would swoon at his feet. The poster image of an immortal rock god. Muscles in his forearms contracted as he tweaked the strings with a relaxed, downright sexy expression that weaved her insides into a hot, throbbing mess.

A stagehand set up a second microphone stand beside the lead singer and Cole moved in front of it. His gaze lifted and snagged hers across the crowd. Silent messages floated through the space between them, conveying vows of love and devotion. And in that moment, there was no doubt he would find her in every lifetime. He would spend eternity searching for her.

Silently, she returned her own vow. She would do the same for him.

With a slow grin, Cole broke their eye contact to count in the band and they started playing as though he were an original member. She nearly toppled off her stool. His voice was heavenly. Not delicate and angelic like she'd expected, but a gritty, soulful vibrato that thrummed through her blood. He strummed his guitar like he owned the stage, and the crowd went crazy for him. But once his gaze found hers again, it never diverted. His intense eyes drew her in until she stood in the center of the dance floor, swaying her hips to the music, completely spellbound.

Cole had so many sides, so many hidden aspects, and suddenly, she wanted to discover them all. Each and every one.

She barely registered the song ending and the crowd chanting for more. Cole was the only thing she saw, as he handed the guitar back and leaped off the stage, striding through the parted dancers until he stood before her.

Blaming it on the margaritas was pointless. Sure, the alcohol gave her a buzz, but that wasn't the cause of the overwhelming need to kiss him. To climb the man like a bookshelf ladder.

When a much slower song began playing, Cole held out his hand. "Dance with me?"

She didn't hesitate. He rested his hands on her hips and she curled hers around the back of his neck. Desire bloomed, overwhelming the alcohol buzz, heightening her senses. Every part of her that touched him sparked with an intense heat that centered between her legs. Breathless tingles spun out of control through her body.

Cole leaned down, resting his forehead against hers as they swayed in time with the music. If only this moment could last forever.

Lost in his touch, she pushed her worries to the back of her mind and focused on the here and now. Cole said he didn't want her to miss out on moments like this. Maybe in her past lives, she had. Maybe he'd found her right before she died. Maybe he hadn't found her at all. Or maybe she'd lived a short life filled with nothing but running from those wanting the book?

Regardless of how or when they met, dancing with him, safely cocooned in his arms, felt right. Nothing had ever felt more destined. As though the entire universe had aligned, granting them this moment of peace.

She rested her cheek on his shoulder, feeling the

steady inhale and exhale of his breath. Back in his bedroom, he'd said he wanted her to touch him, but he didn't want her to hate him once she remembered. She could never. Not now, not ever. Without conscious thought, her hand slipped around his neck to trail along his stubbly jaw. This man, this angel was perfect in every way. He'd done nothing but protect her, keep her safe, reassure her.

His love for her radiated warmth from his chest to hers as though they had a magical tether connecting them.

When her fingers reached his mouth, she brushed her thumb along his bottom lip causing him to suck in a sharp breath. His grip tightened on her hips while continuing to sway them in time with the music. This guy could multi-task like a pro.

Swallowing the nerves fluttering in her belly, she drew back only enough to look at his face. Her thumb continued exploring the thin beard along his sharp jaw, over the dip in his chin, sweeping his bottom lip. Heat pooled in her center, creating an unbearable ache between her legs.

"Evelina..."

Each time he called her by her full name, something splintered inside her.

Life was so cruel. Why couldn't she remember him? Why did he have to suffer until she did?

"I want to kiss you," she whispered so softly it surprised her that he heard.

One hand drifted upward, curving over her waist, trailing along the outside of her arm until he cupped her cheek. This time, she leaned into his touch.

"It's because I'm a rock god, isn't it?"

She laughed, but his expression tightened. Just when she thought he'd pull away, he instead lowered his mouth to hers. Sparks. Heat. Longing. So many sensations and feelings swept through her. Light brushes of his lips, soft nips, gentle caresses with his mouth turned her into a wildfire. His thumbs swept along her jaw maddening the sensations. But still, he held back a part of him. She felt the restrained need he refused to unleash in his shaky touch.

Still cradling her face, he drew back to peer into her eyes.

"I won't hate you." Her breath quickened when her gaze dipped to his wet lips. "I never could. In this life or any other."

His eyes darkened to almost charcoal, burning with an intensity that shivered through her. Whatever he searched for, he must've found because without a word, he unleashed that raw need and crushed his mouth on hers.

This kiss was anything but gentle. The complete opposite. When he slipped his tongue between her lips, drawing a moan from her, he tightened his hold on her face and deepened their kiss. His tongue collided with hers in a feverish rush for dominance. If he didn't have hold of her, she'd collapse right there in the middle of the dance floor. Desperate, needy, she flattened herself against him. He moaned, devouring her mouth as though it were his lifeforce. As though he'd searched the desert for centuries and she was his first taste of water.

Oblivious to anyone else around them, she surrendered to every sensation happening between them. Her hands tightened around the back of his neck, holding him in place. Her center ached and pulsed with a heightened need she'd never experienced. Good lord, this man could kiss. The things he did with his mouth should be illegal.

When she gasped for air, he moved his lips to her neck while his hands trailed down her waist to squeeze her hips. He lightly nipped and sucked, drawing an embarrassing moan from her.

Every sensation intensified. The lights above them pulsed brighter, the music louder yet muffled at the same time, the air thicker, more humid. Fire burned through her. Starting deep within, it spread like an out-of-control wildfire, obliterating everything in its path. No...not fire. Light. Heavenly light. Closing her eyes, an iridescent white light glowed behind her lids filling her with warmth and countless emotions.

Protection, comfort.

Home.

Even dizzy with lust, she knew without a doubt, those emotions came from Cole.

Sharp pain sliced through her side. She cried out.

Cole jerked back, his eyes wide and alert, searching for the threat. "What is it?"

Her back bowed. The pain. It stole her breath. Someone had stabbed her in the ribs. No, her spine. The fury radiated through her bones making it impossible to distinguish where the pain began and where it ended.

She cried out again. Her knees buckled.

Clawing her side, she tore at her shirt, desperate to find the source of the agony. The world swayed. Cole swept her into his arms, racing through the crowd. Her vision dotted. The once colorful, bright lights disappeared as Cole carried her into a room, muffling the music when he slammed the door closed.

He eased her onto the vanity near a washbasin.

Within seconds, the pain eased to an afterburn, allowing her to finally catch her breath.

She ripped off her shirt. "Something's burning me."

"There's nothing—" Cole gently lifted her arm. "What the fuck?"

"What? What is it?" She twisted to the mirror.

He leaned closer, inspecting her ribs. "What is that?"

She peered in the mirror. "It's a tattoo, but..." Lifting her arm higher, she inspected the ink starting below her breast and ending just above her hip. The vibrant colors shimmered as though they came alive under the light.

But that wasn't what stilled her heart.

Vines wove around the colorful stack of books, with a scatter of colorful blooming petals that hadn't been there when she'd gotten the tattoo.

At her touch, the petals...shimmered.

She screamed, jerking back from the mirror. The vines twisted around the books, winding themselves into a tight knot while the blossoms continued to bud.

Bile rose in her throat.

Had Dash slipped something in her margarita?

"Please tell me you see that," she asked Cole.

He brushed his finger along one of the thicker vines, and it reacted, coiling between the others. "It can't be."

Now that the pain had subsided, leaving a strange tingly sensation beneath her tattoo, she could focus on Cole's words. "What can't be?"

He ignored her question, leaning in closer to inspect the ink. "When did you get this?"

"Jemma and I got tattoos together when we graduated college after a rather eventful margarita night." Clearly, nothing good came from margaritas. "Can you stop for a minute and catch me up because I'm starting to freak out. How the hell did someone tattoo a vine on my ribs without me knowing. And more importantly, how is that vine…alive?"

Cole straightened, and something in his gaze threw a bucket of ice over her. "The vines are protectors."

Protectors? She'd heard of such things in books, but they were for witches, not research assistants.

Were they for Nuriel, too?

"Is it protecting me?"

Through the mirror, she stared at the vines laden with petals. As though sensing her gaze one petal bloomed open beside the pile of title-less books.

"I think it's protecting the book."

She gaped, her gaze darting between the tattoo and Cole. "The book? As in *the* book?"

His fingers curled around the edge of the counter as he bowed his head. "That's why we can't find it," he mumbled to himself. "It's been on you this entire time."

On her?

"Wait. What? You think the book, the one we're searching for, is this tattoo? That's ridiculous."

He shoved away from the counter. "Not think, Evie. I'm sure of it. You haven't only hidden the book in this lifetime. My bet is you bound your soul to it."

CHAPTER TWENTY-FIVE

Cole

What a fucking nightmare.

Cole slumped on the grass beneath a shady tree at the Guardian property a few feet from Evie while she chugged some water before dropping the bottle on the grass by her feet. Going by her permanent shellshocked expression, he had half a mind to replace that water with alcohol.

Alcohol didn't fix things, he wasn't that naïve, but it sure as Fate took the edge off.

They could both use some of that right now.

Last night, after discovering Evie had somehow bound the book to herself, he'd misted them straight back here, and all day, they'd been trying to help Evie conjure her magic. He and Raine had taken turns with no luck. Now, Willow joined the party.

Talk about a sick twist of Fate. If she had any hand in this…No, he couldn't think of that right now. He had to figure out how to separate Evie from that damn book. He couldn't destroy it with her soul bound to it.

"Again." Evie extended her arms, palms facing up.

Beside her, Willow raised her own. "Close your eyes and focus on your heartbeat. The steady thrum of your pulse until that's all you can hear."

Of all the immortals he knew, Willow had the most

experience with summoning disconnected magic. After all, a similar thing had happened to her.

"Now, relax, visualize opening your chest, a gateway to your soul. Allow your blood to flow freely through every cell." Bright sunburnt orange sparked in Willow's palms. "When you feel the moment that your blood heats, when you're so full of light you might explode, exhale and expel the power."

Willow's magic burst from her palms until it surrounded her in a golden halo.

Hope soared through him as he stared at Evie's palms, sending her all the mental energy he could muster. "Relax, baby girl. Try to relax."

He held his breath as her shoulders lifted on a deep inhale...Nothing. No spark. No light. No magic.

Evie opened her eyes, and the disappointment gutted him. Between the three of them, they'd tried everything, and they still couldn't release Evie's magic.

She threw her arms up. "Why can't I do this?"

He stood, crossing to her. "It's not easy. Especially when you have to learn how to summon your magic before you can use it."

"But clearly I've already summoned it if I somehow bound a goddamn book to me."

Jemma launched from her spot on the grass and waved her cell in the air. "Check this out."

Her friend angled the phone for Evie to see. Like a magnet, he drew closer.

When he and Raine had questioned Jemma about their tattoos, she'd said they found the random image on a fandom wizardry site on the internet. Whatever the Fate that meant. Magic existed in the mortal world but tattooed protectors with angelic powers? Unheard of. At least, he thought so.

As Jemma scrolled, reading bits out loud from the site, he curled his hand around the back of Evie's neck, gently massaging her tense muscles. Sighing, she peered up at him, and his heart melted. She was all he'd ever wanted and somehow, each lifetime, something kept them apart.

No more. He'd made a vow to end this so Evie could find peace, and he'd do exactly that.

Only now, his plans took a detour. He couldn't destroy the book. He couldn't end any link to her curse because if he did, he'd destroy her soul in the process. And if Blaine found out, he'd use it as leverage to get him to hand over Evie like some lost treasure.

He was back to square one.

Jemma pointed to the cell. "Here. This refers to familiars. Which sounds the same as a protector."

Raine snatched the cell to read. "They were originally made from…" She glared at Evie. "You're half Fallen. Where did you get angel blood?"

Angel blood? Why the Fate would she need blood from an angel?

"I have no idea," Evie answered. "I didn't even know this world existed until Cole found me."

Raine threw a dagger, slamming it into a nearby tree trunk. "It's time to use your shadow magic Azrael and unlock her memories. Stop screwing around."

"They're not cloaked, Raine," he snapped. "They're…broken."

Willow cleared her throat. "Maybe let me? I was able to rejuvenate Raine's memories, maybe I can help with Evie's?"

"That would be great," Evie replied, stepping over

to Willow.

He snagged her arm. "No. Rejuvenating memories could cause more harm than good. What if the process is painful? What if it causes a migraine?" *What if the memories make you hate me?*

Evie's softly cupped his cheek. "Cole, at some point, I'm going to remember. And at some point, you need to trust me. Trust us. Have faith that no matter what I do or don't remember, what we feel here and now is what matters."

Her beautiful eyes, so full of that trust and faith she spoke of, were no match for him. They never were. In each lifetime when he reached this fork in the road, he always chose the safer option. The path which protected his soulmate. But now, he could no longer fly the path of least resistance. Again, and again, he reminded himself this was her last lifetime, this was their last chance. He'd battle this storm, with Evie by his side, and trust they'd find a way through it.

Together.

Swallowing down his fears, he placed his hand over hers in a silent vow that he would trust them even if he didn't trust Fate to intervene. When Evie's memories returned, and history told him they would eventually, he hoped she remembered all their lifetimes, not only their last moment in Hell. He hoped she felt his love for her in his lingering glance, every casual touch. He hoped she saw how every choice he'd made had been for her.

With a slight nod, he switched hands and moved behind her so Willow could step closer. Nausea rolled through him like the poison of a thousand souls as Willow placed her palms at Evie's temples. The orange glow began gradually until it intensified, flowing from Willow's palms in a steady stream between them. Never did he let go of Evie's hand. He held on, clutching her hand tight, her anchor. Her soulmate.

Evie squeezed her eyes shut, her face tensing while Willow's Ariel magic pulsed.

Seconds felt like hours. How long would it take? What memories would rejuvenate first? Which ones were so broken not even Willow could repair them?

Evie shuddered, the pain on her face intensifying. Her once steady pulse accelerated. Color drained from her cheeks…

"Stop!" He shouted right as Evie screamed and her legs gave out.

He toppled to the ground with her in his arms.

"Baby girl, can you hear me?" He stroked her cheek. "Evelina?"

Time stood still as he waited for her to respond. He wasn't ready for her to remember and definitely not for her to die. Not when they'd made the most progress in all her lifetimes. He still had so many things he wanted to say, to do, to apologize for.

Willow crouched beside him, touching Evie's forehand. "She'll be okay. It's just shock."

"How can you be sure? She's not immortal, Willow. She's half mortal. What if this permanently harmed her?"

Evie groaned, her eyes fluttering open before closing again. Wrapping his arms tighter around her, he gathered her against his chest, resting his chin atop her head. "I'm here, baby girl. I'm here. You're going to be okay."

"It's mine," Evie mumbled. "Spells."

Someone swore. Probably Raine.

"What are yours?" He brushed damp hair from her face.

Evie groaned again, her body curling in a ball in his lap. "It hurts. The pain…make it…stop."

"Shh." He kissed her head before standing with her still cradled in his arms. "You're going to be okay. I've got you."

After a curt nod to Willow, he strode back inside the mansion carrying Evie up to his room. At this point, he couldn't care less about what she did or didn't remember. What mattered was taking care of his soulmate.

Just as he reached the door to his room, Evie murmured something, barely coherent. But the words stopped him dead in his tracks. Relief he'd felt a second ago vanished in an instant, replaced with a sickening churn. "Evie, what did you say?"

Her head rolled to one side. "It's my blood."

CHAPTER TWENTY-SIX

Cole

Had his bed always been this lumpy? Were the covers too heavy? Cole checked the thermostat for the tenth time in three minutes just in case the temperature had changed. It hadn't.

Placing the back of his hand on Evelina's forehead, he checked her clammy skin. All seemed normal for a mortal, but what did he know? He was an immortal angel. Both Aric and Willow checked on Evie during the night, and they both agreed she only needed rest. But how could she be fine? Willow had used magic to rejuvenate Evie's memories. Was that even safe for a mortal?

A soft knock drew him away from the bed and to the door, where he found Raven standing in the hall.

"Hey, my man. How's Evie doing this morning?"

Cole softly latched the door behind him as he joined Raven in the hall. "I don't know. Fine, I guess." He sagged against the wall. "I knew this day would come, but I hate that she's hurting."

Raven nodded, hands shoved into the pockets of his black jeans. "Any word on what she remembers yet?"

The nausea from earlier resurfaced when he thought of Evie's words before she'd passed out. "I think she has angel blood."

"How?"

He thought back to the first time he'd escorted Evie's soul to the Heavens and how furious Fate had been. At the time, it had struck him as odd, but the more he thought of it, the more he must've missed something. Even more so now after Evie mumbled about the spells being hers.

"Fate cursed Evie because she performed the spell. All along I thought Fate created the book and Evie found it, but what if...Evie created the spells. What if the book is hers? What if Fate...created Evie?"

Raven swore under his breath. "A Chosen? You think Evie is a Chosen?"

"It makes sense. A Chosen is a mortal created using Fate's magic. They possess her magic in their blood. Protectors are created using angelic blood, and Evie said her blood made the protection spell." The more he spoke it out loud, the more convinced he became. "Nuriel are half mortal and half Fallen Raziel. The mortal part of Evie is a Chosen, I'm sure of it."

A long, quiet moment extended between them until Raven spoke. "If she was a Chosen, one of us would've been assigned for her protection."

Cole pushed off the wall the pace the carpeted hall. "You did. Think about it. You protected her in each lifetime when I couldn't be near her. I protected her because she was my soulmate. What if Fate destined Evie to write the book, but instead of using it for whatever Fate intended, Evie used it for herself? That would piss Fate off enough to curse her and destine her soul to Hell." He paused, turning back to Raven. "What if Fate intended for Evie to give the book to Blaine all along?"

"No way. Evie first died long before Blaine Fell. That theory would only be possible if…"

"Fate already knew Blaine would Fall."

Raven raked his fingers through his hair. "Fuck."

"Exactly. If that's what Fate planned, this won't end until she gets what she wants."

A soft, barely audible groan came from inside his room, and he turned his head toward the door.

Raven tipped his chin. "Go, take care of her. We'll talk more after."

"Thanks, brother."

As he reentered the room, Evie's eyes fluttered open. His heart stilled. Flatlined right then and there. Never would he deserve such a female for a soulmate. He'd tried for centuries to earn her love, to be half the immortal, the man, she deserved. But would he ever reach that standard? By defying Fate, all he'd ever done was cause Evie never-ending death and heartache. Yet, year after year, century after century, he kept striving for that goal. And he'd continue until the realms ended and he breathed his last breath.

She would always be worth it.

Evie blinked a few times as he rounded the bed to sit beside her. "What…happened?"

When she tried to sit up, he wrapped his arm around her shoulders and tucked a pillow behind her. "Any pain? Headache?"

Even though she shook her head, he still wanted to cocoon her in his wings to protect her. But would she want his touch now that she might've remembered?

Instead, he swiped a bottle of water from the nightstand and placed the straw at her lips. "Here, drink."

"Thank you." She cleared her throat after a small sip. "The last thing I remember was...Willow." Her eyes widened. "The book."

"Shh, we don't need to talk about the book right now. You need to focus on recovering. Tampering with memories is...I'm still not convinced it's worth the risk."

Inside, his mind was at war with his heart. Sure, he yearned to know everything Evie remembered, to confirm his theory or prove how outrageous it was but carrying her to his room as she slipped in and out of consciousness had once again reminded him how fragile she was. Half mortal. Destined to die at twenty-five.

In two days, he'd lose her again.

Nothing, not even destroying the book, was more important than this time with her.

Evie smoothed her hand over his shoulder. "I'm fine, really. Nothing hurts. I want to tell you everything I remember in case...well, in case I don't get a chance."

A vise constricted his ribs, squeezing all remaining air from his lungs. How could he be so wrong? Evie wasn't a fragile half mortal. She was tender, brave, fearless. Time and time again, she died in his arms and reincarnated, never losing hope, never giving up. She was a warrior. About time he treated her like one.

Cupping her cheek, he leaned in until their foreheads touched, feeling fucking privileged to share the air she breathed. "I'm here. You're here. I'm not going anywhere without you, Evelina."

After a long moment, he drew back and nodded for her to continue.

"I remember…my first life…how it all began." Evie placed her hand over his, lowering them to her lap.

Air solidified in his throat, thickening, making it impossible to speak. Too long, he'd wondered about her origins, how the book came into her possession, connecting the clues each lifetime until they painted a picture. But he'd never heard the story from Evie.

Perhaps there was a reason she'd never told him. After all, knowledge was power, and with it came great responsibility.

Now though, he'd face that with his head held high, and his wings at the ready.

Evie gave his hand a squeeze, returning his focus. "Creatures like the ones at the antique shop attacked my village, killing all but a few. I felt helpless. Hollow. I should've done more to stop them, but my spells weren't strong enough. That night, a woman appeared in the forest. White light surrounded her as though she glowed. I remember feeling the beams pulse inside me when I neared her."

The vise from earlier squeezed harder, slicing through his flesh. *Fate.* It had to be.

"She said one day someone would eliminate the creatures. I remember thinking, so what? I need help now, not later. But I also remember having this feeling, this…desire to trust what she said."

Bile rose in his throat, and it took all his strength to remain calm. "What else did she say, Evie?"

"She told me my blood would amplify spells in my grimoire, and when called upon, I would use my magic for the…chosen one."

Chosen one?

What the actual Fate?

"What happened next?" He forced his voice to remain steady. "Do you remember anything else?"

She pulled back her hand, but he tightened his grip not wanting her separated from him. Not now, not ever.

"Days later, I don't remember how many, more Fallen attacked the village. I waited for the savior, but when they never showed, I took matters into my own hands." Her gaze dipped to their joined hands, and he gave her a reassuring squeeze. "I used my blood to cast a binding spell for everyone in the village. To combine our powers."

"Baby girl..." Pain sliced right through his damn heart. "That much power..."

She lifted her watery gaze to his. "It killed me."

Throwing off the blanket, he scooped her up into his lap, wrapping her in his arms. *Save. Protect. Love.* Three words that had continually repeated in his mind for centuries.

"You did what you had to, to protect the ones you loved," he murmured, tangling her wavy hair between his fingers.

She drew back. "How could you say that? My actions created this curse. I didn't wait for the so-called chosen one, I didn't wait for someone to save my village, I defied the angel by taking matters into my own hands and as a result, no one survived. Not even me. And you..."

He captured her face in his hands, holding her steady. "I found you. I don't care how many lifetimes we must endure until we get our happily ever after, what matters is I found you that night. And I will find you again and again, in every lifetime after this, for as long as we both still exist." His thumbs brushed over her damp cheeks. "I love you, Evie. I've loved you forever."

She sank into his embrace, her eyes awash with tears. "I'm sorry for putting you through this."

"I regret nothing."

For centuries, he'd longed for her final life, for her torture to end, and now that he knew the truth…he'd give anything for more time. More opportunities to worship her, to prove his worth. To show her how much he loved her.

In that moment, something shifted between them. Not shifted, awakened. As though they laid both their souls bare, no secrets, no one-sided love, no skirting around the truth to protect her memories. It felt…liberating. Exhilarating. *Destined.*

He could take on Blaine, and Fate if needed, because he and Evie were a team. They always had been. The strongest of all teams.

Soulmates.

Her fingers trailed along his jaw, over his bottom lip. "I remember you, too. Flashes of each time you found me." She moved his hands and held them against her breast, directly over her heart. "I feel it. How each life I fell in love with you."

The clamp around his ribs shattered and finally, he inhaled a full breath. The first in centuries. And with each subsequent breath, the warm light in his chest intensified.

Love.

"You…loved me?"

He'd felt it in their connection, the underlying pulse in his blood each time he found her, but that had been their soulmate bond luring him in. Not her. Not

Evie. Many lifetimes he'd told her how he felt, but she never said it back. She never told him.

And how he longed to hear it.

Her mouth pressed against his in a gentle kiss. "I love you, Cole. I've loved you in every life."

When she drew back, he fisted her hair and crushed her lips against his. He never took their time for granted, and he wouldn't waste any more worrying about their future. Together, they'd face the storm. Together, they'd survive. Together, they'd live out their eternity.

If Fate intended for Evie to somehow help Blaine, then Fate had better come up with plan B. No way would he ever let his soulmate go again.

He would kill anyone who tried to harm her.

Using his grip on her hair, he tilted her head back so he could trail his lips down the side of her neck, nipping and kissing her soft skin. In that moment, he wanted to taste every inch of her body. Bask in the sounds of her cries, her pleasure. Finally, seal their soulmate connection the way he craved since they'd first met.

He moved his hands to her hips, easily changing her position to straddle him. *Fuck.* With her heated core pressed against his straining hardness, he almost blacked out.

Their heavy breaths collided between them as he stared into her eyes, finding each spec of bronze, all the glittery gold. His heart had never felt so full. So complete.

"I remember us kissing." Evie glided her hands over his shoulders and down his arms. "But I don't remember us ever…"

His own hands slipped beneath the hem of her shirt, thumbs circling her smooth belly capturing each of her shivers and storing them in his memory. "Because we haven't."

Countless times, he'd imagined her naked beneath him while he peered into her eyes, losing himself inside her. But they'd never had the chance. And now, he'd never been so thankful for missing that opportunity. He never wanted her to forget their first time together.

"Ever? That's…sad."

His hands drifted higher up her ribs, stopping just shy of her bra. "Sad?"

"Yes, sad. For centuries you've met me, fell in love and watched me die, over and over, yet never experienced the passion between us." She leaned forward, mere inches from his face. Her warm breath whispered over his lips, and he stifled a moan. "You've never made love with me."

"No one."

She searched his eyes, brows slightly furrowed. "No one? You've never…?"

Venturing higher, he glided his thumbs over the lacy fabric encasing her breasts. "All those firsts belong to you, baby girl. Only you."

"I want them. All of them." Evie swept her lips over his jaw. "I want you."

That familiar sharp pain in his chest threatened to rear its ugly head. For so long, he'd ached to hear those words. To have her choose him rather than the book. In this life, everything seemed so upside down. And even though he knew at some point they'd have to figure out how to separate her from the book, and how to stop Blaine from getting his hands on it, in this moment he wanted to forget it all. To drown in her scent, to bury himself deep inside her until they no longer cared for the outside world.

Since first finding her, he'd yearned to mark her as his, to seal their soulmate bond. He'd waited for her.

But…if she remembered flashes of her lives, of how it all began, surely, she also remembered her final words to him in Hell.

I'll never forgive you…

Swallowing hard, he forced himself to face his final fear. To banish all the remaining barriers between them. "I don't want you to…regret this."

"Every memory I have of us involves you protecting me. I feel like every choice you've ever made has been for us." She tugged the hem of his shirt up and over his head before tossing it on the floor. Her heated gaze burned a path over his bare chest, firing his blood to boiling point. Their bond streamed so much light between them it would fuel his soul for all eternity.

"I don't blame you. And I will never, could never, regret being with you, no matter what happens in our future." Her soft fingers caressed down his chest, halting at the straining bulge in his jeans. "I want to be with you, Cole. I want you to make love to me."

Sure, he was immortal, but he was also still a male. No male, definitely not one who'd waited centuries for his soulmate, could resist forever.

At some point, he stopped fighting. Gave in and trusted their bond, their love, rather than running from his fears. In this lifetime, he'd take that chance rather than never knowing the outcome.

He eased his mouth to hers, kissing her with all his

years of longing. All the emotion he'd kept locked away inside. He swept his tongue over her bottom lip, and she opened for him, deepening their kiss as her hands explored his bare skin, drawing gasps and shudders from him. Her touch, her taste, her scent consumed him, overloading his senses until he felt ready to burst. Heavenly light, soft, warm, bloomed between their souls, anticipating their joining. He couldn't get enough. Part of him wanted to savor every second, to make it last forever, but another part, desperate to have her naked beneath him, wanted to throw her down on the bed and have his way with her until she screamed his name to the Heavens.

Lowering his hands to her hips once more, he tore off her shirt, feasting his gaze on her lacey burgundy bra before smashing his mouth against hers. Their kiss was more urgent, raw. Hunger built between them. He cupped her breasts, pinching her puckered nipples, capturing every moan with his mouth to store away in his memory forever.

Bliss. Intoxicating bliss. Nothing described the sensations consuming him. He wanted to drown in them all and never come up for air.

Evie rocked her core up and down his hardness, making his head swim. More. He needed her now. Things turned hazy. His brain stopped working, or something in her touch just flat out shut it down. Instead, his heart took control.

Breath heaving, she wriggled off his lap to stand between his open legs. Holding his gaze, she drew in her bottom lip. His brain would never function again. Forever more, lust had taken control of his actions. Of his movements.

Time stood still when she reached behind and undid her bra, letting it fall at her feet. Next, she shimmied out of her jeans and panties to stand before him naked. He could explore her body all day and never discover all the hidden treasures. Shapely hips, rounded breasts that would fit perfectly in his hands, thighs he couldn't wait to have squeezed around his head as he tasted her.

His soul combusted. Died and returned to the Heavens. And he hadn't even begun.

Was it dangerous to be this aroused? His cock strained against the zipper, almost painfully. When he popped the button on his jeans, Evie's gaze darkened, ablaze, tracking his every move.

Standing, he stripped off his jeans before sitting back down. Evie moistened her lips, gaze still locked on his straining length. He gave it a stroke, sweeping his thumb over the head, relishing in her throaty moan.

"You want this, baby girl?"

Instead of answering, Evie lowered to her knees, bracing her hands on the inside of his thighs. His body warred with his heart. Fate, he wanted to experience her mouth wrapped around his length. He'd waited so long to be inside her. But the image of her on her knees before him, as though bowing to him, didn't sit right.

He tucked his hands beneath her arms about to lift her to her feet. "I don't want you like this. You bow for no one, including me."

"You said all your firsts are mine." A groan vibrated through his middle as she leaned in, sweeping her hot tongue up the outside of his hardness. "I'm not bowing before you. I'm giving you one of those firsts."

He'd thought he died earlier. Clearly, he was

wrong. Nothing killed him quite like watching Evie lick and kiss her way over his hard flesh. When she tilted her head to look up at him through her dark lashes, his heart burst open from a swell of emotions he couldn't identify. Slowly, she lowered her mouth over him.

Sensations exploded around him, and he couldn't refrain from tangling his fingers in her hair, applying slight pressure as she moved up and down. Fate, he'd never experienced something so spectacular, so enchanting. So overwhelming. Every cell in his body ignited making his eyes roll to the back of his head.

"Your mouth." He groaned, fisting her hair. "It's so perfect."

When Evie shifted position, taking him deeper, panic spiked through him. He refused to finish before things had even begun. They'd waited too long for this moment.

Fighting through the fog, he scooped her to her feet with a growl. "I want to finish inside you. I *need* to. Tell me what you like. Show me."

She licked her lips, eyes drunk with lust. He knew the feeling well. "Touch me."

Taking her hand, he guided her to straddle his lap once more, widening his thighs, opening her even farther. One hand slid down her hips before dipping between her legs. So hot. Fingers clawed his shoulders while he stroked her center, circling her bundle of nerves, spreading her wetness.

"So beautiful." He leaned forward to kiss along her neck and collarbone. "I've imagined touching you countless times."

Never could he have imagined it would feel this good. To have her trembling with need. To experience it after so long.

Greedy for more, he slipped a finger inside her heat, then a second, just to hear her gasp turn into breathy moans. In and out, he slowly pumped all the while, watching each heated shiver and twitching muscle on her beautiful face tense and tightened on the edge of release.

How had he gone lifetimes without touching her? How had he resisted for so long? Now that he'd experienced this between them, he could never go back. He'd never have enough of her taste. Her touch.

Fate, he wanted to see her fall apart just so he could put her back together again and again.

CHAPTER TWENTY-SEVEN

Evelina

How could something be so familiar, feel so natural, right, even though she'd never experienced it before? Peering into Cole's deep gray eyes, she swore this was where she was meant to be all along. A deep-seated knowledge that every choice she'd ever made, in every lifetime, had led her back to him.

Star-crossed lovers who'd finally found themselves.

Soulmates.

Heaviness in her chest stole her breath at the thought that he'd waited for her. Not just waited to find her. Waited for her. The thought of him being with someone else, as irrational as that was, caused a twist in her gut. He'd waited for this moment. For them to finally be together.

As he worked her into a wild frenzy where she couldn't distinguish between up and down, her connection to him streamed through her blood. Bloomed inside her chest. Warmth, like she'd never experienced, pulsed deep within her.

Comfort. Love. A sense of belonging.

She remembered his voice throughout the centuries, each time he'd found her, every time he'd told her who he was. Each time she'd caught him glancing her way, his eyes filled with yearning. For her. For them.

Without realizing it, her soul had searched for his for as long as he'd looked for her.

Heated shivers racked her body as he stroked her into oblivion. Despite her thighs trembling, clenching, threatening to topple her over, Cole held her safely in his arms as she dived over the edge. Her forehead sagged against his, breath punching in and out. Forever. She wanted this forever.

Slipping his fingers out, Cole murmured praise in her ear, wrapping his arms around her, drawing her flush against him. Vaguely his straining length registered against her belly which made catching her breath all the more difficult.

Fingers burned a path down her spine, lightly squeezing her hips before trailing back up. Never had she been this turned on. Despite his limited experience, no man had ever soared her to such dizzying heights. She only wished she'd known, remembered him, so she could've waited also.

Fire collided with the tingles bursting throughout her blood, pooling once again in her core. Before she knew it, she began rocking on his thick hardness, desperate to ease the increasing ache. She tunneled her fingers through his hair, leaning back to peer into his eyes.

Emotions soared through her, so many she couldn't pinpoint each one, but they filled her with lust. Desire. A yearning to give herself to him.

"You're incredible," Cole whispered, brushing the hair back from her face.

Lifting slightly, she slid herself down the outside of

his length, watching his eyes darken to deep pools of smoldering gray.

One second, she straddled his lap about to kiss him, the next, the world spun before her back bounced on the soft bedding. Cole prowled up between her legs. Dark desire burned in his eyes with an intensity that should scare her. Instead, it made her belly flip flop.

"The things I want to do to you…" His heated gaze roamed her naked body, sprouting another wave of shivers.

Reaching up, she cupped his jaw, bringing his focus to her. "Show me."

He held her gaze for several heartbeats and once again, all those pent-up emotions she'd sensed lingering beneath the surface felt ready to burst. Need. She needed him. Needed to have him in every way. Needed him to show her.

When she dragged her thumb over his lips, he drew it inside his mouth, twirling his tongue, sucking, before releasing it, heightening every sensation until the ache between her legs erupted.

But this was his first time. Not just with her, but with anyone. Even though he portrayed confidence in all areas she'd witnessed, surely, he was nervous. Worried? Was he waiting for her to take the lead? Now, she was no sex god, had only been with a few guys, mainly during college, but she was the experienced one here. Did he need her to guide him?

"Hey…" He lightly stroked her face, down the column of her neck. "Where did you go just then?"

"Nowhere." Slipping her hands from his face, she smoothed it over his shoulders, down his firm pecs. His answering low grumble kept her fingers moving south but she couldn't quite reach. "I want you to feel comfortable."

He drew back, his dark brows set in a deep frown. "I may be inexperienced in the bedroom, baby girl, but you're mine. Your soul and your body are in perfect sync with mine. I'm savoring the moment, that's all. Making sure it's real."

Gosh, didn't that set her heart aflame once again. This man. Could he be any more perfect? *No.*

"I'm here. This is real." Her fingers trailed up and down his chest. "We're real."

A devastating grin curled on his mouth a second before he reached between them and placed himself at her entrance. The steady thrum of anticipation peaked making her shift, desperation clawing at her center. Slowly, ever so slowly, he pushed inside.

The world around her exploded.

Orbs of brilliant white light burst from within her as Cole gradually set a steady rhythm, his gaze never straying from hers. Wonder. Amazement. All the colors of the rainbow, and new undiscovered shades, blended between them. His brows drew tight in an expression somewhere between pain and relief.

"I want this to last forever." He leaned forward, tunneling his fingers through the back of her hair. "But I'm so fucking impatient to claim you."

That brought a smile to her face. How could two people be so in sync?

Soulmates.

"Stop holding back. I won't break."

A feral look burned in his eyes before he drove deeper, drawing a throaty moan from her.

Her breath quickened, as each thrust careened her

closer and closer to the peak. Her body trembled, having surrendered somewhere along the way to their connection, the need, the yearning to join with him, wrapped itself around her insides, her chest, her flesh. To give him not only her soul, but her body. Her heart.

When she reached for him, he braced his forearms on either side of her head and kissed her heartbreakingly slow.

Her heart swelled beyond belief.

Died right there in the bed.

As his tongue swept hers, and his hips ground down with each thrust, tears welled in her eyes.

Cole stilled. He stroked her jaw, her cheek, swiping a stray tear with his thumb before taking her mouth once more.

"I feel it, too, baby girl. Don't be afraid to fall." He kissed her cheeks one by one. "I'll always catch you."

Before she replied, he took her mouth again, this time deeper. More demanding. As though all that emotion they couldn't label came crashing down around them. A tidal wave breaking over the jagged shoreline. Fire swept through her senses. Midnight, dark roses in full bloom, a familiar scent she now linked to her many lives. Once, she'd thought it reminded her of darkness. But now, with Cole inside her, his heavy weight pressed all around her, memories rushed to the surface.

A mossy forest. A crystal-clear stream trickling over rocks. An angel, standing before her with majestic, silvery-gray wings unfurled behind him. He lifted his head, capturing her with his equally dark eyes.

Hers.

Here and now, Cole kissed her deeper. In a rush,

the new memories swept through her, cocooning them in light until the world outside this bedroom no longer existed. They weren't in the Guardian house, they weren't chasing a magical book, they weren't running out of time. They were two soulmates who'd finally found each other.

Tears streamed down her cheeks. Not sadness, but an overflow of emotion her body and mind couldn't grapple with. Cole captured every one of them with his lips or a brush of his thumb as he continued sliding in and out.

Tiny sparks sizzled over her skin, waves of heat rolling through her blood. When the pleasure almost broke her, Cole trailed his wet lips down her throat, thrusting harder and deeper. Millions of glittery stars sparkled in her vision as she sped toward the edge, knowing she was safe in his arms. That he'd catch her when she fell.

And that, he did.

Over and over, she clenched him, riding the never-ending waves, her body floating to a place somewhere above the Heavens. She wanted to stay there forever. Just her and Cole. Hand tightening on the back of her neck, he rolled his hips with one more deep thrust before his shuddering breath collided with hers in the space between their mouths. She stared into his cloudy eyes as he kissed her, whispering sweet words of endearment at the column of her neck, her mouth, her eyelids.

Still inside her, he rolled them over, flipping her on top to ease her head on his chest. She sighed, the steady thrum of his heart in time with his.

Nothing had ever felt so powerful. So...whole.

Complete. Forever. How had they never joined their bodies before in such a powerful way? They'd known each other for countless lifetimes and never experienced this passion. This union.

In the stillness, Cole tightened one arm around her back, using his freehand to toy with her hair, twisting it between his fingers, placing gentle kisses on the top of her head. She could stay here all day.

All year.

Until the reminder of her upcoming birthday barged in and tore away all the warm and fuzzies.

Cole must've sensed the change in mood because he kissed her head, clutching her tighter. Nothing could distract her enough to forget the truth. Sooner or later, they had to face reality.

Before letting her sour mood rub off on him or worse, he asked her about it, she wriggled free from his grasp to lay alongside him. A degree of separation.

Raising on one elbow, Cole brushed his finger down her shoulder, causing a painful ache in her chest. To think, only a few weeks ago they'd met in the library of Blaine's castle. Even knowing now that they were soulmates, the feelings, the connection between them seemed so…beyond this world. Impossible to comprehend, only feel. And wasn't that the truth? Trust her feelings, trust in them. Her soulmate.

Sure, her upcoming birthday, the day she supposably died, wasn't ideal. But what if they could stop it? What if there was a way to prevent her death? A world where Cole didn't have to watch his soulmate die. A world where they could both be happy?

The pain sharpened. Cole had experienced each of her deaths as if it were his own. She'd do anything to prevent a repeat. First, she needed to know how.

"Cole?" She lifted her gaze to his. "How do I...die?"

CHAPTER TWENTY-EIGHT

Cole

Was it possible for an angel to stop breathing? Because Cole swore in that moment, his lungs gave out and refused to do their job of inflating again. He couldn't inhale, nor answer.

Fate. How the Heavens did he answer?

"I'm sorry. Sometimes I...sometimes I forget you witnessed all those deaths firsthand and how painful that must've been." Evie sat up, tucking the blankets beneath her armpits. A good thing because not seeing her bare breasts definitely aided in keeping him focused. "I'm thankful I don't remember. I shouldn't have asked. I just thought maybe if I knew how I died, I could figure out how to stop it from happening again."

She lifted her gaze, stirring ominous clouds in his heart.

She'd hate him. In Hell, before her last reincarnation, she'd vowed to never forgive him if he found her again. And now she wanted him to tell her how she died? How, in each lifetime, he killed her. Prickles erupted beneath his skin. There hadn't been enough time for him to prove how much he loved her, how sorry he was for putting her through all those deaths. Of course, their soulmate bond would always connect them, bring them together, but that didn't mean she'd suddenly forgive him. Nor would it make her love him.

Then again, he kept returning to the fact that this life was her last. Each previous reincarnation, he'd ached to know more about her. Hold her closer. But had somehow resisted, knowing that when he finally ended this curse, he could enjoy those moments. Now though? Now all he wanted was for her to know he'd told her the truth. Bared his heart. Only then could he do enough to earn hers in return. He wanted to free them both of this...pain. Of the regret.

Only the truth achieved that.

"Don't apologize. It's difficult to...Maybe it's best if I just say it? Rip that feather out."

At her nod, he sat up with her, pooling the blankets at his waist while he relaxed against the headboard. She took his hand, granting him the reassurance he needed. Suddenly, too much space separated them, but it helped him to concentrate. Ensured he said the right words. If nothing else, he owed her the whole truth.

Seeking her forgiveness was better than endless deceit.

He scrubbed his free hand over his stubbly chin as he carefully chose his words. "In each new life, Blaine finds you first. I don't know how he manages it, but...he does." His jaw tightened at the countless memories of always finding her too late. "By the time I find you, Blaine has already convinced you to search for the book for him. You're already...invested."

Not only in the book. One lifetime, by the time they met, Evie had also been invested in Blaine, too. He'd ended Evie's soul far too early that lifetime and the pain would haunt him for eternity. But the idea of

Blaine touching his soulmate had made him want to burn down the entire realm.

Each lifetime, that Fallen had toyed with her emotions, her life, her fucking soul. A heavy sense of dread sank into his blood. All Cole ever did was play catch-up. No longer. That ended now.

Her curious frown turned those ominous clouds into a vicious storm.

Light strokes of his thumb on the back of her hand simmered his bubbling anger. "Blaine needs you for one purpose. To cast a spell. After he's in possession of the book, he'll no longer play nice."

"What if I learn how to cast the spell and then do what he wants? Obviously, it's inside me somewhere. After that won't he leave us alone?"

Us. Last century, that word felt like such a foreign concept. Yet, the closer he pushed toward the finish line, the more he imagined a future for them. Was Fate cruel enough to rip it all away at the last moment? *Yes.* Especially now when he had no bargaining power. Now that Evie had somehow bound the book to herself, *inside* herself, he was back at square one. All those centuries of planning, hoping, trusting his plan, were for nothing. He couldn't destroy the book. He couldn't hand the book over to Fate. Hell, it was never hers to begin with. As far as he could see, handing Evie over to Fate was his last remaining option.

He'd burn his soul before he did that.

"I suspect the spell he needs you for, you won't…" *Survive.*

Hope dimmed in her eyes, filling his lungs with coal.

"What will happen when he finds out the book

is…me?"

That lump expanded inside his throat once again. Would it ever disappear?

He tugged her closer, removing the cold distance between them. "He'll find a way to activate the spell and your power, regardless of the outcome."

She peered up at him for a long moment. "That's why you don't like him near me. Each life, you protect me from him. You save me."

Fate. He almost threw up right there in the bed. Save her? Protect her? Those were traits of a half decent soulmate. Him? He was a selfish bastard. Reckless. Sure, he'd saved her, protected her, but only because he couldn't stomach Blaine taking her soul to Hell. Using it for his own agenda. He also couldn't stand the thought of Fate cursing him and Evelina for hundreds of years only to pave a path that led right back into her hands. An existence without her wasn't worth living. She was the reason he awoke each day, the reason he continued escorting souls in case he somehow missed her in mortal form.

Selfish.

"No. I…take your soul before Blaine does."

He refused to acknowledge her sharp inhale. Ignored it like it never happened. Yes, Blaine was the villain in this version of her world, but he was equally the bad guy. He didn't save her. He ended her life. Time and time again.

A soft touch on his forearm made him lift his gaze. Big mistake. Her eyes softened until all the hazel flecks melted together into a pool of gold.

"You take my soul? You…kill me?"

Fuck. Hearing her say it opened flood gates inside

him allowing nothing but regret and self-loathing to fill every crevice.

Instead of words, he nodded. What could he say? He'd told her from the beginning that they were soulmates. Never did he say he was worthy of her.

"Why?" she whispered.

"Because Fate destined your soul to Hell, and I've spent every lifetime preventing it from ending up there. Blaine won't grant you the same mercy. If it serves his purpose, he'll take you to Hell in a heartbeat." He tipped her chin with his finger. "I'd rather you live a thousand half-lives than none at all."

He'd make no apologies for keeping her soul permanently out of Hell. One day, he hoped that when he retrieved the book first, Fate would have no choice but to grant his request. Evelina would enter the Heavens. Even if he couldn't, at least he'd give her peace. But now…

"Cole…" Her voice softened even more.

Tiny threads inside his heart threatened to unravel when her eyes washed with tears. He didn't mean to upset her. But he couldn't lie. Ever.

Now was that point.

"I'm so sorry."

He drew back. "What for?"

"That to save me, you need to…do that."

Stunned. His brain couldn't even formulate words. How…how had she twisted his words to make it sound as though he'd done her a favor?

"That must be a painful burden to bear."

She wrapped her arms around his middle, resting her cheek on his chest. They were quiet for several heartbeats.

Finally, the words he'd held back for so long made it out into the world. "Blaine will do whatever it takes to retrieve the book. I'll do whatever it takes to save you."

****

They spent most of the day curled up in each other's arms until exhaustion eventually lulled Evie to sleep. When the warm puffs of breaths on the crook of his neck steadied, he carefully untangled their limbs to slip out of bed, tucking the covers tight around her. Of course, he stood at the end of the bed for a few precious moments staring at her peacefully asleep. Committing the image to memory. The soothing rise and fall of the covers spread over her shoulders, her dark hair splayed on his pillow, the light flutter behind her closed eyelids. How her lips fell slightly open. The solid thump of her heartbeat right alongside his.

But the need to capture this moment was more than seeing her in his bed for the first time. It was the sensations taking place behind his ribs. The fullness, the continual beams of light bouncing from one side to the next. The expanding ache when he thought of losing her again.

He was a damn fool to think he loved her in previous lifetimes. Until this moment, he hadn't even known what love felt like. He'd loved Evie through their bond. But now...now he loved Evie with his whole heart. Every cell in his body, every breath he took, more and more with each passing moment.

Losing her wasn't an option.

He'd never recover.

Forcing himself to turn away, he slipped out the door, wandering down the hall until he reached the war room where he found EJ and Raven seated at the table.

"Come on in, Reaper." EJ waved him over.

He'd moved into the Guardian mansion only a few weeks ago. How could so much have changed within such a short time frame?

A slow smirk lifted the corner of Raven's mouth, reminding him again of the resemblance to Blaine. "About fucking time."

Of course, Raven could sense the completion of his bond with Evie. No doubt by the brightness of his soul now that it had reunited with its other half. Once again, warmth swelled in his chest. Waiting, longing, the centuries of pain and regret, had all been worth it for one single night with her.

He pulled out a chair opposite EJ and joined them at the table. "Feels so surreal, you know? After all this time."

"I hear you. Those girls capture our souls like nobody's business. We've all been there. Except for River." EJ downed his soda in one gulp. "His soul is in a frickin' committed relationship with fluorescent clothing."

Raven barked a laugh. And just like that, any awkwardness he'd expected to feel after sealing his bond with Evie drifted out the open door. They all knew Evelina was his soulmate. Unlike him, they all probably assumed one day they'd seal their bond.

He nodded at the laptop open in front of EJ. "Found something?"

"Nothing," Raven replied. "EJ has been scouring every web-thing trying to find a mention of how to undo protectors."

The earlier warmth in his chest dulled. Replaced

with tightness when he remembered all the events during the last twenty-four hours. Specifically, how said book was now inside Evie.

He leaned back in the chair, wishing a cupcake or three would magically appear in front of him. "I don't think we can."

"Why not?"

"Somehow...and I'm still not sure how, Evie bound herself to the book. Or more accurately, bound the book to herself using her blood to amplify her magic."

EJ whistled, closing the laptop.

"I think in her last life, right before she...died and the book vanished, she cast a binding spell on it, linking it to her soul. It's now inside her. Evie is the book. I think the protector guards the spells."

Silence and stunned looks greeted him.

Raven braced his forearms on the table, leaning forward. "How will you destroy the book if it's inside her?"

"Clearly, I need a new plan."

"I'll say."

Finding and destroying the book had been his goal in this lifetime from day one. Now the thought alone made him nauseous. How could he even consider destroying something connected to his soulmate? How had he missed that important fact all this time? The book had always been a part of Evie. He'd been a fool to think it had ever belonged to Fate.

He'd condoned Evie to lifetimes of reincarnation not knowing the full story. Though, did it even matter? If he'd known what she'd done before her death, how she'd died, that she'd unwittingly defied Fate, he still would have fought for her. He still would have stood beside her, battling her enemies one at a time, fighting for them. Their ending. Their eternity.

Giving up wasn't in his soul. And giving up on his soulmate wasn't even an option.

For Evelina, for Rosaline, Cicely, Nora and all the other reincarnated versions of his soulmate, he'd fight until the very end.

He straightened in his chair. "Willow helped her remember her past lives."

Usually, Evie remembering her past was the beginning of the end. The point where she remembered why she needed the book, and how her soulmate had ended her life time and time again. But it also signified the beginning of them. Of trusting in one another, showing their true selves. No longer hiding behind shadows and secrets.

The time where they fell in love.

Raven reached for his drink, both him and EJ remaining silent.

"Fate never wanted the book. She told Evie how to amplify her spells and that one day, she'd help the chosen one destroy the Fallen."

He still couldn't get over the fact he'd had it all so wrong.

"The chosen one?" EJ frowned. "Who the hell is the chosen one?"

Raven took a long draw of his drink, the ice clinking in the glass as he swirled the amber liquid. "Blaine. He has the Empryen. A weapon capable of ending Zath. When that happens, his next target will be Fate."

"You're fricking kidding me." EJ grabbed another

soda from the nearby mini-fridge and popped the top. "Blaine? Surely, Fate didn't intend, long before Blaine even Fell, for Evie to help him destroy the Fallen? That would require serious planning, even for her."

He'd thought the same, but somehow, it all made sense. Why Blaine wanted the book, how he knew Evie's location each lifetime long before Cole found her. Why Fate had kept her distance, waiting for Evie to fulfill her chosen path. The thoughts made him want to rage. "As far as I'm concerned, Blaine can have at it. Fate stole centuries from Evie and me. She's played us every step of the way. A big chunk of my soul yearns for Blaine to defeat Fate, but I'm fucking compelled to prevent it."

Not literally compelled, but because his soul aligned with the Heavens, he couldn't allow anything to destroy Fate. Even after she ruined his chance with Evie over and over again.

Raven gave his shoulder a squeeze. "I know. When Tayla died, a piece of my soul returned to the Heavens with her. You saw me, you know how dark it got. I know it's not the same, fuck, if I had to go through that every fifty years I'd never recover. But in the end, I put one foot in front of the other. I kept waking up, showing up. And somewhere along the way, a thought hit me." He swirled the ice in his glass. "Fate doesn't do shit for no reason. We know she exiled us to save Blaine. We know while he's in Hell he's siphoning angelic power from those he recruits. We also know that he's the Sareal. The protector of the Heavens. And now, he has the ultimate weapon. Fate has a lot of plans in action, and it wouldn't surprise me if we haven't discovered them all."

Lowering his head, he thought of all the events that had happened since Fate banished the Guardians from the Heavens. Raven was right. Fate's plans began long before any of them even realized.

"This is Evie's last life. There's more at stake this time."

Raven nodded. "There is for all of us. My advice, enjoy at least a moment of peace with your soulmate while you can. Because once Blaine realizes Evie is the book, he'll come for her. And none of us know how it will end."

CHAPTER TWENTY-NINE

Evelina

Crossing the lawn, Evie found Jemma sprawled out on a blanket beneath the sweeping branches of the cherry tree. Afternoon sunlight filtered through the heavy branches laden with pale pink flowers, the scent drifting in the crisp air. She'd woken alone in Cole's bed and even knowing he disappeared on angel business she hadn't been able to squash the pinch of disappointment at his absence.

She slowed her steps as Jemma lifted her head.

"Hey, Evie-Eve. Come sit. We have a lot to catch up on. Starting with..." She narrowed her eyes, attempting her most ferocious stern face. "Where have you been all day?"

She couldn't hold back the grin.

"Tell me!" Jemma squealed, patting the space beside her for Evie to sit.

She lowered to the blanket and crossed her legs, catching a glimpse of a picture opened on Jemma's phone. "Are you still researching protectors?"

"Ah, sure, yep." Jemma turned her cell over, face down. "I want all the deets. Don't leave anything out. I bet he was amazing."

She thought back to the feel of Cole's hands and his mouth on her body, how everything had felt so right being with him. Come to think of it, being with him had been predestined since the moment she first saw him at the masquerade party. Last night was one more step in their path. "He's…I don't even know how to describe it, Jem."

"Start with telling me how not so angelic he is in the sack."

She barked a laugh. "Trust you to want those details."

"Guilty."

Her gaze drifted to the distant pine forest, recalling how worshipped Cole had made her feel. Not only when he was inside her, but how his words, the adoration on his face had made her feel emotions she'd never even dreamed of. "Being with him was…so much more. So intense." She briefly covered her face with her hands. "I had tears. Actual tears."

Jemma screwed up her face. "He's that bad?"

"What? No."

"It was good crying?"

"Yes." She playfully smacked her friend's shoulder. "You know what I mean. Being with him was different. I know he said that we're soulmates, and I sense a connection to him, but being with him felt…destined. It's hard to describe. I felt everything he did as though we were one."

Jemma gave an exaggerated sigh. "So romantic."

"I've never believed in soulmates. Well, that's not true. I never considered the possibility before. It seems so fairytale-ish. So…you."

"It is so me." Jemma laughed before picking up her phone. After a few swipes on the screen, she held it out for Evie. "It's real though. I found this. It talks about an ancient binding spell between two souls. Or more accurately, a tether between two hearts made from one soul. The idea seems beyond this world, but the term has been used forever."

She tossed the concept around in her head while she toyed with a silky blade of grass as she gave Jemma the condensed version of what she remembered of her past lives. "I remember loving him, fighting to hide the spells, the sense of dread with each approaching birthday." She placed her palm over the center of her chest trying to quell the building ache. "He told me that he's the one who takes my soul."

"As in he kills you?"

She nodded. "He's done it for centuries. A timeframe I can't even comprehend. Every time I turn twenty-five, he takes my soul to reset the curse." She wound the blade of grass around her finger until the tip turned white. "I just slept with the man who will take my life. Does that make me a bad person?"

"Why does he do it?"

"He said to prevent Blaine from taking my soul to Hell. He thinks Blaine needs me to cast a dangerous spell that I'll...die from. And then my soul will end up in Hell permanently."

Jemma blew out a low whistle.

She tossed away the grass. "I literally have days left to live and instead of figuring out how to expel this magical book from me, or how to stop Blaine, or how to not die, all I can think about is Cole. What it feels like for him to repeat this over and over. How devastating it must be to have to kill his soulmate to save her." She swallowed pins. "Is he relieved? Is he sad? Does he want it all to end?"

Jemma rested a hand on her knee. "I doubt he's relieved, Eve. I'd say he dreads the countdown as much as you."

"I wish…I wish I was who they all thought I was. Who Fate thought I was. A Nuriel, who can amplify her magic to save the world. Instead, I'm just…me."

Jemma tapped her hot pink nail on Evie's knee. "Maybe all you need to do is believe you're that person. This Fate angel sounds like she knows a thing or two. Maybe you need to trust your path. Besides, Blaine can't be that bad, can he?"

Before she responded to that absurd statement, a swoosh of air behind her made her spin around as Cole landed on the grass. His large gray wings unfurled, gracefully at ease behind his back. His gaze pinned her, sending ripples of heat through her blood. He was magnificent. How he wore those black jeans as though they were tailored for him, and the white fitted T-shirt, with some band slogan splashed across the front, left nothing to her imagination. Even his stubbly jaw and disheveled midnight black hair made her fingers itch to touch him. If she stopped for a second, dismissed the facts and evidence she usually relied on, if she only listened to the steady hum deep within her, she'd find her answer.

Cole took her soul in each life to save her. He gave her mercy. He made sure he reset the curse, that she reincarnated, so they could be together once more. For him, the never-ending grief would be unimaginable.

Cole stepped forward and outstretched his hand. "Come with me?"

Her heart thudded.

Jemma nudged her in the back. "Believe,

girlfriend. Believe in who you are."

She shot her friend an eyeroll before standing to place her hand in Cole's. Even if she didn't believe she was this badass Nuriel, she believed Cole's story. Their story. She trusted him to show her their path, not some angel who appeared to her centuries ago with a cryptic message that only resulted in her death.

"Where are we heading?"

With his free hand, he lightly stroked the side of her cheek with the back of his fingers. "I want to show you where it all began."

Bending down, he pressed his mouth against hers. Every kiss with this angel was better and different from the last. Back in the bar, he'd kissed her with so much raw heat she'd wanted to climb him like a bookshelf ladder. In the bedroom last night, his kiss had made silent promises and vows for their future. Now, his mouth sealed with hers as though she were his only lifeforce. He didn't kiss her or sweep his tongue over hers. He devoured her. He drowned in her.

As only a soulmate could.

Her body molded to his, sunk into his embrace, craving more. His soul called to hers, captured her, reinforced their unbreakable connection.

Not caring that Jemma was nearby, Evie curled her fingers through the back of Cole's hair, fisting it. He moaned, drawing her closer until his growing hardness pressed flush against her belly.

This kind of fire between them was too much. At any moment, her body would combust, burning them where they stood. How had they both lived without it?

Jemma cleared her throat. "Should I leave or are you two going to come up for air?"

Reluctantly, she eased her mouth from Cole's, but he refused to release her, locking his arms around her. The yearning and intensity reflecting in his steel-gray eyes fluttered all the way to her toes. It vowed endless pleasure, endless nights. Unending love.

"Ready?" he asked, his gravelly voice sent an indecent shiver through her middle.

"Excuse me?" Jemma interrupted again. "What time should I expect you two love birds home?"

A sinful grin curled at the corner of Cole's mouth. "Don't wait up."

CHAPTER THIRTY

Cole

Cole materialized by the banks of a peaceful river with Evelina tucked close by his side. He would've preferred to fly with her in his arms, but it was too risky. Especially this far from the Guardian residence.

For a thin slice of time, he craved peace from the ancient war. From forces beyond his control. He yearned for time with his soulmate. Raven had made him see sense. In each of Evie's previous lives, they'd never had the chance to bond. He'd never had an opportunity to court her, let alone seal their soulmate connection and offer her his whole heart.

For the next few hours, he'd push thoughts of Evie's impending birthday, the battle with Blaine, and the knowledge that Fate would intervene at any moment, and make up for lost time.

Starting where it all began.

Holding Evie's hand, he led her a few yards up the riverbank to a grass patch overlooking the gently flowing river. Heaviness settled in his chest. The spot hadn't changed a damn bit. Sure, the undergrowth had thickened, trees had no doubt died with new saplings having taken their place, but the essence, the tranquility, remained the same. Snowcapped mountains looming on the horizon reflected in the deep blue water.

He hadn't returned here since that day, the one where he lost her before their future had even begun, because the pain had been too great. But now, standing in the very spot where he'd lifted her lifeless body off the ground, he realized his error. This was the beginning of their story. Not each time Evie reincarnated. Right here. This small patch of land, where her blood had seeped into the earth, was where he'd vowed to fight the Heavens, to fight Fate herself, to grant his soulmate peace. Even after all this time, that vow had never faltered.

Much like their bond.

Evie peered out over the river. "Are we in Canada?"

He nodded, pointing to a spot at his feet. "This is where I first found you. You were lying face down on the pebbles with the water lapping at your singed fingers." He paused, swallowing the stones in his throat as the memories clawed at his chest. "At first, I didn't believe you had died. Why would Fate create a soulmate for me, only to take her away? But then, I got angry. I'd failed you. For twenty-five years, you'd walked this realm, and I hadn't known. I didn't find you."

Evie snaked her arm around his waist to lay her head on his chest. "No one's to blame. We both didn't know."

He kissed the top of her head, breathing in her scent.

"I remember this river. My village was on the other side."

"It's mainly untouched forest now, with a few private residences and further west, hiking trails mortals use during the summer months."

He'd asked EJ to research the area before bringing Evie here in case it was now a small town or vacation destination full of tourists. To his relief, the area remained secluded.

"I'm scared, Cole."

A wild urge swept through him demanding he slay her fears. If only it were that easy.

"What will happen when Blaine comes for me? Will you…?"

Thank Fate she didn't finish that sentence. Ever since he'd told her that he took her soul each lifetime, he'd regretted it. She shouldn't have to carry that knowledge. But more than that, he hated withholding the truth. Especially when she'd opened her heart to him without knowing.

He tightened his arms around her. "I won't let anything happen to you. Don't underestimate the lengths I'll go to protect you."

"That's kind of romantic in a twisted way."

He drew back enough to see her face. "I've had almost five-hundred years of practice and still can't get it right."

"I think you're doing a mighty fine job this lifetime."

"Oh, yeah?" He brushed his lips over hers, lingering to capture her moan. "Tell me more."

She angled her head so he could trail his lips down her neck. "Seriously though, I don't want to…die."

Cradling her face in his palms, he peered into her eyes. "For today, choose to live. Choose to be with me."

When she gave him a slight nod, he kissed her

again before taking her hand to lead her away from the river up a small rise to an estate he'd secured for the night. A summer home for a wealthy mortal family mostly hidden in the wilderness.

Today, he'd spoil her. Create new, happy, forever memories for them to cherish regardless of the outcome.

Evie tugged his arm. "What is this place?"

"It's ours. For tonight."

If they made it through this, if Evie somehow survived or even if she could leave the Heavens, he'd make an offer for the entire estate, one the current owner couldn't refuse. If not, he'd never return here again.

"Our first life began in this forest. I want it to be a place of happy memories for us."

Her grin was contagious as they walked hand in hand up the outer stairs to the spacious deck, overlooking the river and the breathtaking mountains beyond. Despite having materialized to the mortal realm thousands of times, places like this still stole his breath. Fate's magic created such beauty. How she could be so cunning and manipulative, he'd never understand.

At the far side of the deck, he curled up with Evie in his arms on a circular outdoor couch, draping a throw blanket over their legs. They lay there content, watching the low clouds drift across the dusk sky, the occasional hawk. Such a mortal activity but moments like this were so foreign, so new to him, and he loved every second.

He loved her.

His heart had never felt fuller, not even when he'd

first found her. Or the first time he'd met her after she reincarnated.

Night closed in, darkness chased away the light and the solar lights turned on around the deck, still they lay together. From what the owner had told him, there were at least five bedrooms inside, spacious living rooms, fully stocked kitchen, but none of that appealed to him because it meant breaking the tranquility of their moment.

A cool breeze picked up and he lifted the blanket farther up Evie's shoulders. Leaning down, he kissed the top of her head and hoped for the millionth time they made it through this.

Or at least Evie did.

"This place really is beautiful. I love it," she murmured, snuggling into the crook of his arm.

He lightly stroked his fingers up and down her side. "I love you."

At her sharp inhale, he wanted to punch himself. So many times, he needed to remind himself that he'd had lifetimes to fall in love with her. Each life only added to, amplified, his love from the previous. Even though Evie remembered some of her previous lives, in this life she'd only met him a few weeks ago. He shouldn't expect her to feel the same. But at the same time, he wanted her to always know how he felt. For him, their soulmate connection meant everything.

He tightened his hold around her. "I'm sorry. I didn't mean to—"

Evie wriggled free from his grasp to twist and face him. He searched her gaze for hints that she felt the same, even though he knew he shouldn't. "When I first met you, I felt an instant connection. Sure, I was attracted to you, but it felt deeper than that and I think I fought it because I didn't understand our bond."

He swept loose strands off her forehead, his heart doing flips. "And now?"

A slow smile brightened her cheeks. "I love things...red velvet cupcakes, the smell of leather-bound books, the joy of finding an ancient artifact, margarita Fridays. What I feel for you in here,"—she took his hand to press it over the steady thump of her heart—"feels so much stronger than love. It makes me feel...whole."

For so long, he'd yearned to hear those words from her.

Even though Fate had warned him that this was Evie's last life, that things would be different, he failed to realize how much. Evie was stronger, wiser, more open and accepting of his world than any other lifetime. In previous lives, she'd told him that she loved him, but it had been right before he'd taken her soul. The moment when she realized what was at stake and that their only option was for her to return. To reset the cycle and try again.

But hearing her say those words here, now, curled up in each other's arms with no danger or urgency looming over them, gave him more hope than any other time.

Cupping the back of her neck, he pulled her closer and eased his mouth to hers, kissing her with everything he had. No words could ever describe how much he loved her, how even when they were apart, she was always his first thought. How her soul resided right beside his until the end of time. His tongue stroked hers, eager, impatient. Hungry.

When Evie climbed onto his lap, straddling him, he took a second to soak in her beauty. Her swollen lips, the pink dusting her cheeks, the freckle near her temple.

"I feel this...hum, right beneath my skin." Her hands tunneled through his hair, fisting. "Like at any moment, I might burst."

He knew that feeling all too well. Magic. He'd heard the other Guardians talk about how sealing the soulmate bond intensified their soulmate's angelic powers. Evie had struggled to connect with her magic, but now...maybe now that they'd sealed their bond, she could access it.

"It's your magic. Release it, baby girl. Let it free."

"I don't know how."

Holding out a palm, he called forth his Azrael shadows. Long tendrils of dark clouds rose from his hand, swirling upward to the glittering deck lights. He directed them toward Evie, floating around her, skimming her arms. She leaned back, her keen gaze studying the shadows as they circled her, cocooning them in a pool of shimmering heavenly magic. Each time they brushed her skin, tingles swept over his limbs, jolts of electricity bursting from each tiny hair on his body.

"Do you feel it?"

Evie lifted her hand, sweeping it through the shadows. "It's like little sparks all over me."

In the next breath, he released more shadows, pouring them from his hands. One second, they shimmered over the surface of her skin, like a coating, the next the shadows seeped inside her. Much the same way he removed a soul, his shadows sank beneath her skin, swirling through her blood until they become one with her.

She gasped, turning her hands over. "I feel them. I feel you...beneath my skin. It's so...strange."

He grunted, not even sure what to say.

For him, he fought every second not to succumb to the thrill and devour her mouth right then and there. Having his shadows embrace her, consume her, did something wicked inside him. Pride, possessiveness, love all mingled together in a hot mess of emotions he struggled to contain.

Evie lifted her chin to the night sky. "I feel alive. Buzzing. Like my whole body is on fire. Awakening."

Oh, Fate. He felt the same. Using his shadows had never felt so damn good. "Close your eyes, baby girl, let the shadows rise from within."

As she slowly closed her eyes, he did the same, focusing on the tether connecting them. Tiny white sparks erupted from deep inside her soul, calling him, luring him closer. His shadows obliged. In the next breath, his darkness collided with her light, exploding into a fiery blast that shook the deck beneath them. Their eyes flew open at the same time.

A spectacular explosion of light surrounded them. Wind whipped Evie's hair into her face, but she didn't bother to hold it back, too focused on the tornado of magic encircling them. But something was inside the light...was that...words? Pictures. Colors and symbols he'd never seen before. Surely, that wasn't the...

Holy Fate.

Evie reached up, sifting her hand through the gusts flying around them. Light sparked, reacting to her touch as her fingers entwined with the symbols. Above her hand, in the center of the wind tunnel, words and symbols connected in slow motion, forming lines of script. Lines and lines. Everywhere. From all directions. As though someone had removed words from a book and tossed them into a tornado.

All at once, Evie snatched back her arm. The wind ceased. The light vanished. The words disappeared. His empty shadows were the only thing left.

Wide eyed, he stared back at an equally shocked Evie. "You…released the book."

CHAPTER THIRTY-ONE

Evelina

With greater ease each time, Evie once again summoned her magic and...the book. Words and complex symbols floated in the air before her, and she practiced grasping them one by one to form sentences. Spells. Blaine had been right when he'd told her the book was old. Old-old. The oldest thing she'd ever seen. Maybe even older than her first life. The symbols triggered memories, though they weren't of this world. Cole had recognized some of them from an old angelic language, rarely used by angels anymore but others he'd never seen. Either the Heavens created the language and passed it on to her or...she'd created it.

While she continued to practice, weaving her fingers between the words, Cole paced up and down the deck, cell to his ear, talking to one of the Guardians. Black shadows fueled with dread and anxiety rolled off him and through their bond, sinking heavy in her stomach. Over their lifetimes, she'd witnessed his concern, anger, worry, but this...this was an entirely other level. Just when she'd thought they were making progress, this happened.

Dragging her focus back to the book scattered in the night air around her, she held her hand still, allowing the words to...come to her. Although she didn't recognize all the symbols, as they passed through her fingertips, she registered them. Felt them. Their meaning, their intention. They whipped through her mind as though speed reading a textbook, creating old and new spells, until one made her stomach clench.

Symbols weaved together into a spell right before her eyes. A blood ritual. Memories slammed into her mind. Her. Her village. The soul-deep urge to save everyone she cared for. Her desperation.

At the center of the spell was one illuminated word. Nuriel.

Her.

She'd chosen the spell thinking it would protect her village. Combine their magic so they could fight the Fallen and survive. But this ritual wasn't only for binding magic. Unknowingly, she'd attempted something much more powerful...

A chill swept over the base of her neck, raising tiny hairs. In an instant, her magic stopped, and the words disappeared. Her vision wavered before righting again. Cole's urgent whispers to the Guardians ceased. So did the dread rolling through their bond.

She scrambled off the day bed. "Cole?"

Along with everything else, he'd vanished, too. Had he misted to the Guardians without telling her? Eerie silence laced the air. Even the night creatures, and gentle breeze rustling the forest below had stopped. Something was wron—

A creak in the hardwood flooring made her turn.

Blaine.

He casually leaned an arm on the railing, peering out into the night as though he lived here. "Hello, love."

The dread she'd experienced earlier from Cole now

belonged to her. "What are you doing here? Where is Cole?"

Blaine waved a hand in the air before looking at her. "You're actually here, with me, but it's rather complicated to understand."

As discreetly as she could, she glanced through the uncovered window. Still no sign of Cole. Where was he? Had Blaine waited until the exact moment Cole misted? Had he gone for help?

Had she somehow summoned Blaine with her magic?

Did he know?

She backed up a step, closer to the door.

"No need to fret, love. I'm just here to have a chat about the pesky book that seems to keep alluding you." Blaine's chin lowered slightly, his dark eyes narrowing. "Unless you wish to tell me that you've finally located it?"

Shit. Where the heck was Cole?

Retreating another step, she bumped into the couch. Only now, a woman about her age lounged on it, inspecting her neon purple painted nails. Black hair with purple streaks peeked out from under the hooded sweatshirt, and the woman wore black lipstick and the thickest, blackest eyeliner meticulously painted around pale blue eyes. Clearly, she'd never recovered from her teenage goth phase.

The woman lifted her gaze and winked. Holy shit. Did her eyes flash red?

"Don't worry about Ebony, she's along for the ride." Blaine paused, his lips twisting as though deep in thought. "Technically, she is the ride, but that sounds rather strange, don't you agree?"

That made no sense. But she wasn't about to agree with him.

"What the hell is going on?"

Blaine tsked. "He really should keep a better leash on his soulmate. After all these centuries, he still hasn't learned."

Moving in the opposite direction, she sidestepped closer to the stairs, contemplating bolting through the forest, even knowing she'd never outrun an immortal who could mist to her exact location.

"Now, be a good girl and tell me where the book is. I've waited long enough. Even my patience has a limit." Blaine prowled forward. "I've let you have some fun, now your time is up."

She swallowed. If Blaine had done something to Cole when he arrived, she was on her own. Giving him the book though or telling him that it was inside her wasn't an option. She needed to stall until she figured out her next move. "I don't have it."

Unease swirled in her gut. Where was Cole?

Blaine narrowed his eyes, as the prickles at her nape intensified, then threw his head back and laughed. Deep and throaty. "Oh, love. Nice try but I happen to know you've found it."

"I don't know what you've heard, but you're wrong."

She turned to make a run for it, but Blaine snagged her arm in a fierce grip.

"Don't lie to me." Crimson flames flashed inside his pupils. "I see your soulmate failed to inform you that I can tell when you're lying." He lowered his voice to a deadly whisper that shivered up her spine. "I bet he also failed to mention that I can *make* you tell me."

Around her, the landscape warped again, just like before Blaine appeared. It rippled, as though someone had thrown a pebble into a calm pond.

Ebony raised her hands in the air, pushing against an invisible force. "He's trying to wake her."

"Hold it," Blaine snapped. "Now's not the time to slip up."

Shrugging out of Blaine's grasp, she stumbled backward. "What the hell is going on?"

"You're in a dreamwalk, love." He dismissed her gasp with a wave. "Don't fret, you're fine. Let's skip to the part where you give me the book. After all, you did agree to find it for me. Then we can run off into the fiery sunset. Though, the sun doesn't set in Hell, so I guess you'll just run off into the fire, but you know what I mean."

Dreamwalk? Fiery sunset?

Hell?

She'd come too far to fail. Everything she remembered about her past lives, everything she'd learned in this new one. How far her and Cole had come. How much she longed for more time with him. She couldn't give in now, she couldn't let Blaine win. She wouldn't.

In all the great battles, there came a point where the war shifted. The moment where the fighters knew they would win or lose. Until recently, she'd been unknowingly fighting on both sides. Now, she'd planted her allegiance firmly on one side. She wouldn't betray Cole. He'd sacrificed so much for her already. He'd taken her soul each lifetime, so the book didn't end up in Blaine's hands, so her soul wouldn't end in Hell. Leaving now with the Fallen would make all those centuries of sacrifice for him pointless. Worthless. They were soulmates. They belonged together, now, and forevermore. She would fight for him as he'd done for her.

At the top of the stairs, she lifted her chin. "I'm not giving you the book."

Blaine threw his head back and laughed again, this time the sound tightened around her throat. "Did you hear that Ebony? Evelina thinks she's not giving me the book."

Ebony inspected her long, painted nails. "That sounds like her problem."

Blaine abruptly cut off his laugh. "Don't you think he's suffered enough? Having to take your soul again and again because you refused to hand it over?" Flames once again flashed in his dark eyes making her skin prickle. "This doesn't end until you give me the book. Mark my words. Next time, I won't ask so nicely."

Before she knew what happened, Blaine shot forward and shoved his palm against her forehead. Pain sliced open her skull. Hot. Fierce. Never-ending. She screamed unable to escape his hold as one memory burned her mind.

CHAPTER THIRTY-TWO

Cole

Cole shook Evie's shoulders harder, trying to rouse her. Her eyes remained open, dazed, unblinking, as though she'd fallen into a trance while he spoke with Raven. How? Had she accidentally cast a spell? Had the power been too much?

Why the Fate wasn't he watching her more closely?

He knew this would happen. For the first time, he'd let his guard down, let them enjoy moments, make memories. He should've stuck to the plan.

With his arm supporting her back, he lay her down on the couch and gently lifted one side of her shirt. The ancient vines coiled around the tattoo on her ribs, alive, aware, individual blossoms budding and blooming as though the beginning of spring. Minutes prior, before Evie summoned the book, it had been dormant. Had it taken on her power?

Was it warning her? Protecting her? Was it a link to her magic?

"Evie." He jostled her shoulders again with no response.

What if Fate had recalled her soul? She had the ability and the power to do so. If Evie was a Chosen, one wave of Fate's fingers would summon Evie's soul to the Heavens. No, he still sensed her soul there, bright light streaming back and forth between them. If Fate wanted Evie in the Heavens, she would've taken her soul by now. Which meant, Evie hadn't yet fulfilled her Chosen path.

More evidence her casting a spell or, Fate forbid, aiding the chosen one, was in her future. A future he had to figure out how to prevent. Alter her path so she could—

Evie shot upright with a scream, clutching his shirt and yanking him forward.

Unfurling his wings, he wrapped them around her, cocooning them in a safe haven as she sucked in gasps of air. "I've got you, baby girl. You're safe."

"Cole…" Her voice croaked, her wet cheek dampening his shirt.

He rubbed his hand up and down her back, using the motion to also calm himself, because right now, his jaw felt ready to shatter. Someone had hurt his soulmate while he stood not three feet away.

"Shh."

How had that happened?

With her tucked in his wings, he scanned the deck and beyond. Nothing. He sensed no Fallen or even mortals. Her magic must've spooked her or, as he thought earlier, perhaps she unknowingly cast a spell.

Once her breathing settled, he drew back slightly to see her face, wiping her cheeks with his thumbs. "What happened?"

The pain in her eyes sliced him in the gut. He recognized that look. More accurately, he remembered it. The one he'd witnessed when he visited her in Hell right before Fate reincarnated her for the final time.

"You remember."

She didn't need to answer, he sensed the truth in their bond. Now, countless emotions seeped between them. Anguish. Hurt.

Regret.

That last one stabbed him in the heart. They'd endured more than one lifetime of unimaginable heartache, but he hadn't regretted a single moment. Not when it came to Evie. For her to feel that now, deflated any hope he had stored for their future.

While the circumstances of how and when she remembered were always different, the outcome wasn't. She'd push him away.

She'd make him choose the book over her life.

In the past, he'd always done exactly that. Until they figured out how to destroy the book, without destroying her, they kept restarting. After all, they'd always known they'd get another chance.

Not now. Not this time.

Evie looked up at him through her dark, wet lashes. "This is my last life."

He nodded, the sharp blades in his throat preventing words.

"I told you not to find me. But...you did."

Those blades landed in his gut and sliced him into two. Yes, he'd found her. Even thinking that he wouldn't pissed him the Fate off.

One wing knocked a hanging lantern straight off the rafter when he shot to his feet, smashing it on the floor. Not that he gave a shit. He'd avoided this conversation. Riddled himself with guilt. No longer.

"What would you have me do?" Shadows swirled from his hands without a thought. "I won't fucking give up on you. On us. Ever. Do you hear me? My soul is dead without you. I will always find you. And I will never…*never*, walk away from us. Not for anything."

Her steady gaze held his while he stood there, breath punching in and out.

Had he said too much? Had he overstepped? Pushing her wasn't something he wanted, but he needed her to know the truth. How he felt. He hadn't endured centuries of watching her die, of taking her soul from her body, for her to think he wasn't in this for the long haul.

Everything he'd ever done had been for her.

Slowly, she rose. He held his breath as she moved toward him, stopping a mere inch away. Her sweet otherworldly scent surrounded him, called to him, lured him even closer until she tilted her head back to maintain eye contact.

"I know." She reached up and eased her palm on his cheek. "I know."

Any other time, he'd allow his shoulders to relax, wrap his arms around her and squeeze her tight. But distracting himself with her touch wouldn't resolve this conversation. They needed to be on the same page if they were to defeat Blaine, and Fate, and what felt like the entire damn realm.

"I remember the hurtful things I said to you." Her eyes washed with unshed tears, and he fought every cell in his body not to comfort her. To reassure her that everything would be okay in the end. But…he couldn't guarantee that any longer. "I also remember each of our first meetings. How my heart fluttered, how the world fell from beneath my feet. How each time I heard your voice, my chest flared with brilliant light." Her gaze dipped before returning to his. "I also remember, vividly, the pain in your eyes each time you had to take my soul."

Her voice cracked at the end, and he lost the battle, pulling her into his arms. "Please don't cry. I can't...I can't watch you cry." Her chest quaked and he tightened his arms, returning his wings around her as an extra layer of safety. "I'm so fucking sorry."

When she drew back to look up at him, he wiped away her tears. "No. I'm sorry. I'm sorry I made you do that in each life. I'm sorry I bound the book to me. I'm sorry I cast that original spell."

Those sharp blades were back. Right in his damn heart.

"You fought for your destiny. Your village. For us."

She shook her head. "It doesn't matter anymore. Blaine is done waiting."

His jaw tightened, blood suddenly red hot and alert. Though he sensed no Fallen nearby, he still scanned the deck and surrounding forest just to be sure.

"He somehow dreamwalked me to him."

"Fuck."

That explained Evie's trance-like state earlier. He'd witnessed it when Hailee dreamwalked.

Releasing Evie, he grabbed her hand ready to mist. "We need to get back to the Guardians. It isn't safe here."

"Wait. I...need to tell you." At his nod, she continued, "I don't want you to go through that again."

"I've already told you, baby girl. For you, I'll do anything."

Evie's chest rose with a deep inhale. "Before you

came to see me, that last time in Hell, Blaine spoke to me."

He figured Blaine had gone inside Evie's chamber, he just hadn't wanted to think of it. Not then, not now.

He steadied his voice. "Tell me what he said."

Determination roared into her eyes as she lifted her chin. "He told me that if I didn't give him the book this lifetime, he'd destroy your soul...as well."

****

For most of the next day, Cole held back on one side of the entertainment room, while Evie sat on the couch across from Hailee. Never had he felt so out of place. One half of his soul, a decent chunk, cried out at their distance, urged him to sit beside her. Hold her hand to comfort her. Yet, he planted his feet firmly in place. His soulmate needed him to be strong, but his entire world crumbled around him while he was helpless to stop it.

Somehow, Blaine had always been one step ahead of him, and if it weren't so ridiculous, he'd swear Fate had aided the Fallen. That, or Blaine had an ally in Fate's inner circle.

He cast his gaze over the Guardians gathered in the room. His brothers. No. They wouldn't betray him. But who else?

Fate's plan aligned with Blaine's. He was sure of it now. Going against Blaine also meant challenging Fate which they all knew would result in consequences. He'd told Evie he'd do whatever it took to save her, and he damn well meant it. To hell with the consequences.

On the couch, Hailee jolted out of her dreamwalk.

He gravitated closer. "Did you connect with Ebony?"

EJ, who'd accompanied his soulmate in the dreamwalk, gave him a grim look. Boulders tumbled through his gut taking out everything in their path.

"I did," Hailee replied, twisting to face him. "But she wouldn't tell me Blaine's plans, only that it involved the king of Hell. I don't think she fully understands what she's gotten herself into because she seemed…remorseful."

EJ scoffed. "I wouldn't go that far, sweetness. She's still a Fallen."

"She didn't seem remorseful when she dragged me into a dream with Blaine where he threatened to kill me and Cole," Evie snapped.

Once again, he lost the battle to keep his distance, perching on the armrest beside her. Suffering hundreds of lifetimes clearly wasn't enough for Fate. The queen of the universe wanted him to pay for his insubordination until his last breath.

Raven stepped forward, hands in the pockets of his jeans. "She needs to extract the book so we can destroy it. It's the only way to stop Blaine from getting his hands on it."

That idea had crossed his mind more than once, but where would that leave them? Facing the wrath of Fate? Even if Evie somehow removed the book from herself, she'd still bound her soul to it. Blaine still needed Evie's magic to cast the spell. Fate still intended for Evie to aid the chosen one. Still, still, still.

All options would still destroy her soul. She'd still die for the final time. And when that happened, he'd have to trust Fate would grant Evie entry through the shimmering gates. If she was a Chosen, like he thought, Fate wouldn't destine Evie's soul to Hell for her final life.

But could he stomach taking her soul one final time, knowing the curse wouldn't reincarnate her?

"No." He grunted.

The door flung open so fast it bounced against the wall. River rushed into the room in a swirl of neon green with Raine a few steps behind.

"We have an idea." River halted by the couch. "Complete an immortality spell."

A fist squeezed his lungs. Where had the air gone?

"Hear me out." River continued farther into the room. "If you can bind your souls together, with more than a soulmate bond, Evie will be able to live past twenty-five."

"Might, not *will*," Raine added.

"And then what?" The rasp in Evie's voice broke his heart. "Blaine chases me for eternity instead?"

River's green eyes illuminated as brightly as his damn shirt. "Negative. Then we destroy the book and hope you survive."

CHAPTER THIRTY-THREE

Evelina

Evie shivered on the couch even though seconds before, she'd considered tearing off her jacket. Before her, were those she'd met only a few weeks ago, a best friend she'd known half her life, and her soulmate whom she had met more times than she could count. A gathering of people supporting one another toward a common goal. Loved ones. Family. During her short time here, she'd slowly become part of their family, slipped into their routines and movie nights as though she'd always been one of them. A sense of belonging wrapped tightly around her shoulders. Yet, now, she'd never felt so lost.

While Raine, River and the other Guardians spoke back and forth about an ancient immortality spell River had once heard of, she sat there with numbness spreading through her bones.

If she'd never used her blood to amplify the spell...She lowered her head. No point dwelling on that choice. She had gone against Fate, not waited for the chosen one and taken matters into her own hands.

And failed.

Her actions resulted in a curse of epic proportions, spanning hundreds of years, torturing not only her but Cole, too. It all started with her. Cole hadn't asked for any of it. He'd done nothing but find his soulmate dead, lying by a riverbank. And ever since, he'd paid an unimaginable price. Time and time again, he'd sacrificed his happiness to save her soul. To give her another life.

She'd done this to him.

Chills swept down her spine, turning her blood cold, until her jaw ached.

Despite him perched on the armrest beside her, his hand a heavy weight between her shoulders, she couldn't look at him. Couldn't stand to witness the deflated hope in his eyes.

Feeling it flow through their bond was enough.

This was it. Tomorrow was her birthday. They were out of time. Memories of her forcing Cole to take her soul each lifetime, to restart the curse, flashed before her eyes. His pain. His heartache. His vows to always find her, to always save her.

An invisible hand squeezed around her neck. She couldn't stay in this room any longer and pretend to be part of the solution when she was the problem.

While the conversation continued around her, she silently slipped out the room, heading to…she didn't know where. She needed air. Somewhere to clear her thoughts so they stopped leading to one destination.

Warmth bloomed at her nape as Cole followed her, but she didn't turn around, instead quickened her pace. His presence constricted her ribs. She couldn't breathe.

"Evelina…"

She sucked in rapid gulps of air. How would she fix this? How could she save him? How could she repay him for the centuries he'd dedicated to saving her?

His hand seared her shoulder. "Stop."

When her legs buckled, his strong arms snaked around her waist. This immortal. This perfect man, who'd done nothing but be patient, loving, forever choosing her.

He'd continue to save her, no matter the cost.

But what happened when the cost was too high?

Who would save him?

Midnight blooms scented the air seconds before soft wispy shadows twisted around her torso, encompassing her and Cole in a cocoon. Safety. Security. Peace.

Cole didn't say a word, simply curled his body around hers and rested his cheek against hers until her breathing settled and the invisible hand around her throat loosened a fraction.

Slowly, she turned within his embrace to peer up at him. The chokehold returned.

He lifted one hand and swept it over her cheek. "We'll make it through this. I know we will."

"How? How can you be so sure?" Tears burned her eyes. "My birthday is tomorrow, Cole. Tomorrow. Blaine needs me with the book. Even if we figure out how to remove it from me, he still needs me. He needs the magic I've only just figured out how to summon."

Cole cupped her face in his firm, surprisingly smooth hands. "From the very first moment I saw you, I knew you were mine. I won't let Blaine harm you. River thinks the immortality spell will work."

"You can't know for sure. What happens if it doesn't? I die tomorrow anyway? Or worse, you have to take my soul, so Blaine doesn't get the book?"

"I'd do it for you." He leaned his forehead against hers. "I'm going to speak to Fate."

"You can't. She cursed us, remember? After I used the binding spell without the chosen one."

He wiped her tears away with his thumbs. "Trust in me, baby girl. Trust in us that we'll make it through this, that's all I ask."

His warm lips lowered to hers, kissing her softly at first. Deep, gravelly sounds reverberated from Cole's chest, seeping into hers. As his tongue swept over hers, she surrendered. To everything. Every intense emotion streaming through their bond, the tenderness of his lips against hers, his soft hands on her face, the security and safety she found within his arms.

Cole would always do whatever it took to ensure her safety. But who protected him? Who put him first? Who saved him when he was about to make the biggest mistake of his immortal life?

Her.

She loved him. She'd loved him for countless lifetimes. In a way, hadn't she known that all along? As the realization struck her, the intensity of their kiss heightened. Cole tugged her closer, pressing his body flush against hers while he claimed her mouth, not just in this lifetime, but for all the others they'd missed. Her hands fisted his shirt, desperate to rid them of the barriers standing between them, needing his skin against hers.

With shadows still surrounding them, Cole gripped her thighs and lifted her off the ground, locking her legs around his waist. A few strides down the hall and he shouldered open a door, slipping them inside a small bathroom.

They barely broke for air when her feet touched the cool floor. Clothes came off in a blur. Before she knew it, she was on the vanity with Cole between her legs. He devoured her mouth. Kissing her with the kind of raw passion people would write tales about for centuries to come.

No longer was she reading ancient texts about tragic lives, lost loves, failed kingdoms. She was living it. Experiencing it first-hand. Drowning in it.

Heat tingled her fingertips as her magic flared, blending seamlessly with the shadows still swirling around them, bursting pure white sparks into the gray mist. Cole's mouth trailed wet kisses down her neck as she lost herself in their magic. The two of them joined in more than body and soul.

Each sensation pooled in her core, burning and aching, yearning. She rolled her hips, desperate for more of him, to fill her in every way, but at the same time, never wanting him to let her go. He groaned in the crook of her neck, reaching between them to stroke her center, stoking the fire until it almost burned her alive from the inside. Her head fell back against the large ornate mirror. Light flooded the room. Glittery gray shadows.

Their magic.

Their souls.

Overcome with emotion, the pleasure snuck up on her, thrusting her over the edge into a dangerous freefall. Tiny pinpricks of light burst in front of her eyes as Cole slid inside her, his arms quaking under his gentle restraint.

She didn't want gentle. She wanted to feel. For all those emotions to crash between them like a vicious storm. A wild, destructive tornado, taking everything from them in one dangerous sweep. She wanted to burn this moment in her memories for ever.

Lifting her hand, she brushed her thumb over his bottom lip. "Take me, Cole. Make me feel."

The already hot, humid air thickened. Something flipped behind his dark, gray eyes.

"You'll feel that you're mine, baby girl." Clutching her ass in his hands, he held her gaze as he slid out before thrusting back inside, harder, and deeper each time until he stretched and filled her, sprouting delicious tingles over her skin. "You've always been mine."

Shadows darkened, scattered with flashes of light. A midnight storm. And like those storms, he didn't relent. His fingers dug into her ass, holding her in place as he drove into her heat. Sweat trailed between her shoulder blades, her back squeaking up and down the mirror with each plunge.

Never-ending. No beginning or end. Only a middle. Only them. She found her soulmate in his scent, his shadows, their combined magic, the intensity of him inside her, the promise of forever in his eyes.

Regardless of what happened tomorrow, this would be their forever. Right now. This would be the moment they remembered. The point in time where she made Cole know, without a doubt, that she loved him.

That for once she'd chosen him, not the book.

That she'd saved him.

His body stilled when she lifted her hands to his stubbly jaw. "I love you."

A knife stabbed her chest, shredding it to pieces. She ached to give him everything he deserved, everything *they* deserved. If only she had the power.

She curled her fingers in the back of his hair. "I

love you. I've always loved you," she murmured over and over again until he believed it.

With a growl, he crushed his mouth against hers, plunging inside her and flinging them into the epicenter of that storm. Tremors wracked her body as brilliant white light exploded in the small bathroom. A collision of hearts and magic. Souls uniting.

As their breathing settled, Cole drew her tight against his sweaty chest, his chin atop her head. "We'll make it."

This time, she wasn't so sure.

CHAPTER THIRTY-FOUR

Evelina

After their stopover in the hall bathroom, Cole had carried her to his room where he wrapped her in his arms tucked in his warm bed until she pretended to fall asleep. At which point, he'd slipped out of bed, dressed, and snuck out the door, no doubt thinking he could fix their situation.

He couldn't. Only one path made sense and he had no control over it.

She lay there staring at the ceiling, wracked with nerves for a whole four more minutes to make sure Cole didn't return. Back when she'd first met him in Blaine's castle, he'd confessed his fear of Falling. Not until now did she fully understand what that meant. He didn't fear falling off a second story balcony and plummeting to his death. He feared becoming like Blaine. A Fallen. Losing himself without her. He feared that taking her soul each lifetime would eventually break him. And when that happened, her soul would do the same. But didn't he remember that her soul renewed every lifetime when she reincarnated? No matter what happened, what she made Cole do, her soul always found its way back to him.

Their bond always saved them.

Now, she had to trust it would save them one final

time.

Throwing back the covers, she dressed before opening the bedroom door enough to scan the hallway. Not a soul. Muffled voices drifted from the opposite end where the Guardians often met around that board table. Thankfully, Jemma's room was in the other direction.

As quietly as she could, she tiptoed down the hall before slipping inside Jemma's room.

"Jem?" she whispered.

A bedside lamp flicked on, and she blinked a few times to adjust her vision. Her friend sat cross legged in the center of the bed with scraps of paper scattered around her. Prickles erupted over her nape making her pause. "Were you…sitting in the dark?"

Jemma dismissed her worry with a wave of her hand. "I do my best thinking in the dark."

Uh, no she didn't. Jemma hated the dark. Even more so when she was alone.

Jemma shoved a handful of papers aside for Evie to join her on the bed, but she kept one piece tightly clutched in her fist.

"What's going on, Jem?"

Her friend blinked a few times before plastering on a wide smile. "I'm waiting for you, of course."

Her heart raced as she eyed the mess surrounding her friend, including the broken pens littering her side of the bed. "Are you all right?"

Jemma ironed out the piece of paper in her hand before presenting it to her.

Now that she remembered all her lives, she recognized the scribbled symbols. "It's a summoning spell. How did you know wh—"

"Such a simple spell to summon anyone you want."

Summon.

Anyone.

Her earlier unease and her many questions regarding how Jemma knew the spell, flew out the window as an idea struck. She almost laughed. Such a simple solution. Why hadn't she thought of it?

"Do you have someone in mind?" Jemma asked, leaning closer, almost too eager for her answer.

Something flashed in her friend's eyes, so quickly she probably imagined it. Jemma shoved the page at her.

"Actually…"

Cole had been through enough. If this was truly her last lifetime, then she'd already decided that she wouldn't make him go through the horror of taking her soul again. Once was too much. Twice? Eight times? No. The regret and self-loathing in his eyes the second before he ended her life would haunt her for eternity. Let alone having to feel that daily forever and ever.

She wouldn't put him through that again. This time she would save him. Save them. She'd hand over her soul so he didn't have to take it for the final time. Because if she didn't make it through this, if she didn't reincarnate, no way she'd let him suffer that guilt for all eternity. Even if an immortality spell worked, they still had the matter of destroying the book. And something told her that the consequences would be greater.

An image of Cole sitting on the couch across from her appeared in her mind. His guitar rested in his lap, gently strumming the song he'd written for her. Her heart had never felt so full, so complete. So whole.

She wouldn't take that risk. Not on a "might." Not

with Cole's soul at stake.

Their love had bloomed from lifetimes of memories, secret moments, first kisses, stolen glances. Now was the time to trust their bond. Have faith that no matter what happened after this, all that history would bring them back together.

Mind made up, she twisted to face Jemma. "Do you think I'm strong enough to summon Blaine?"

The corner of her lip lifted in the slightest smirk. "Oh, I'm positive you can."

A sudden drop in temperature made her shiver. A warning? Or had Cole somehow sensed her decision, and any second now he'd kick down the door to stop her?

Her pulse skipped and she shot off the bed. "Do you think Cole can sense my magic?"

"Probably." Jemma stood before her, shoving the paper into her hands. "Better hurry."

Swallowing the unease in her throat, she peered at the spell scribbled on the paper. This version missed two critical steps compared with the one she remembered from her original grimoire, but the basics were there. Enough that it triggered her memory.

How had Jemma known the spell? Had she researched it?

It didn't matter. Her friend was right. She needed to hurry before she changed her mind or worse, Cole busted down the door.

She uncapped a nearby pen and made a quick adjustment to the spell before laying it on the floor to crouch in front of it. Magic buzzed from her fingertips as the words danced in her mind. Incarnations. Ancient magic she'd lost touch with lifetimes ago now came back to life with only a thought. The familiar at her ribs stirred, twisting vines around the tattooed book, she felt it pulse and shimmer with each movement. But she didn't need the book. Not for this spell. Not one she'd used a handful of times during her first life, after Fate had approached her, trying to summon the chosen one. Though, she hadn't known his name before.

Closing her eyes, she conjured an image of Blaine. One from the masquerade party where he stood in front of all those gathered in the grand ballroom looking…otherworldly. Powerful. She hadn't noticed it at the time, but now the image clearly portrayed his black eyes. Pits of darkness so alluring everyone bent to his will.

How had she not pieced it together before now? How had she not recognized him?

White hot power intensified beneath the surface of her skin. Sizzling. Tingling. As though she sat too close to the open fire and any moment, her clothes would incinerate. In her mind, she pictured Blaine in the distance with his back to her. The air wobbled, distorted, before settling once more. Towering pine trees. A crescent moon low in the dark sky. As though in slow motion, Blaine turned to face her, and her stomach twisted. His eyes flamed with crimson fires. A menacing aura of hellish power surrounded him.

Death.

Every lifetime she'd arrived at this moment, this junction in her destiny where she considered giving Blaine the book. Just to end it. To live in peace. But each time, she'd reneged and instead, convinced Cole to make her forget. To take her soul.

No longer.

She ended this now.

The faith Cole spoke of, that he'd begged her to have in him, in them, hummed inside her as fiery as the flames burning in Blaine's eyes. She had faith in Cole. Faith they'd find a way back to each other. Faith he'd forgive her for this choice.

Faith she was strong enough to survive.

Blaine swept his arm and bent over at the waist into a regal bow. "Evening, love."

"I have the book."

No need for small talk. The quicker she conceded, the quicker she left the mansion undetected.

"I knew you'd come to your senses."

She didn't feed his ego by agreeing. "How do I get to you?"

He motioned to something behind her, making her peer over her shoulder. Her stomach lurched. The Guardian mansion. Blaine was in the forest.

"Step outside, love. I'm waiting."

Evie jolted, her eyes flying open. Her magic ceased. With her heart thumping against her ribs, she scurried off the floor and darted to the window. Darkness covered the grounds. She couldn't see a damn thing. But something, an eerie sense someone watch her, skated down her spine. Pressing her face to the glass, she scanned the tree line.

A single, tiny flame sparked to life making her gasp. The light flickered over Blaine's face.

She spun to Jemma, standing by the bed. "He's here. Outside."

Her gaze lifted, and the same crimson flames flashed inside her unblinking eyes. "You better get out there before those pesky Boy Scouts save the day."

Ice froze her blood.

"Jemm—"

Someone thumped on the bedroom door, startling her. "Jemma? Evie?"

Cole.

Oh, no. He knew. He knew she'd summoned Blaine. He'd stop her.

Lifetimes flashed before her eyes. His pain. His regret. She couldn't back out now. Not when she had the chance to save him from taking her soul again.

Jemma glided to the balcony door. "Step outside, love."

Her gaze darted between the slider and her best friend and all at once, everything became obvious. Even if she wanted to trust River and the immortality spell, Blaine had always been one step ahead. He wouldn't allow her to walk away from this. Too much was at stake. If she stayed, not just her but the Guardians, her friends, her soulmate, would pay the price. Blaine wouldn't stop until he had her and the book.

Cole banged on the door again. "Let me in before I bust down this fucking door."

She loved them too much. All of them.

Jemma pulled open the slider and motioned to the balcony.

It all happened at once. Frigid air stole her breath. Menacing shadows exploded through the door sending splinters in every direction. Jemma collapsed to the floor. Evie stepped out onto the balcony.

Blaine snagged her arm and misted her away.

CHAPTER THIRTY-FIVE

Cole

"Evie," Cole roared as he launched over the balcony to hover in the air, searching for her. For Blaine. Even though he knew that asshole wouldn't have hung around. Blaine was long gone, and he had no way of tracking him.

That Fallen had taken his soulmate right out from underneath him.

How the hell did he even get this close to the mansion? Raine had assured the Guardians the Raziel spell prevented Fallen from entering. And he was damn sure the barrier didn't commence at the glass sliding door.

Raven hovered in the sky beside him, wings flapping. "Which way did they go?"

He'd been downstairs speaking with Raven when he sensed a change in Evie's blood. Felt her magic swell inside him as if it were his own. At first, he thought she'd been practicing, but then worry and fear had slammed into his chest, making him gag, before a feeling of...acceptance. Fucking acceptance. Evie had decided to leave, and she'd accepted the consequences.

Right before he'd sensed Blaine.

He raked a hand through his hair, tugging at the long strands. "Blaine didn't fly. He fucking misted."

Silence. They both knew what it meant. Blaine could've misted Evie anywhere, in this realm or another. If he could only lower his pulse so his brain functioned better, he might be able to track her through their soulmate connection. If Blaine took Evie to Hell, he was a dead Fallen. He didn't give a damn what Fate would do, he'd end that Fallen in a heartbeat.

Willow shouted, and he and Raven spun to find the Ariel waving them over from Jemma's balcony.

As they landed, Willow urged them inside. "It's Jemma,"

His legs wouldn't work properly. Through the open door, he spotted Jemma slouched on the floor with her back against the bed, Aric beside her doing all the talking. Jemma's gaze darted around the room as though she didn't know where the Fate she was. Perhaps she'd hit her head when she collapsed as he busted down the door? In the split second he'd entered the room, he'd focused on only one thing: saving Evie.

His priority wasn't a mortal. His soulmate was out there with a Fallen. Blaine may not have harmed Evie before, but in previous lifetimes, he'd also never had the book and Evie. This was uncharted territory. No one knew what Blaine would do next.

He jumped onto the balcony railing, scanning the grounds once again even though he knew Evie wasn't there. From within, he called forth his shadows, concentrating on his soulmate bond to locate her spark. Her soul's unique signature.

"Cole," Raven interrupted. "You need to see this."

He almost ignored the Guardian until he saw the grim expression on Raven's face. Withdrawing his wings, he followed Raven back inside the room where he found Willow comforting Jemma. Raine spoke in hushed tones to Aric by the door.

"What is it?" he snapped. He didn't have time for this. He needed to save his soulmate. Didn't they understand that?

Raven motioned to him while speaking to Jemma. "Do you know this guy?"

What the Fate? What a ridiculous…Prickles scraped down his spine when Jemma frowned, scanning his face without a single ounce of recognition.

No. It wasn't possible. Even if Blaine had the power, he couldn't have tampered with Jemma's memories, not in the time between him sensing Blaine's presence and busting into the bedroom.

He stepped closer.

Jemma had been fine when he and Evie left the entertainment room earlier. He'd also sensed no other Fallen on the property besides Blaine. Yet, something had happened for Jemma to forget who he was. Unless…

No. No, no, no. If Blaine…

The sudden silence in the room buzzed in his ears.

All this time…Right under their wings…

That level of deceit burned a hole in his stomach. But had Blaine acted alone, or did he have help?

Towering over Jemma, he struggled to contain his anger. "What's the last thing you remember?"

"I don't know what's happening." Her eyes darted left and right as she shot to her feet. "Where am I?"

Holding out his hand, he called his shadows, fully prepared to suck out Jemma's memories, but Raven snagged his arm. Jemma squeaked, retreating until her back hit the wall.

He shrugged out of Raven's grasp. "Tell me what you remember."

"Cole," Willow interrupted. "Give her a second."

"I don't have a second," he roared. "Don't you understand? Blaine has Evie."

Willow flinched.

Aric stepped forward. "Calm it down, man."

Frustration clawed inside his gut, twisting his organs. "I need to…"

"I…" Jemma said, squeezing her temples. "The last thing I remember is attending a masquerade party with Eve—" She sucked in a sharp breath. "Where's Eve? Jesus, what have you done with her?"

Behind him, Raven swore.

Willow ushered Jemma to sit on the edge of the bed, laying a gentle hand on her shoulder. "Evelina will be fine. If there's anyone who can find her and keep her safe, it's Cole."

Find her? Keep her safe? He'd done a shit job of it so far, hadn't he?

"This entire time, Blaine has been in Jemma's mind." He spun to Raven, on the verge of tearing apart the room. "He manipulated this entire fucking thing."

Everything they'd said in front of Jemma. Everything she'd seen. Blaine now knew it all.

His stomach roiled.

How had they missed this?

He tore at his hair. Either that or he broke things. The air in the room squeezed his lungs, burned down his throat with every inhale until his vision swayed. He needed to find her before Blaine extracted the book and ended her soul.

He stormed back onto the balcony.

"Hold up." EJ darted through the doorway. "Speak to me, Reaper."

Instead, he unfurled his wings, inhaling ragged breaths that snagged in his lungs. Fury rolled through him in destructive waves. "Blaine took her. Took her right out from under our wings."

"Then let's bust down Hell and get her back. I owe you a trip."

"This won't be so easy, brother." As he inhaled a ragged breath, he thought back to when he'd aided EJ in a similar situation, escorting him to Hell to rescue Hailee. "Fate protected you. She tied my shadows to you so your soul didn't blacken. She won't help me. She's the one who cursed us."

Raven joined them on the balcony. "Blaine wouldn't have taken her to Hell. She's mortal. It would end her life instantly. He wouldn't risk it."

Evelina was still mortal. Wasn't she? Despite the clock passing twelve only minutes ago, every fiber in his body told him Evie was still alive. Today...was her birthday. Instead of dreading the task of taking her soul today, he paced back and forth trying to figure out how to save it.

Tingles erupted over his cheeks as the blood drained from his face. "Blaine has the Empryen to kill Zath and now he has the book. Once he uses Evie's power, she's useless to him."

"Not if you get to Zath first."

He stilled, turning his attention to Slater, leaning against the door frame with his arms crossed.

"And then what?"

Slater's mouth hitched ever so slightly at the corner. "Save your soulmate."

A crazy plan materialized in his brain as the seconds ticked by. They were both Azrael. They could both enter Hell without Falling. They could also both enter Zath's realm. And maybe, just maybe, he could capture the king of Hell and use him to bargain for Evie's freedom.

Any other lifetime, he wouldn't risk such an idiotic plan. But in this life, he had nothing left to lose.

****

Evelina

Evie landed with a thud on the hard ground, her knees taking the brunt. Not the graceful misting she'd experienced with Cole. Darkness dotted her vision but the stale, smoky air stuck in her lungs was a dead giveaway that they were no longer at the Guardian mansion. Brimstone. Reminding her of the desolate fires of Hell.

As she lifted her head, more of the ground appeared, followed by jean clad legs, and scuffed black boots.

"You all right down there, love?"

Blaine.

Once, she'd found his voice alluring. Deep, gravelly, with that bad boy British accent. Now...it made her stomach knot. He wasn't a bad boy. He was the villain.

Part of her bet he even embraced the title.

Lifting her gaze to meet his, darkness retreated even farther until the beginnings of a room materialized in her peripheral vision. Soft light flickered over Blaine's sharp jaw, giving him an unearthly aura. All these centuries, she'd run from him, hid the book so he couldn't find it, and now here she was...with him.

Refusing his outstretched hand, she pushed up from the ground to stand. "Where am I?"

"Neither here nor there. The location isn't important."

The nothingness faded away as Blaine turned his back to her and strode into the room. She waited until it fully materialized. Dark furniture, a grand hearth with a low fire crackling inside flanked by floor to ceiling bookshelves overflowing with ancient brown tomes. The room reminded her of the local history room in one of the libraries she'd worked in.

The only thing missing was a sliding ladder for the bookshelf. Because who didn't want one of those?

Blaine stilled, facing the hearth. "Now that you've located the book, we can move on from this long and tiresome game."

"Tiresome game?"

He didn't answer.

"That tiresome game is my life!" She raised her voice, hoping to anger him. Maybe get through to him. This wasn't a game to her and Cole. This was their lives.

Blaine spun, and she almost wished he hadn't. Deep crimson flames flickered inside his pupils as he prowled toward her. "Your life? You mean your mortal life? Because immortality wasn't in your future. That book you so casually hid for centuries was never yours to keep."

She retreated until the back of her legs hit a low table.

"And now you think I should…what? Apologize? Drop to my knees and beg your forgiveness for taking back what's mine?" He encroached her space, so close she felt the flames in his eyes singe her cheeks. "Fate intended that book for me. Not you. Don't think for one fleeting moment I will cower to your,"—he circled her face with his finger—"sad little state, so you can live yet another lifetime. I'm done waiting."

His words, the unsaid threat, clenched her ribs.

Blaine narrowed his dangerous eyes at her for a long moment before he blinked and the flames vanished, along with his threatening demeanor.

"Right, now that the unpleasantries are out of the way, let's get started."

He looked at her, as though he expected her to click her fingers and change her mood as quickly as he. If only she could. This guy was insane.

She needed to keep her wits about her if she wanted to survive. Blaine may think she would hand over the book, but he had no idea what she truly planned. If he did, she doubted he'd keep her alive.

She swallowed and wiped her clammy palms on her jeans. *Think of Cole. Think of Jemma.* "Why do you need the book?"

"Oh, goodie. Now you're interested." Blaine relaxed on an armchair, a glass appearing in his hand filled with ice and golden liquid. "You will perform the binding spell contained in the book to immobilize the king of Hell. Then, I will end him."

She blinked. Bind? Immobilize? End?

"Why me? Why not a different Nuriel?"

Blaine gave an annoyed sigh. "Because you're one of a kind. Haven't you figured that out yet? Fate paved this path for you long before you were even born."

"What if I refuse to cast the spell?"

He took a long, slow sip. "Try. See what happens."

How anyone could deliver death threats with a smirk was beyond her. "I can't hand over the book. It's…"

"Part of you. Yes, I already know. I do not care how you extract the spell, or cast the binding, only that I get the outcome I want."

Questions sprung to mind, along with a strange sense of calm. Confidence. Blaine needed her, something that worked in her favor. He wouldn't end her soul before she performed the spell. Also, Fate had destined her for this path all along. Had Cole known that? Or suspected it? For an unknown reason, hadn't she also sensed it? The impending doom each time she reincarnated, the ticking clock every time Cole found her, the compulsion to help Blaine find the book. The signs had all been there, only she didn't see them at the time.

Now, her eyes were wide open.

"Why did Fate intend the book for you when I possess the magic?"

Those flames flared to life again before disappearing just as quickly. "You naïve little mortal. Fate had you contain the spells in a book so I could construct this exact moment. I'm not the chosen one, *you* are. *You* will aid *me*." He waved a hand at the hearth and the flames roared to life. "Now, stop wasting my time."

Her? The chosen one?

Blaine's power was like a heavy weight, tightening around her chest, allowing only the slightest inhale before crushing her lungs again. She remembered the day Fate appeared to her as though it were yesterday. The spell, Fate's instructions, how she told her to wait until the chosen one came for her. She'd assumed Fate had meant someone else, but maybe all this time she'd been waiting for herself to...become who she was destined to be.

The last time she performed the binding spell on her coven, the power killed her. But that wouldn't happen now. Not now when she knew the truth.

Now, the spells spoke to her, they were more than magic, like a second life vibrating beneath the surface of her skin. As though each individual spell was written only for her. Strong. Powerful. Fueled with knowledge and experience, encased in a protective bond.

She narrowed her eyes, watching Blaine as the missing piece clicked into place. "You need me to cast the spell because you don't have the power."

He took another long sip of his drink, seemingly unfazed by her accusation. "Some magic is even older than me."

Whispers echoed in her mind, her grandmother telling her stories as a child. Stories of lost ancient magic, of star-crossed lovers powerful enough to end the realm. Not her and Cole, they hadn't even met yet. Then who?

Warmth swirled through her blood at the thought of Cole and how his shadows had melded with her magic as though the two powers had become one.

One.

Soulmates.

Is that why she felt stronger?

"Say I perform the binding—"

"Which you will."

"Then what? I die?"

Blaine tilted his head, studying her for a quiet

moment. "Your death is inevitable, love. You were never destined to harness that much power and survive. Your mortal form isn't strong enough, even with Chosen blood."

"So you want me to do something for you that will kill me?"

He shrugged one shoulder. "Precisely. Because it will save your soulmate from having to watch you die again. What a grand sacrifice."

She stepped forward, about to give him a piece of her mind, when goosebumps sprouted along her arms before the woman from her dreamwalk appeared out of nowhere. Ebony? A fitting name for someone so...dark.

Ebony eyed her with a scowl before turning to Blaine. "Everything is ready."

Blaine placed his empty glass on the floor and stood, shrugging off his leather jacket. "It's time to topple a king."

CHAPTER THIRTY-SIX

Cole

Heat buffeted his cheeks the moment Cole materialized in front of the fiery gates with Slater right beside him. Usually, the ornate iron bars and crimson flames didn't faze him. Today, however, he…stared at them. He couldn't speak for his Azrael brother, but he sensed Slater was just as apprehensive. He didn't make a habit of traveling inside Hell if he didn't need to, opting to escort souls to the gates before departing again. Too long in this realm would taint his soul and he risked becoming a Fallen. Yet, over the past few centuries, ever since finding Evie, he'd spent more and more time behind those gates. Taken more risks.

Now…he risked his soul to face down the king of Hell himself.

Lifting his head, he stared at the flames stretching high into the darkness beyond the gates. He'd meant every word when he told Evie he'd do anything to save her. Did she not believe him? Or had she intentionally left with Blaine thinking she was saving him? He didn't need saving. He only needed her. If she'd given him more time, he could've figured out a way to save them both.

Slater withdrew the dagger from the sheath strapped to his thigh and inspected the blade. "I'm not one for sappy speeches, but I wanted to tell you that I get it. What you're doing."

A hard lump expanded in his throat. It wasn't too long ago that the Azrael beside him had found himself in a similar situation. "Let's hope it's not for nothing."

He resumed his stare off with the gates, willing his feet to step forward while battling his angelic urge to flee.

"Fighting for someone you love will never be for nothing."

He couldn't look at Slater, instead giving him a curt nod before moving toward the gates. On their approach, the wrought iron swung inward and side by side, they entered Hell.

Time passed differently in Hell and too soon, he lost all concept of how long they'd been walking. Sweat beaded his spine from the sun looming over him. Thick sulfur suffocated his lungs. Constant screams pierced his ears. Usually, he blocked it all out for the short time he traveled between realms but this time it clawed beneath his skin making him wanted to tear holes in his flesh.

He picked up the pace with Slater in tow.

Two Azrael stalking the streets of Hell wasn't an uncommon sight. But given he had a long list of enemies in this realm, and Slater's more recent switch to the light side, they couldn't afford to become complacent. To avoid unwanted attention, they took back alleys and less common gateways. By the time they reached an abandoned building on the far outskirts of upper Hell, he was ready to rip someone's head off.

Preferably Blaine's.

He and Slater paused by the crumbled mess of

ancient brimstone, surrounded by sand and volcanic rock. Nothing but desolate landscape existed for as far as they could see. No one came out here, unless they knew this gateway existed.

The gateway to Zath's lair.

One way in and one way out.

Fate had told him the location of Zath's lair centuries ago. Long before he'd first found Evelina. Long before he...before he even knew why she'd told him.

Back then, he'd had no reason to know where Fate imprisoned Zath. But Fate had known all along that he'd arrive at this destination. She'd set the entire path in motion.

Had any of his choices in the past made a difference? Could they still?

He turned to Slater. "If things turn ugly in there, vow to me that you'll return to the Guardians. Even if I don't."

Slater narrowed his dark eyes. "Not sure I can do that. Raine made me vow to bring you back, no matter what."

Something expanded in his chest. "If this doesn't work, if I can't save Evie, I don't want to..."

Slater held out his hands, calling forth his shadows. Black swirls lifted from his palms, thickening, and darkening until they resembled an angry storm. "Less talking, more action," he said right before he stepped through the gateway.

Damn Azrael.

Regardless of what Slater promised his soulmate, Cole wasn't leaving without Evie. If she died here, so did he.

****

Evelina

Evie had to stall them. Do something. Anything. Because when this was over, she…she was over. No more curses or reincarnations to bring her back. Dead. Forever. Familiar panic twisted in her gut. The same panic that arose each lifetime Cole had told her they were out of time. The moment when she'd witnessed him shut off his emotions, preparing himself to take her soul. He'd reassure her that they'd see each other again. That he'd find her each and every time.

But now…Cole wasn't here. He wasn't holding her hand, whispering loving words in her ear as he urged her to close her eyes. He wasn't giving her the strength she needed to do what was right.

He wasn't…here.

So desperately she craved an end to this, only now, all she thought of was Cole. How he felt when she'd left with Blaine so he wouldn't have to take her soul again.

"I'm a patient Fallen, I've had centuries in this hellhole waiting for the moment to act." Blaine approached her, his heavy footsteps seemed to rebound off the walls in the dreamlike landscape. "But your stalling is becoming irritating. I'm a little underwhelmed to be honest. I expected an epic display of power from you. After all, your mortal ancestors were a force to be reckoned with." Blaine raised his palm, the center sparked to life, fueling a deep crimson flame. "Wield your magic, Nuriel. Now."

She was out of time.

Swallowing, she held out her palm. Before, when she'd accessed the book's spells, Cole's shadows had swirled through her blood, seeped into every cell in her body until they were one with her. When they connected with her soul, her own magic had roared to life. Only then had the book revealed itself. But she could do this without him. Even now, far apart, she sensed his shadows inside her, melding with her magic, fueling the light in her soul.

Closing her eyes, she remembered Cole's steely gray eyes as he peered down from on top of her. How he bit his bottom lip as he strummed his guitar. How tiny creases appeared in the corners of his eyes when he laughed. The glimmer in his eyes as he fed her cupcakes. How her heart lit on fire each time he captured her gaze from across the room.

The love in his eyes when he claimed her.

Heat flashed through her limbs, sparking at her fingertips before her magic burst from her.

She snapped open her eyes.

Hovering in the air around her, just within reach were the spells. Golden, glowing words, weaving through the air as though floating in the ocean. She reached out, waving her hand through the letters, a buzz sparking at her fingertips, extending all the way up her arm. The words gravitated closer, surrounding her as Cole's shadows had once done.

She caught Blaine's stoic expression through the glimmering words. "You can't see the words, can you?"

He narrowed his eyes, and something told her he wouldn't admit the weakness. Or power imbalance.

"I see your power, the glowing halo around your mortal form. I have no interest in seeing the spells."

If he couldn't see the spells, how would she know she'd cast the right one? Or...wouldn't he?

As though her thoughts were one step ahead, a spell gravitated in front of her face. Would it work? Was she powerful enough to cast it?

Blaine gave her a short dagger. "On my command, you will bind Zath's powers."

She mentally pushed the spell aside as another jumble of words reorganized themselves and moved within reach. Sweeping her hand through the letters, the spell drifted through her mind. The incarnation, the power.

The warning she'd ignored the first time.

Once she locked onto the spell, she nodded to Blaine. She'd do his bidding, she'd bind Zath. But Blaine was naïve if he thought she would roll over and accept her death. She'd died enough lifetimes already.

Not this time.

Blaine held her gaze for a long moment before turning to Ebony. "Dreamwalk us to the soon-to-be former king."

CHAPTER THIRTY-SEVEN

Evelina

Darkness. Thick, inky darkness coated her skin in a slimy film as the vines at her ribs stirred to life. She felt them coil between the book and fan out across her belly, up over her breast, inching toward her neck. Tiny bursts of power popped beneath her skin where each budding blossom opened. Before long, the thickening vines extended up her neck and down her arms until they encompassed her entire torso, pulsing and shimmering with power.

Magic.

Bursts of sparks tingled her fingertips as though the magic were static electricity waiting for an anchor. It continued building, intensifying while Ebony lowered her head and closed her eyes. The room waivered before transforming to…

She sucked in a breath. Her magic reacted, spitting bolts of white from her fingertips.

Ebony had dreamwalked them to a desolate landscape with a sole castle. What was left of it. She recognized the ancient structure from her memories. Though, in her memories, the grand castle had once stood proud and strong, surrounded by lush green foliage and thick jungle. This version though, with massive holes in the stone walls, a dark sun beaming down on the landscape, was the complete opposite. Harsh lands, large black volcanic boulders, bubbling lava in a nearby river. The scene sent chills down her spine.

Blaine nodded to Ebony. "Very good. Now bring him to me."

Ebony raised her hands and the landscape wobbled slightly again, as though she'd contained the three of them inside a bubble. A giant bubble floating above a volcanic river, just waiting to pop. Was this the only thing keeping her soul alive in Hell? Or did the vines covering her torso protect more than the book?

Slowly, on the far side of the bubble, the surroundings changed once more until they were no longer outside the ruined castle, instead, inside the crumbling walls where...Oh my gosh. Bile rose in her throat, and she stumbled backward.

Zath. It must be him.

Gradually, his form materialized, one rotten limb at a time, the oversized throne he sat on building around him. Constructed of charcoaled...bones. *Gag*. The sharp points extended high above Zath's head, spearing the flaming sky. But the bones weren't what shocked her most.

Once the dreamscape formed completely, Zath stood. Behind his back, gossamer crimson wings fanned out, oozing with a thick red substance. Surely that wasn't blood. Maintaining control over her magic almost slipped when he turned his head, exposing decomposing bones and sinew inside an open festering wound.

She covered her mouth. If she survived this, the nightmares alone would haunt her for eternity.

The devil depicted in literature had nothing on the imagery before her.

"What is the meaning of this?" Zath demanded, his monstrous voice booming off the crumbled walls.

"Did you miss my invitation?" Blaine stepped forward, half blocking her view, his tone bright and chirpy. "Oh, right. My bad. It's a surprise party. Surprise!"

Towering over them on the top of the raised altar, Zath lowered his chin. Flames licked the tips of his wings, snuffing out almost immediately after igniting. Black scars marred what was whole on his sweat-glistened torso. "Leave."

"That's not very hospitable of you." If it weren't for the medieval sword now dangling from Blaine's hand, she'd freak out about his casual approach to such a monster. "Anyone would think you didn't appreciate visitors."

Zath narrowed his crimson eyes at Blaine. "I said *leave*."

Beneath her feet, the stone rumbled. She shot a glance at Ebony, who still had her head down, arms out, channeling whatever power she had to control this...dreamscape. Is that what Ebony had done? Dreamwalked them in a magical bubble to Zath?

"No can do, *Your Highness*," Blaine spat the title, prowling forward with the tip of the sword scrapping along the stone making her spine shudder. "You see, a long time ago, you picked the wrong side. You challenged her. You *changed* her. For that you will pay the ultimate price."

Zath's sickening chuckle churned her stomach. "You can't end me, you despicable Fallen. Nothing is more powerful than I. And she knew that. Why do you think she banished me here?"

Blaine reached the base of the steps leading up to the throne. Zath didn't move, and he no longer looked surprised, though his assessing gaze darted to the sword in Blaine's hand.

"There's only one who is more powerful, and it's not you."

Bind his magic. She gasped when the words appeared in her mind. *Now.*

Now was her time to end this. To save Cole, to save herself, to save *them*. Now was her moment to end the curse, centuries of suffering, long forgotten memories, and needless sacrifices. Using the dagger, she sliced both palms before dropping it on the ground to raise her hands in the air. She summoned the spell. The words tumbled in the air, weaving in and out themselves, lost in a whirlwind of magic. Her hair whipped in front of her face as she drew on more power, searching the mass of letters for the right spell. Grasping it with her mind, she called it forward, reorganizing the letters until she read the words aloud.

Warmth pooled at her nape. A familiar tug in her chest making her glance to one side, far in the distance. Cole. He flew toward the castle, his menacing shadows swirling around him as he darted between the bubbles of popping lava. Her heart soared at the same time as it sank. How did he find her? Could he reach her? If he tried to stop her, this would all fail.

Do it. Blaine demanded. *Now.*

Outside the bubble, she had to believe Cole was safe. He couldn't reach her. Not within the dreamwalk. She needed to follow this through.

Dragging her attention from a nearing Cole, she refocused on the spell, chanting the words as her magic swelled and droplets of her blood hissed when it splattered the ground. Zath descended the stairs, one stumbling step at a time, closing in on Blaine, but she blocked it out. She blocked everything out. Ebony standing beside her, Cole racing toward her, how the earth rumbled beneath her feet.

Soon, the words became one with her magic, blending in a stream of bright white light. The blossoms, once attached to the tattooed vines on her torso, lifted from her skin, twirling together in a tendril of light. Once fused together, she shot the ropes of magic toward Zath, wrapping around his body until it bound his arms and wings by his side.

"It's done," she gritted, holding the tether tight.

Her chest burned. Flames from Zath's wings zinged her magic.

Zath roared, struggling against the shackles, only visible to her. "What have you done?"

"I'm doing what should have been done millennia ago when you deceived her. She took mercy on you. I will not."

The constant jerking gradually weakened her ropes, loosening them until Zath almost yanked one wing free. She channeled more magic into them, strengthening them, but the power...it scorched her blood, opening an inferno inside her. An invisible blade sliced down her center, making her stumble. If Blaine didn't hurry, this much power would...kill her.

She'd known that. Hadn't she accepted the risk she might not survive? This spell had killed her once before, why would now be any different? Why did she expect a different outcome?

Cole's distant roar echoed in her ears.

She squeezed her eyes shut before snapping them open with renewed determination. He couldn't witness this. He couldn't see her die, it would kill him.

"Hurry," she snapped at Blaine.

Blaine ascended the steps, now in front of Zath. "On your knees."

Zath's knees crashed on the stone floor with a sickening crunch.

"Not so powerful now, are you?"

"I'll tear off your wings and feast on them." Zath thrashed against the restraints, fury making him foam at the mouth.

The air wobbled and she shot a glance at Ebony. The Fallen's chest punched in and out while tight, deep grooves lined her forehead.

"Blaine..." she yelled. If he didn't hurry up, their protection in the dreamscape would fall apart.

Blaine moved behind Zath and raised the sword, the etched black letters pulsing in the firelight. "Bye-bye."

Before Zath reacted, Blaine slashed down either side of Zath's back and a second later, his wings thumped onto the ground.

The ground quaked as Zath roared. Lava erupted from a distant volcano.

Finally, Blaine swung the sword in a high arc before plunging it through Zath's chest. Sickening screams pierced her ears. Thousands of them. Light illuminated Zath, intensifying, flooding his blood until his entire form glowed with a blinding white light.

Unfazed, Blaine yanked the sword out and stepped

back.

Light erupted in a nuclear blast sending her flying backward into a stone wall. Pain exploded in her back as she hit the trembling ground. The world outside the bubble collapsed. Fire balls shot from the sky. Enormous crevices split open in the earth swallowing gulps of lava and rock.

Vaguely, Cole's shouts broke through the ringing in her ears. He slammed his fists against the magical bubble, trying to puncture it. Beside him, Slater threw his shadows. The dreamscape wobbled, but still held firm. They wouldn't succeed. Somehow, she knew that.

While Ebony had control of their dreamwalk, Cole couldn't reach her. But if it broke while they were in Hell, she would...die.

A jolt through her shoulders made her look at where Zath's body disintegrated in the light. As the last pieces of his flesh exploded into mist, the tendrils of her spell snapped, recoiling toward her like a shimmering rubber band. Blaine stood beside the throne, watching with a strange mix of wonder and...resignation.

Resignation?

The spell. The magic.

If the tendrils collided with her, she'd die. This was the moment. She remembered it from last time. Already, she struggled to contain the sheer amount of magic she'd expelled, when it hit her, the force would be too much.

They spiraled toward her. Any second now, they'd reenter her body.

Cole would witness her death again.

Not this time.

She was the chosen one. And this lifetime, she

chose to live.

Seconds before the mystical shackles reached her, she snagged another spell from the words still tumbling around her. The incarnation that called to her after Blaine had misted her. She thought of Cole, of them, of everything they could be, and chanted with everything she had. The world around her slowed, sounds, eruptions, screams, it all faded into the distance. Staring at the shackles, as they shot toward her, she laced her words with every hope for the future, her love for Cole. From within her, his shadows rose, blending with her magic.

When the magic slammed into her chest, she threw her head back with a scream. Shadows erupted from her mouth, spewing into the air, colliding with her magic. Blinding white light stole her vision as the bubble dreamscape encasing the three of them ruptured.

Her body convulsed.

The last thing she saw before the explosion of light swallowed her whole, were the shadows she'd conjured, anchoring to their intended target.

Blaine.

****

Cole

Flames plummeted from the sky, raining doomsday around the cone of magic preventing him from saving his soulmate.

The scene played out before his eyes, and he was helpless to reach her.

He roared, slamming his shadows into the magic from above, attempting to penetrate it while he screamed for Evie to stop.

The spell, the intense magic, would kill her. He

sensed it.

When the dark gray shadows erupting from within her ruptured the magic bubble, he swooped down toward Evie, but Slater snagged his shoulder.

"Don't touch her yet. Her magic will burn your soul."

He shoved out of Slater's hold. "I don't care."

Fireballs continued shooting around them, singeing his wings and clothing as he dodged them. His sole focus: reaching Evie.

He swooped passed Blaine standing beside the throne with the Empryen in his hand, and vaguely registered Ebony unconscious on the ground, but they weren't his priority.

The Empryen wouldn't only kill Zath, it would destroy all realms connected to the once king of Hell. Including this one. He needed to get Evelina safe before the realm collapsed with them in it.

His feet skidded on the trembling ground as he landed beside Evie, scooping her up in his arms. Her head fell back over his arm, her body limp, her skin too hot. Whatever magic she'd harnessed had already taken its toll. But the absence of a pulse drove him forward. He wouldn't give up. Not now, not ever.

Cradling her in his arms, he spun, finding Slater kneeling beside an unconscious Ebony, her limbs twisted in an unnatural way.

Innocent casualties.

Fury burned a white-hot path directly to Blaine. "Was it worth it?" he screamed at the Fallen.

"This was always our path."

"I don't give a shit about paths. Look at what you've done."

He stepped forward but thought better of it. Engaging Blaine only prologued his time in the crumbling realm. For all he cared, the Fallen could go down with Zath. Two Fallen, one blast.

He glanced at Slater, back at Blaine, then finally, to Evie limp in his arms.

His soulmate.

His everything.

Another explosion erupted outside the castle walls, prompting him into action.

"Slater," he shouted over the booms as he took flight, heading to the distant gateway.

Slater shot to the sky but stopped and backtracked, scooping Ebony off the ground to throw over his shoulder. They soared above the broken cobblestone path, leaping through the gateway right as the realm collapsed.

Cole stumbled into Hell, landing on a mound of volcanic rock with his lifeless soulmate still in his arms, his breath heavy.

Slater launched through the gateway a split second later followed by puffs of dust and debris as the exit sealed shut. "That was fucking close."

If he weren't so out of breath, he'd reply.

Slater lay Ebony on the ground, staring down at her. "I'm so conflicted. Leave her? Take her with us? Either way, I think I'm screwed."

Cole laughed. He had to. Otherwise, he'd go delirious. "A reformed Fallen with morals."

"Shut the fuck up, Shadow."

The decision to leave Ebony or not made no difference to him. Despite being Hailee's twin, Ebony had aided Blaine in taking Evie and for that, she could

345

rot alongside him. But a niggling sensation told him that ending Zath was only the beginning. Did ending Zath's reign make her worthy of saving. Wasn't every Fallen worthy of redemption?

How the Fate did he know?

He adjusted his hold on Evie, pulling her tighter in his arms.

Deep inside he knew she'd died trying to save him, to prevent him from having to take her soul for the final time. Yet, here he was, once again holding his lifeless soulmate in his arms, the grief threatening to drown him. But by aiding Blaine to end Zath, had she completed her Chosen path? Would Fate grant her soul entry into the Heavens? That was his only hope. Still, after everything that had happened, he could still bargain for her peace.

Standing, he looked at Slater. "I need to mist Evie to the gates."

Still staring at Ebony, Slater waved him off. "Go. I'll meet you back in the mortal realm once I figure out what the hell to do with her."

He turned but paused to glance back. "Thanks, brother."

Before Slater replied, Cole unfurled his wings once more and took to the sky, flying as fast as he could to the nearest exit, hoping Fate was prepared for his arrival.

CHAPTER THIRTY-EIGHT

Evelina

Blurry summer sunshine basked her skin in a warmth like no other. A comforting weight wrapped around her middle while the hint of sweet floral notes drifted in the air. A gentle breeze tickled her nape, whispering loving words for her ears only. Hang on. That wasn't right.

"Evelina." Cole's voice cleared her foggy mind, bringing her into the present.

She blinked a few times, scanning the pillowy white landscape as he kissed her neck, his arms tightening around her from behind. "Where are we?"

"The Heavens, baby girl. We're at the gates."

As though conjured by thought, the air rippled a few feet away. Gradually at first, giant shimmering gates appeared out of nowhere, stretching high into the cloudless sky. They glittered with a kaleidoscope of colors, scattered with millions of gems, extending in both directions as far as she could see. Power buzzed in her blood. Soothing, tranquil, calming.

She sifted through her most recent memories, slowing down her final moments to figure out what happened. How she'd ended up in the Heavens. She could've sworn she sensed the shadows inside her latch onto Blaine's soul. Even now, she sensed the power.

But if the spell had worked, she would've lived, not...died.

But she hadn't.

She twisted in Cole's embrace to place her hand on the hard set of his jaw. "I thought I could do it. But I mustn't have had enough power."

He cupped her cheeks, his silvery-gray eyes peering deep into her soul. "We're here together, that's all that matters." He placed a soft kiss on her forehead. "We fought until the very end. I don't regret the time we had together. Not one second."

How could he say that? Time and time again, he fought to save her, and when it mattered the most, she'd failed. "What happens now?"

"I need to know the gates will open for you, that you've completed your Chosen path."

He stood, helping her up as though his words were final.

"What?" She hadn't faced Blaine, and then Zath, channeling more magic than ever before, for him to give up. Now wasn't the time to concede. Not after all they'd been through. "I'm not entering the gates. Not unless you're coming with me."

"I can't, baby girl. Fate exiled me when I first refused to take your soul to Hell." His heavy sigh splintered her heart. "You need to enter alone."

"You're giving up?" Pressure squeezed her ribs.

He took her hands in his, holding them against his heart. "All I've ever wanted is you, but I won't allow your soul to wither away out here until it's nothing but dust. We've been sitting outside the gates for a long time. I thought she'd come, that I could plead with her, but she didn't. It's over." He pressed his lips on the back of her hand, and that crevice in her heart tore open. "You deserve all the peace behind those gates. I'll find you again, I vow to you. This isn't the end of our story."

Just like every other lifetime.

Every damn lifetime ended with something tearing them apart.

Leaning down, Cole kissed her slowly as though he savored each touch, each gentle stroke of her tongue, each breath colliding between their mouths. Each time they kissed felt like the first, and this was no different. Emotions burned through her, igniting the now familiar soulmate bond between them, filling her with light. But as his fingers tunneled in her hair, angling her head to one side, another power hummed, something she'd never felt before, building in her blood—

Cole stilled. He drew back, his dark brows furrowing. Pinching her chin, he tilted her face left and right, searching for something unknown. She felt different, but could he see it? And if she felt it, did that mean the spell worked? How could she tell?

"What did you..." His frown deepened. "Evie, what did you do?"

"I..."

A rush of balmy sea breeze ruffled her hair as the Heavenly gates swung inward to reveal a stunning angel with glorious white wings. She levitated an inch above the ground with her elegant floral gown floating behind her in a long train.

Fate.

The angel glided forward, halting at the perimeter of the gates. "Azrael."

Even her voice drifted through the air as though

carried by a thousand angels.

"Fate." Cole bowed his head. "Evelina aided Blaine to end Zath. I beg you to grant her entry into the Heavens. She's done what you intended."

"Perhaps it's best that you do not make assumptions regarding what I did or did not intend."

Fate hovered before them, silent, almost like an apparition of a goddess. Atop her head, the cherry blossoms in her crown constantly bloomed new buds to replace the withered ones that simply misted away, much like the blossoms connected with her magic had. Even more evidence her magic stemmed from Fate's.

Fate's sharp gaze snapped to her. "It seems you have once again altered your Chosen path. Not unlike the first time you harnessed magic before your time."

Prickles danced over her limbs.

At this point, what could Fate do? Banish them? Curse them? Nothing the angel did could be worse than what her and Cole had already endured for centuries. Yes, she'd cast a spell she sensed was forbidden, but all she wanted was to break the curse. Grant them a chance at a normal life together. But it hadn't worked. Now, they had nothing left to lose.

Backing down or cowering to Fate wouldn't change the past. Nor would it aid their future.

Lifting her chin, she smiled. "I stand by my decision."

Fate's eyes flashed with silver. "This...rebellion of yours will end in one of two ways and I look forward to the outcome. After all, I now have an eternity to watch it play out."

Without another word, Fate turned her back on them and glided into the distance, her gown fluttering behind her until the gates closed, blocking their view.

Hang on…

I now have an eternity…

"It worked?" she squealed, spinning to Cole and latched onto his shoulders. "It worked!"

Excitement made her dizzy.

"Slow down, baby girl. What the Fate just happened?" Cole stared at her for the longest moment, his expression a mixture of wonder, shock, and a healthy dose of confusion before his eyes crinkled at the edges. "The immortality spell. But River said that spell required an immortal soul and Fate's magic."

She nodded, unable to contain her smile. "When the binding spell recoiled after Zath perished, I had two choices. Either I let the power slam into me, which would've killed me like my first death, or I diverted it. So…I anchored it to Blaine's soul while casting a second incarnation. I'd already spilled my blood which amplified the spell, and for some reason, I just knew my magic linked to Fate's."

"You did it." Cole wrapped his arms around her, lifting her off the ground to lock her legs around his waist. "I love that you're immortal, but I'm not keen on it being linked to Blaine's soul. Not one bit."

"He's now the king of Hell. As long as he's alive, the spell will hold." Cole tucked a strand of hair behind her ear. "I think he knew what I was about to do. Right before I diverted the power, he looked me straight in the eye and nodded. As though he, I don't know, gave me permission or something."

Cole's chest expanded with a deep inhale. "The old Blaine, before he Fell, would've done anything for those he cared about. But now…"

"Maybe the old Blaine is still in there somewhere, hiding beneath his Fallen exterior."

"I hope so."

She rested her head on his shoulder, their breathing in sync with one another, their hearts beating as one. And beneath their joined souls, another essence flickered in the background like a distant beacon, present but never drawing close enough to grasp.

Blaine.

Sure, he portrayed the villain in all her lifetimes, but something told her that one day, he'd reveal his true self and it would send a shockwave through the realms.

Eventually, when fatigue crept in, she murmured against Cole's chest, "What now?"

Cole kissed the top of her head. "We go home. The Guardians have work to do, and I suddenly have a vested interest in ensuring they achieve their mission."

"Home."

That sounded damn good.

Cole eased back and cupped her face. "Yes, baby girl. We're finally going home."

EPILOGUE

Cole

Cole strolled the hallway on the second floor of the Guardian mansion, with a lightness in his chest that he hadn't felt for centuries. Actually, he couldn't remember the last time his soul had felt this rejuvenated. Having recently returned from escorting souls, it usually took him hours, if not days, to recover from the side effects. But this time, something was different, and he had an inkling as to what.

Evie.

His soulmate.

She'd completed her Chosen path. She'd broken their curse.

Fate hadn't spoken those words, nor had she openly invited him back into the Heavens, but he felt the restored connection. The heavenly light cleansed his soul each time he thought of home.

His long-forgotten home.

No longer was he forced to wander this realm in between escorting souls. For the first time in centuries, the Heavens welcomed him back into the fold and…he didn't go.

Raven had also invited him and Evie to permanently reside with them at the Guardian mansion, which after about two seconds of consideration, they'd

353

accepted. He'd given his word to aid the Guardians in their mission to return Blaine to the Heavens. A mission he once thought impossible. Now though, he had faith that anything was possible. After all, he'd thought he and Evie would be forever trapped in an endless loop of finding each other only to lose each other shortly after. Again and again. But now, they were in the same realm at the same time…for as long as they chose.

Grateful didn't even come close.

At the entrance to the entertainment room, he held back and soaked in the scene before him. Raine, Aric, Tayla and River, converged around the pool table heckling one another. EJ busy behind the bar, chatting with Raven. Soft rock music played in the background filling him with the urge to grab his guitar and serenade his soulmate in front of the entire room. Not tonight though. Tonight, he had something else planned for them.

Speaking of soulmates…

Finally, his gaze drifted to the leather couches, where Evie lounged with the others, her best friend perched on the armrest by her side. When she threw her head back and laughed at something someone said, euphoria soared through him, streaming a brilliant white light into his soul.

He never dreamed he could feel this…whole.

As though sensing his presence, Evie looked his way, her beaming smile making the golden flecks in her eyes sparkle. How had he gotten so lucky? She was all he'd ever wanted, and now he not only had her, but this sense of completeness he'd trade for nothing.

His previous duty to aid the other angels when they called on him had recently also taken on a new dimension where he now considered them not only his friends, but his family. All of them safe and protected, together under one roof.

As much as he could stand on the outskirts with a full heart, watching his soulmate in her element forever, he'd planned something for them. For her. And if he didn't hurry, he'd miss the chance to surprise her.

Instead of barging in and interrupting the others, he hitched his chin for Evie to come to him. After excusing herself, she walked over, him drinking in her every step.

"Did you just get back?" she asked, clutching the front of his shirt to pull him down for a gentle kiss.

"A little while ago, but I had something to do first."

Her hands snaked around his back, slipping beneath his shirt, drawing a contented sigh from him. "Oh, yeah. What?"

Reluctantly, he unhooked her arms to lead her into the hall and downstairs. "I'll show you."

Outside, on the gravel drive of the Guardian mansion, as the sun lowered behind distant mountains transforming the sky into an array of pink, he withdrew a black satin scarf from his pocket and twisted Evie around to tie it over her eyes.

"Ooh, are you taking me to an actual sex club this time?"

His blood flamed at the memory of her reaction when she'd thought the bar was a sex club. Maybe he should change the location of their date. No...something told him she'd appreciate the place he'd chosen more.

Bending down, he grazed his mouth up her neck,

lingering for a heartbeat to capture her scent and lock it away in his soul. He'd never tire of having her in his arms. Nor would he ever take their moments for granted. Finally, Evie could live the life she deserved and never had the chance to in any of her previous reincarnations.

"Not tonight. Some place better," he whispered in her ear.

"Now, I'm really intrigued."

Wrapping his arms around her, he placed a soft kiss below her ear before misting them.

Dusty tomes, rich with history, scented the air the second they materialized in the upper rear section, right before closing time. A shiver quaked her body as he undid the scarf, letting it flutter to the floor.

Evie gasped. Then squealed.

He slapped a hand over her mouth. "Quiet, baby girl, otherwise the security guards will hear us."

A playful spark replaced the earlier heat in her eyes as she scanned the rows and rows of shelves, leaning over the banister to take in the entire view.

"You..." Excitement danced in her bright eyes as her gaze darted between him and the overflowing shelves, soaking it all in. "I...this is..." She lowered her voice to a whisper. "We're in the Jophael College Library."

In his opinion, the most impressive library in the mortal realm.

Towering shelves overflowing with rich mortal history, arched stained glass windows depicting prominent events in literature, and a grand staircase extending to secluded areas such as the one he'd misted them to, hidden from prying eyes. But he barely spared all of it a glance with Evie standing before him.

Fate, his chest couldn't inflate any more without bursting. Seeing her this excited, this joyful, made his existence worth living.

Mortal voices drifted up from the first floor, fading in the distance as the main doors to the library closed right on cue, followed by heavy silence.

Evie pushed off the railing to saunter toward him. "You snuck us into a library at closing time?"

"Our union began with a book of spells. It's only fitting that our eternity begins surrounded by ancient tomes as old as our story." He lowered his voice to a husky growl. "Plus, I heard you had a thing for hiding in the restricted areas of the library after hours."

"Jemma." Evie rolled her eyes, but she couldn't wipe the smile off her face.

He lifted one shoulder. While her friend was still recovering, piecing together the time in which Blaine had possessed her mind, she'd remembered everything before she met the Guardians. And when he'd sought advice on planning this evening for Evie, Jemma didn't hesitate in revealing Evie's secret fantasy to lock herself in the library overnight with a hot date.

Only tonight, he planned activities for her that didn't involve reading.

Taking her hand, he yanked her forward until he captured her in his arms, where he vowed to keep her forever.

"I hope you remembered snacks," she murmured, her cheek against his thumping heart.

"I sure did." Twisting, he motioned to the container full of red velvet cupcakes Hailee had baked for them. Well, she'd baked them, and he'd swiped them from the kitchen right after she iced them, leaving a thank you note.

Backing to the single armchair situated by a full-length paned glass window, he tugged Evie onto his lap.

Nerves fluttered in his gut when he took her face in his hands, peering right to the heart of her soul. "For so long I thought a happy ending wasn't in our future. When you came into my existence, you'd already departed this realm. I'd already lost you without even knowing. But your courage, your bravery, united us back together, no longer living the twisted existence Fate cursed us with." He paused, catching his breath. Did the library's ventilation system suck out all the oxygen after closing time? "I love you, Eveline, with every cell in my body, and I want to spend an eternity proving I'm worthy of our bond."

Leaning down, he lifted the lid on the cupcakes and grabbed the chosen one, offering it to Evie. The one in the center with the simple gunmetal gray band squished into the velvety icing. "This band is fused with Purah, water from the Eternal Fountain, and blended with my shadows."

Raine had helped him craft the band in secret.

Tears pooled in her eyes as she blinked at him. "Are you...asking me to marry you?"

"I'm asking you for forever. Offering a token wielded with my magic to symbolize my eternal commitment to you. Something we've never had the luxury of before now. With a side of sugar."

Those tears slipped down her cheeks as she chuckled and sobbed at the same time. He hadn't meant to upset her. Had he got this all wrong? The gunmetal color was dark, but surely not ugly.

"Cole…"

He wiped the tears away with his thumb. "Don't cry, Evie. Cupcake calories don't count as an immortal, I swear."

She laughed harder. Swiping his finger through the icing, he trailed it over her bottom lip, on her cheek, on the tip of her nose. Each time, licking it off, capturing all that sweetness mingled with her scent. It worked, drying up her tears, making her giggle. But it also drove him into a frenzy. If he could calm down enough, he'd throw that damn cupcake over the railing in favor of freeing both his hands to tear off her clothes.

Evie moaned, angling her head as he nuzzled her neck, licking off the last spots of icing. "Say yes, baby girl."

"Yes." His breath hitched when she smiled. "Always, yes."

Pausing only to slip the band on her finger, icing and all, he dumped the cupcake on the floor before capturing her face in his hands, devouring her with a claiming kiss.

Two of his greatest loves: cupcakes and his soulmate, together at last. For eternity.

A word about the author…

Cassie Laelyn is an international bestselling paranormal romance author living in Queensland, Australia, with her husband and their two BMX-crazy boys.

She spends her days writing swoony otherworldly bad boys in need of redemption and a gut wrenching happily ever after…unless there's a looming deadline. In that case, she loves binging on TV shows, daydreaming at the beach, and curling up listening to the rain!

Join Cassie's newsletter (www.cassielaelyn.com) for exclusive free content, character interviews, giveaways, and new release information. You can also stalk @cassielaelyn on Facebook, Instagram, TikTok, BookBub and Goodreads. http://cassielaelyn.com

Thank you for purchasing
this publication of The Wild Rose Press, Inc.

For questions or more information
contact us at
info@thewildrosepress.com.

The Wild Rose Press, Inc.
www.thewildrosepress.com

www.ingramcontent.com/pod-product-compliance
Lightning Source LLC
Chambersburg PA
CBHW072308020726
47501CB00002B/444